Dixie Hart

WILL N. HARBEN

Dixie Hart

Will N. Harben

PO Box 2211
Fairfield, IA 52556
www.1stworldlibrary.com
First Edition

LCCN: 2007927862

Softcover ISBN: 978-1-4218-4584-5
Hardcover ISBN: 978-1-4218-4500-5
eBook ISBN: 978-1-4218-4668-2

1st World Library Literary Society

Giving Back to the World

"If you want to work on the core problem, it's early school literacy."

- James Barksdale, former CEO of Netscape

"No skill is more crucial to the future of a child, or to a democratic and prosperous society, than literacy."

- Los Angeles Times

"Literacy... means far more than learning how to read and write... The aim is to transmit... knowledge and promote social participation."

- UNESCO

"Literacy is not a luxury, it is a right and a responsibility. If our world is to meet the challenges of the twenty-first century we must harness the energy and creativity of all our citizens."

- President Bill Clinton

"Parents should be encouraged to read to their children, and teachers should be equipped with all available techniques for teaching literacy, so the varying needs and capacities of individual kids can be taken into account."

- Hugh Mackay

TO THE MEMORY OF THE LATE RICHARD WATSON GILDER, WHOSE KINDLY APPRECIATION OF THE CHARACTER OF "DIXIE HART" WAS MY INSPIRATION IN WRITING THIS BOOK

CHAPTER I

In a blaze of splendor the morning sun broke over the mountain, throwing its scraggy brown bowlders, spruce-pines, thorn-bushes, and tangled vines into impenetrable shadow. Massed at the base and along the rocky sides were mists as dense as clouds, through the filmy upper edges of which the yellow light shone as through a mighty prism, dancing on the dew-coated corn-blades, cotton-plants, and already drinking from the fresh-ploughed, mellow soil of the farm-lands which fell away in gentle undulations to the confines of the village hard by.

"A fellow couldn't ask for a prettier day than this, no matter how greedy he was," Alfred Henley mused as he stood in the doorway of his barn and heard the gnawing of the horses he had just fed in the stalls behind him. A hundred yards distant, on the main-travelled road which ran into the village of Chester, only half a mile away, stood his house, the eight rooms of which were divided into two equal parts by an open veranda, in which there was a shelf for water-pails, tin wash-basins, and a towel on a clumsy roller. A slender woman, with harsh, sharp features, older-looking than her thirty years would have justified, and a stiff figure disguised by few attempts at adornment, was sweeping the veranda floor, and in chairs propped back against the weather-boarding sat an old man and an old woman in the plainest of mountain attire.

For a moment Henley's eyes rested on the group, and he sighed deeply. "Yes, she's my wife," he said. "I owe her every duty, and, before God, I'll stick to my vows and do what's right by her, come what may! She was the only woman I thought I wanted, or ever could want. They say every cloud has a silvery lining, but my cloud was made out of lead—and not rubbed bright at that. I reckon, if the truth must be told, that the whole mistake was of my own making. Whatever the Creator does for good or ill, He don't seem to bother about hitching folks together; He leaves that job to the fools that are roped in. Well, I'm going to stick to the helm and guide my boat the best I can. I made my bed, and I'm as good a sleeper as the average."

Here the attention of the man, who was tall, strong, good-looking, and about thirty-five years of age, was attracted by the dull blows of an axe falling on wood, and, looking over the rail-fence into the yard of an adjoining farm-house, a diminutive affair of only four rooms and a box-like porch, he saw an attractive figure. It was that of a graceful young woman about twenty-two years of age. Her hair, which was a rich golden brown, and had a tendency to curl, was unbound, and as she raised and lowered her bare arms it swung to and fro on her shapely shoulders.

"Poor thing!" the observer exclaimed. "Here I am complaining, and just look at her! A stout, able-bodied man that will grumble over a mistake or two with a sight like that before his eyes ain't worth the powder and lead that it would take to kill him. Look what she's took on her young shoulders, and goes about with a constant smile and song on her red lips. Yes, Dixie Hart shall be the medicine I'll take for my disease. Whenever I feel like kicking over the traces I'll look in her direction. I'd jump this fence and chop that wood for her now if I could do it without old Wrinkle making comment."

Her work finished, the girl turned and saw him. She flushed a shade deeper than was due to her exercise, and with the axe in hand she came to him. Her large hazel eyes held a mystic charm behind the long lashes which seemed actually to melt into the soft pinkness of her skin.

"Good-morning, Alfred," she greeted him, her lips curling in a smile. "I know this ain't where you sell goods, but I thought it might save me a trip to town to ask you if you keep axes at your store. This old plug of a thing is about as sharp as a sledgehammer."

"I've got a few poked away behind the counters somewhere," he laughed, as he always did over her droll and original speech, "but the handles ain't in them, and that is a job for a blacksmith, if they are ever made to hold. Let me see that thing." He took the axe from her, and ran his thumb along the blunt and gapped edge. "Look here, Dixie," he said, "I thought you was too sensible a farmer to discard good tools. This axe is an old-timer; you don't find such good-tempered steel in the axes made to sell these days, with their lying red and blue labels pasted on 'em. Give this one a good grinding and it will chop all the wood you'll ever want to cut. Let me have it this morning. I've got a grindstone at the store, and I'll make Pomp put a barber's edge on it."

"Of course you'll let me pay—"

"Pay nothing!" he broke in. "That nigger is taking the dry rot; he's asleep under the counter half the time. The idea of you delving in the hot sun with a tool that won't cut mud! You oughtn't to chop wood, nohow. You ain't built for it. Your place is in the parlor of some rich man's house, leaning back in a rocking-chair, with a good carpet under foot."

"That's the song mother and Aunt Mandy sing from

morning to night," the girl smiled, showing her perfect teeth. "They want me to quit work, and get some man to tote my load. I reckon if the average young fellow out looking for a wife could see behind the hedge he'd think twice before he jumped into the thorns."

Henley laughed again, his eyes resting admiringly on her animated face. "I reckon the gals wouldn't primp so much either if they could see the insides of their prize-packages," he returned. "I reckon neither side is as wise while courting is going on as they are after the knot is tied. Folks hereabouts certainly have plenty to say about me and my venture."

There was a frank admission of the truth of his remark in the girl's reply. "Well, if I was you, I wouldn't let anything they say bother me," she said, sympathetically. "Mean people will say mean things; but you've got friends that stick to you powerful close. I've heard many a one say that in taking your wife's father-and mother-in-law to live with you, and treating them as nice as you have, you are doing what not one man in ten thousand would do."

"I don't deserve any credit for that—not one bit," the young man declared. "I'm not going to pass as better than I am, Dixie; I'm just human, neither better nor worse than the average. I reckon you've heard about how I happened to get married?"

"Not from *you*, Alfred," the girl answered, in a kindly tone. "I have often wondered if the busybodies got it straight. I've heard that you used to go to see your wife before she married the first time."

"Yes, me and Dick Wrinkle was both after her in a neck-and-neck race, taking her to parties, corn-shuckings, and anything that was got up. Hettie never was, you know, exactly pretty, but she had a sort o' queer, say-little way about her that caught my eye. I was a gawky boy, as green as a gourd, and never had been about with women. Dick was just the opposite: he was a reckless, splurging chap that dressed as fine as a fiddle, wasn't afraid to talk, joke, and carry on, and he could dance to a queen's taste; so he naturally had all the gals after him. I was afraid he was going to cut me out, and I was fool enough to—well, I used to hope, when I'd see him so popular in company, that he'd make another choice. And he might—he might have done it—for he was the most wishy-washy chap that ever cocked his eye at a woman; he might, I say, if me an' him hadn't had a regular knock-down-and-drag-out row. He was drinking once, and said more than I could stand about a hoss trade I'd made with a cousin o' his, and it ended in blows. The crowd parted us, and he went one way and me another; but after that he hated me like a rattlesnake, and he told her not to let me come there again. He might not have made that demand if he had thought it over, for it sorter give 'er a stick to poke 'im with. She used to say nice things about me to egg him on, and he often went with her for no other reason than to keep me away. Well, you can see how it was. She wanted to beat the other gals, and he wanted to outdo me, and, in the wrangle, they got married one day all of a sudden."

"And you felt bad, I reckon," Dixie Hart said, sympathetically.

"I wanted to die," Henley answered, grimly. "I cursed man and God. That gal was my life. I was as blind as a bat in daytime."

"Then I've heard," the girl pursued, "that he neglected her and finally went off West with Hank Bradley, and almost quit writing to her."

"Yes," Henley nodded, "and she moped about home as pale as a dead person, and never seemed interested in anything that was going on. All that didn't do me any good, I'm here to tell you. Her trouble become mine. I toted it night and day. I wasn't fit for work. I was as nigh crazy as a man could well be out of an asylum."

"Then the news come back that he was dead?" The girl leaned on the fence and looked down.

"Yes; Hank Bradley come home, and told how Dick was blowed away in the awful tornado that destroyed that new town in Oklahoma. Hank had helped hunt for his body; but it never could be identified among the hundreds that was picked up, and so his remains never was brought home. That one fact nearly killed Hettie. I'm talking plain, Dixie, but me and you are good, true friends, and I want you, anyway, to understand my fix. I used to watch her taking walks all by herself in the woods, always in her thick, black veil, and bowed over like, as if she was under a heavy load. I reckon no woman the Lord ever constructed is quite as attractive to the eye uncovered as she is partly hid, for we are always hunting for perfection, and so nothing under the sun seemed to me to be so good and pure and desirable as Hettie did. I even gloried in the attention she paid his mammy and daddy. I thought it was fine and noble, and that it gave the lie to the charge that women are changeable. I don't want you to think that I rate her any lower now, either, Dixie, for I don't. She's a sight better woman than I am a man, and I certainly dogged the life out of her till she agreed to marry me. She told me fair and square at the start that she'd always love him, and I told her that it wouldn't matter a bit. It hurts my pride a little now, but that ain't her lookout. Folks say she's odd and peculiar, and that may be so, too, but she was that way all along, and it's a waste of time to criticise anybody for what they can't help."

"I've always liked her," the girl said. "She certainly attends to her own business, and that is more than I can say for my chief enemy, Carrie Wade. Alfred, that girl hates the ground I walk on, and yet she keeps coming to see me. She has me on her visiting list so she can devil me. She has no work to do at home, and so she comes over to nag me. She never has a beau or gets a thing to wear without trotting over to tell me about it or flaunt it in my face. She even makes fun of me for having to work in the field, and is actually insulting sometimes. I'd shut the door in her face, but it would only please her to think she'd made me mad."

"She's more anxious to get attention from men than any woman I ever laid eyes on," Henley declared, resentfully. "When drummers come to sell me goods, she scents 'em a mile down the road, and is in the store pretending to want to buy some knickknack or other before they open their samples. I oughtn't to talk agin a lady, Dixie, but she lays herself open to it, and is so much like a man in some things that I forget what's due her as a woman. She has such a sneering way, too. That reminds me. I heard her mention my name when I passed you and her at the spring the other day. I couldn't hear what she said, but from the way she snickered I knew she was poking fun. I caught this much: she said that I was the only man on earth who was fool enough to do something or other. I couldn't hear what it was, and I didn't care much, but—" Henley broke off, and for a moment his eyes rested on the averted face of his companion.

"I don't carry tales," Dixie finally said, with a touch of embarrassment, "but I've a good mind to tell you exactly what she said, Alfred, so that you won't think it is worse than it really was. It wasn't such an awful thing, and she was laughing more at her own smartness than at you. She said—she said you was the only man under the sun who had gone so far as to adopt a step-father-in-law. Now, that wasn't so terrible, was it?"

A sickly smile struggled for existence on the face of the storekeeper, and his color rose. "Well, that was a new way to put it, anyway," he said. "I think I could laugh hearty at that joke if it was on some other fellow, and I'm glad you told me what it was. I didn't know but what she was saying something even nastier than that."

"She really said some *nice* things," Dixie went on, diplomatically. "She said it was good of you to give a home to the Wrinkles, and—"

"As I said just now, I won't take credit for that," Henley broke in; "in fact, I'd have refused if I could have done it. It come as a surprise, and it almost knocked me silly. I'd counted on Hettie doing a good many odd things, but I never expected that. So when she come home from the camp-meeting, where there had been such a big religious upheaval, and said she'd met the old man and woman there, and that they both looked so lonely and peaked and ill-fed that she felt like she was acting unfaithful to Dick's memory in living in one county and them in another—well, that's the way it happened. I confess I never thought the pair looked so bad when they come over, for they was awful cheerful, and seemed to 'a' been fed on the fat of the land. Hettie told me afterward that she'd been sending 'em all her spare change, so that was explained. You'd never know the old woman was about unless you stumbled over her in the dark, for she is as quiet as a mouse, and never says a thing nor listens to anybody but him. He's all right. The old man's all right. I really think I'd miss 'im if he was to leave. I never like to encourage him too much, but I often laugh at the jokes he plays on folks. People poke fun at me for having him around, but he drives off the blues sometimes. He showed me what to expect from him the first day he got here. He come down to the store, and walked in and looked around till he saw the tobacco-boxes behind the counter, and he went to 'em and pulled a plug off of each one, and smelt of 'em and looked at 'em in the light. Then he took the best one and sidled over to me. He run his hand down in his pocket, and I thought he was going to pay me for it, but he was just hunting for his knife. He grinned as he clipped a corner off the plug, and stuck it betwixt his short teeth. 'You'll find that I'm a great chawer and smoker, Alf,' he said. Then he axed me if I had such a thing as a empty dry-goods box about, and when I pointed to some in the back-yard that I was saving to put seed-corn in, he said he'd take one and wanted me to have the horses and wagon sent over for a pig they had left. 'I wouldn't send for it,' he said, 'but it has got to be a sort of pet. Its pen used to be right at our window, an' me an' the old lady miss its squealing, especially in the morning. It is as good as an alarm-clock.'"

The girl wiped a smile from her merry mouth. "Excuse me, Alfred," she said, "but it does seem powerful funny. It must be the way you tell it."

"I'm glad it's funny to *somebody*, and you are more than excusable," he said, dryly. "If I could get as good a joke as that on an enemy of mine I'd never kill 'im in a duel; I'd keep him alive to laugh at."

"You didn't say whether Mr. Wrinkle paid for the tobacco or not," Dixie reminded him, expectantly.

"Well, I'll tell you now that he didn't," was the answer, "nor for a pocketful of red stick-candy which he took from a jar. He said it was for his wife's sweet tooth; but if she got any of it she met him on the road home, for he was chucking it in at a great rate as he walked away."

They both glanced toward Henley's house. They saw the subject of their remarks emerge from the kitchen door, and hang his slouch hat on a nail on the veranda, and reach for the dinner-horn.

"He's going to blow for me," Henley smiled, as the spluttering blast from the horn rang out and reverberated from the mountain-side. "Breakfast is ready. He eats like a horse at all times, and is as hardy as a mountain-goat. I'm going to call him 'Kind Words.'"

"Kind Words"? Dixie looked up inquiringly and smiled. "That's as odd as Carrie's 'stepfather-in-law.' Why are you going to call him that?"

"Because," and Henley glanced back as he was moving away, "the Sunday-school hymn says, 'Kind words can never die,' and I know old Wrinkle won't."

CHAPTER II

As Henley, the axe in hand, approached the house, his stepfather-in-law, with considerable clatter, was hanging the horn on its nail.

"I noticed you was talkin' to Dixie Hart at the fence," he said, as he discarded his quid of tobacco and stroked his grizzled chin, on which a week-old beard grew. "Well, if I wasn't no older'n you are, an' was as good-lookin', which maybe I ain't, I'd chin 'er over the fence mornin', noon, and night—married or unmarried. Man laws was made to keep us straight, I reckon; but when the Lord Himself lived on earth they wasn't quite as bindin' as folks try to make 'em now. A feller, in that day an' time, could be introduced to a new wife every mornin' at breakfast, if he could afford to keep a drove of 'em, and still be looked up to as a wise man and a prophet."

"Dixie was talking about buying a new axe," Henley answered, "but I told her this one was good enough, and that I'd make Pomp grind it."

"She's as purty as red shoes," old Jason said. "And if she hain't had a load to bear, no female ever toted one. Talk about justice! Why, Alf, that gal hain't had a thimbleful sence she was a baby. She has set out to make a livin' fer a mammy that can't hardly see where she's walkin', and an aunt that is mighty nigh tied in a knot with rheumatism, and she is doin' it—bless yore life!—better'n many a man could in the same plight. Folks say she's already paid old Welborne half on that farm, and that before long she'll own it, lock, stock, and barrel. As you may 'a' noticed, I sometimes poke jabs of fun at women, but I never do at her. Somehow I jest can't. I was a-settin' right back of Carrie Wade an' some more frisky gals at meetin' last Sunday when Dixie come in an' tuck a seat on the bench ahead of 'em. I don't let women bother me, one way or another, but I got rippin' mad at that gang. They was makin' sport of her. One of 'em re'ched over an' felt of the ribbon on the pore gal's hat, and then they stuffed the'r handkerchiefs in the'r mouths and come nigh bustin' with giggles. Them sort think they are the whole show, with their white hands, smellin'-stuff, and the'r eyes on every man that passes, while a gal like Dixie Hart is overlooked. I've stood thar at the gate and watched her out in her corn or cotton in the br'ilin' sun with her hoe goin' up and down as regular as the tick of a clock, while the other gals was whiskin' by in some drummer's dinky-top buggy or takin' a snooze flat o' the'r backs in a cool room."

"Is breakfast ready?" Henley asked, with an appreciative nod in recognition of remarks he did not wish to prolong, as he leaned the axe against the front gate and ascended the steps.

"Sech as it is," the old man answered, taking another tack. "When me an' Jane decided to come here to reside, Hettie was goin' to do wonders in the cookin' line. She was particular to ax just what our favorite dishes was, and you may remember how she spread herse'f the fust three days after we was installed. It was like a camp-meetin'. You couldn't think of a single article that she didn't have ready, in some shape or other. But after 'while hot things quit comin' and cold uns appeared that had a familiar look, and now me and you and all of us set down to the same old seven and six. Well, my jaw teeth ain't as good as they used to be, and I make out by soakin' my bread-crust in my coffee. Hettie says she's goin' to have me an' Jane both fitted out with store sets. Folks that have tried 'em say they beat the old sort all holler—that you kin crack hickory-nuts if you have both upper and lower and git a fair clamp on 'em and use yore muscles."

Henley turned into the big dining-room, where his "stepmother-in-law," a diminutive woman, sat at the foot of the oblong table dressed in faded black, even to the poke sunbonnet which, worn indoors and out, completely hid her wrinkled face. Mrs. Henley, as he seated himself on the side of the board opposite Wrinkle, came from the adjoining kitchen carrying a steaming pot of coffee, which she put by her plate at the head of the table, and sat down stiffly. The smooth floor of the room was bare save for a few rugs made of varicolored rags. The walls had a few cheap pictures on them—brilliant old-fashioned prints in mahogany frames, and some enlarged photographs in tawdry gilt. The wide hearth of a deep chimney was whitewashed, as was also the exposed brickwork up to a crude mantelpiece on which towered a Colonial clock with wooden wheels, ornamental dial, ponderous weights, and a painted glass door.

Mrs. Henley had not always been so unattractive; her dark eyes were good and her face held the glow of fine health. She had added to the severity of her sharp features by the too-elderly manner in which she parted her hair exactly in the centre of her high brow and brushed it sharply backward to a scant knot behind. She wore constantly an expression of one who was well aware of the fact that vast and vague duties to the dead as well as to the living rested on her and which should be performed at any cost. She was not usually talkative, and she had few observations to make this morning. As she nibbled the hot biscuit, upon which she had daintily spread a bit of butter, she allowed her glance to rove perfunctorily over the three plates beyond her own. She asked Wrinkle if his coffee was strong enough, and the gap in the black bonnet if the mush was too lumpy. From the bonnet came a mumbling content with the yellow mass into which cream was being slowly stirred with a quivering hand. Wrinkle seemed more ready in the use of his tongue.

"I hain't got no complaint to make," he said. "Especially sence Alf said t'other day at the store that coffee was on the rise. I was curious to see how this batch would sample out. I reckon when the market takes a jump storekeepers has to take a lower grade to keep customers satisfied with the price. But it won't work ef they are as good a judge of the stuff as I am. I parched this lot myself and picked out heaps o' rotten grains."

"They wasn't rotten," Henley explained, authoritatively. "They was water-stained by a wet crop-year, that's all. You was throwing away good coffee."

"Good or not, the chickens wouldn't eat it," argued the tangled head. "I know, fer I watched 'em. They was hangin' round the kitchen-door and would run every time I throwed out a handful, but they didn't swallow 'em any more'n they would so many buckshot. But prices nor nothin' else will ever git right, if I am any judge, till we git free silver. I tell you, Alf, that man Bryant is the biggest gun, by all odds, that ever belched fire in the defence of a helpless nation, and when them dratted Yankees tricked 'im out of the Presidency they put the ball an' chain o' slavery on every citizen of this fair land. Bryant told 'em that sixteen to one would do the work, and what did they say? Huh, they said he was a fool and didn't know how to figure. I tell you if he was a fool, Solomon was a idiot. Who was the'r brag man up in Yankeedom?—why, Abe Lincoln—an' what did he ever do but set back in the White House and tell smutty jokes, while the rest o' the country was walkin' on its uppers, eatin' hardtack, sweatin' blood, an' spittin' out minnie-balls. *That* man"—Wrinkle swallowed as he pointed the prongs of his fork at the crayon portrait of Henley's predecessor, which, with shaggy mustache and partially bald pate, in a new oaken frame, hung near the clock—"that man was a Bryant supporter from the minute the sixteen-to-one proposition electrocuted the world to the day of his death."

"Electro*fied*," corrected Mrs. Henley. "You oughtn't to use words out of the common. People don't understand them hereabouts."

"Well, they ought to grow up to it," Wrinkle grunted in his cup. "I read more'n they do, I reckon, an' sometimes a word tickles me till I git it out."

Henley ate his breakfast in silence. He was known to be a good talker himself, but he seldom indulged the tendency when Wrinkle was present. The meal over, he took his hat and went out. The road passing the farm-house led straight into the main street of the village, and along it he strode in the soothing, crisp air. His store stood on the square which encompassed the stone court-house. The store was a plain wooden building which had never been painted, but had received from time and the weather a gray, fuzzy coat which answered every purpose. It was about eighty feet long by thirty in width, and had a porch in front, which was reached from the sidewalk by a few steps. Ascending to the door, Henley unlocked it and proceeded from the rather dark interior to unscrew the faded green window-shutters. These thrown back on the outside, the light filled the long room, displaying two rows of counters and shelving. The right-hand side was devoted to dry goods and notions, the left to groceries, hardware, and crockery. Henley went on to the rear, where, by lifting a massive wooden bar from iron sockets, he opened a door in one side of the house. Next he took up a water-pail from an inverted soap-box, and, emptying the contents, he went to the well in the adjoining yard, a fenced enclosure which contained a conglomerate mass of old junk, broken-down wagons, buggies, agricultural implements, and other odds and ends which the merchant had bought very low or taken in some sort of exchange for new wares whereby they had cost him practically nothing. Returning with the water, he had just seated himself at his desk in the rear when his clerk, James Cahews, entered at the front, busied himself putting out some samples of hardware on the porch, and then came back to his employer. He was tall, well built, had very blue eyes, yellow hair, and a sweeping mustache which was well curled at the ends. He was without a coat and wore a blue cravat and a shirt of fancy cotton which matched none too well.

"You beat me to the tank again, Alf," was his jovial greeting. "I would have got here sooner, but I stopped to drive Mrs. Hayward's cow in for her. The blamed huzzy took a notion to prance about over the school-house lot, and the old lady is too near-sighted to see which way to turn and was afraid she'd get hooked."

"No hurry, no hurry," Henley said, as the other took up a battered tin sprinkling-pot and, filling it from the pail, began to dampen and sweep the floor, after which he lazily wiped the counters with a soiled towel.

"Pomp will be here after a while," the clerk said, pausing near where Henley sat, his glance thoughtfully on the sunlit ground in the yard. "I come by his cabin. He said he had to run for some medicine for his wife, and I told him I'd sweep out for him. Them dern niggers had rather take medicine than eat ice-cream at a festival. I don't know that it's anybody else's business," he went on, after he had stood the broom in a corner and was wiping the top of Henley's desk, "but thar is considerable talk going around that you intend to take a trip to Texas."

"I'm thinking seriously of it," Henley admitted. "I've heard of a deal or two in land out there that I want to get a finger in. You know, Jim, that I don't really make my best trades here in this shack; nothing worth while seems to come this way. I reckon it's because this country is old and settled. In a new, undeveloped section like that out there big things is continually happening. The general impression is that a trading-man can make more amongst ignorant folks than amongst keen traffickers, but it is a mistake. Folks that ain't born with the flea of speculation wigglin' in their brain-pans won't never let loose of nothing. It is the feller that is eternally on the lookout for opportunities that will sell the shirt off his back to raise money when he thinks he sees an opening. Then there ain't no fun nor Christianity in making money out of a fool. I want to know that a feller is up to snuff and fairly in the game, and then I'll swat 'im if it is in my power. It's been the ambition of my life to get the best of old Welborne across the street there. He's made his pile off of widows and orphans, and if I ever get him under my thumb I'll crack every bone in his hide."

"Traders that have the knack of it like you have, Alf, are simply born that way," Cahews smiled. "I never had any turn of that sort. I can talk an old woman into buyin' a dress pattern off of a shelf-worn bolt of linsey, or a pair of shoes too tight for her, but this way you have of buying a feller's wagon that breaks down in the road and having it patched up by a blacksmith that owes you money, and selling the wagon for more than it cost new—well, as I say, I don't know how to do it."

"I believe myself, as you say, that the trading turn is born in a feller," Henley laughed, reminiscently. "I know I was swapping knives 'sight unseen' when I was wearing petticoats. I had a stock of old ones and I kept the jaws of 'em rubbed up bright. My daddy used to whip me for it. He was one of the best men, Jim, that ever wore shoe-leather, and he never could stand to see one neighbor get the best of another. He was dead agin all the deals I made when I was growing up, but I learnt him the trick and showed him the beauty of it before I was twenty."

"You say you did?" Cahews sat down and eyed his employer eagerly.

"Yes, it come about through my fust hoss-trade," Henley smiled. "It was this way. Pa was on the lookout for a hoss to do field-work, and he let everybody know he had the money, and a good many came his way. He wasn't any judge of hoss-flesh, and a gypsy, passing along, stuck him—burned the old chap clean to the bone. It was a flea-bitten hoss that was as round and slick as a ball of butter, and as active under the gypsy's lash and spur as a frisky young colt. The gypsy said he had paid two hundred for him, but, as he was anxious to get to his sick wife in Atlanta, he would make it a hundred and fifty and be thankful that he'd made one man happy. The old man was his meat. He told him he only had a hundred and twenty-five, and—well, the gypsy was a smooth article. He wanted to get his eye on the cash. He said a whole lot about havin' had counterfeit money paid to him, an' that he had to be careful, and with that Pa went to the house and got the money and spread it out before the skunk to prove that it was all right. And in that way the chap got his hands on it. He shed some tears as he put it into his pocket. Pa said he kissed the hoss square betwixt the eyes and rubbed him on the nose and went away with his head hanging down."

"I catch on," the clerk broke in, deeply interested; "it was stolen property, and your Pa had to give 'im up."

"No, the titles was all right," Henley answered, dryly. "The time come when Pa would have greeted any claimant with open arms. The hoss had the disease traders call 'big shoulders.' I was a mile or two off when the calamity fell, but somebody told me Pa'd bought a hoss, and I come home as fast as I could. I found Ma and Pa out in the stable-yard, and he was fairly chattering over his wonderful bargain, and what a kind heart the gypsy had. Pa saw me and grinned from ear to ear.

"'Say, Alf,' he said, 'you are always making your brags about knowing hoss-flesh; what do you think of this prince of the turf?'

"I walked round in front of the animal to size him up, and my heart sunk 'way down in my boots. 'Pa,' I said, 'it looks to me like he's got "big shoulders."'

"'Big nothing!' Pa said; but when he stood in front and took a squint I saw him turn pale. 'Big shoulders, a dog's hind-foot!' he grunted, and he was so mad at me that he could hardly talk. He put the hoss in a stall and jowered at me all that evening, and at the supper-table he clean forgot to ask the blessing. The more he feared I was right the worse he got, till Ma had to call him to order by putting the family Bible in his lap and making him read and pray. I couldn't help laughing, as serious as it was; for while we was on our knees the thought struck me that he ought to ask the Lord to bless that gypsy and restore his wife to health. Well, I was right. Early the next morning, after a good night's rest and plenty of water and feed, we found the hoss lying down. He'd get up and go about a little whenever we'd prod 'im, but he'd lie down whenever our backs was turned."

"I've seen hosses like that," Cahews remarked, "and they might as well be shot."

"That's exactly what Pa decided to do, after two weeks' nursing and cajoling," Henley laughed. "He come in to the breakfast-table one morning with his rifle in his clutch, a sort of resigned look in his eyes.

"'What are you going to do, Pa?' I asked him."

"'Why, I see that danged thing has got on one of his lively spells,' he said, 'and I'm going to shoot him while he's at his best. If there is any hoss-heaven, he'd make a better appearance like he is now than at any other time. I've had my fill. The sight of that hoss peeping out betwixt the bars every day at meal-time and lying on a bed of ease the rest of the day is driving me crazy. He'll be on his way in a few minutes if I can shoot straight.'"

"'No, don't kill 'im,' I said, my trading blood up. 'Let me ride 'im to town while he's lively and maybe I can git rid of him. I might get a few dollars for his hide, and that would be better than having to dig a hole to put 'im in.'"

"'No, don't kill 'im here,' Ma said, for she had a tender heart—God bless her memory—and so the old man hung his gun up on the rack and went to eating, almost too mad to swallow. Well, after the meal was over I saddled the hoss and rid into town at a purty lively gait. It was really astonishing what a decent trot the thing could take at times. You see, I'd heard that Tobe Wilks, a big hardware man at Carlton, who had a plantation in the country, was looking for a hoss, and I thought I'd see what he'd say to mine. I was jest a boy, but I'd hung around hoss-swappers enough to know that it never was a good idea to be the first to propose a trade, and so I hitched at the post in front of Wilks's store and went in. I bought a pound of tenpenny nails, that I thought would come in handy in patching fences at home, and while the clerk was weighing 'em up I saw Tobe leave his chair behind a counter and go out and walk around the hoss. Finally he come to me and said, said he: "

"'Alf, does your Pa want to sell that stack of bones out there?'"

"'He don't,' says I, 'fer the hoss is mine; he gave 'im to me.'"

"'Oh, that's it!' said Wilks; 'well, do *you* want to sell him?'"

"'Well, I ain't itchin' fer a trade,' I says, and I paid no more attention to Wilks, pretending to be looking at some ploughshares in a pile on the floor, till he come at me again. "

"'But you *would* sell him, wouldn't you?' he asked."

"'Well,' I said, slowlike, as if I had some difficulty in recalling exactly what we'd been talking about, 'I had sorter thought that a good mule would do the work I have to do better than a hoss.'"

"'What would you take for him?' Wilks come at me again, and he looked kinder anxious. 'I want a hoss to send out to my plantation. They are needing one about like yours.'"

"'It will take a hundred and fifty of any man's money to buy him,' I says. 'Friend nor foe don't get him for a cent less.'"

"Well, we went out to the hoss, and Wilks got astraddle of him, and, sir, he took him round the square in the purtiest rack you ever saw shuffle under a saddle. I saw Wilks thought I was his game, for his eyes was dancing as he lit and hitched."

"'How would a hundred and forty strike you, cash down?' he said."

"'I'm needing the other ten,' I said. 'I'm a one-price man. I know what I've got in that hoss' (and you bet I did), 'and you can take him or leave him. I didn't start the talk, nohow.'"

"'Well, we won't fight over the ten,' he said, 'but here is one trouble, Alf. You are under age, and I don't often trade with minors. I don't know how your daddy may look at it, and I'm going to make this deal before witnesses so there won't be any trouble later.'"

"'You'll not have any trouble with Pa,' says I. 'I'll guarantee that.'"

"Well, Wilks called up two of his clerks to see the money handed to me, and with the wad of bills in my pocket I lit out for home. But the nearer I got to the house the more I got afraid Pa wouldn't endorse what I'd done, and so I felt sorter funny when him and Ma met me at the gate, their eyes wide open in curiosity to know what I'd done."

"'Well, what did you do with the hoss?' Pa wanted to know."

"'I sold him,' says I. 'I let him go to Tobe Wilks for cash.'"

"'Cash the devil,' says Pa. 'How much?'"

"I drawed out my roll and fluttered the bills in the wind. 'A hundred and fifty,' I said. 'If I'd asked less he'd have been suspicious and backed out.'"

"Well, sir, Pa was plumb flabbergasted. He leaned against the gate-post and puffed for air, and Ma was the same way. But he wouldn't touch the money. 'It's plain open-and-shut stealing,' he said, when he riz to the surface, 'and we are simply going to hitch a hoss to the buggy and take the money back.'"

"Well, it looked like it was no go. I argued and produced evidence till I was black in the face, but Pa just kept saying he wouldn't sanction no such deal, and Ma she agreed with him. So you bet I felt like a whipped school-boy as me and him set side by side and drove into town. He was bewailing all the way that he'd fetched into the world an only son that was no better than a hog-thief in principle, an', if I didn't change, me 'n him would have to part."

"When we got to the square I saw Tobe Wilks standing in the door of the store, and I saw that he was mad. At first I thought he'd found out about the hoss, but I saw it wasn't that as soon as he reached the buggy."

"'Now, I'll tell you right now,' he said to Pa, when the old man drawed the roll out and started to hand it to him over my legs. 'You sha'n't come here and try to back down in a fair trade like that. I made it before witnesses, and your boy said he had your consent. I've sent the hoss out home, and I don't do business that way.' Pa tried to get in a word, but Tobe 'ud cut him short as soon as he opened his mouth, so the old man couldn't do anything but wave the money at him."

"'If you get the hoss you'll do it by law,' Tobe went on, fairly frothing at the mouth, 'and I'll put your boy in the pen for selling stolen property. You can't browbeat me, you old hog.'"

"'Old hog!' I heard Pa grunt in his beard, and he stuffed the roll down in his pants pocket. Now Pa wouldn't take advantage of his worst enemy in a trade, but he'd fight a bosom friend if he was insulted. And before I could bat my eyes he had lit out of the buggy, and him and Wilks was engaged in a scrap that'ud make two wildcats go off and take lessons. The town marshal run up and parted them by the aid of bystanders, and some of 'em persuaded me to drive Pa home. He was a good, holy man, but he cussed all the way, and ended by saying that Wilks never should see hair nor hide of that money. And he never offered it back again, neither, and him and Wilks never spoke for two years. Pa bought a fine Kentucky mare with the money, and used to chuckle every time she'd pass him. He got so he thought hoss-trading wasn't the worst crime on earth."

"And what became of the hoss?" the listener asked.

"I never knew," Henley answered; "men don't advertise such things when they go against them. But one day, during election, Tobe asked me to cast a vote for his son, and I promised to do it, and we got kinder friendly. As he was leaving me he turned back and laid his hand on my shoulder and said, 'Alf, I've wondered many a time what in the name of common-sense your Pa wanted with that hoss.'"

"'So have I,' said I, and he went one way and me another."

Pomp, the negro porter, was entering the door, and with a laugh Cahews turned to meet him.

CHAPTER III

The gray light of early dawn had taken on a faint tint of yellow, and the profound stillness of the air, the vast quietude of the mountain foliage and drooping corn-blades gave warning of the fierce heat that was to follow.

Dixie Hart turned her head drowsily on her pillow and opened her eyes and closed them again. "Oh, I could sleep, sleep, sleep till doomsday," she said to herself. "I wish I didn't have to get up. I'd like to take one day off. I could lie here flat on my back till night. But, old girl, you've got to be up an' doing."

She heard the clucking and scratching of her hens, the chirping of the tiny chickens, and the lusty crowing of her roosters in their answering calls to neighboring fowls, the neighing of her horse in the stable, the mooing of her cow in the barn-yard.

"They are all begging me to hurry," she mused. "They don't want to sleep; they've had their fill through the night, while I had to be up. Well, repining don't make good dining, and here goes."

She dressed herself, went out on the little kitchen porch, bathed in fresh, cool well-water, and, with a coarse towel which hung from a nail on the door-jamb, she rubbed her face, arms, and neck till they glowed like the reddening skies.

"My two women, as sound as they pretend to sleep, are crazy for their coffee," she smiled, "but they've got to wait, like people at a circus do, till the animals are fed. The older folks get, the earlier they go to bed and the earlier they rise. Heaven only knows where it will end. If mine could get their suppers early enough they would say good-night at sundown and good-morning when it was so dark you couldn't see 'em in their night-clothes."

"Dixie, is that you, darling?" It was Mrs. Hart's voice, and it came from the open window of a tiny room with a sloping roof which jutted out from the end of the kitchen.

"Yes'm. What is it, mother?"

"Nothing." A thin hand drew a white curtain aside, and a pale, wrinkled face, surrounded by dishevelled iron-gray hair, appeared above the window-sill. "I just wanted to know if you was up. I heard you through the night. Your aunt was suffering, wasn't she?"

"Yes, she couldn't sleep," Dixie replied, as she spread the damp towel out on the shelf where the coming sun's rays would dry it. "She says she sat too long at the spring yesterday. I got up and rubbed her arms and chest twice with the new liniment. It smells like it's got laudanum in it; but it didn't deaden her pain."

"I'd 'a' got up myself," Mrs. Hart said, in her plaintive tone, "but I can't see good enough to help."

"It's well you didn't," Dixie said, lightly, "for you'd just have made double trouble. I'd have laid down my patient and let her grin and bear her pain while I was trotting you back to bed and making you lie there. Don't you ever get up and go stumbling about in the dark while I'm attending to anything like that."

"I think I'll get up and make the coffee while you are feeding," Mrs. Hart said. "Mandy nearly dies waiting for it to come after she wakes up."

"That's right, lay it on her," Dixie laughed, impulsively. "You are getting like a ripe old toper who is always begging whiskey for somebody else. You let that coffee-pot alone. The last time you tried your hand at it you put in a double quantity of corn-meal and couldn't understand why it didn't have a familiar smell as it was boiling."

"I believe a body does become a slave to the habit," the old woman agreed. "The other day you was over at Carlton, and left enough already made for dinner, I accidentally spilled it, and me and Mandy went nearly crazy. It was one of her bad days, and she couldn't get up, and I couldn't find the coffee."

"I remember," Dixie answered, "and you both swigged so much at supper to make up for it that you wanted to talk all night. Oh, you two are a funny lot! But you've got to wait this time, sure. I'm going to feed these things and stop their noise."

She had reference to half a hundred fowls, young and old, that were squawking loudly and fluttering on the steps and even the porch floor. She disappeared in the kitchen and returned in a moment with a dish-pan half filled with corn-meal, and into this she poured a quantity of water, and with her hand stirred the mass into a thick mush. This she began to throw here and there over the yard like a sower of grain till the voices of the fowls had ceased and they had fled from the porch. Then she took up a pail of swill in the kitchen and bore it down to a pen containing a couple of fat pigs and emptied it into their wooden trough. Going into a little corn-crib adjoining the stable and wagon-shed, she brought out a bucketful of wheat-bran and fed it to the cow, which stood trying to lick the back of a sleek young calf over the low fence in another lot. "I'll milk you after breakfast," she said, as she stroked the cow's back. "The calf will have to wait; I can't attend to all humanity and the brute creation at the same time. You'll feel more like suckling the frisky thing, anyway, after you've filled your insides."

The sun was above the horizon when she had breakfast on the table in the little kitchen. She stood in the space between the cooking-stove and the table and attended to the wants of the half-blind woman and the all but helpless aunt. The biscuits she had baked were light and brown as autumnal leaves, the eggs fried with bacon in thin lean-and-fat slices would have tempted the palate of a confirmed invalid. The aroma of the coffee floated like a delectable substance through the still air.

"It's going to be awfully hot to-day," Mrs. Wartrace, the widowed aunt, remarked. "I hope you are not going to hoe in the sun this morning."

"Huh!" Dixie sniffed, as she sat down at the end of the table and began to butter a hot biscuit, "and let the crab-grass and pussley weeds literally choke out the best stand of cotton I ever laid my eyes on. No, siree, not me. I'd hire hands, but all the niggers have gone to town where there are more back-doors to live at; no, there is nothing for me to do but to look out for number one. See here, you two women don't seem to be able to look ahead. I've paid for half of this farm in the last three years, and in two more I'll own it. It is a good thing as it stands, but when I'm plumb out of debt we'll take it easy and set back in the shade once in a while. Alf Henley is a keen trader and knows what values are, and he told me not long ago that he believed a railroad would head for Chester some day, and, if it comes, my land would sell for town lots. Let's let well enough alone and be thankful for the blessings we've got. That's right, Aunt Mandy, drain it to the dregs and I'll fill it again. I knew I'd hit it exactly right this morning by the color of it."

Breakfast was over, and Dixie, aided by the fumbling hands of her mother, was washing and drying the few dishes and putting them away in the safe with perforated tin doors, which was the chief piece of furniture in the room, when the front gate opened and closed with a metallic click of the latch, and a visitor hurried along the little gravelled walk to the front porch.

"It is that meddlesome Carrie Wade," Mrs. Wartrace looked into the kitchen to say. "She's got on a new muslin, and has come over to show it, even as early as this."

"I'm not going to stand at the door and knock like a stranger," the visitor cried out, as she entered the little front hallway and rustled back to the kitchen. "Hello, Dix; Martha Sims and me are invited to spend the day over at Treadwell's. You know the new lumber-camp is there, and there's some dandy fellows working at it. They are going to give a dance, an' told us to send Ned Jones over with his fiddle. Oh, we are going to have a rattling time. We agreed to get up early. It seems funny, don't it? It's been many a day since I saw the sun rise."

The speaker was a tall blonde about Dixie's age. She was thin, inclined to paleness, and had a nervous look.

Dixie was drying her hands on a dishcloth, and she turned upon the visitor, surveying her carefully from her rather worn shoes to the newer dress and gaudily flowered hat with its tinsel ornaments and flowing pink ribbons. She knew full well that her neighbor had come for the sole purpose of showing her finery, and was secretly gloating over her misfortune in having to remain behind, and yet she allowed this knowledge in no way to affect her demeanor.

"You'll have a glorious time," Dixie said. "It's going to be a fine day for a picnic and dance."

"How do you like my dress?" Miss Wade asked, turning round for the inspection.

"It's very pretty, and pink suits you," Dixie answered, touching one of the folds of the skirt.

"It's entirely too long in front," Mrs. Hart said, as she bent forward and squinted sidewise with quite a visible sneer. "You'd look powerful funny walking along kicking up the skirt behind. With a veil on nobody could tell whether you was going or coming. Take my word for it—that stuff'll fade, even in the sun. You won't get more than one or two wearings out of it."

"Oh, do you think so?" The blond face fell. "I was a little afraid of that myself, and maybe you are right about the fit behind, too."

"Mother doesn't know what she's talking about," Dixie said, with a reproachful glance at her parent, who frowningly hovered on the verge of another criticism. "It is the way you've put the flounce on, Carrie, that makes it look that way in front. Wait, let me pin it up."

"Pin it up, I say!" Mrs. Hart sniffed. "You'll never get it to look decent that way. Nothing but making the whole thing plumb over will do any good. You ought to have got you a new sash to go with the muslin; weak-eyed as I am, I can see the dirty, faded edges agin the new cloth. The two don't go together. In war-times it was considered excusable to botch things that way, but not in this day and time when all *industrious* folks can get what's needed."

Dixie looked up regretfully, and a flush of embarrassment climbed into her fine face as her mother, accompanied by her silent sister, swept stiffly from the room.

When Carrie Wade had left, after her by no means triumphant call, Dixie went to her mother, who stood in the yard under an apple-tree, still with a frown on her really gentle face.

"You oughtn't to have said all that, mother," Dixie said, as she leaned on the smooth handle of the hoe she was going to take to the field. "After all, she was in *our* house."

"And come in it like a yellow-fanged snake with its forked tongue fairly dripping with poison," was the ready retort. "She come to gloat over you as she always has since the day you cut her out of that young man. She knowed you were going to work at home to-day, and she had the littleness to traipse over here to try to make you feel like you was missing something awful grand. If I hadn't left the kitchen I wouldn't have stopped with what I said about her flimsy dress. I'd have told her that if she'd stay at home more, and keep the holes in her stockings darned, and her underclothes cleaner, she'd stand a better chance roping in some fool man. I'm plain and outspoken, and I resent sneaking hints and false grins as quick as I do slaps. I'm tired o' you doing the way you are, anyhow. I want you to be like the rest of the girls. What do we care about owning this farm. Her daddy can't buy a knitting-needle on time, and yet they live as well as anybody else, and she thinks she is a grade higher than the rest of us."

"Don't you let it bother you, Muttie," Dixie said, tenderly;

indeed, she was always moved by a demonstration of her mother's love, and her eyes were moist as she put a caressing hand on the gray locks of the little woman. "We are going to see it through. When the farm is plumb paid for we'll make Carrie so sick with our fine doings she'll wish she was dead."

"It is mighty hard," the old lips quivered, and the gaunt, blue-veined hand was raised to the dim eyes. "I can't stand to see that girl going to places you can't go to. I simply can't, that's all."

"I could have gone, mother," Dixie remarked. "I didn't tell her, for I knew exactly what she would say, but Hank Bradley met me on the way home yesterday and offered to drive me over there. He says he knows all the lumber crowd well."

"Hank Bradley—did he want to take you?" cried Mrs. Hart, "and you wouldn't go?"

"I couldn't, mother. You know every girl that has ever kept company with him has been talked about. I don't like him. I can't stand him. He's a bad man, mother—a gambler, a drunkard, and an idler. He doesn't care for the characters he has ruined. He's fast running through the money his mother left him; he's no good."

"I don't know that you did exactly right," Mrs. Hart said, with the indecision and bad logic into which her ill-fortune sometimes drew her. "I know what he is well enough, but you are able to take care of yourself, and you lose so many chances by being so particular. He knows your true worth, and I've knowed men even as bad as he is to be reformed by loving a good girl."

"I ain't in the reforming business," Dixie laughed. "I'd

rather fight crab-grass and pussley weeds, and I'm off now. You go back in the house and set down and don't talk about the picnic. I sha'n't even think about it. I never bother about anything when I get warmed up."

Without a word further the two parted. Mrs. Hart stood on the little porch, and Dixie crossed the stretch of green meadow-land and climbed over the rail-fence of her cotton-field. The long rows of succulent plants, as high as the girl's knees, seemed breathing, conscious things to which she was giving relief as she smoothly cut away the tenaciously encroaching weeds and deep-rooted grass, the heaviest bunches of which she took up and threshed against the hoe-handle and left in the sun to die lest they be revived by some shower which would beat their roots into the mellow soil again. The sun rose higher and higher till it was poised almost directly over her head, and its rays beat more fiercely down upon her. The almost breathless air was as hot as a gust from the open door of a furnace. Her hands, in her heavy, knitted yarn gloves, were moist and red.

In the distance, and nearer to the village, rose the white, pretentious house of old Silas Welborne, the money-lender and the uncle of Hank Bradley, to whom she owed the remaining payment on her land. Almost day and night it stood before her as a mute reminder of her difficult undertaking. This morning, in the golden light, against the mountain background, it seemed an inspiration, as a flag of peace might appear to a tired soldier. Hank Bradley was the orphaned son of old Welborne's sister, and he lived in his uncle's home in lieu of any other that was available. He had made trips to the West and had remained away for indefinite periods, the last being the time he had come home with the carelessly announced death of his companion, Dick Wrinkle. The uncle and nephew were an incongruous pair: old Welborne, with his miserly grasp on the vitals of half the county, and the devil-may-care Bradley, whose wild ways made him the constant talk of the community. Old Silas gave no thought to the fellow's reform. As the administrator of his sister's estate, he doled out honestly enough the various sums in rents, dividends, and interest to which the young man was entitled after his liberal fees as administrator had been deducted, and even smiled when told of Bradley's reckless and almost criminal escapades. Henley had once remarked in his keenly observant way that Welborne, being the next of kin, would be glad to hear that his nephew had died with his boots on in some one of the lynching affairs to which Bradley was suspected of being a party.

Dixie had reached the farthest end of one of her longest cotton-rows, and was turning to work homeward on another, when the branches of the bushes of a near-by coppice parted and Bradley, with a fowling-piece on his arm, appeared.

"Good gracious, you *are* a queer girl!" he laughed, as he advanced to the low fence and climbed to a seat upon it. "Working here like a corn-field nigger in sun hot enough to bake a potato, when you could have been gliding through the shade behind my horse—to say nothing of the picnic and dance when we got there."

She pushed back the hood of her bonnet and smiled faintly.

"Driving and dancing ain't paying debts," she said, "and there is no other time to do this work. You know your uncle well enough to understand what he expects of folks unlucky enough to be on his books."

"That's another thing I can't understand," the young man said, bracing his heels on one of the rails, and, with his gun across his lap, he began to twist his stiff brown mustache, while his dark eyes rested with growing warmth on her trim figure. "What in the name of common-sense do you want to own land for?"

"What does a body want to *breathe* for?" Dixie asked him, sharply, "or own the duds on your back, or the grub you eat? Why, it is simply to be independent. I wouldn't quake and shiver every time that old man meets me if I wasn't in his clutch. I ain't afraid of anybody else, but I am of him, and why? Because he's got me where he can do as he likes with me. The last time I went to explain why I couldn't meet the payments exactly to the day, he growled like a bear, and said if I didn't look sharp he'd sell the roof over my head."

"Well, we needn't talk about him," the handsome daredevil said. "What I want to know is why you'd rather hoe cotton in weather like this than go with me to a jolly picnic. Why, Dixie, you don't begin to know your power; you could do as you like in this world, if you only would. You are the best-looking girl in the county, and you grow prettier every day. The blood of life is in your veins; you haven't got the sickly, palish look that the girls have who stay indoors half the time. You've got a clear eye, a good figure, and a complexion that society women would give big money for."

"You needn't begin all that again." The girl lowered her head and half raised her hoe to strike at a weed near a stalk of cotton. "I know what I am well enough. I was born with a load on me, and I'm going to tote it till I get to a dumping-place. My good looks won't set the world on fire."

"Well, they have set *me* on fire," Bradley laughed, significantly. He lowered his feet to the ground on her side of the fence and leaned his gun against it. "Say, this sun will actually blister us; let's go down to the spring."

"No spring for me to-day," she said, grimly. "I see Aunt

Mandy on the back porch now. She'll hang out a towel in a minute. That's the signal that it is half-past eleven by the clock. I've got to go cook dinner."

"Well, I'll walk over with you."

"No, you mustn't."

"Why?"

"Because I'd rather you wouldn't—that's all."

"I declare I believe you mean that, and I won't push myself on you, Dixie. You know how I feel about you, and you oughtn't to be so dadblasted rough with a fellow. I think about you night and day. I didn't come out to shoot anything this morning. I simply couldn't get over the way you turned me down yesterday. I lay awake last night thinking about it, and so I waited for you this morning. I stayed in the bushes over there watching till you hoed up here. I don't believe I'll ever get over feeling that way, and I am not going to give up. I'm going to keep hoping."

"There goes my towel!" Dixie said, as she laid her hoe across her shoulder. "I must go. Don't follow me, Hank. I don't want her, or anybody else, to see me out here with you."

"Then come out to the fence this evening, after supper, won't you, just a minute?"

"No, I can't—I never leave the house after dark. They need me at home."

"Blast them, what have they got to do with you? You are already a slave to them. Well, good-bye. You'll change your mind some day."

He held out his hand with a smile, but she refused to take it.

"You won't even shake hands. Why, what is the matter with you? I can see that you are mad at me by the twitching of— Do you know, Dixie, you have the most maddening mouth and lips that a woman ever owned? Say, shake just once to show that we are friends."

"I won't. I did it once and you held me and tried to kiss me. I'll tell you now in dead earnest, Hank, you must never try that sort of a thing again. I mean it, as God is my judge, I do."

"I never will while you hold a hoe in your grip," he jested, with a thwarted smile, as she turned from him.

He stepped back to his gun and stood watching her as she plodded homeward. "I can't help it," he said, a dark, desperate look on his face. "I simply can't quit thinking about her. I've got staying qualities, and no man ever gained his point that paid the slightest attention to a woman's moods. Right now she may be wishing she'd gone to the picnic."

CHAPTER IV

"Jim, how's your courting getting on?" Henley asked his clerk, half teasingly, one sultry afternoon, as the two were finishing a game of checkers on a board from which the squares were almost obliterated by the constant sliding of the black and white pants-buttons which were used for checkers.

"Don't ask me, Alf," Cahews answered, with a sickly smile. "I'm afraid she's too much for me. We ain't a bit nigher the altar than we was a year ago when I begun. Sometimes I think she is willing, and then ag'in I don't."

"I kinder thought you looked worried the last time you took her to ride," said Henley, sympathetically. "I felt sorry for you. She looked mighty chipper in her finery as you whisked by, but you was down in the mouth. Looked like you was on duty, and that was all."

"Somehow I don't much blame her," Cahews sighed, "but it looks to me like she is having too good a time running here and there to want to settle down. Sometimes I git blue and think she is just holding me as a safe thing to land on while she looks the field over. I have to stay here and attend to business and see her gallivanting in her ruffles and flounces with every drummer and lightning-rod agent that comes along."

"Maybe you ought to sorter lay down the law, at least on that particular point," Henley submitted, delicately. "I've heard my step-daddy-in-law say that a woman was born to be commanded, and when they ain't they hop to t'other extreme and just loll about in their abuse of a feller's good-nature. I don't know—that's the old man's view. You might give out a decided order or two, Jim, and see how—"

"Not to a woman you are tryin' to marry," said the clerk, quite firmly. "Sech a thing might be done to an army of soldiers or a red-handed mob at a lynchin'-bee, but not to a gal that makes you feel like you are sinking down in a mire whenever she looks you in the eyes. No, Alf, not to a gal as purty and sweet as a bunch of roses, and that knows it, and is in the habit o' being told of it as regular as eatin' and sleepin'. A gal like that sort o' feels 'er oats, as the feller said. She knows she's the stuff, and she loves to be told of it as much as a cat loves to sleep in the sun."

"Well, I'll be dadblamed if I'd tag after her without *some* substantial hope," Henley opined, wisely. "Life is long and life is earnest, and beauty is only skin deep, anyways. It seems to me—*now*, at least—that if I was out on the hunt for a helpmeet I'd look to the *solid* qualities in a woman just as I would in a man I wanted to work with. I'd study her character, her pluck under trying circumstances, her industry, and her all-round good-nature. The shape and face and furbelows, eyebrows and color of bangs, would be the last consideration."

"I never hear that from any but married men," Jim said. "They sing that song till they bury their wives, and then they turn to boys again and pick the youngest and prettiest they can lay their hands on."

"I was just thinking, Jim"—Henley seemed unwilling to combat the last assertion. His eyes rested thoughtfully on a sunny spot before the open door—"you see, I've got a little neighbor that—"

"I know—Dixie Hart! I know who you mean," the clerk broke in. "She's all wool and a yard wide, but I never run across her till after I'd got in with old man Hardcastle's daughter. I wouldn't talk to just any stray person this away, Alf, but me and you was boys together, and you've always been my friend. She's got me, Alf—I don't exactly know how—but she could crook her little finger at me and I'd make for her side—yes, sir, I would, through flame and smoke, if the world was coming to an end."

The talk had grown serious; there was a moist gleam in Cahew's blue eyes, and he snuffed as if he had a cold. Henley was glad of the interruption brought about by the arrival of a stranger who entered the front door and came back to them with swift, steady strides. He was fat, middle-aged, short, had a round, smooth face, and in removing his straw hat to fan his pink brow he disclosed a very bald head.

"I don't know whether you gentlemen are in need of anything in my line," he said, as he drew a big book of illustrations from beneath his arm and opened it on Henley's desk. "But I was givin' yore town and vicinity the one and only chance of its life to git the only true and artistic thing in marble. I'm agent for the Adamantyne Tombstone Company, of Tennessee. We own the only quarry of snow-white, non-grit, pristyne Parian rock on this side of the blue ocean, and we have in our employ the best and most world-renowned chisel-artists that ever breathed the spark of life into inanimate matter. Now, just set where you are, gentlemen—don't move—and I'll show you a beauty—a tombstone that will make a man want to die—if he's able to pay the price."

He held his book of illustrations open before Henley, whose

eyes were twinkling mischievously as they rested on his clerk.

"I'm not in the market," he said, without a smile. "I wouldn't buy any but a second-handed one, and then it would have to be so cheap that a dead man would kick it off of his grave in disgust. You've got in the wrong box. If you'll look about amongst the junk I've got in my back-yard you may find one or two lying about."

"I see you've got a streak of fun in you," the agent said, good-naturedly, and at this instant old Jason Wrinkle entered and sauntered back to the group. He seemed to recognize the stranger, for the two exchanged nods of greeting. "I'm still at it, you see," the salesman said. "I'm going to give all a chance. How about you, sir?" and he turned to Cahews. "I may find you serious, if this man ain't. Death is beautiful when it is properly looked at and provided for."

"I don't need anything in that line," Cahews said, with a flush.

"You *might*, Jim," Henley broke in, with a grin, "if you don't git cured of that complaint you was telling me about just now," and Henley winked almost imperceptibly to any one not familiar with the tricks of his face. He bent his head and smiled behind his broad hand. "I'll tell you, sir," he went on to the salesman, after another sly wink at Cahews, "none of us here happen to want anything in your line, but there is a rich old codger across the way—Mr. Silas Welborne—who will trade if you'll stick to him long enough. He's got dead kin with no sort o' tags on 'em. You might have to talk to him all the evening, and even follow him home, but you'll sell him if you understand your business. He's powerful soft-hearted, for one thing, and if you'll tell him a tale or two in the eloquent tongue you was rolling off just now he'll place a dandy order. I'll give you that as a pointer."

"Well, I'm much obliged to you, sir, and thank you kindly," the agent said, as he closed his book. "I'll look him up. I'm doing a big business here. Your people don't seem to have had a chance to invest in my line in no telling how long. Good-day."

"Good-day," Henley echoed, and he endeavored to hide the mischievous smile that was playing about his mouth. In a chuckling undertone he said to Wrinkle and Cahews: "I'd give a pretty to see this oily-tongued chap holding down that crusty old miser. A tombstone is the last thing on earth that Welborne would want to think about or talk about. I'd love to be there and see 'em meet."

Cahews laughed and sauntered toward the front, and old Wrinkle sat down in the chair just vacated and tilted it back against the door-jamb.

"That is a sorter good joke," he said, his small eyes on Henley, "considering the man you mean it for, but as I stood thar hearin' you concoct it I couldn't help thinking if you knowed what a joke this self-same peddler had got off on you you'd not be exactly in the mood for fun—at least not in the grave-rock line."

"What joke are you talking about?" Henley asked, incredulously, his face falling into seriousness. "I have never laid eyes on this chap before."

"I reckon not, but you'll know him the next time you see him; I'll be bound you do, even if you are a mile down the road an' he's round the bend with his back turned to you. The truth is, I just followed him down here to see who he'd strike next. He's been to our house, Alf. He slid in there just after you come off, and set on the porch and begun his palaver. He has a different way with women than he has with men. He seems to know that women are soft on some lines, and chiefly on preachin' and buryin'. He'd picked up a list of folks round about here that had lost kin, and he had me and Jane down on it on account of Dick. Now, it seems that when he gits to a place he goes to the graveyard and looks for stones to tally with his dead list, and when he don't find any he makes a note of it; so, you see, havin' Dick's name down, an' not knowin' the full particulars, he hunted us up, thinkin' we was unsupplied in his line. So, you see, that's why he made sech a leech of hisse'f on our porch."

"Huh, I see," Henley frowned—"I see."

"I can't begin to describe all the chap done or said," Wrinkle resumed. "He riz and walked and ranted, an' prayed an' sung an' mighty nigh called up mourners. I thought them two women would bust out cryin' once or twice, but they belt in tiptop through the hottest of the wrangle. Then I thought I'd put a stop to it, and I up and told him, I did, that he'd made a mistake, an' that we didn't need a thing of the sort—that Dick's body never was recovered, and so on. Then what do you think? The skunk was actually flabbergasted, and didn't know what to say. But he was game, and knowed thar was some way out of his trouble. He said, 'Wait a minute—don't bother me!' an' he shet his eyes tight, an' set thar with his head hangin' down for fully five minutes. Then he looked up an' said, 'I was jest tryin' to recall the good lady's name that had the same trouble, pine blank, as your'n, but it slips me somehow.' An' with that he said it was the custom all over civilized Christendom, in such cases as our'n, to erect a suitable monument jest the same, havin' a plot the right length an' width set aside, with both head and foot rock, and, if a sermon hadn't been preached already, one ought to be on the day the stone was put in place an' consecrated. I 'lowed sure them women would see how plumb silly it was, but they listened like they was gittin' the only directions to the Golden Shore, and begun to look at the pictures in his book like they thought the skunk was savin' 'em from death, destruction, an' disgrace."

"You don't mean to tell me they actually went and ordered—" Henley began, but his voice trailed away into indistinctness. He could only stare at his tormentor hopelessly.

"Only a little one fur five hundred dollars," Wrinkle said, with evident enjoyment. "They had a lots o' trouble pickin' out the design amongst all the doves, broke-off pillars, seraphims, an' angels, but they finally got what they wanted. Not a tear was shed, if you'd stood off a few feet, out o' earshot, you couldn't 'a' told but what they was pickin' out a pattern fer a weddin'-dress or buyin' tickets fer a side-show. After they got under headway I couldn't say anything—they had sech a solemn way about it, and then I couldn't help but be fair and think if I'd been in Dick's place they would have gone through exactly the same antics, an' been jest as liberal in showing due respect. Hettie says it is all to come out of her own money that she had when she married you. She was particular to mention the fact, and I think that showed a sensible streak, for a fool would know you oughtn't to be expected to stand sech expense, and so long after you took her, and that being a thing that would naturally belong to her past career, too. After the agent had gone off I set thar, an' Hettie told me what she was goin' to do. She don't intend to spare expense to do the thing plumb right. She's goin' to send away off for a high-priced reverential orator to give the discourse, an' intends to have evergreens hung all over the church. I don't know whether she designs to have all the business houses in Chester closed that day, but she'd naturally expect you and Jim to shet up an' take it in."

"So this is the joke you said that man had got off on me, is it?" Henley snapped out, irritably.

"Well, I reckon it mought not appear exactly in the same light to you, Alf," answered Wrinkle, "as it would to somebody who'd be more inclined to laugh over a thing of the sort. You was gettin' off what you called a good one on old Tight-fist just now by puttin' this chap on his track, and I reckon you'd have no call to git mad if Welborne made it tit for tat an' fired back at you. You wouldn't be justified in killin' 'im, you know, if he was to take a notion to send you a big bouquet o' flowers out o' his gyarden all tied up in black ribbon with a cyard sayin' he's sorry to hear of the sad loss in yore family, an'—"

"Ah, you make me sick, with your eternal chatter!" Henley burst out, angrily. "I don't care what them two silly women do. I'll not be here to witness such tomfoolery. I'm going to Texas, to be away several months."

"So I've heard," Wrinkle said, a trifle more mildly, "but you'll be missin' some'n out o' the general run, if I'm any judge. Thar may have been sech a thing sence the flood as a married woman callin' out all hands to solemnize her first husband's demise while she's still wearin' the weddin'-clothes bought by her second, but it's a new *wrinkle* on me, an' I hain't makin' what you mought call a pun, nuther."

Abruptly leaving the old man, Henley joined his clerk at the front.

"I get so mad at that old chap sometimes I could kick him," he said, in an angry undertone. "Nothing under the sun is sacred to him."

"He's gettin' old and childish," Cahews answered. "I sorter love to hear 'im chatter. Some o' the things he says about folks and their peculiarities sound powerful funny."

"Well, they don't to me," burst from Henley, "and I'll tell you another thing, Jim—enough of a thing is a plenty, and while I'm away—" but Wrinkle had approached, and, passing behind the counter, he was tiptoeing that he might reach a candy-jar on the top shelf.

"Looks like I'm about yore only candy customer, Jim," he said to Cahews. "Thar hain't been a stick took out o' this jar sence I was here Monday. I laid one crossways on top just to see. I'd order a fresh lot if I was you. This is gettin' dry and crumbly. I can suck wind through a stick the same as a pipe-stem."

CHAPTER V

One clear, warm morning a week later Henley stood in the little porch in front of his store and glanced up the street which gave into the road that led on to his farm. In the store Cahews was nailing the top slats on a coop of scrambling, squawking chickens, and with a pot of lampblack and brush was marking it for shipment to Atlanta. In a cloud of dust in the rear, Pomp, the negro porter and all-round servant on Henley's farm, was turning the handle of a clattering machine for the separation of chaff from grain. And while his eyes were resting on the road the storekeeper saw a horse and wagon come around a bend and slowly advance toward him. The horse was a poor beast of great age, and the wagon was none the better for wear. It had lost all its original paint, the woodwork was cracked by the weather and the sun. Its four wheels ran unevenly; some of the spokes were missing, and its bolts and rods of iron rattled in holes worn too large.

"By Gum, it's Dixie Hart, and she's fetching in a load of produce," Henley muttered; then he called out to Cahews: "Say, Jim, get through there and stop that nigger's clatter. We are going to have a visitor. The fairest of the fair will be here in a minute."

Henley stepped down to the edge of the sidewalk and bowed and smiled to her as she drew rein. In her new straw hat and clean, well-ironed gingham she looked decidedly well. She was radiantly bright, and smiled merrily as she extended her hand and shook his over the rickety fore-wheel as she leaned forward from the dilapidated, sagging seat, the springs of which rested on the sides of the wagon-bed.

"I told you I'd be in," she laughed, "and, if the market is off to-day, back I go to my shanty. Nothing but the best prices catch me."

"About as favorable now as any time," he said. "What does your load consist of?" he ran on, jovially, as he glanced behind her at the bags, boxes, coops, pails, and jars.

"Odds and ends," she laughed. "I've got to make a payment to old Welborne on my debt. You and Jim had better give me tiptop bids all through or I'll peddle the truck from door to door and steal your trade right from under your noses."

Henley smiled good-humoredly as he walked round the wagon opening boxes and bags and making notes with a pencil on a scrap of paper. Then he told her what he would pay for each item.

"Is that as good as you can do?" It was a question she always asked, and she did so now more from habit than for any intention of disagreeing with him.

"That's the top-notch, Dixie," he said. "We couldn't do that, but we've got customers that simply won't eat butter and eggs that don't have your brand on 'em."

"I believe you," she said, laconically. "I've met 'em myself. They pass by the house from Carlton sometimes in their fine rigs and ask me why I don't start a milk-and-butter farm. I may do it if I ever get out of debt. I've got sense enough to know it would pay, and pay big, considering that there ain't no such business established. Well, Alfred, I'll take your offer. I don't like to dicker with first one store and then another, and I know you've been straight with me in all my dealings. I'll trade out part of the amount. I've got a few tricks to buy in your line."

"Well, alight and come in and set down," he said. "Jim and Pomp will unload and weigh and measure. I'll make Pomp mind your hoss."

"Oh, old Bob will stand all right!" she laughed, as she put her gloved hand on Henley's shoulder and sprang lightly to the ground. "He's moved all he wants to to-day. It would take a switch-engine to budge him an inch. See 'im nod? He knows what we are talking about."

Henley led her through the long room to his desk in the rear, and gave her a seat near the open door as the clerk and the porter went out to the wagon. She took off her hat and pushed back her luxuriant hair with her fingers.

"You go on with your work," she said; "don't mind me."

He applied himself to some writing he had to do till Cahews came with a slip of paper on which he had noted the weights, quantities, and values of the things she had brought, and with a polite bow he handed it to her.

"Look it over, Dixie," Henley jested. "Old man Hardcastle's daughter has rubbed a rabbit-foot on Jim so that he can hardly add two and two. Besides, he is always rattled when he's waiting on a pretty girl."

"Well, he won't rattle any more than a green gourd round me, if that's the case," Dixie said, as she began to run over the figures, her lips moving as she counted on her fingers. "I know in reason it's correct," she said, extending the slip to Cahews. "No, wait a minute," drawing it back and looking at it again. "If I'm not powerfully mistaken, Jim, you are swindling yourself out of twenty cents on the string-beans. There was one peck instead of two."

"I told you Jim was rattled," Henley continued to jest. "But I won't discharge 'im. I'd pardon him if he was to set the store afire, under the circumstances. I've seen him wash his hands in the kerosene tank and wipe 'em on his clothes just after Julia Hardcastle driv' by in a hug-me-tight buggy with a drummer."

"Well, I wouldn't blame him much," Dixie smiled in her sympathy for the embarrassed clerk. "She is nice and pretty, and one town-girl that isn't stuck up. I like her. She wants to have a good time; she likes attention and good clothes, and I'm sure I'd be just like her if I had half the chance. She called to see me the other day, and Ma and Aunt Mandy fell in love with her. They think she has lots of common-sense, and they know. I had another call. Carrie Wade waited till she saw me go to the field to work, then she come over and asked if I was at the house. Ma told her where I was, and she come over the clods grumbling like a spoilt baby about getting dust on her shoes. What do you reckon she wanted?"

"I can't imagine," Henley answered, as Cahews, flushing with delight over the compliment to the maid of his choice, moved away.

"She come to cut at me," Dixie said, as she took the pile of silver into her hand which Henley was extending. "As she stood there between the corn-rows holding up her skirt she said she was going over to the lumber-camp again with Martha Sims to another big all-day blow-out. She said she was to start early and had so much fixing to do that she wondered if I'd spare the time to wash and iron a muslin dress for her. She said she'd pay well for it, because my things always looked so nice."

"Impudent thing!" Henley said; "she ought to have, knowed better than that."

"She *did* know better, and that's exactly why she said it. She intended to let me know where she was going, thinking it would break my heart. She admits she is bent on getting married, and says she knows I'll live and die an old maid. She hates me, Alfred; with all her soul she hates me. She will never rest satisfied till she sees me plumb down and out. It all started through no fault of mine, too. You remember that young preacher, Mr. Wrenn, that boarded about in the families three years ago. Well, she made a dead set at him. She literally tagged after him everywhere he went till folks here in Chester was laughing about it and calling her his little dog Fido. They say he got so he'd run and hide every time she'd turn a corner. Well, he stayed at our house two weeks, and, of course, we all tried to make him as comfortable as we could. I give you my word that I never was alone with the fellow more than five minutes in all the time he was there, but I'll admit he hung around considerable—that is, with us all."

"I remember the fellow," Henley said, deeply interested. "I had a talk with your Pa about him not a month before he died. Your Pa said he couldn't see why you was so offish. The fellow made no beans about how he felt, and when the report went out that you had turned him down folks wondered powerful, for all the girls was setting their caps for him."

"I was too young to have good sense, I reckon," the girl said, shrugging her shoulders. "Pa was alive, and we did not want for anything. I never dreamt I'd have such a load on me as I've got now. Then I had a foolish notion about love, anyway. I'd been reading novels, and got an idea in my silly head that when a girl met the right person she went through some sort of dazzling regeneration; and as I didn't feel anyways peculiar when Mr. Wrenn was about I thought I ought to wait, and I told him so. I'll never forget that young man's face. I've thought of it thousands of times, and been sorry."

"And Carrie Wade found out about it?" Henley was leading her along gently and sympathetically.

"Why, he told her himself—told her to her face in a crowd of young folks at Sunday-school the next day, and the worst part of it was somebody in the bunch that didn't like Carrie joked her about it. The whole thing has gone out o' folks' minds by this time, I reckon; but Carrie never laid it aside. It rankled and still rankles. She gloats over my hardships and makes a point of flaunting her good luck in my face, and is eternally telling me of her chances to get married. She's half crazy on the subject, and thinks every one else is like her. I know one thing, Alfred Henley, when I do slip off the coil of single blessedness she'll be madder than a wet hen without shelter on a cold December day. And she won't have long to wait neither—there! I've gone and let the cat out of the bag, but I don't care. I'd trust a friend like you with my life. You talk pretty free to me, and I can to you."

"You don't—you can't mean to—to say that you have got some 'n of the sort in view, Dixie?"

"Well, you just lie low and watch," she laughed, significantly. "I let one chance pass me, and I don't intend to be such a fool again. I can use a stout, willing, and able-bodied man in my line of business. I've got two old women to support and a big debt to pay, and I'm about to the limit of my endurance. I might have put it off, but I'm itching to see my prime enemy's face when I march him out to meeting. It's all on the quiet, and is going to be a big surprise. I never let my folks on to it till just the other day. That reminds me. I want one of your blank envelopes. I've written to him, and

I'm clean out of envelopes and want to mail the letter before I go home."

She flushed slightly, and her long lashes rested on her pink cheeks as she drew a folded paper from her pocket and held it in her lap with the money he had given her.

"You don't mean it!" Henley cried in astonishment. "Why, you take my breath away; but, of course, I'm glad. I certainly can congratulate the lucky fellow."

"Ask 'im whether it would be in order before you do." She reached for his pen and dipped it, and began to address the envelope as it lay on her knee.

"And that letter is to him, you say?" Henley said, wonderingly.

"Well, it ain't to no *girl*," Dixie smiled, with an arch, upward glance. "Stamps and paper cost too much such times as these to waste 'em on women."

"I'm curious to know what sort o' chap you've decided on," said Henley. "What does he look like?"

"He's a pig in a poke." She had finished writing and was drawing the gummed flap of the envelope across her smiling lips. "I never laid eyes on 'im in my life. What do you think of that? But that part must never get out. I want Carrie and all the rest to—to think, you see, that I got acquainted with him in—in the regular way. She never would get through talking if she knew the full truth, and that is nobody's business but his and mine. You may think I am a born fool, Alfred, but for the past six months I've been corresponding with a fellow in Florida. But he's all right. Don't you worry; he's *safe*, and that is a lot to say in this day of trickery and strife. It all come about by accident. I've got a cousin—Tobe Chasteen—working down there in an orange-grove, and now and then he writes me a letter. Well, in one he wrote that a nice fellow down there wanted to write to some girl up in Georgia, and asked me if I'd answer. So, just for fun, and to kill time, I agreed, and so it started. He writes a good, flowing hand, and has plenty to say, and I got interested in the whole thing. He sent his picture, and wanted one of me. So I put on my best outfit and had a tintype struck off under that tent on the square and sent it to him. It was a frightful daub, I tell you; but he liked it, or said he did; he said it was fine, and if the goods come up to the sample that was all he could ask. I've got his in my pocket. I don't tote it about all the time, but it happened to be in the pocket of this dress. My two women want it to stay in the clock, so they can get it out and peep at it when I'm in the field. They are more crazy about him than I am. They sneak and read my letters, and ask ten thousand questions about him. There are some of his long epistles that I wouldn't show 'em for money—they are so silly. At first we just wrote about what was going on, but he kept edging closer and closer, and I never, in so many words, told him to let up. Once he drew a round ring in the middle of a blank page and asked under it if I couldn't guess what was in the middle of it. I looked close and could see a greasy splotch when it was held sidewise in the light. That kinder disgusted me, and I drew a ring in my answer, and told him there wasn't anything in mine, and never would be. He must have liked what I said, for he wrote back that it was cute, and that he'd bet I was one girl that never had been kissed. Well, he can think that, too, if he wants to. It won't do him any harm. I say all this was going on, but I never dreamt of closing the deal till I got in this present money-tight. You see, I wrote him about my financial trouble, and he said he had saved up some money and that he could wipe out all my obligations, and that me and him together would make a fine team on the farm. He wrote so kind, too, about Ma and Aunt Mandy, and said he'd always want 'em with us. You see, I felt grateful, and, considering everything, I think I acted wise—don't you?"

Henley half nodded, and tried to meet her frankness with a smile that was free from doubt. At this juncture Pomp came back with a telegram. It was an order from an Atlanta hotel for a quantity of eggs and butter. Henley read it and handed it back. "Tell Jim to quote the lowest cash prices," he said, absent-mindedly.

"But it's a order, suh," said the negro.

"Oh yes; I see it is. Well, ship it; it's all right."

"Would you like to see his picture?" Dixie asked. She had taken the crude tintype from her pocket and held it in her lap.

"Yes, I would," Henley replied, and he took the picture and looked at it. He didn't like it. A keen, quick reader of men's faces, he saw what had escaped her less experienced eye. There was something that bespoke prodigious vanity and lack of principle in the low brow, over which the coarse, black hair was plastered down so smoothly; in the heavy, carefully waxed, curled, and perhaps dyed mustache; in the small, conscious eyes, set close together; in the grossly sensuous mouth, from which a weak chin receded.

"He ain't as purty as he thinks he is by a long shot," Dixie remarked, rather lamely, for she was slightly chilled by Henley's failure to comment favorably on the picture, "but he has a good heart. He is a church member in fair standing, and has a Bible class of young ladies in Sunday-school, and was once proposed for superintendent, and lost out because he was unmarried and too young. Oh, I've thought it all over. I'm not jumping without looking for a spot to light on. I thought I could carry my load through, but I had to give in. I can't perform miracles, Alfred; I'm just clay, and the wrong gender of that. If I could keep temptation out of my way I might keep on, but I can't run against Carrie Wade's sneers. I'd rather strut by her house with a husband that was able to take me in out of the wet than anything else I know of, and I want to rest. I want to sleep one night without dreaming of old Welborne's flabby jaws, blinking eyes, and harsh voice snarling at me. Folks may say such an arrangement ain't customary—that it is out of the common—but it seems to me that everything about me is out of the common, anyway, and why shouldn't this fall in line? Customs are just what the most folks want to do. Custom don't look after the under dog in the pack. But when right is on a body's side there is no need to fear, and there won't be a shade of wrong in this if I have anything to do with it. I've made up my mind to do a wife's part in every sense of the word, and let it go at that—nothing risk, nothing have. I never used to think I'd ever marry a man I never saw—in fact, when I was young and silly I used to see myself strutting by whole regiments of fellers all making signs to me to come be his darling, but that was when my eyelids was glued down and before they was jerked open by trouble. Marrying with me in this case is an open-and-shut business proposition. I read somewhere that it is worked that way among high-up folks in France—though the dickering takes place between the parents of the contracting parties; and as I know a sight more about what to do than Ma, why, it was all right for me to take it in hand. Peter is an orphan, and I'm the head of a family, and so there was nobody else concerned. My two women are getting old and plumb helpless—more like children than grown-ups. They may live a long time. I certainly hope they will, for they are all I've got; but they are actually getting so that they don't want to budge out of the house, even as far as the fence. They are afraid a little sun will kill 'em dead. But, Alfred, I don't somehow like the way you look about it. You don't take it like I thought you would. I know in reason that you wish me well, and—"

"I don't know that I have a right to say a thing agin it," Henley broke into her now hesitating words. "But I must confess I'm sorter stunned, Dixie. I've always felt like a big brother to you, and pitied you a good deal, and now—well, you see, I reckon it is natural for me to be sorter afraid that you may be making a mistake in what you are doing. I feel like begging you not to do it, and then ag'in I don't, for I've always made up my mind that marrying was one thing no outsider could decide about. I have been dead agin marriages that afterwards turned out tiptop, and you know I didn't show such far-reaching wisdom in my own case as to set myself up as a judge."

"Well, you needn't have any fears on my account," Dixie smiled, assuringly. "I know what I am about, and I ain't the back-out kind. It's too late, anyway; the day has been set. For the last two weeks I've been giving every spare minute to the making of my outfit. It is a good one. I was determined to give Miss Wade a treat. I do things right, and I've spent some cash. My trousseau will attract attention, and I reckon Peter won't be ashamed. But it is to be kept quiet. Don't you say a word to a soul. A week from to-day I'll drive in and meet the up-train and haul my bridegroom home in my wagon. We'll eat dinner at our house and then drive over to Preacher Sanderson's and have him tie the knot. Now I'll go down in front and buy a few things and mail my letter and hurry home."

"Wait a minute, Dixie." She was moving away, and he stopped her, standing before her, a grave look in his eyes. "Surely it ain't as dead sure as that?"

"Yes, it is, Alfred; it's settled—plumb settled."

"But—but," he pursued, anxiously, "if you didn't like him

when you see him, you wouldn't marry him?"

"Oh, that's a gray horse of another color," she smiled. "I think I'll like him; but if I didn't—well, if I didn't, I'd pay his way back to Florida, and beg off."

Henley made no further protest. He sat at his desk and bowed his head in troubled thought as she tripped lightly away.

"What a pity!" he mused. "She deserves the best in the land, and this fellow looks like a worthless scamp."

CHAPTER VI

That evening after supper, while the sultry dusk hung heavily over the land, shutting out the few lights of the village and obscuring the near-by mountain, Henley took his chair into the passage, and, without his coat, he leaned back against the weather-boarding and lighted his pipe. He had not been there long when his wife, having finished her duties in the kitchen, came out and stood over him. Accustomed to her varying moods, he saw by her attitude that she was displeased.

"Pa told me something I don't like," she began. "I tried not to pay attention to it, but it was so unexpected, so unheard-of, so plumb disrespectful, that it hurt me. He said you told him you was going to Texas to keep from being here during the—the memorial service next month."

"I told him no such thing," Henley retorted, with an effort to control his rising temper. "I can't be responsible for the slap-dash way he puts things. I don't like his eternal gab, nohow."

"Well, you must have said *something*," Mrs. Henley pursued, probingly. "He never makes up things out of whole cloth. He is not that way."

"Well, I suppose I did say something," Henley reluctantly

admitted. "He was nagging the life out of me at the store about what you intended to do, and holding me up to ridicule, and I reckon I did say that I wouldn't be here—that my business would keep me in Texas. As for that matter, I told you about the trip long before this queer—long before you decided to do this—this thing."

"I know just how you said it," the woman threw back, sharply. "I know what you've thought all along about Pa and Ma being here, and me loving 'em and caring for 'em. You do your best to hide it, but you can't."

"Well, if I do my best, what more could you expect?" Henley asked, with more logic than patience.

"I'd want you to keep your promise to me," Mrs. Henley said, crisply, and she bent lower over him and fixed her offended eyes on his. "You told me before we were married that you'd promise never to object—you even said you admired me for my feelings, and that it proved to you that I had stability and strength of character—that you wouldn't have a wife that would ever forget her dead husband."

"Well, I have kept my promise," Henley said. "I am not sure that I knowed just precisely what I was doing when I made it, but I've kept it. As for attending his—his funeral services at such a late day, that is another thing. I don't see how you could expect it."

"You don't?" she flared up. "Will you tell me if there would be anything to be ashamed of in your being there? Would a divine service of that sort disgrace you? Would it besmirch your character?"

"No, and nobody said it would," Henley managed to fish from his addled brain. "But I simply thought, somehow, that it would look better for me to be out of the way.

Funerals and the like are generally attended by mourners, and, well, where would I come in? I reckon my proper seat would be with you and the—the rest of the family on the front bench, if it was anywhere. It would look funny for me just to be a looker-on from the back part of the house, and I'd feel like a dern fool in front. A dern fool—you may not know what that is from experience, but you ought to from observation; you've had one under your eye for some time."

"Well, you simply don't approve of it," the woman returned, resentfully. "You can set there, blessed with good health and life, and plenty to eat and wear, and actually begrudge the little mite of respect that is paid to the helpless dead. In being overpersuaded and marrying you I was untrue to him and his memory, and now you make it worse by opposing a simple little ordinance that is due every person on earth, high or low."

"It ought to have been done earlier, and before I got—got mixed up in it, if it was done at all," Henley said, trying to speak mildly and, even, pacifically.

"I know that now," Mrs. Henley said, in a tone of such deep self-reproach that her stare softened and wavered; "but it wasn't thought of. I never knew it was the style till this man come along and told me; but that is no reason I shouldn't make amends, late as it is. It is all the better proof that Dick is remembered. But you can go to Texas." The stare hardened and became fixed again. "Folks will say you are jealous and mean, and that I was an unfaithful fool for listening to you, but I will have to stand it."

"Well, I'll simply be obliged to be away," Henley said, doggedly. "The business won't be put off, and—and—"

"And you are a heartless brute!" the gaunt woman cried, as she whirled from him and strode into the house.

A few minutes later there emerged from the near-by door of the kitchen the real instigator of the present dispute. He trudged across the passage, drawn down on one side by the weight of a dripping swill-pail which he was taking to the pigpen, descended the short flight of steps, and turned back toward Henley. He stood for a moment hesitatingly, the pail wiping its dripping exterior against his baggy jean trousers. Then he said: "I've got a thing or two to say to you, Alf, if you will oblige me by steppin' down to my pen so I can stop that hog's squealin' long enough to hear myself talk. One at a time, I say, an' let it be me."

"By all means," Henley answered, ambiguously, and he joined Wrinkle on the grass and they walked down the path together to the pigpen in a corner of the rail-fenced cow-lot.

"No use enterin' a talkin'-match with the whistle of a crazy steam-engine," the stepfather-in-law strained his lungs to say, and he grunted as he raised the pail to the top rail of the pen and cautiously tilted it to let the contents run into the wooden trough.

"Now, that's more like it," he said, his voice rising above the suction-pump noise of the hungry animal. He lowered the empty pail to the ground, and with a paddle began to dig out the mushy sediment from the bottom and throw it into the trough, as a mason might mortar from a trowel. "The truth is, Alf, I've got an apology to make to you, and I didn't want to do it up thar before them women. The other day when I said that about old Welborne a-sendin' you a bunch o' flowers to decorate Dick's grave I wasn't actually thinkin' about you as much as I was about Welborne an' his close-fisted ways. Of course, now I think of it again, it *would* be a good way for 'im to git back at you for yore joke in sendin' the tombstone man to him, and I catch myself lafin' every time I think of it, and the way you'd look if he did, but—"

"What the devil do you mean?" Henley broke in, testily. "Here you are startin' in to apologize for a thing and going over it again word for word? Have you plumb lost your senses?"

"Was I doin' that?" Wrinkle asked, blandly, though even in the twilight Henley could see that his eyes were twinkling. "Well, I'm sorry again, and I'm just man enough to say so, Alf. I'll apologize as many times as you like. I'll keep on till you *are* satisfied. But you must listen. You are a-gittin' powerful touchy here lately, and it ain't becomin' in a man of yore dignity. It will git so after a while that I can't express any sort of opinion to you without a fist-fight. I was goin' on to say that I was jest thinkin' of old Welborne's quick wit in every emergency that set me to wonderin' that day how he might act in sech a case. They say everything is grist to his mill—that he turns every single thing that drifts his way into profit great or small. And that day after you railed out at me in the store I went across the Square to see how yore joke would terminate. The door of his dingy little office was open, an' I could see the grave-rock man inside bendin' over old Welborne at his little table, pointin' at the pictures in his book and sweatin' like a nigger in a cotton-gin. But what struck me most of all was the glazed look in old Welborne's eye; he looked like he wasn't hearin' a word the fellow was spoutin', but was thinkin' o' some'n else plumb different. I walked on and hung about outside till the tombstone man come out. He was as mad as Hector. I seed he was, an' stopped 'im in a offhand way and axed him what luck.

"'Luck hell,' says he—he used the word, I didn't—'I talked to that dried-up old mummy,' says he, 'fer an hour jest to find that he was settin' thar all the time figurin' in his head about a speculation I'd made 'im think of while I was talkin' to him.'"

"The agent was so mad that he wouldn't explain what the

speculation was, but I heard it that evenin'. Hank Bradley was tellin' it to a crowd at the post-office. You know Hank makes all manner of sport of his uncle behind the old skunk's back. He told a tale, too, that I'd never heard. It seems that old Welborne's mother-in-law died, and Welborne went to a undertaker to buy 'er coffin. He picked out a fifty-dollar one, and talked and talked till he finally got the pore devil down to forty. Then he said:

"'You'd sell two for seventy-five, wouldn't you?'

"'I reckon I might,' the undertaker said, 'but you only want one.'"

"'I'll need another 'fore many months,' old Welborne said. 'My father-in-law won't last long. I'll take one now at thirty-seven-fifty and the other when the time comes.'"

Henley laughed, despite his displeasure. "That is just like him," he said, "and I believe every word of it."

"His present speculation takes the rag off'n the bush," said Wrinkle. "The talk of the gravestone man started him to thinkin' about what thar might be in that line for him, and he recalled that he owned ten acres of ground on a rise in the edge of town which he had bought at a tax-sale for twenty-five dollars. The very next mornin' he had a feller diggin' post-holes an' puttin' a fence around it with a main gate that had a big curvin' sign over it with the words 'Sunnyside Cemetery' on it, and I'm told that he has been all over town tellin' folks that the *old* graveyard is too low and soggy to be half decent, and that his'n was a great improvement. He intimated, too, that nobody but blue-bloods could git the'r names enrolled, and thar has been a powerful scramble for places, even by folks that have no idea of dyin' yet a while. You see, Alf, I got a good many particulars at fust hand, for he was out here to see Hettie in regard to accommodations for Dick, and I heard all that was said. Accordin' to Welborne thar is to be a wholesale movin' right away and choice quarters will be scarce, right when they are in the most demand."

"I suppose she—I suppose my wife—"

"Yes, she bit, Alf, and took a full mouthful at that. Welborne told her he was givin' her the pick of the whole thing because she was startin' the ball rollin', an' her fine marble would set the place off. She selected twenty foot square under a weepin'-willow, which he said had a rock bottom and the best view of the town. It only set her back two hundred round plugs, but she had that much left in the bank, and seems powerful well, satisfied. I wouldn't 'a' fetched all this up, but I 'lowed you'd like to know what a big thing growed out of yore little joke that day. I love a good joke myself, but when one's turned on you in a sort o' wholesale way, it don't feel the best in the world."

"There is no joke about it; it's outright stealing!" Henley had reference to Welborne's part of the transaction. "Any man can get money out of fool women, if he's mean enough to take advantage of their silly whims."

"I often wonder about you an' me an' the whole bunch of us here at the house," Wrinkle said. "Not one of the four is blood kin to the other, and yet here we are all wedged together as tight as young catbirds in a nest. Folks say the hardest question on earth is how to live, and yet to me it's been as easy as fallin' off a log into soft sand. Me 'n Jane never counted on Dick for any sort of aid, an' yet it was through him that we are provided for—in fact, he was so wishy-washy and helpless that we was glad to have him tie up with a woman that had a few dollars. He went in for a high old time, and he had it. I couldn't object—I was that way myself. He was as bad after gals as a drummer, and in his sparkin' days, as maybe you know, he could have had his pick. I couldn't keep from hearin' you an' Hettie talkin' in the passage jest now, and when she come into the light mad enough to bite a tenpenny nail in two I saw thar had been a row. Her notion to have you on hand at sech a time as that may seem odd, but women are all odd. They want what other women can't have, and I reckon Het thinks it would be a sort o' feather in 'er cap to mourn in public over one husband while she's leanin' agin another that is ready an' willin' in every way."

"I reckon we've talked long enough about it," Henley said, frigidly, and he glanced toward the lights in the farm-house.

"Yes, I reckon so," returned the gadfly. "As for me, I never was able to see how Het could accuse you of bein' jealous of Dick, when—"

"Jealous fiddlesticks!" Henley snorted. "I never was jealous of a *live* man, much less a dead one."

"It would *seem* that way," was all the support Wrinkle would give to the claim, as he took up his pail and started back to the house. "I didn't say you *was*, but Het seems to size it up that way."

Left alone, and with hot fires of resentment raging in his breast, Henley sauntered along the fence till he was behind his barn. His change of position brought him within a few yards of Dixie Hart's cottage, and he suddenly heard her voice. She was speaking to some one. Peering through the deepening darkness, which was broken only by the gleams of a few random stars, he saw her inside her yard at the gate, and leaning on the fence from the outside was the tall, well-clad form of Hank Bradley.

"You are not going to treat a feller as mean as that," Bradley was heard to say, in a gruff, pleading tone, "when I've been begging you so many times."

"I can't let you come in now, and I can't go to ride with you, either," Henley heard her answer, as she stood well away from the fence. "I've got good and sufficient reasons, and I hope you won't ask me any more."

"I'll keep on asking till the crack of doom," Bradley said, in a voice that shook. "You know I'm not the weak-kneed kind. The Bradley stock hold on like bulldogs. When they take a notion to anything they want it, and they keep on till they get it. So look out, Dixie Hart. I'm not to blame; your eyes burn holes in me and set me on fire. The more you turn me down the more I think about you."

"Well, you mustn't come any more," Dixie said, firmly. "Good-night."

Henley saw her move across the grass and vanish in the cottage. He heard Bradley stifle a surly exclamation of disappointment, and saw him turn and walk off slowly toward his uncle's house.

"Poor girl!" Henley said to himself. "In all her troubles she has to ward off a dirty, designing scamp like that; but she's doing it like a queen, an' no harm can touch 'er. And she's going to get married! She is going into the treacherous thing absolutely blindfolded, and the Lord only knows what will come of it. It's a risk for the best, and under the best conditions—it may prove to be the final stroke that will knock out her wonderful courage. God have mercy on her!"

CHAPTER VII

On the day set for Dixie's wedding Henley had occasion to go to the little express office, adjoining the old-fashioned brick car-shed in the village, to see about a shipment of produce which had been incorrectly marked. And as he was returning he saw the girl seated in her wagon in the open space between the station and the hotel.

Henley knew what it meant. She had come to meet her lover. She happened to have her glance fixed on some point in the opposite direction from him and did not know that he was near. He hesitated for an instant, and then decided that he would not intrude upon her privacy. There was something in her attitude of bland and helpless expectancy that probed the deepest fount of his sympathy.

"Poor, brave little woman!" he mused, as he turned his back upon the scene and moved on toward his store. "She's having her dream like all the rest. She may get a fair cut of the cards, and she may not. He ain't very promising material from the looks of his picture, but it wouldn't be fair to judge him by that. He may do his part, and the Lord knows she needs help. I'm too big a failure in the marrying line to object or offer advice."

Reaching his desk, he applied himself to the writing of some letters pertaining to his intended trip to Texas, but the pathetic sight he had of the girl at the station thrust itself between him and his task. She was his faithful friend. He loved her almost as if she had been a sister; she had confided in him; only he and she and her little family knew of what was to take place to-day. How strange to think that she would no longer be as she was! The wife of a man she had never seen, of a man whose full name Henley had not even heard.

Just then the still air was stirred by the sportive whippoorwill's call with which the young engineer of that particular train always announced with the locomotive's whistle his approach to Chester, and later there was a sound of escaping steam and the slow clanging of a bell as the train drew up in the shed. Only a moment's pause, and the train was off again.

It occurred to Henley that as his store was on the most direct way to her home Dixie would naturally drive past it on her return, so he went to the front, taking pains to stand back a few feet from the entrance that his position might not appear to be by design. He was glad that Cahews and Pomp were busy in the rear, and he became conscious of the hope that no stray customer would interrupt him at what seemed such a grave and important moment. Time passed, and still old Bob and the ramshackle wagon were not in sight. Henley cautiously ventured to the door, whence he glanced down the street. He saw the wagon. It was now at the door of the post-office, but no one was in it. With his hip-joint loose the animal swayed and sagged against one of the shafts, the reins hanging from his rump to the ground.

"They've stopped to get the mail," Henley said in his tight throat; "they'll be out in a minute. I'll take one peep at 'im, anyway."

But Dixie emerged from the narrow doorway of the little

building alone. She was reading a letter, and she groped slowly across the sidewalk to the wagon, where she stood till she had finished it. Even at that distance Henley could see that she was pale, and he fancied that her hand and step were unsteady as she mounted to the spring seat and reached for the reins. Henley receded farther into the store, actuated by a vague intuition that she might not care to be seen, and he was glad that he had not intruded upon her, for, as she drove past the store, she did not glance toward it, but instead looked steadily in the opposite direction.

"The fellow didn't come, and she's had bad news besides," Henley mused, and he now stood in the doorway and looked after the shackly vehicle as it moved slowly away in the beating sunshine. "She's bad hit by something or other," he said, anxiously. "I've never seen her look like that before. Some'n has gone wrong."

He did not see her for three days. On the evening of the third day he was standing at the door of his barn. It was growing dark. The coming night had robed the mountain-peaks in gray, and put them out of sight. Old Wrinkle was singing "How firm a foundation, ye saints of the Lord!" as he trudged back to the house, swinging his empty swill-pail. The door of Dixie Hart's cottage opened, and in a narrow frame of firelight she stood peering out toward him. Then he saw that she was coming. She moved swiftly, and with a sure step, till she paused at the fence which separated her land from his.

"I've been wanting to see you, Alfred," she said, in a low, changed voice. "I had no excuse to go to the store, and—well, I didn't think that was exactly the place, anyway to—to say what I had to say. You haven't spoke about what I told you to anybody—I know in reason that you haven't, but—"

"I'd cut off my right arm first," he declared, earnestly. "What you said that day was as sacred to me as if it had come from on high and my very salvation depended on it."

"I knew that," she said, softly. "I only said that to—to sort o' get started. I'm all upset, Alfred; I'll get right after a while, but things are all crooked now. I've had trouble—I reckon a girl might call it that and still have self-respect. I've had heaps of unexpected trouble."

"I was afraid some'n had gone wrong," Henley found himself able to say, "not hearing any more, you see, about—about what you talked of that day."

"I'm going to tell you, and then dismiss it," Dixie said, her pretty lip twitching, the dark curves under her eyes lending sharp contrast to their fathomless lustre. "I had everything ready, and went to meet him, but he didn't come. I went to the post-office and got a letter. He was—was taken sick—so the letter said. He was pretty bad off. In fact, Alfred, the truth is, he's dead; the—the fellow is dead."

Her head was down; she had folded her arms on the top rail of the fence, and she rested her brow on them. He was wondering if she was crying and what there was for him to say, when she suddenly, and quite dry-eyed, looked up and said: "But that must be a secret, too. Nobody knows about it except my home folks, and nobody must. I'd give plumb up if Carrie Wade was to flaunt that in my face and start it going over hill and dale."

"It's too bad," Henley ventured, as nearly upon what he considered consolation as his knowledge of her rather questionable bereavement would justify. "What was his complaint?"

"You mean, what ailded him?" Dixie asked, an incongruous

flush battling with the pallor of her face and becoming observable even in the starlight. "Why, you see, Alfred, I didn't get full particulars—a body never can, you know, at a time like that—and in just a letter—but you can depend upon it that it was sudden."

"Maybe it was what they say is so common now," Henley pursued, awkwardly—"heart failure."

"Or weakness of the backbone." He was sure that she smiled impulsively, for she quickly covered her mouth with her hand and lowered her head to the fence again, and for a moment he stood staring at her and wondering if the calamity had caused her to be hysterical. Suddenly she looked up again and said:

"I reckon you think I ought to act different—that I ought to cry and take on—but I can't. You must make what allowance you can. You see, I never saw him in my life, and, well, it was just a wild-goose chase that started in nothing and ended the same way."

"I see," Henley ventured, "but I'm sorry. Death is bad enough, in any case, but to be called away without a minute's notice and on the eve of—"

"Well, you needn't be sorry for me—you needn't waste pity on me," Dixie broke in with irrelevant warmth. "You'll find me doing business at the same old stand, man or no man. If we can just keep this silly caper from getting out I'll be thankful. So far, I've got along by myself, and, outside of wanting to flaunt a husband in Carrie Wade's face, I don't know as I'll be particularly disappointed. I can keep on at the plough and hoe, rain or shine, and—" Her voice had trailed away into indistinctness, and he saw her lower lip quivering. She suddenly turned and hurried away.

He saw her vanish in the lighted doorway, and he stood overwhelmed with blended perplexity and sympathy.

"She's trying to keep a stiff upper lip, but she's hit, and hit hard—harder'n I thought possible in her case," he mused. "She never saw the feller, but she may have had a sort of a idea in her head of what he was like, an' the loss is as keen as if she had knowed him a long time, maybe keener, for the gloss hain't been rubbed off by actual acquaintance, as it has been off of me and most other married folks. I reckon my wife has put the gloss back on Dick Wrinkle, if it was ever off, and I've got a rival in the spirit-world that nothing earthly could ever hope to match. They say absence works that way, and when I get to Texas maybe she will look back on all I've done to keep peace and harmony betwixt us and appreciate me more than she is doing now. I say maybe, for, on t'other hand, she may be glad to have me away, and when I get back I may find that her whole heart is in the empty grave she is bent on digging and adorning at such a great outlay."

CHAPTER VIII

The next afternoon, as Henley was on his way home from the store, and was passing a corn-field owned by Sam Pitman—a farmer of weak character and sullen disposition who had been a moonshiner as long as the law had permitted the business to yield profits—he was surprised to see Dixie near the centre of the field. She was bending over something or somebody, and, fearing that an accident had happened, he hastily climbed the fence and walked rapidly over the ploughed soil toward her. He could not make out what the object of her attention was till he was quite near, and then he saw that it was a little boy about ten years of age who was seated on the ground and, till now, hidden by the corn-stalks and their succulent blades, which, as he sat, rose higher than his yellow, ill-kempt head. Dixie heard Henley's step and turned a very grave face on him.

"It's the poor little orphan Sam Pitman adopted by law the other day," she informed him in a gentle aside, as her hand rested tenderly on the child's head, which was supported by his frail knees in their ragged and patched covering. "I've had my eye on him all evening. He's hoed out all this since dinner." She waved an indignant hand over the patch of corn immediately about them. "I couldn't have done more myself, and I know what work is. Yes, I was watching him, and awhile ago I saw him stagger an' fall. He'd fainted from overheat. I come as quick as I could. I got water in his hat and dashed it on him—look how wet it made him, but it revived him. He wanted to work on, but I made him stop and set down. He's timid and shy before you, but me 'n him are great friends, ain't we, Joe? He helped me hunt eggs the other day"—she was running on now in a tender, caressing tone—"and I gave him some of my pie. He could crawl to places I never got at before, and we raked in a peck that would have been a dead loss, for I've already got too many broods."

"I heard Pitman had got a boy," Henley said, guardedly, "and I wondered what the Ordinary meant by turning such a little fellow over to a man like him. It seems like there was only one or two applications, and the boy had to be sent somewhere right off. Do you feel better now, Joe?"

"Yes, sir," the child answered. "It wasn't nothing. It didn't hurt a bit."

Henley caught Dixie's quick upward glance. "Ain't it pitiful?" she said, with a shake of her head and a catch in her full voice. "Huh, 'didn't hurt,' I say! You dear little boy!"

With a brave smile the lad stood up to the full height of his spare frame. He was still pale, and his hair was matted down over his brow by the douche it had received. His little, cotton, checked shirt was open at the neck, disclosing a rather low chest. He stooped down and picked up the hoe, which was of the regulation size and weight used by men. Dixie was protesting against his working more that day, when, looking behind her, she saw the foster-father of the boy approaching.

"What's the matter here?" the farmer growled, eying the group distrustfully with his small gray eyes under pent-house brows. He was short of stature, sinewy, and grizzled as to head and bristling beard.

"Miss Dixie says the boy fainted," Henley answered. "I saw her here, and come over to see what was wrong. The little fellow don't look overly stout."

"Nothing's the matter with 'im," Pitman retorted, visibly angered by what he regarded as the interference of outsiders in his private affairs.

"Well, I know he fainted," Dixie said, calmly, "but we won't argue about it. I'll tell you one thing, though, Sam Pitman, if this thing goes on—I say, if Joe is overworked like this any more—a single other time—and it comes to my knowledge, I'll take you smack-dab to court. I don't meddle in things that don't concern me, as a general thing, but I'll take this in hand and I'll clutch it tight."

"You'll do wonders," Pitman sneered, but with a guarded glance at Henley, who had, on one occasion, knocked him down in some dispute over a debt at the store. He turned to the boy and took the hoe from him. "You go drive up that cow. I'll finish this patch myself, and don't you dare come back and say you can't find her, nuther. If you know what's good for you, you fetch 'er home."

Leaving Pitman at work in the corn, and with the boy trudging homeward, Henley and Dixie made their way out to the road. At the fence he threw down several rails and aided her to step over the remaining ones. When he had put the rails back in their places and joined her he was struck by the altered expression of her face.

"I've wanted to see you all day," she began, her grave glance on the ground, "and it looks like this meeting is providential. I want to get it all plumb out, Alfred, and have it off my mind. I don't know when a thing has bothered me so much. It seemed like such a little thing at the time, but a whopping big one now. You 'n me have been too good friends, Alfred, to let deception of any sort whatever come between us. Please don't look at me so straight; I'll never get through it if you do. You think I'm as good as the general run of girls, I'll be bound, and yet I ain't."

"I'll take the risk on that," he laughed, incredulously. "I know what you are—you are true blue. You've just showed the stripe you're made of. In a minute you'd have fought that skunk back there like a mad wildcat. For the time, at least, you was loving that pore boy as if he was your own."

"We are not talking about that—that's nothing," she said. "No woman that is half a one could see the dreamy blue eyes of that lonely boy, and know what he's going through, and not want to hug 'im up to her breast and pet 'im and comfort 'im. I saw him the day Pitman fetched him here. He sat out under the trees all day long. I watched him from my field, and I could see 'im wiping his eyes on his sleeve. He kept it up from morning till night. Sometimes, Alfred, I doubt the goodness of God Almighty. I know it's a sin to say so, but I can't help it. I've talked a heap to Joe off and on, an' he's had more put on 'im than a grown person ought to bear. Poor thing! he misses his Ma. From what he says I judge she was good and tender. I had a queer dream the other night. I seemed to see a woman in my room; she was crying, and, as plain as I can hear yore voice this minute, I heard her say: 'Don't let 'em abuse 'im—he's weak and he can't stand it,' and with that she seemed to melt away. But that is clean off the track. I've got a confession to make to you, and I am so ashamed I hardly know what to do. Alfred Henley, I've told you a lie—a cold, deliberate lie. Can you respect anybody that will tell a lie?"

"Well, I wouldn't have much respect for myself then," he said, his eyes large in wonder over what she was driving at. "I've lied as many times as an average clock can tick in a lifetime. I've told a dozen lies to sell a pair of shoes, and forty to sell a hoss."

"Hush joking," she said. "Listen. When I told you that fellow was dead I was lying. I didn't intend to fool you, but I got in an awful tangle, and you had to take your chance along with the rest. When I went to the train that day and that fool didn't heave in sight I smelt a mouse. I went to the post-office and got a letter from him. It was the most wishy-washy concoction that was ever put on paper. He never, at any time, had marry in the back of his head. He was just seeing how far he could go with me to pass time. Some men are that way. They are powerful interested till they get a girl to commit herself, and then they begin to twist and turn or call it all off on the spot. As long as I kept this 'un in doubt he wrote the softest gush that ever flowed from a pen. But when I wrote that I was ready—actually ready and waiting—well, that was another proposition. He plumb lost his nerve."

"The scoundrel!" Henley burst out, grown red in the face. "He is below contempt. I was afraid he was a sneak the minute I saw his picture. I'd have stopped you if I'd known how."

"Well, it was nobody's fault but mine." Dixie was trying to divest her brave voice of a certain quavering. "Folks say I've got a long head on me—you amongst 'em—but if any God-forsaken female on this round globe ever made a bigger fool of herself than I did that whack I'd like to shake hands with her. I shall see myself setting in that wagon in my new togs waiting for that train to blow—I'll see that sickening sight till I draw my last whiff of air. Oh, you don't know! Being a man, you can't understand what a woman's pride is. Fate has hit me hard licks, but letting me get my outfit ready, clean up the house, and cook enough ahead to last a week, and come to town with my own hoss and wagon to haul a trifling man to the altar who was *jest joking with me*—well, that's what made me lie."

"God knows, it was enough," Henley answered in his throat. "The banners toted by the angels have such mottoes as your lie on 'em."

"I was forced to it to protect myself," Dixie said. "You see, Alfred, Ma is kind o' high strung and liable to fly off the handle and talk before folks. She thinks I'm all right, and she'd have raised the roof off the house and let all the country know my plight if I hadn't acted, and acted quick. I drove home slow that day and studied up a plan. Death was the only thing that would do any good, and so I killed him. I liked that part of it, anyway. I wouldn't have lied to you, but I'd done it so often at home, and with such a straight face, that it had got to be a settled habit. But I jumped from the frying-pan into the fire in one way, for they both weep and wail over him—think o' that, and me feeling like I could pull his ears clean out of his head and stomp 'em into the ground."

"Oh, they take it that way!" exclaimed Henley.

"That's what they do," said the girl. "I attend that fellow's funeral sixteen times a day. They want me to put on black—to put on—huh! when the fool has already made me spend my last dollar on an outfit that—shucks! Well, you see what I've got my foot into. I had actually to clap my hand over Ma's mouth the other day while Carrie Wade was there making her brags to keep Ma from telling of my great loss. Carrie would see through it, you know she would, and I'd never hear the end of it. Ma was dead bent on letting folks know, till I worked a trick on her. I told her, I did, that men didn't like to marry widows, and if I ever expected to get a husband I must keep Pete's death quiet. With that understanding they both agreed to hold their tongues. But it's funny, ain't it?" she ended with a laugh—"you with your tombstone trouble at home, and me with a dead bridegroom to look after, and one that treated me like a hound-pup in the bargain?"

Henley laughed now, for she was laughing. "I'm not going to let mine bother me any more," he said, "now that I've heard what you are going through."

"And you'll forgive me for the lie I told you?" she asked anxiously, as she turned to leave him at a point where their ways parted.

"I would for a million of its sort," he said, fervently. He raised his hat and smiled, and stood watching her till she was out of sight in the apple-orchard she had to traverse to reach the cottage.

CHAPTER IX

Henley had been away nearly a year, his absence being protracted by various business enterprises. Letters to Jim Cahews in regard to the store, which Cahews was admirably managing, contained humorous accounts of the various deals which Henley had put through. At one time he had bought a roller-skating rink, which was sold by auction at a great sacrifice because the town was too small to support it. Henley had bid it in, packed it up, and shipped it to a thriving young city, advertised a big opening, and sold it for a handsome profit while the novelty was at its height. On another occasion he was the highest bidder on the scrap-iron in a stove-foundry which had been destroyed by fire, and he made a handsome "speck" through his ability to guess more nearly than any of his competitors the weight of the refuse. There was nothing he would not buy if the price was right, he wrote his clerk, except *tombstones*, and Cahews understood, and answered to the best of his ability and tact that the public had long since ceased to talk about that unfortunate little matter, and when Henley returned he would perhaps never hear it mentioned.

The stepfather-in-law had used less diplomacy in the account he had forwarded to Henley on the day following the great occasion. Wrinkle was as fond of writing as he was of talking, and he fairly basked in the sunshine of the letter he sent. He read it aloud to himself as he walked to Chester to post it, pausing now and then to scratch out a word or to add one with a pencil as the paper lay on his raised knee. This is the way it sounded to his pleased ears:

"DEAR ALF,—I take my pen in hand to address these few lines to you to let you know that we are all well, and hope you are endowed with the same and many like blessings. Nothin' unusual is goin' on here right now. It is as quiet as the day after camp-meetin'. Dick's funeral was preached yesterday. The weather was tiptop, and nothin' was lackin' to make it a plumb success. Hettie got us out of bed before a single streak of day had appeared. We put on our clothes by pine-knots. The preacher she sent away off for, because she was bound to git some'n extra, was installed at the hotel. He is a wheel-hoss; he dressed as fine as a fiddle, with a plug-hat and dashboard shoes, and had a long jimswinger coat that come to his knees. The paper said he was the silver-tongued orator of the entire Cherokee pulpit, and printed his picture, and said he'd been paid a handsome figure by one of our wealthiest citizens to take part in the memorable occasion. I cut the artickle out to send to you, but forgot an' lit my pipe with it. I'll try to git another, but they are hard to find, as all hands seem to be keepin' 'em for future generations to look at. I seed ten men all readin' one at the same time in a gang at the sawmill t'other day. They seemed to consider it funny, but I didn't. I don't see how a thing as solemn as that affair was could be funny.

"We et our breakfast by candle-light, and then set around and had nothin' to do till startin'-time. We went in the two-seated spring-wagon. I was the only one in our layout not draped from head to foot in black. I couldn't see the women's faces, and as they didn't say a word I couldn't estimate the extend of their grief. I reckon you can guess, anyway. You know 'em. You never saw sech a stream o' folks in all yore born days. You'd 'a' thought it was a public hangin', and every livin' soul had to take a special peep at us as we driv along. As well as I could make out through her veil, Hettie seemed to like bein' so conspicuous, for she axed me to drive slow an' go through the main street, which ain't the nighest way to the church. When we got thar the house was packed as tight as dry apples in a cider-press. But the front bench was all our'n. Nobody dared take it, although more'n half of it was empty, an' folks was settin' in the windows. I had trouble with Hettie, for she made me throw my chaw o' tobacco away, and I found I was settin' right over a wide crack in the floor, too. I wouldn't 'a' damaged a thing, an' could 'a' done it without bein' seed.

"Then I made her as mad as Old Nick by a little mistake of mine. While I was hitchin' up the wagon Old Bay bit a whoppin' big gap out'n my straw hat, and it was so comical-lookin' that Ma told me not to wear it. That was easy enough to say, but I didn't want to go bareheaded, so I begun to look about the house for some'n to put on, and hid away amongst Het's knickknacks I found a hat that used to belong to Dick. It was jest my size, and so I put it on an' thought no more about it till we was all settin' in church. It was on my lap, and all at once I seed Hettie lift up her veil an' squint at it; then she heaved a big groan and snatched it and put it out o' sight. She'd have blessed me out on the spot, I reckon, if the singers hadn't set in. I was a sight goin' home without a thing on my head, but she wouldn't listen to reason, an' kept it stuffed all in a wad under her arm. She said I had no feelin' or I wouldn't have done sech an outrageous thing.

"The preacher was all right, but he'd bit off more than he could chaw. It seems from report that he went around Chester to find out statements that he could work in about Dick that would sound nice and suitable; but for some reason or other—maybe because everybody was so excited, and maybe because they was naturally backward before sech a shinin' light—but, as I say, he run short on information. When he come to that part of his talk he looked actually teased. He floundered about considerable, an' drunk a lot o' water, but he done the best he could. He said Dick was a devoted husband and father, and got red when he corrected the last part, and said a Divine Providence had seed fit to take 'im away purty early in the game, and that the poor fellow hadn't really had a chance to show what was in him. Looked like he was determined to say some'n nice about Dick, so he gave a few backhanded licks at the Republican party and the nigger-lovers of the North, an' wound up by sayin' that the late lamented had been a stanch Democrat an' worked at the poles as hard to overthrow graftin' and Yankee oppression as any man in the fair Southland. He got through somehow, but, betwixt me 'n you, Alf, I don't think Hettie thought she got her full money's worth, for she was countin' on a wonderful display of poetry and highfalutin' things that would be remembered an' placed to her credit for a long time afterwards. He got his foot in it several times. Once I heard Hettie sniff mighty nigh loud enough for him to hear it. It was when he said life wasn't what it was cracked up to be, nohow, and he didn't doubt that Dick was a sight better off where he was at than here in this earthly wrangle. I thought to myself, I wonder what Alf would say in his far-off retreat to a statement of that sort.

"The marble monument looks all right in Welborne's new graveyard, an' he has a right to be proud of his enterprise. The ground is bein' mapped off in great shape. He's had grass sowed all over it and laid out avenues and sidewalks, and thar's some talk of a fountain.

"That Dixie Hart's a corker. She's not mealy-mouthed about anything. The day before the funeral Hettie was talkin' to her at the cow-lot, and axed Dixie if she was goin' to take it in. Dixie quit milchin', and stood up straight and said: 'No, I've got better sense, and you ought to be ashamed of yoreself. You've got a good husband, and you don't appreciate him nigh enough.'"

"I thought it was funny that Het didn't fly off the handle, but she stood and tuck it, and seemed to be set back a peg or two. Me 'n her went to the house together, an' I looked for her to rail out on me, anyway, but she set on the porch like she had a lot to think about till bed-time. I made up my mind then that Het jest loves to do things that other folks don't approve of, an' that Dixie had set 'er to wonderin' if she hadn't gone a little bit too far.

"But the old gal is all right. She has tuck a new turn, as I wrote you in my last. She keeps boarders in the two spare rooms mighty nigh all the time, and she is figurin' expenses purty close. Sometimes it is a rovin' peddler at day-rates or a fruit-tree agent by the week. I can't say I like it overly much—though thar is somebody to talk to at odd times when they are through work—for she don't seem to feed quite as well when she's bein' paid as before money begun to come in. She seems to want to lay up scads for some reason or other; maybe it is to try to git back the cash she has spent on her odd notion. I don't know, an' I ain't sure she does herself, but she's as close as the bark on a tree. Jim says she's runnin' a separate account at the store, an' makes 'im figure everything she gets at bare cost in market—freight not included. I heard her tellin' a lightnin'-rod peddler that that was where she could cut under the Chester House, which didn't have no store nor credit to speak of.

"Who do you think was here last week? Why, Ben Warren, Hettie's bach' uncle. He stayed all night, an' occupied yore room. He says he's got two thousand acres in his plantation over the mountain, and the finest residence in the State—keeps a dozen hosses an' all the old niggers that his daddy used to own. He's thirty-five, an' still on the turf, but he told us he was at last engaged to a Baltimore lady that he had been settin up to for lo these many years. He's goin' to have us all spend a week over thar before long. He thinks a lot of Het, an' wants her to fix up his house for the bride. Het's lookin' forward to it. He couldn't stay over for the funeral, but he said she was showin' by her act that women was not forgetful of the past, and that it made him feel more secure in the venture he was about to make. He'd been inclined to doubt females to some extent, he said, and he was goin' to let Het's conduct stand before him always as a proof of how deep a woman's affections can be when they are tested.

"Now, take care of yourself, Alf, and come on home. These cool, green mountains are good enough for any man, an' you know what is said about a rollin' stone. So long. I sign myself, with my best respects,

"Yours truly,
"JASON WRINKLE.

"*P. S.*—The same old crowd of jolly loafers make the store headquarters, and they are, if anything, worse 'n when you was the king-bee o' the bunch. They git off a fresh joke on somebody every day. I got off one on Jim that he didn't like a bit. Jim is still holdin' on to old man Hardcastle's gal like grim death, an' in order to cut a special dash he's got to sendin' his things to the steam laundry at Carlton. T'other day at the post-office the nigger that delivers for the Express Company, an' can't read, showed me Jim's package of socks, drawers, shirts, an' the like, that had just come, an' axed me who it was for. With as straight a face as if I was lookin' a corpse in the eyes, I p'inted out Hardcastle's house an' tol' 'im to take it thar. Then I writ with a pencil on the kiver these words, 'Please restore missin' buttons and stitch up holes.' Then what did I do but hike back to the store an' set an' wait. Miss Julia sent the stuff a-whizzin' to Jim by a nigger woman that works for her folks. The things was all tousled up in a big basket, an' she fetched along a note that made Jim turn as white as a cake o' tallow. He left me in charge an' run over an' explained matters to the best of his ability, but it's the talk of the town, an' not a soul has suspicioned me. If you don't want to git knocked flat you'd better not mention a steam laundry in Jim's presence.

"J. W."

CHAPTER X

Alfred Henley was coming home. Jim Cahews announced it one morning to a cluster of farmers and chronic loungers at the store, and the news rapidly spread through the village and country-side, and various comments were made. He was going to do a man's part and try to put up with the cranky woman he had married, said the men. He was heartily ashamed of himself, said the women. He had got over his silly pout and was coming home to make amends for his conduct in living so long away from a woman who had shown such beautiful constancy to her first and, perhaps—as it looked now—only love.

Dixie Hart heard the report on her way to the post-office, and, needing a spool of cotton, she went into the store.

"Yes, he's headed this way," was Cahews's confirmation of the news. "The truth is, Miss Dixie, if I'm any judge of a man's letters, Alf's actually homesick. He wants the mountains he was fetched up in. He writes about his lonely days and nights, when his speculations don't keep him busy, an' says they don't have anything out thar but pesky north winds an' sand-storms. He might have stayed away longer, as it was, but one little thing I wrote him turned the scale. You know that measly ten-cent circus that was to show here last month got stranded. The performers all quit and footed it home, an' the sheriff levied on the thing, lock, stock, and barrel, an' is to sell it piece by piece at public outcry Saturday week. Alf wrote me that a sale of that sort was exactly in his line, and that he'd try to be on hand. He didn't think anybody here would have any money to invest in such truck, and he'd have his own way. He said about the only man hereabouts that he'd have to contend with would be old Welborne, but he would risk him. He don't often allude to home matters, Miss Dixie, but I think Alf counts on havin' things up at the house a little smoother than they was when he went off."

"And maybe he will," the girl answered, thoughtfully, as she turned away.

The only boarders Mrs. Henley had at this time were a certain young married pair, Mr. and Mrs. Thomas Allen, who had arrived only a week before with a baby not yet a month old. Allen was a travelling sewing-machine agent, and boarded his wife and child at some farm-house while he drove about the country in a buggy with a sample machine to instruct women in the use of it and take orders.

When Mrs. Allen heard the report that Henley was coming back, she was considerably disturbed by the thought that she and hers might not be wanted any longer. She nursed her fears all the morning, and finally, with the infant on her arm, she went out to Mrs. Henley, who was in the back-garden gathering cucumbers for the dinner-table.

"I reckon I'd as well come to the point an' be done with it," Mrs. Allen began, timidly. She was thin, had blue eyes and faded blond hair, used snuff, as was indicated by the brownish deposits in the corners of her mouth and her stained teeth. "I want to speak to you about yore husband."

"Well, what is it?" Mrs. Henley asked, as she drew herself up and peered at the speaker from the hood of her sunbonnet, and rested her pan of cucumbers on her hip.

"Why, they all say he's comin' home," said Mrs. Allen. "I've heard yore father-in—I mean, I've heard old Mr. Wrinkle say that yore husband, never havin' had children, can't abide babies, an' I got bothered. My little darlin' don't cry much—in fact, compared to most babies, it's a purty good un. It did cry some just a minute ago, but that wasn't its fault. It was mine. Like a plumb fool, who certainly ought to have had more sense, I was takin' a dip o' snuff from my box as I come out of the house, an' a sudden whiff of wind round the corner blowed a speck of it in the little thing's eyes. You know it stings like ackerfortis. We are goin' next week, anyway, you see."

"Well, you needn't let my husband's coming hurry you off," Mrs. Henley answered, as she reached out to a bean-pole and bore down on it that she might fasten it more firmly in the soil, and it was impossible to judge whether there was resentment in the tone. "He's coming back of his own free will, and if he stays he'll put up with the house just as he finds it. Nothing will be turned topsy-turvy, you may be sure. His room is where it always was, and it ain't likely to be changed."

The conversation was disturbed by the appearance of the baby's father, who emerged from the house and was on the way to the stable to feed and water his horse. He wore a ready-made suit of clothes and a scarlet necktie which clashed sharply with his blond hair and mustache. He was almost as young as his wife, and he beamed proudly on the red human lump in her arms as he paused for a moment. He smiled warmly on Mrs. Henley when his wife playfully informed him that they would not have to move till their week was up.

"Well, I certainly am glad to hear it," he declared. "I'd hate to look for a new place just for a day or so, an' I've got so I feel sorter at home here. Me an' yore father-in—(excuse me)—I mean, me 'n Mr. Wrinkle have high old times. Even if I went to board somers else I'd come here an' set of an evenin' to hear him talk. He drives off every spell of blues I have. He is the beatenest man to get off jokes I ever knowed, to be as old as he is. Just now he walked clean over to Pitman's to tell that crusty old cuss that thar was a cow inside his lot fence, an' when Pitman come down hoppin' mad with his shot-gun full o' pease yore father-in—(excuse me)—Mr. Wrinkle p'inted to Pitman's own cow an' said, 'I wasn't lyin' to you, Sam; thar she is.' He was laughin' just now an' said he had a joke in store for Mr. Henley when he got here. I tried to git it out of him, but he wouldn't say what was in the wind."

That evening, after supper, as the night was warm, the Allens, with the child asleep on a pillow in a chair between them, were seated out under the trees in front of the house, when Wrinkle slouched across the grass to them. He was chewing tobacco, and frequently pressed two fingers over his lips and between them spat with considerable accuracy at various shrubs and tufts of grass about him. Even in the twilight they could see that his small eyes were twinkling with suppressed amusement.

"I thought once, Allen," he chuckled, "that I wouldn't let you in on this joke, but I'm afraid I won't sleep if I don't tell somebody. I don't mind lettin' you two in on the quiet, but I wouldn't tell Hettie for any amount. You see, this un's a baby joke, an' it may be a tender point with her, not havin' a baby, an', in fact, never havin' had one up to date, although she's had two husbands in her day, an' resided with each one a sufficient time."

"So it's a baby joke?" Allen said. "Well, that interests *me*."

"That's what it is," the old man said, dryly. "You'd enjoy it if you knowed Alf. The gang at the store was eternally laughin' at 'im about babies. They could shet 'im up tight by jest gettin' a nigger nurse-gal to tote a lusty one back to his desk while he was at work. Once one of the gang sent 'im a tin rattler by mail, an' they was all thar to see 'im open it. He took it all in good fun, too; he's one joker that kin stand one on hisself. You may 'a' noticed that Hettie is a sorter odd woman in some ways. Well, she's more peculiar on the husband line than any other. Alf's been off now goin' on ten months, an' she hain't once put pen to paper for him. So the few lines that has gone from this shebang has been writ by yours truly. Alf hasn't writ to me much, but I've kept 'im posted. He didn't write me he was headed this way, but I got it from Cahews. As soon as I heard he was comin' in a week or so, I set down to write how glad we was. I was in my room j'inin' your'n at the time, an' all at once it struck me that it would be a royal welcome to greet 'im with some sort o' joke, an' while I was tryin' to study up some'n yore baby rolled out o' the bed an' struck the floor with a thump. It was as quiet as a stick o' wood fer a minute till it ketched its wind, an' then it set up a scream like a Comanchy Injun, an' right thar I got my idea. I determined to write Alf that he'd become the daddy of a bouncin' baby boy. But I had to go about it right, you see, for I knowed Alf would smell a mice if I brought it out bluntlike; so, knowin' that I'd have time to hear from him ag'in before he started, I jest ended my letter by sayin' that I didn't intend to take no hand in the little cold spell betwixt him an' his wife, but that I felt bound to say that after she had laid down her pride to write him *sech important* an' *delicate news*, for him to take no notice of it whatever was enough to hurt and offend any woman. He bit. He took my bait an' hook an' line, broke my pole, an' run up-stream. He writ by the next mail—said he hadn't got no letter from Hettie, an' axed me what the news was. He was so anxious to know that he said he was goin' to stop a day or so in Atlanta, an' wouldn't I oblige him by sendin' my answer thar? You bet I did. I'll do a friend a favor whenever I kin. I told 'im Alf Junior was a buster, had a yell on 'im that would do for a fire-alarm, an' was already keen enough to know the difference betwixt a bottle with a rubber neck an' the rail thing. So thar it rests. He hain't got no use for babies, an' he'll be as mad as Tucker, but when he finds out it's jest a joke he'll be happy enough to set up the drinks."

"Gracious, surely you didn't go as far as that," Mrs. Allen cried, casting a jealous look at her sleeping infant and sweeping it on to her grinning spouse.

"Didn't I, though!" Wrinkle spat, gleefully. "Alf has often said I couldn't fool *him*, an' we'll see—we'll see this pop."

"It certainly is a corker," Allen declared—"that is, if he swallows it."

"He's already done it," sniggered the stepfather-in-law. "I writ a document a Philadelphia lawyer and a Pinkerton detective combined couldn't pick a flaw in. I hedged it in with roundabout reasons an' facts, tellin' 'im he'd 'a' had letter after letter about how the baby was thrivin' if he'd just answered Hettie's first official proclamation, and so on, and so on. Folks, I can hardly wait. He'll git here to-morrow night, an' we'll have the fun of our lives. I hope you two won't say a word—at fust, anyway. Leave it all to me."

CHAPTER XI

The following afternoon about dusk the mail-hack, which usually brought a few passengers over from Carlton, put Henley down at the gate. The Allens, the Wrinkles, and Mrs. Henley were seated on the porch, and all stared expectantly except the wife of the returning man, who rose suddenly and retired into the house. Henley was tanned, wore a more stylish suit of clothes than had been his wont, and a broad-brimmed hat. As he advanced up the walk, swinging his bag in one hand and a bulky parcel in the other, the observers noted that he was flushed and smiling complacently.

"Durn it all!—dad blast his pictur'!" Wrinkle ejaculated, "I'll bet he missed my letter. He wouldn't look tickled that way if he'd got it. Well, the fun is off. If I was to tell 'im now he'd know I was lyin'."

The new-comer was at the bottom of the steps now, and, depositing his things on the grass, he came up with his hand extended.

"Well, here I am," he cried, as he clasped Wrinkle's hand and shook it cordially. "I never was as glad to strike Georgia grit in my life. I feel like a old soldier back from war. As I drove over and saw the sun in its bed of yellow behind the mountains I felt like I was flying through space. This country is good enough for me, and I'll prove it by sticking to it in the future. Where's Hettie? But, first of all, I want to see that baby. Trot him out—bless his soul!—trot him out."

Profound astonishment showed itself in every face. Only old Jason seemed capable of rising to the situation. For barely an instant he floundered, and then his small eyes began to twinkle, his voice held a rippling, unctuous quality as he laid his hand on Henley's arm.

"Oh, you mean *little* Alf," he faltered. "Why, he's—he's in thar asleep on the bed. We-uns—the last one of us—'lowed you'd raise big objections. You always seemed to have mighty little use for anything o' the sort."

"Huh!" Henley grunted, an honest flush spreading over his face. "That's another matter altogether. There are babies and babies in this world. This one's got different blood in 'im—this one's *mine*! If I've made light o' having little tots, I wasn't talking about *him*, for he hadn't come. Where is he? Let me see 'im. I won't wake 'im. I'll walk easy, an' not say a word."

"Well, step this way." Wrinkle cast a bubbling glance of warning at Mrs. Allen, who had risen resentfully, and motioned her back into her chair, and, with a comical strut, he led Henley into the room occupied by the child's parents. Near the door, in the dim light of a sputtering tallow-dip, on a tiny bed lay the sleeping infant. Wrinkle, choking down his amusement, took the candle from the mantelpiece and held it over the little face. "You can't see the favor so plain while its eyes are shet," he chuckled, "but when it grins an' winks it's you to a gnat's heel."

"Gewhilikins, ain't he a corker!" Henley said, worshipfully, under his breath, as he leaned over the bed.

"I wouldn't wake 'im now." Mrs. Allen stood in the doorway, quite erect and cold in her bearing, and there was no one but the deluded man who failed to detect her frigid tone of offended ownership. "This is his sleepin'-time; if he wakes now he'll fret all night, an' Mr. Allen has to git his rest or he can't git up early an' do his work."

"I see," said Henley, politely. "I heard Hettie had taken some boarders. I know she'd hate to have the little thing keep anybody awake."

"Sh! not yit, for the Lord's sake, not yit!" Wrinkle whispered, as he slid along, to the bewildered mother. "Don't spile it all."

"Well, let's go back on the porch," Henley said. "I've got some'n to show you. What you reckon I've got in my bundle? Come take a look." He led them back into the outer dusk, and descended to the ground for the parcel, which, after hastily cutting the string, he opened on the steps. The others stared in astonishment at the pile of toys, little dresses, flannels, dainty caps of lace, and shoes and stockings.

"What did you go an' buy all them things for?" Wrinkle asked, rendered serious for the first time by the realization that his jest had at least cost more than he had intended.

"Because I wanted to, that's what for!" Henley laughed, proudly. "Do you reckon I was going to come away from Atlanta empty-handed when I was right where so many things could be had? I showed your letter to Mrs. Moody, who keeps the house I stopped at, and she took me down-town and helped select what was best. She said every single article would come in handy, and she ought to know—she's the mother of nine. Lord, I wish I'd got here earlier, before his bed-time. I tried to git the driver to hurry up, but first one thing happened, then another. I want to see what the little chap 'll do with this rattler; these blamed little bells set up a jinglin' noise every time the hack struck a snag."

During this monologue the machine-agent was silent, a dark frown of indecision on his face. As for his wife, she looked as if she had bartered her child's birthright for something that had disagreed with her mental digestion. Jason Wrinkle, however, reflections on the cost of his joke for the moment set aside, seemed to have fallen into his happiest mood. Unable to disguise his merriment at such close range from his victim, he had slipped out into the yard, and Allen could see him writhing in the folds of darkness as he slapped his thighs and raised his heavy boots in a soundless dance of joy.

"Well, I'll go find Hettie." Henley took up the parcel, and, with it in his arms, he clattered thunderously through the hallway back to his wife's room. There was candle-light in the room, and he saw her hastily turn toward a window as he entered and threw the things on her bed.

"Well, here I am," he announced, the ring of elation still in his voice. "I don't blame you for hiding from me, Hettie. I've acted like an old hog, and I've come back to say so."

She turned toward him, an expression of surprise struggling on her thin face, but it had never been her way to show affection, and she made no offer even to shake hands. However, he had put his arms round her and kissed her cold cheek.

"You've just come?" she said, tentatively, as she drew stiffly from his embrace.

"Just a minute ago. I had to see the baby the first thing. I couldn't wait. The old man showed him to me. Ain't he great? I hain't seen his eyes yet—he was sound asleep. I reckon that boarder-woman helps you with him; she seems to thinks lots of him, and be powerful particular. I didn't get your letter about its coming, Hettie. I'd have written at once—you know I would. It was lost, I reckon. The mails don't run right always. The old man wrote me, and it certainly was like a thunderclap. I'm mighty proud, Hettie. You see, I'd given up hoping that a baby'd ever come to us, an'—"

"To *us*?" The woman stared and drew herself more erect. "What do you mean? Are you crazy? You've seen babies before and never went on at such a rate. I don't care for it. I haven't once touched it since it come. I don't like its mother any too well, and she is such a fool about it that—"

"Its *mother*?" Henley gasped. "Why, ain't it *ours*—ain't it yours and mine? The—the old man wrote me that—" Henley's voice faltered and sank. His lower lip hung loose from his teeth and quivered. With a furious shrug Mrs. Henley turned from him to the curtainless window against which the outer night pressed like a palpable substance. She could hear him behind her panting like a tired beast of burden. For a moment there was an awful silence in the room, then he broke it.

"My God, he made a fool of me!" he groaned.

"And you made one of *me*," the woman threw back from the window, "and before them all!" She sneered, as her glance fell on the pile of gifts on the bed. "This is what you come back for? Any other man would have had too much sense to be so easily fooled." She strode to the table and picked up the candle, for what purpose he did not know, but it slipped from her fingers and fell to the floor and went out. He heard her groan, and the slats of the bed creaked as she sat down. Thankful that the darkness hid the evidences of shame on his face, and not daring to trust his voice to further utterance, he went out of the room. As he passed through the hallway he heard a low cry from the infant on the right, and its mother crooning over it. No one was on the porch. A vast weight of misery and chagrin was on him. He sat down on the steps and fumbled in his pocket for his pipe. But his nerveless fingers broke the only match he had, as he attempted to strike it on the step, and, holding his pipe before him, he sat staring into space. He had a hunted sense of wanting to avoid forever all human contact; an intangible shame burned within him, drying up the tender emotions which so recently had swayed his being.

Suddenly his glance fell on his valise still resting on the step where he had left it, and, rising, he clutched it as he might the hand of a friend. The next instant he was striding over the grass to the gate. To shun the village, the lights of which winked sardonically in the distance, he crossed the road, climbed the fence and was in the meadow which lay between his land and Dixie Hart's. Blindly he trudged through the high weeds and grass, now wet with dew.

Cruel, cruel—a joke, a mere joke, as such things went with the shallow and light-minded, and yet it was a tragedy. For several days, in the highest realm of fancy he had revelled in the first joys of fatherhood, only to have it end like this. He paused on a slight rise of the ground and looked back at the outlines of the farm-house, and cursed it and its inhuman inmates. As he dug his nails into his palms and gnashed his teeth, he swore that the surrounding mountains, so false in their late promises, should never see him more; the wide, free world should be his solace, if solace could be had.

Suddenly, as he stood, he became conscious that there was a moving blur before him, as if some portion of the general darkness, by some trick of vision, had been rendered more compact and animate. Then he saw that it was a cow, and immediately in the animal's wake appeared another blur. This was the form of a woman. In a mellow, soothing tone she called out to the cow, and Henley recognized the voice. It was Dixie Hart. Instinctively, and shrinking even from her, he started on, but she suddenly cried out:

"Don't go, Alfred, you haven't said howdy to me. You aren't going to treat an old friend that way, I know."

Putting his valise down at his feet, he stood speechless while she advanced to him, her hand extended from beneath the shawl which enveloped her head and shoulders. "How are you?" She seemed to avoid seeing his valise. "I'm powerful glad to see you back home."

He made an effort to speak, but there was a dry tightness in his throat which made him doubt his command of utterance. His only response was the dumb clasping of her hand, and to it he clung, unconscious of what the act implied, as a proof of weakness.

"I knew you had got back," she went on, her face uplifted, her friendly fingers tightening on his. "That old mischief-maker told me. I didn't come out here after the cow. That was just a dodge to keep anybody from talking about me being away from home after dark. I had to see you. I knew you needed a friend, and I'm one, Alfred—I'd sacrifice anything on earth to help you. You've been a true friend to me, and I want to be to you. I know all that happened back there."

"You say you do?"

"Yes, Mr. Wrinkle come and told me. He was laughing, but he let up, for I opened his eyes. He hasn't had such a tongue-lashing since he was born. The fool, the fool—the silly fool! You mustn't mind, Alfred. You really mustn't."

"Mind?" he muttered. "My God!"

"Oh, I know!" she went on, still soothingly. "It is awful looked at from *your* standpoint, but that ain't the thing. We must consider the intentions of folks before we take offence. Why, Alfred, that old busybody hasn't yet got it through his head that any living man could object to a joke like that. Nothing under high heaven was ever sacred to him; you must have noticed that in the time you have known him. He'd make a jest out of the death of his closest kin. He told me once that to think anything was wrong in this world would be to deny God's goodness to mankind. When I told him just now that he had overstepped the bounds of reason and good sense in what he done, he simply wouldn't believe it. He said you knew how to give a joke and take one, and that he liked you better than any living man. The Allens are going to leave soon. Alfred, you mustn't go 'way like this—you just mustn't."

"There's nothing else to do."

"Oh yes, there is." She laid her hand on his arm, and gazed persuasively into his eyes. "You've got your duty to perform —your duty to your wife, Alfred."

"Huh, to her!" he sniffed.

"Yes, to *her*," Dixie went on, simply and yet eagerly. "I'm sorry for her, Alfred. To most folks she seems peculiar, and yet God made her that way just as He made you and me like we are, and, moreover, she can't help being like she is. You told me once that you didn't think she had ever quite got over her love for her first husband, but that you counted on that when you married her. Well, all the queer things which she done while you was away, that folks thought was so funny, come from her idea of her duty in that direction. If I read her right, she thinks, somehow, that she proved herself untrue to—to the dead by marrying again, and she's let it prey on her mind. But that is over with. I think she is afraid now that she went too far."

"You think so?" Henley breathed hard.

"Yes, I lost patience with her myself during it all, and give her a piece of my mind one day. If she had been plumb sure she was right she'd have got mad, but she didn't. She took it different from what I expected. She never had paid any attention to me before, but after that day she made a point o' coming to me. She never would bring up the subject again, but she'd stand and talk with as much respect as if I'd been some old person. She looked like she was ashamed, and wanted to let me know in some other way than telling me in so many words. No, you mustn't go 'way like this, Alfred. It 'ud never do. She ain't to blame for that old man's joke, and she ought not to suffer for it. She was glad you was coming back. A woman can read a woman, and she couldn't hide it. It looked to me like she is glad to get a chance to act different and do her part. If you was to go off on top of this thing it would humiliate her awfully. A great deal would be said, and it would all heap up on her as the prime cause. You are the noblest man I ever knew, Alfred, and you won't go and do as big a wrong as this would be, and in such thoughtless haste. A man never can decide on a correct course when he is upset like you are now, and you'd live to regret it. Then think of yourself. You was plumb homesick for these old mountains, and was glad to get back."

"How did you know that?"

"A little bird told me." She quoted the saying with an arch smile. "You wanted to get here in time to be at the auction sale of that broke-down circus, and you'll miss a good thing if you go. The horses are in bad shape, owing to poor feeding and hard use, but there's big come-out in 'em. Nobody else here will have the ready money, and you'd have a clean walk-over."

"What else have they got besides hosses?" The trader's eyes twinkled with an interest that broke through the stupor that was on him.

"Oh, lots o' odds and ends; you wait and see. Tote that valise back in the house, Alfred, and don't do what you'll be sorry for all your life. If you was to leave like this to-night it would be harder than ever to come back, and you'd have to do it sooner or later. You know I'm giving you good advice."

"Yes, I know it—before God I know it," he said, fervently. "You are the best friend I've got, Dixie. No, I don't want to go back to Texas." His strong voice shook and he coughed to steady it. "I never want to roam about that way again. I forced myself to stay out there day by day. That was one mistake, and I ought not to make another on top of it. You see it right, Dixie. You see it right."

"Then there is little Joe," she reminded him. "He is still having a hard time with Sam Pitman, and the little fellow has almost counted the hours since he heard you was coming. He dotes on you. He still has the money hid away that you left for him. He says he is going to keep it till he's a man. Oh, it was so sad! Alfred, he started to run away one night awhile back, after Pitman had whipped him for planting the wrong seed-corn. I happened to meet him down the road. He had a little bundle under one arm and a pet chicken I had given him under the other. I stopped him and got him to go back. I couldn't bear the thought of having him so far away from me and unprotected. I told him that, and it made him break down and cry. Then he let me kiss him; he never had before, he's so bashful, and, well"—her eyes were glistening and her tone was husky—"the next morning I saw him in the field bright and early. He was doing the hardest work there is on a farm—digging sprouts with a heavy grubbing-hoe. But he was cheerful."

"You made him go back, just as you are making me do," Henley said, swallowing a lump in his throat and forcing a smile. "You were right in his case, and right in mine. You are my best friend. How goes it with you? We've talked enough about me."

"Same old seven and six," she answered, with a shrug. "Still fighting with the world and Carrie Wade. She's a worm in my flesh that is on a constant wiggle. She nags me more now because she is more miserable herself. She don't even get as much attention as she did. She used to go after it, but the men have headed her off. The fellows at the lumber-camp got to laughing at her for the way she done. She's got down to little boy sweethearts. She's been making eyes at Johnny Cartwright, and the little fool—he ain't more than seventeen, eight years younger'n her—is clean daft about her. Poor old Mrs. Cartwright is awfully worried. The little scamp declares he is engaged to Carrie, and, instead of giving the report the lie, she actually seems proud of it."

"But how about your marrying?" Henley questioned.

"Me? Oh, I've got my trousseau ready, every stitch of it, including hat, gloves, stockings, and what not."

"You don't tell me—well, that *is* news!" Henley exclaimed in surprise.

"Well, it ain't to me," Dixie laughed. "You see, Alfred, it is the same old outfit that I laid in a year ago and keep in storage. It hain't exactly the latest wrinkle as to style, but I could cut away and add a flounce here and a ruffle there, and not have so much cash to lay out as I did when I missed fire that time. But I don't think I'll get to use it soon. Field-work in the broiling sun and setting on a divan with a dinky fan to your face and a young man to peep over it don't hitch, somehow. And I'm still deep in debt to old Welborne. He's the only man I make love to, but I don't get a cent off for my smiles; he growls and grumbles every time I see him about hard times and the like. But I'll pay out one of these days. As you pass it in the morning I want you to just take a look at my stand of cotton; if the drought will let it alone I'll make five bales. Now I must go. I know you'll keep your promise, so I ain't going to worry. Good-night."

"Good-night," he echoed, and as she moved away in the darkness he took up his valise and turned his face toward the farm-house. "She's right," he muttered. "God bless her, she's plumb right."

CHAPTER XII

The Allens had gone, taking with them the baby things, which Henley had prevailed upon them to accept. He sank into his accustomed place at home and at the store as naturally as if he had been away only for a day. The news of his return drew around him many of the motley ilk who made trading and swapping both a business and an avocation. They seldom dealt with him, to be sure, but it was a liberal education to hear his experiences, and even better to see him actually make a deal. On his first day at home he had bought a lame horse for the small sum of fifty dollars, after he had delivered a free lecture about the great "American Cruelty to Animals Association," as he called it. And, with his eyes on the owner, he gave it as his opinion that in a more enlightened community a man who would ride a horse in that condition would be dragged straight to court, and maybe imprisoned for life. When the animal was his, and the ex-owner had gone to buy a ticket to go home by rail, Henley winked at Cahews and said: "I know how to cure that hoss's leg. I paid two dollars to learn in Fort Worth from an Indian hoss-doctor. Two hundred dollars wouldn't buy 'im right now."

It was the loquacious stepfather-in-law who revelled most in Henley's sayings and doings, and he regaled his wife and Henley's with accurate and vivid reports of them. One morning he came into the sitting-room, where the two women sat bent over a quilt on a big, square frame, their needles going methodically up and down.

"You mought guess one million years," he panted, as he bent over them, that he might feast on their facial expressions, "an' not guess what Alf Henley's gone an' done."

They raised their faces and stared, and the wizened raconteur smiled as he stepped to the open fireplace, shifted the paper screen to one side, carefully spat, and then, replacing it, returned to his coign of vantage.

"I don't know, and care less," Mrs. Henley answered, though her poised needle and steady gaze belied her words. "He's done so many fool things in his life that I'd not be surprised if he'd gone off in a balloon."

"That's equal to sayin' you give it up." Wrinkle again applied himself to the screen and fireplace, and returned shuffling, his tobacco-quid in his hand. "Well, you've heard about the dime circus that was to show here a month back, an' couldn't because all the actors hit the grit an' left the manager to settle with the sheriff for debts that follered it all the way from Boston?"

They had heard every detail of the matter innumerable times, and only stared and gaped as they awaited further revelations.

"Well, Alf Henley is sole owner an' manager now," was the bomb which exploded in Wrinkle's hands. "He's the John Robinson and P. T. Barnum of the whole capoodle."

"You don't mean that he has actually gone off with—" began Mrs. Henley, but was checked by the old man's smile of correction.

"Well, he ain't, to say, actually *started out* yit," the old man grinned. "You know he'd have to git performers, tight-rope walkers, hoop-jumpers, bareback riders, an' the like, an' these mountain clodhoppers ain't in practice. But I'm here to state to you two women if he kin git clowns to furnish as much fun fer a dime and a seat throwed in as he give that crowd this mornin' he'll be rich enough to throw twenty-dollar gold pieces at cats in no time. I seed the whole shootin'-match. I was in the store when the nigger boy come by the front janglin' a bell an' totin' the red flag with a sign on it, an' Alf sent Pomp out fer one of the circulars that had a list of the items. He looked it over, an' then re'ched for his hat, an' me 'n him went down to the court-house yard whar the whole thing was spread out, piled up, an' haltered. It was like Noah's Ark washed ashore an' lyin' thar to dry. Thar was six hosses so thin you could read through 'em without yore specs, three big road-wagons heavy enough to haul steam-engines on, the little, teensy pony with a bob-tail that the clown driv' in the procession, an' the little red-an'-green streaky wagon that he rid in. Then thar was the heavy iron den on another big road-wagon that the lion stayed in till he starved to death, a whoppin' pile of planks that was used for seats, an', last of all, the big canvas tent.

"The entire town an' country was on hand, nosin' about an' crackin' jokes on the fat manager who had come up from Atlanta to attend the sale an' was lookin' as seedy as a last year's bird's-nest. But I'm here to tell you that when Alf Henley come stalkin' down, lookin' sorter indifferent, like he always does when he has a notion to trade, that crowd pulled in its horns an' waited."

"The fool!" Mrs. Henley ejaculated. "Making a public exhibition of himself."

"Well, I've often wondered about that very thing," Wrinkle said. "I sometimes think he tries to make folks think he is a fool to suit his aims, an' ef he ain't a natural-born one it oughtn't to be belt agin him. I admit I was puzzled on that point this mornin'. I stuck to his heels, bound to see 'im through. He'd sniff at one thing an' turn away from another as if it didn't smell right; he'd kick a pile of stuff with contempt an' walk on, an' he grinned to beat a heathen idol at the mere sight of the lion-cage an' pony an' cart, an' then he just squared hisse'f around same as to say, 'Well, I'm in pore business, but I'll jest stand here an' see if anybody will be fool enough to bid on such truck.'"

"You know Sheriff Tobe Webb is a dry-talkin' cuss, anyway, an' I had to laff when he got up an' begun his harangue, fer all the world like a feller in front of a side-show tryin' to drum up a crowd to see a passel o' freaks on the inside. Tobe had the fust item led out fer inspection—a bony hoss that tried to lie down, an' Alf spoke up an' wanted to know if he was a stump-sucker.

"Fred Dill up an' said, 'The man that buys 'im will be the sucker,' an' everybody laffed, Alf as big as the rest.

"'I think I know whar I could sell his hide,' he said, an' bid ten dollars. Then somebody—or it may jest have been the show-man's bluff—raised it to fourteen, an' then Alf went 'im a dollar more an' got the hoss."

"Another one to feed and doctor," sighed Mrs. Henley.

"I say another," Wrinkle chuckled. "He got all six at about the same figure. Nobody was biddin' agin 'im except old Welborne, an' he was so mad he couldn't stand still. They say he had been countin' on havin' it all his own way, but Alf come home an' turned his cake to dough. Next come the three road-wagons. Some o' the farmers was interested in 'em, but they was too heavy fer field-work, an' though Tobe mighty nigh tore the linin' out o' his throat yellin' agin it as a plumb outrage, Alf raked 'em in at about the cost of the bare iron in 'em.

"The next item was the lion's cage, an' a big laff started, for Fred Dill told Alf that it was entirely too clumsy fer a baby-carriage, an' I knowed then that my joke was goin' the rounds, an' I backed away a little, fer I didn't like the way Alf looked. But he was still in the game, an' he walked up to the cage an' ketched hold of the bars an' sorter shook 'em. It had one of the same heavy wagons under it in good condition, an' I believe Alf was tryin' to attract attention from the wagon, for all the time Tobe was talkin' an' sayin' the cage would be a good thing fer a man to lock his wife up in to break 'er of the gad-about habit, Alf was examinin' the iron slats an' the bolts an' bars. It had a big door an' wooden sides that could be tuck off or left on, an' Dill advised Alf to buy it an' turn gypsy, an' roam about tradin' here an' yan. But Alf got the thing at his own bid, an' sorter sneered as he writ down the price on the scrap of paper in his hand."

"For Heaven's sake, what fool caper did he cut next?" Mrs. Henley demanded, in a tone of impatience.

"Why, he bought the pony an' little wagon fer ten dollars, even money, an' it was all I could do to keep the baby joke from risin' ag'in. I could see that Dill was about to spring it, but I shook my head at 'im, an' he kept quiet. I reckon he thought thar was no use rubbin' it in. Then everybody got to watchin' the nigger helpers stretch out the big tent at the sheriff's orders. It was stout, new cloth, an' it glistened like a patch of snow in the sun, an' driv' the crowd back on all sides in a big ring. I reckon everybody thar thought Alf surely would balk at a thing like that, but it looked like the fun folks was pokin' at him had got his dander up. Jim Cahews had closed the store an' come down, an' I seed 'im nudge Alf an' heard 'im say, 'I believe I'd let that item slide, Alf, the cloth has been cut on the bias, an' the seams are so stout that it never could be sold by the yard.'"

"'Shet up, I know what I'm about,' I heard Alf whisper, an' then he yelled out to the sheriff, 'Put up the pile o' planks along with it; nobody wants a' old rag as big as that.'"

"The sheriff agreed, an' both lots went in as one. It was a sharp trick of Alf's, for he had found out that a photographer was thar from Carlton to go his limit on the tent, but lumpin' it in with the planks sorter upset the chap's calculations, an' he didn't have the look of a man that could figure quick. He shuck all over as he bid ten dollars, an' while the sheriff was yellin' 'Goin'! goin'!' Alf stooped down an' felt of the canvas. He found a clean hole that looked like it had been cut, an' run his finger through it an' laffed an' said, 'It wouldn't do to hang it up to dry, the wind 'ud blow it to pieces, but I kin use the planks, an' I'll resk a dollar more.' The photographer got scared, an', while he was stoopin' down tryin' to feel o' the tent, Alf ketched the sheriff's eye an' said, 'I'll withdraw my bid if you don't hurry. I'm wastin' time.' The sheriff yelled out an' told the photographer it was agin 'im, but he look scared wuss 'n ever an' shuck his head, an' that ended it. Alf wasn't in as big a hurry to git away as he had let on, neither. He set a couple o' niggers to work stackin' up the planks in neat piles an' rollin' up the tent. He sent the hosses to the pasture back o' the store, an' told Pomp to give 'em a good rubbin' down, an' to put some o' his famous hoss-tonic in the'r feed."

"A circus!" Mrs. Henley said, with a sniff. "A circus, and me the daughter of a Baptist preacher."

"Well, he ain't raily goin' to put the thing on the road," Wrinkle said, seriously. "He counts on sellin' it off piece by piece. I went back to the store when he did. I was afeard, at the start, that he was cracked in the upper story, but I've sorter switched around. Old Welborne come in an' had his say about the snag Alf had at last struck in his overeagerness to have some'n to do now that he was back, an' went out as mad as the very devil about some'n or other. Jim an' me set down back at the desk an' watched Alf figure up. He looked tickled, and after a while he said:

"'Jim, I'm glad I got back. I know now that Texas ain't no place for my talent. It's overrun with sharp-witted Jews an' keen Yankees that know values down to a gnat's heel. But here in these mountains these yokels git scared clean out o' the'r senses when a dollar has to change hands. Do you know,' says he, 'that I'm out less'n two hundred this mornin', an' at a low estimate I have got a thousand dollars' wuth o' truck?'"

"'I don't know, Alf,' Jim said. 'I'm with yore judgment, as a general thing, but not on this deal. I was lookin' at them hosses t'other day in the court-house yard, an' the Chester brass-band come along. Now, a average hoss,' Jim said, 'will either git scared or break an' run at a sound like that, but three o' them things you got this mornin' struck up a regular jig an' capered about the lot kickin' up the'r heels as if they was in a ring jumpin' over red strips o' cloth.'"

"Well, folks," old Wrinkle continued, "you kin always tell a born trader by his not bein' in a hurry to unload, an' Alf is that way. While we all was settin' thar Pete Hepworth come in at the front, an' while he was on his way to us Alf said: 'You fellers hold yore tongues. That feller is itchin' fer a deal; I had my eye on 'im at the sale.'"

"Pete leaned agin the platform-scales an' talked about the weather an' crops, an' then he said, kinder offhand, to Alf: 'I had a sort o' idea o' biddin' on that pile o' old planks, but when the sheriff lumped 'em in with that fine tent it let me out. I want to build me a cowhouse an' wagon-shed.'"

"'I didn't care for the *tent*,' Alf said, an' he filled his pipe from a china bowl on the desk an' made Pomp fetch 'im a match. 'It was them planks I was after, an' I was bound to have 'em. They are smooth, ready-dressed, long-leaf, heart-pine boards, one an' a quarter by ten, with the ends sawed square an' seasoned by folks settin' on 'em under cover for three or four years—never had a nail driv' in 'em, nuther.'"

"'Well, I never thought they was as good as all that,' Pete said, 'but what are you holdin' 'em at?'"

"'I hain't thought much about it,' Alf said. 'I hain't much of a hand to jump at a trade. It railly does my eyes good to look at lumber like that these days when the best timber you kin git is full o' sap an' worm-holes. How would twenty-five dollars for the pile look to you?'"

"'Why,' said Pete, with a funny look at me an' Jim, 'you only paid eleven for the tent an' planks together.'"

"That hain't got a thing to do with yore deal an' mine,' Alf said, an' he turned an' axed Jim some'n about shippin' some chickens to Augusta that Jim didn't seem to know how to answer."

"'I think it is purty steep,' Pete said. 'I've got time to build now, an' it 'ud take a month to git an order sawed out at the mill, so I'll have to take it'; an' as he was countin' out the cash he laffed an' said: 'I've got an apology to make to you, Alf. Back at the sale I remarked that you was a born idiot, but I don't believe it now. You are a big fish amongst minnows.'"

"An' when Pete had left Alf winked at us an' said, 'You fellers lie low an' watch, an' if I don't double my money on every item I bought to-day I'll buy new hats fer you both.'"

CHAPTER XIII

The purchase of the circus furnished amusement for the village for many a day afterward. During the month that followed the event every citizen who had any appreciation for the droll things of life looked in at the store and had some dry remark to make in regard to the deal. Fred Dill, the clerk of the court and wag of the place, had a new suggestion to make each day as he went to his work. There were certain village freaks he declared who would be drawing-cards on the road and who would work simply for their board and clothes.

But Henley was wisely keeping his own counsel. His underlying wisdom began to show itself one day early in June when there was a widely advertised sale of horses in the square. Farmers came for miles around to sell, swap, or buy, and buyers for city persons were on hand with plenty of ready money. The strangers in town saw nothing remarkable in the fact, but the knowing ones stood open-mouthed when Henley's negro assistants led six well-groomed horses into the square. The Chester band played in the balcony of the court-house, and Henley's exhibit kept gay and sprightly step to the music, as if glad to be once more in their accustomed element. The mane of each animal was decorated with a blue ribbon bow, to which was fastened a card holding the price asked. In no case was it low, and yet when the day was over Henley had completely sold out, and in the presence of many admiring witnesses whom he could hardly shake off he had banked a prodigious roll of currency.

The tide of opinion had turned. From ridicule it had swept with eager-eyed conviction to vast local pride in Henley as a native product. From that day on the remaining items of the circus property were regarded with growing interest. Would Henley actually triumph all through? became the question the villagers asked one another as if it were a game they, themselves, were playing. There was much general discussion over what, after all, really was the "hardest stock" of the lot, and the general consensus of opinion had decided that it was perhaps the three wagons, which were too heavy and cumbersome for any ordinary use. And this view was held till one day when the well-dressed representative of a gang of men working on a new railway over the mountain came and took a look at the wagons. They were almost too heavy, he said, but they might be made to answer his purpose in trucking ties along the new road. He had offered twice as much as Henley had paid for them, and yet the latter's laugh of open derision could have been heard across the street.

"I see you don't want my wagons," he smiled, as he cordially patted the stranger on the shoulder. "You want your company to spend their money on them light, painted things that bust in the sun and break down if you run 'em on anything but a plank floor."

The customer thought too well of himself to realize that he was under Henley's spell. "How much do you hold them at?" he asked.

Henley mentioned a price which was fully four times what they had cost him, and he did it in a tone of supreme contempt for the smallness of the figures. He added that he would never dream of letting them go so low, but that he had no place to store them and didn't care to ship them to Atlanta.

"Well, I'll take them," the man said. "I reckon neither of us will lose by it."

"Well, *you* won't, there's one thing certain about that," was the agreeable seal Henley put on the deal as he watched the railroad man draw out his check-book.

"I really did need one more," the purchaser remarked, "and I'm sorry you only had three."

"Hold on, hold on," Henley said, as the other was shaking the ink down into the tip of his fountain-pen. "Let me study a minute. You see that lion-cage standing on that vacant lot across the street. Now, I'll tell you what I'll do. The wagon the cage is on is pine-plank like them you've bought. The lot it stands on belongs to Seth Woods, the shoemaker; his shop is right around the corner behind the post-office. I put the thing there without his consent, intending to move it right away. I can't get away from here right at this minute, but if you'll step in and ask him if he will consent to let the cage rest on his land awhile I'll have a carpenter take the cage part off and you may have the wagon at the same low figure as the others."

It was one of Henley's best dodges—this raising of apparent obstacles between a customer and his own munificent proposals in the customer's behalf. He had learned early in life that nothing so completely clinched a trade as making a party to it work to bring it about. The man's eyes twinkled as he consented. He hastened out and returned in a moment to say that the shoemaker, with whom he had left an order for a pair of boots, was perfectly willing for his neighbor to use the lot as long as he liked, as he had given up all hope of ever being able to build a shop on it, as had been his plans when he bought the property.

"Well, then, you can draw your check for the whole amount," said Henley, in the same uneventful tone that always preceded his reception of money. "I'll let the cage set on the edge of the sidewalk. Maybe I can induce the town council to use it as a calaboose. The one they've got ain't strong enough by half."

The report of the four-wheeled transfer went over the village before nightfall, and the next morning, for the first time, Fred Dill looked in on Henley without a smile or a joke. He eyed the storekeeper, as he stood behind the show-case smoking a cigar, with a new and wondering respect. Fred was beginning to see largely manifested in Henley the very qualities which were wofully missing from his own merry and shiftless make-up. He counted on his mental digits the remaining items of the defunct circus—the tent, the clown's pony and cart, and the lion's den standing open-doored like a wheelless furniture-van across the street. And even while Dill stood there, telepathically apologetic for his past bantering in the presence of so much incarnate shrewdness and foresight, little Sammy Malthorn, the twelve-year-old son of the wealthiest planter in the village, came in, as he had been doing several times a day for a week past. His voice quivered with youthful triumph as he looked eagerly across the show-case at the smoker.

"Well," he announced, "papa says I may have 'em. You can charge it on his account. It was twenty-five dollars, you said."

"Yes, twenty-five to *you*, Sammy boy," Henley laughed easily. "Pomp will go with you to the stable and hitch 'im up. You'd better let me put in a ten-cent box of axle-grease for them wheels. If you haven't got the dime handy I can add it on the bill. I'd hate to see as fine a rig as that going through town squeaking like a rusty wheelbarrow."

"All right," responded the proud owner of the pony and cart. "Pomp will get it for me."

"Good Lord!" Fred Dill said in his throat, and he went at once to Seth Woods's shoe-shop, where there was a group of loafers, and told the last bit of news. "I begin to think, boys," he said, "that Alf Henley is goin' to make the only money that dang circus ever made. Jest think of it—think of a big circus, hippodrome, menagery, an' side-shows tourin' the whole United States an' Canada without a cent of profit, an' a mountain storekeeper in a measly hole like this gitting rich out of its remains without turning his hand over or losin' a minute's sleep. It looks like thar is some'n crooked in the universe."

"It's beca'se the Lord's bent on smitin' sech cussedness with a broad hand," said a long-faced deacon, who had come in to half-sole his own shoes with the shoemaker's tools, and sat soaking his bits of leather in a tub of dingy water.

"I mought take yore view of it ef the reward was bestowed in a different quarter," Fred said, grimly. "But Alf don't go to meetin' any oftener'n I do. Though he kin send up as good a prayer as the next one when they force 'im to it. Boys, I'm curious to see what he will do with the tent an' lion's cage. Nothin' would surprise me now. He's dead sure to git profit out of 'em."

CHAPTER XIV

That very evening Henley took even another step in his amusing enterprise. He returned to the store after supper and sat writing letters till about eight o'clock. Then he got up, brushed his clothes, and made Pomp polish his boots, and adjusted his black string tie before a glass over the water-pail and basin. Then he went out and walked leisurely up the street till he came to the dark stairway of a little public hall over a feed-store. He ascended the steps with a respectful tread and entered the hall. It was furnished with crude unpainted benches and lighted by kerosene lamps in concave-mirrored brackets on the white walls. At the end stood a table holding a pitcher of water, a goblet, and a Bible, and behind the table sat an earnest-eyed, middle-aged evangelistic preacher, who bowed and smiled in agreeable surprise at the new-comer. The room held fifty or sixty men and women, all silently awaiting the beginning of the services. Henley seated himself on the front bench nearest the preacher, and put his hat on the floor, and dropped his handkerchief into it.

The meeting was opened with the singing by the congregation of familiar hymns, in which Henley joined harmoniously with a fair bass. It was known of him that he never declined an invitation to lead in prayer, and on being asked this evening he readily complied. His voice was deep and round and mellow, and the burden of his utterances was suitable to that or any other religious occasion, being a sort of singsong tribute to the eternal glory of humility and submission to the divine will. The prayer was followed by a rousing sermon from the preacher, and, in closing, he called attention, as Henley evidently had gathered from some source that he would do, to the future plans of the organization. The time was ripe for work in the highways and byways—the sowing of seed in out-of-the-way places, and the preacher was to "take the road" with one or two good singers, a cornet-player, and a cottage-organ, and give people in isolated mountain-nooks a chance to hear the Word and profit thereby for their eternal weal.

He had just seated himself and was mopping his perspiring brow when Henley rose and stood hemming and hawing and clearing his throat.

"I want to say in this same connection," he began, "that I plumb approve of this new idea of taking the great and living Truth into remote corners of our spiritually dark land. Here in Chester we are, you might say, basking in the sunshine of Christian civilization, but away out off of the main roads in the mountains the Book hain't read and prayer hain't held except now and then. I heard that you had already entered into negotiations with an Atlanta tent factory to furnish you with a tabernacle, an' I must say it ain't a bad notion, because many a fine bush-arbor meeting has been busted all to flinders by sudden showers that good, stout canvas would shed as well as a roof of shingles. I want to contribute five dollars toward the fund myself; but I'm here to confess to you frankly that I wouldn't like to see the money throwed away. The great majority of them meeting-tents on the market are simply made to sell and not for hard use. They look all right in the sample-room, but they are full of starch to give 'em body, and when they get wet they are about as porous as a fish-net."

"That's a fact, Brother Henley," spoke up the preacher, with a slow and deliberate nod. "We've been looking around and receiving circulars from all sides, and we have found it purty hard to run across a durable tent at a price we can afford; but there was a drummer here from Nashville the other day, and he claimed—"

"I'd advise you to let drummers alone, too," and Henley brushed away the preacher's words with a firm and all-wise hand. "You see, in my constant contact at the store I know 'em all the way down to the ground. They are the most ungodly pack on earth. Most of 'em drink and play poker, an' never look inside of a Bible. The fact is, if I may be allowed to speak of it at such a time, I happened myself, awhile back, to buy a whopping big tent from a stranded show. I thought at the time that some such a need as this might arise, and so I bid it in. To get it, I had to pay for a lot of old planks and such-like, but in doing it I secured a rattling good thing. It was a bargain; but I could let a good organization like yours have it for a sight less than a new tent not halt as big would cost. It would last a lifetime. It is big enough to hold the multitude that ate the loaves and fishes. It was made for rough wear and must have cost a pile of money. I don't know but what we all could agree on a price—that is, if I had any idea of how much your body would feel disposed to—to invest in a tent."

"We have fifty dollars in the treasury," spoke up the preacher, with an eagerness that blended in his face and voice. "Of course, it may not be near enough to—" He blew his nose and coughed.

Henley stroked his face thoughtfully, and he had the look of a man who was making a polite effort to be resigned to disappointment.

"Well, of course, I *had* hoped that I might do much better

than that," he said finally, looking around at the anxious group, "but, as I said at the start, I want to help you along. You know I said I'd contribute five myself, so—to be accurate—we'd better call the price fifty-five. Then I'll take what you've got in the treasury and call it even."

There was a murmur and shuffle of released suspense throughout the hall. The preacher beamed joyfully as he reached forward and shook Henley warmly by the hand.

"There's no use putting it to a vote," he said. "I'll take the responsibility and accept your magnificent offer right now. Brethren, we are in luck. A special providence seems to have been at work through the whole thing. A vain and ungodly enterprise broke down in our midst, and we are, by our act, directing streams of evil into channels of good. In putting this tent to our use we will be turning over the tables of the money-changers, and causing grain of righteousness to grow where tares of evil flourished."

As Henley walked homeward along the lonely road he mused: "I could have run that crowd up to seventy-five as easy as not. They would have raked up the balance, but I reckon a fellow ought to let well enough alone."

Of all the denizens of Chester and its environs, no one had keener enjoyment over the gossip concerning these various deals than Dixie Hart. She had enough of the speculative tendency in her make-up to heartily appreciate the situation in all its phases, and she was glad, too, that her friend had found, so soon after his return home, such good opportunities to exercise his rare gifts. She went into the store only a day or two after the sale of the tent, and found Henley alone.

"So you won out in that venture, after all?" she laughed. "And, if what folks say is true, you made big money."

"I'm not out of the woods yet," he smiled. "There is always a drawback, you know." He pointed through the open doorway to the lion's cage on the shoemaker's lot across the street. "I've still got that thing, and I'm afraid it's going to be a white elephant. I'm sorry, too, for I'd like to make a clean sweep, just because folks bet that I'd lose heavy. I'd give the cage away if I could do it, but, like a fool, I went and said that I'd show 'em that I could turn every item in the lot over at a profit."

"What are you asking for it?" Dixie inquired.

"Twenty-five dollars," he replied. "If I can't sell it like it stands I'll split it up an' use the iron some way or other."

"It would be a pity to do that," the girl said, thoughtfully. "Let me take a look at it."

He stood in the doorway and watched her as she crossed the street in her easy, graceful way, and then he saw her approach the lion's cage, turn the bolt of the door, and look in, and heard the sound of her fist as it rapped against the wooden sides. Then she disappeared. She had entered the cage and was out of sight for several minutes. Emerging, she came directly across the street to Henley, her head hanging thoughtfully, a slight flush on her face.

"You may think I've plumb lost my senses," she smiled, "but I want to buy that thing. I've heard so much about your deals that I'm itching to speculate some myself. You seem to have come to the end of your rope as far as this cage is concerned, and I want to try my hand. They say two heads is better 'n one, if one is a cabbage-head."

"*You?*—good Lord, what could you do with it?" Henley gasped.

"A heap of things," she retorted, lightly. "You've been offering it for twenty-five dollars, and I'm going to take you up. I had just started to the bank to deposit some money, and so I happen to have the ready cash."

She put her hand into her pocket and drew out a roll of bills, but Henley held up his hand protestingly, and flushed red.

"You don't spend your hard-earned money like that and through my foolish example," he said. "I've had experience in all sorts of junk-handling, and what I do is a different matter. Besides, I know there's no money to be made out of that thing. I got the cream out of the deal, and I won't let you throw money away."

Jim Cahews came in at this moment, and, redder in the face than ever, Henley explained the situation.

"Alf's right, Miss Dixie," the clerk joined in. "You'd better take his advice. If there was anything in that old pile of iron he'd have seen it long ago."

But her money was lying on the show-case before Henley's eyes, and she had retreated to the door.

"I've bought it," she insisted. "It's mine, and I'm going to make some money out of it, too. I'm tired of working like a corn-field nigger for puny profits, while you men make jokes here in the shade and get rich at it."

Henley refused to touch the money. His flush had given place to a look of pained concern.

"I can't—just can't let you do it!" he said. "Like a good many women, I reckon, Dixie, you look at the dealings of men from the outside, and are willing to go an' plunge into unknown waters and get ducked and leave your money at the bottom. Profit ain't ever made by getting in at the tail-end of another fellow's venture. I've squeezed this thing dry, and—"

"I'm a more experienced milker than you are," Dixie laughed, "and the cage is mine. There's your money. It's mine, and if I make money out of it I won't have you grumbling, either."

Henley and Cahews exchanged glances of actual alarm.

"What do you intend to do with it?" Henley almost snapped in his impatience.

"Did anybody ask you what you intended to do with it when *you* bought it?" Dixie asked. "You haven't any right to ask. But I'll tell you *one* thing. I'm not going to turn it into a corn-crib, though it would make a dandy, and one that no nigger could steal from. I'm buying it to sell for at least twice as much as I've paid for it, and I want you to watch me. I've been tickled mighty nigh to death over your late deals, and I want to amuse you. I know you'd like to see me make some money, and I'm going to do it as sure as I'm knee-high to a duck."

When she had gone Henley and Cahews stood in the door-way disconsolately staring after her as she walked briskly down the street.

"You see, Jim, I'm afraid I'm responsible for it," the storeke-eper said, with a frown. "She's got a long head for a woman in most matters, but she's had it turned by watching this little game of mine. It is the first time I've ever seen her fly off the handle at all. As a rule she's very cautious, but, Lord, Lord, the idea of paying twenty-five dollars for that thing! Why, if it gets out she'll be the laughing-stock of the town."

CHAPTER XV

The next morning when Henley arrived at the store, Cahews, who with a face drawn long was standing at the front, pointed mutely at the lion's cage. Henley looked and groaned. It bore a pasteboard placard, and the words, in big, irregular capitals:

FOR SALE. APPLY TO DIXIE HART.

"She come in here yesterday evening after you'd gone," Cahews explained, "and borrowed my marking-pot and brush. Then she had me get her the pasteboard, and after she had painted the sign she took the nail-box and hammer and went over there and tacked it up. A crowd of schoolboys was watching, and raised a laugh, but she come away without paying any attention to them. I tried to get her to reason a little, and told her the money was there in the drawer waiting for her to change her mind, but she said she knowed exactly what she was about, and if I'd lie low I might learn a trick or two in business methods."

"She's off—she's away off!" Henley sighed. "And I'm plumb sorry, for she is, in many other ways, as quick as a steel trap and bright as a new dollar."

One morning, two days later, as the storekeeper was at his desk in the rear writing letters, his attention was called by a keen whistle from Cahews, who stood in the front-door wildly signalling him to approach. And going to the clerk, who was now on the front porch staring toward the lion's cage, he saw that Seth Woods, the begrimed shoemaker, had torn down the placard and stood looking into the cage.

"He's mad about it, I'll bet," was Henley's troubled comment. "I reckon folks have been guying him. That railroad man said he consented to let me use the lot. Maybe he lied to close the trade."

"Maybe he did," agreed Cahews; "but look! What do you make of that?"

A negro man with the shoemakers bench on his shoulder had turned the corner and was headed for the cage. "Put it inside an' go back for the rest," they heard Woods order.

Wonderingly, Henley strode across the street and reached the cage just after the negro had put down the bench on the inside and was coming out of the narrow doorway.

"What's the meaning of this?" Henley inquired of the shoemaker.

"Why," and a complacent smile broke through the grime on Woods's face, "it means, Alf, that I'm at last my own landlord. I've been paying old Welborne fifty dollars a year rent fer that little hole in a wall, away back from the square, because I couldn't get enough ahead to build on this lot or get any other shop. I think I've had a stroke of luck, and, strange to say, it come through a woman. Yesterday evening Dixie Hart come in my shop and axed me if I could straighten the heels of her shoes while she set thar. I told her certainly, an' while I was at work we got to talking first on one topic and then on another. She likes my wife an' daughter, an' she said a good deal about 'em. She axed me if

I had any objections to lettin' this cage, which she said she had raked in from you at a big bargain, to set on my lot till somebody come along and bought it. I thought buyin' sech a thing was a powerful quar thing for a young woman to do, but of course I didn't say so to her, for it wa'n't any o' my business. Well, one thing fetched on another till she got to lookin' about my shop while I was trimmin' the heel-taps, an' all at once she wanted to know—if thar was no harm in axin'—what rent I was payin'. I told 'er fifty dollars, an' she whistled kind o' keenlike an' said: 'My gracious! an' got a vacant lot, too, right in the heart o' the square.' I explained to her that I wasn't able to build a shop, an' was afraid I never would be, gettin' old like I am an' so many to feed. Then, Alf, what you think that gal said? As cool as a cucumber in a spring branch, as she set thar wigglin' her toes in 'er stockin' feet, she said: 'You'd better listen to me, an' I'll fix you so you won't have *any* rent to pay. That lion's cage, just at it stands, with the door openin' on the sidewalk, would make the dandiest shoe-shop in seven States. It's plenty wide and long; it is well-roofed with painted sheet-iron, an' would be as tight in cold weather as a jar of preserves. It faces every street that leads into the square, and you'd get twice as much custom there as you do away back here next to this little pig-trail alley.' By gum, what she said struck me like a bolt of lightnin'. I'd examined the cage, as everybody else in town has, I reckon, an' I knowed all about it, so I up an' axed 'er what she'd paid you for it, an' she kind o' dodged my question.

"'Has that got anything to do with it?' she axed, an' I told 'er, I did, that I heard you was offerin' it fer twenty-five dollars. That seemed to set 'er studyin' fer a minute, an' then she said:"

"'To tell you the truth, Mr. Woods, that *is* all I had to pay, but I got it, you mought say, at that figure by the very skin o' my teeth. In a thoughtless moment Alf Henley said he'd take twenty-five, and, knowing what it was railly worth, I yanked out the money on the spot and laid it down. He's a gentleman'—she said—'Alf Henley is a plumb gentleman, but he tried his level best to back down. Jim Cahews will testify that I was actually obliged to leave the money on the counter and walk out before he'd give in.' Is that so, Alf?"

"I am obliged to say it is, Seth," Henley answered, flushing. "Some'n like that actually *did* take place."

"I didn't think she'd fib about it," Woods went on, "and I finally axed her what she'd take, an' she said nothin' less than fifty dollars cash down would interest her, as she had a winter cloak to lay in, an' shoes for three women, an' what not."

"I told her fifty looked purty steep, but she throwed herself back an' laughed hearty. She said my rent in the shop fer one year alone would pay it, and after that I'd be a free man. She said in the summer I could prop up both these flap sides, to cut off the sun, an' the wind would blow clean through. She said the very oddity of the thing would draw trade, that I could have the picture of the lion painted out an' a big boot an' shoe put in place of it. Oh, I can't begin to tell you all she said. She'd 'a' been talkin' till now if I hadn't traded: Besides, betwixt me'n you, she give me a scare; you see I was afraid the thing would slip through my fingers, fer she set in to talkin' about havin' it moved to t'other side o' the square and rentin' it fer a barber-shop, an' she 'lowed, too, that it would be a bang-up thing to sell to a convict-camp to keep chain-gang prisoners in.

"As a last resort, I axed her, I did, if she thought I ought to pay her a clean hundred per cent. profit, an' she said: 'That ain't for you to consider at all, Mr. Woods. You must jest let your mind rest on what *you* are goin' to get out of it. Alf Henley's made money out of it; I must make my part, and you can do the same. It is the way business is run all over the world. As soon as it becomes yours, somebody may come along and pay you a hundred for it, though you'd be a fool to let it go even at that. You are the one man in all the world that ought to hold on to it.' She was right, Alf. I'm tickled over the change. I feel like a new man. You ought to have seen old Welborne's face when I told 'im I was goin' to vacate. He swore Dixie Hart was a meddlesome hussy, an' that she had cheated the hindsight off of me. He said she owed him an' was behind in her pay, an' that he was goin' to fetch 'er to taw."

Henley went back to his desk. There was a flush on his brow.

"Beat to a finish, and by a girl," he mused. "Here I've been thinking I had nothing to learn about trading, and she picks up one of my remnants and turns it over at a hundred per cent. profit as easy as knitting a pair of socks. If I'd lived a hundred years I'd never have thought about that shoe-shop."

CHAPTER XVI

Henley did not see Dixie Hart till a week had elapsed. He had started to drive over to Carlton one morning, when he passed her as she was mending a rail-fence round one of her fields which extended down to the road. She had on a sunbonnet and heavy gloves, and stood in a dense patch of prickly blackberry briers which reached to her shoulders.

"That work's too hard for you," Henley greeted her cordially. "I've done all sorts of jobs on a farm, from splitting rails to feeding a steam thresher, and they are picnics beside what you are now at."

"I believe you are right," she smiled, as she pushed back her bonnet and exposed her red face and neck. "But I had to do it; the pigs have rooted away the rotten rails next to the ground under these briers and got in to my turnips and potatoes. But I've nearly finished, thank goodness."

"I'm off for Carlton," he informed her. "I go every day or so now on business. Is there anything I can do for you over there?"

"There really is, Alfred." She parted the clinging briers and came quite close to him in one of the fence corners which was infested with the wild growth. She had drawn off her gloves, and now thrust a pink hand into her pocket and got out a handkerchief, in a corner of which were tied some coins. "I want you to step into the book-store and get me a Second Reader—the sort they use in the public schools over there. It's for little Joe. I'm learning him to read, and he's doing it as fast as a dog can trot."

"I wish you'd let me pay for the book," Henley ventured, as she put the money into his hand. "You know I've got twenty-five dollars of your cash, anyway. That old cage wasn't worth anything."

"You mean I've got twenty-five dollars of *your* money," she retorted. "Why, I've been ashamed to look you in the face. I didn't act right about it, and I hardly know why I done it. As a friend to you I ought to have told you about the chance I saw and not set in to gain myself. I don't feel right about it. I'd rather you'd have it—I can't feel like it's mine. You'd made money out of all the other things, and you ought to have made a clean sweep of the whole job."

"You are forgetting two main things," he said, gravely, his eyes averted. "You forget that you paid me all I asked for the blame thing, and that if it hadn't been for you I'd not have been at the sale of the circus, anyway."

"You mean—" She flushed knowingly, and avoided his earnest gaze.

"That you stopped me that night, and kept me from doing the biggest fool thing a sensible man ever was guilty of. I've thanked you in my heart, Dixie, thousands and thousands of times. It would have ruined me for life, but you looked ahead and saw it and saved me."

"Oh, well, that's past and gone," Dixie said, touched by a certain new and deep quality in his voice. "I'll keep the money if you want me to. I really need it. Old Welborne got hopping mad at me for ousting his tenant, and simply rowed me up Salt River. Some day I may come to you for legal advice. I want you to look over the document he got me to sign. I want to know more about it than I do. There are too many 'aforesaids' and 'herebys' in it to suit me. I bought that farm with my eyes shut. I was so anxious to own land that I was willing to take the property on any terms. Welborne is getting to be like that old man in the fairy-book that stuck to the feller's neck and never could be shook off till he was made drunk. Welborne never touches a drop, you know, and so he'll stick till death claims him. I'm in an awful mess. I work like a slave from break of day till away after dark, and never seem to move a peg toward any sort of landing-place."

"You really ought to marry," Henley said. "That's exactly what you ought to do. There's many a good man in the world that is actually suffering for the need of the right sort of a helpmeet."

"You hit the nail on the head that whack," she said, quite seriously. "I know I'm better-looking now—when I'm fixed up, at least—than I will be ten years later; and I've got sense enough to know that old maids don't make natural-looking brides. No, I really ought to give the subject more thought. I ain't acting in a businesslike way about it. I ought to put myself on the market, but I let first one thing and then another interfere, and now it seems to be little Joe. I think I've got a sort of mother-love for him, Alfred. He works over in his field, and me in mine, and when it's twelve o'clock I get out my dinner-bucket and call to him, and we both go down to the spring and have a picnic. That's where I learn him to read. If old Pitman was to get on to it I reckon he'd raise a row. Joe fetches his pore little scraps of streak-o'-lean, streak-o'-fat bacon an' hoe-cake along, but I make 'im throw the stuff away. I don't know, but I believe I'd rather see that child's big, hungry eyes as I open that bucket than to be admired by the handsomest young man in the county. I don't know, though—I've never tried the young-man part."

"Yes, you ought to marry, Dixie." Henley, with the true feeling of a gentleman that he ought not to sit while she stood, got out of his buggy and leaned on the fence. "I'm going to confess that I've thought a lot about that very thing since I got home, and, if I'm the judge I think I am, I believe I've run across the very man for you."

"You don't say!" Dixie cried, eagerly. "Well, well!"

"You know I drive over to Carlton every now and then," Henley went on, "and as Jim always has a few pounds of butter, a box or so of eggs, and the like, to send, I take 'em to a store run by a young feller that I always did like. Jasper Long is his name. He got his start by the hardest licks that was ever dealt by a poor boy. He was a half-orphan, and had to take care of his old mother till she died and left him all alone. He drove a dray about town till he was twenty, and with money he'd saved he set up for himself in business. He's the wonder of the town now, for he made money hand over fist. He's hitched on a brick warehouse to his shebang, and buys cotton when it reaches its lowest ebb and holds it till it gets to the top—then he lets loose. Me and him are pretty thick, and when I go over there either I have to eat with him at the hotel or he does with me. Sometimes we toss up head-or-tails to see who pays."

"I've never seen him," Dixie said, quite interested, "but I've heard about him. Carrie Wade said he come out to camp-meeting one Sunday, and was pointed out as a big catch, but she said he was sort of clumsy and awkward in his movements."

"Carrie wouldn't think his gait was so bad if he was trotting at her side," commented Henley. "But Long's all right; he's honest, and straight as a shingle. I'd trust him to act square in any deal, and that's a lot to say these times. He ain't had much to do with women. You see, they've got a sort of stuck-up society crowd over there that don't think he's quite the thing, and so he's out of what you might call the *elyte.* His sort are the kind that always count in any struggle, though. He bunks in a big, wide bed in the back end of his store, and one night when I had to lie over there because the river was out o' banks he made me sleep with him. That was the time I advised him to marry. It pleased him powerful, and he up and told me that he'd been giving the matter considerable thought and investigation. He said that every now and then it would occur to him that precious time was passing, but that he'd been so busy he'd not had time to go at it right. He said that most of the women on any list of the kind he'd seen was fussy and looked lazy and thriftless. Then he come right out and asked me if I happened to know a suitable candidate, and—well, Dixie, I couldn't hold in. I talked as earnest as a preacher at a ranting revival. I had his eye and I helt it clean through. I described you to him and—"

"You did?" Dixie laid an eager hand on his arm and laughed merrily, "What did you say? Tell me exactly. I won't let you leave till you do. Tell me, Alfred."

"Oh, I couldn't do that, Dixie!" Henley flushed to his hat. "I'd make a botch of it. I could talk to him, but I couldn't to you—at least—at least not on that line."

"But you've *got* to do it!" the girl insisted. "I want to hear it. I've always wanted to know what a man would say about me behind my back. I know what women will say, for they will tell you to your teeth exactly what they will behind your back, only worse, if they can possibly do it. Try to remember exactly what you said."

Henley's blood burned fiercely in his tanned face. "I couldn't tell you like I did him, and I hain't going to try. I ain't made that way—some men are, but I ain't."

"You are afraid I'll feel bad about it, I see," the girl said, with well-assumed severity, and she glanced aside that he might not read the look of conscious power in her eyes. "You and me have been such stanch friends that you hate to tell me what a poor opinion you have of me and my looks. I see. I see. Well, I hain't got no right to think anybody would think well of me—you least of all."

"Shucks! If you'd heard me you'd never complain," Henley burst forth. "I told him you was the prettiest thing that ever wore shoe-leather; that you had hair of a reddish-brownish mixture that no man could begin to describe, and eyes so big and deep and drawing-like that a feller couldn't look in 'em without wondering what they was made of, and cheeks and lips as red and ripe and laughing as—"

"That will do," Dixie laughed, pleasurably. "You was determined to trade me off, and you went at it like I was a horse you was trying to get rid of for more than he was worth. Well, what else did you say?"

"Why, I told 'im about your awful struggle against adversity; about the hold old Welborne had on you; about your mother and aunt being helpless on your hands, and about how you wanted to add to it all by helping Pitman's bound boy. But when I told him the other day about the way you bought and sold that lion's cage I thought he would bust wide open. He throwed himself back agin the counter and yelled and clapped his hands. Said he:

"'Alf, that's the woman for me. Every trading man, needs a partner like her. Such women as her are the mothers of kings and presidents and great geniuses. *My* mother was that way; she made me what I am.' And then he railed out against conditions that could make you undergo so much hardship, and said he'd just love to give a girl like you a good home that you could keep neat and clean and in apple-pie order. He said his life was lonely, and that he wanted to see a smiling face at the window when he got home after work. He says he's able to build as good a house as any man in Carlton, and that he already owns a corner lot on Tilbury Avenue, the swell street of the town. The truth is, he wants to take a look at you powerful bad, and I promised him, if it was possible, that I would—"

"Well, I don't know about that," Dixie objected suddenly, and her pretty brow wrinkled. "You know what they say about a burnt child. I've already as good as offered myself to one chap. I didn't come up to requirements, and I don't want to do it again. What you'd say to *him* about me and what he'd actually *think* are two different things. If I was to meet him and I saw from his looks that he didn't think much of your judgment I'd hate you both and feel like scratching your eyes out. I'd make a sensible man a good wife, and I'd do my part; but I'll be hanged if I'll walk up to him wearing a 'For Sale' tag. What you say is mighty interesting, and I may let it bother me a good deal, for a woman owes it to herself to look out for number one, but there is a line of self-respect that a woman can't cross. I'm in an awful mess, and I'd marry to get out of it. You may say what you please about me to him, but that's as far as I'll go."

"You don't think you could send the poor chap some word or other?" Henley ventured, at the end of his diplomacy, as he got into his buggy and took up the reins.

"No, I don't," was the thoughtful answer. "He's a friend of yours, and you recommend him high enough, but we hain't been introduced, and to take any step beforehand on *my* side would be unbecoming of a lady, and that's what I am."

"Yes—of course, and you know best," said Henley, as he clucked to his horse, "but Long will be powerfully disappointed. He's got sort of keyed up over this thing, and it has gone and unsettled him. I reckon he's got a pretty picture of you in his mind, and keeps it before him all the time."

"That's it," said Dixie. "And I wouldn't like to see it turn to a chromo on his hands. I know what I look like to myself, but I wouldn't expect to suit every taste."

CHAPTER XVII

That evening, just after dark, when Henley drove his horse into his barn-yard, he saw Dixie over in her own lot milking her cow. She was a brave, erect little figure as she stood in the soft, black loam. "So, so!" she was saying in her sweet, persuasive voice to the restless animal. "Can't you stand still and keep that pesky fly-brush out of my eyes? Them hairs cut like so many knives when they are flirted about like a wagon-whip. You may as well let me get that milk out of your bag. It will give you trouble through the night if you don't."

Henley turned his horse into one of the stalls, and fed him with fodder and corn in the ear, and came and leaned on the fence behind her. She was now crouched down beside the cow; he could see her brown, tapering arms and wrists against the cow's flank, and hear the milk as it ran into her tin pail with a sharp, intermittent sound. Above the back of the cow, of which she seemed a part in the thickening darkness, loomed up her cottage. There was a yellow light in the kitchen from a bank of blazing logs in the wide-open fireplace. Henley waited till she had finished and stood up.

"Hard at it," he jested. "Day or night, it's all the same to you. I wonder if you work when you are asleep."

"Huh," she laughed, as she advanced toward him, her pail

swinging by her side. "This is my reception-day, and this is my parlor. Won't you come in and set awhile? Take that rocking-chair over near the piano—or maybe you'd rather smoke in the bay-window, where you can get fresh air."

"What's the joke now?" he inquired. "I'm not exactly on."

"Why, you see, you are the second beau I've had right here in the mud, and with these dirty clothes on, in the last ten minutes."

"The second?" he said, wondering what she was driving at.

"Yes," she made answer, as she rested her pail at her feet and stood smiling blandly at him. "Hank Bradley has just left. He come over to invite me to go with a party of girls and boys to the Springs day after to-morrow. I wish I knew exactly what to do in a case like that. I want to go—my! I want to go so bad I hardly know what to do. Mother and Aunt Mandy both think I ought to accept such invitations. I know folks talk about Hank, and say all sorts of things about girls he goes with. But he says he has quit drinking and gambling and wants to settle down. His sister, Mrs. Bailey, is going along to give respectability to it, and it is to be a great blow-out. I've never been on such a trip; they say there is a lot of fashionable Atlanta folks at the hotel, and a fine band, a ten-pin alley, and a lawn-tennis court, and I hardly know what all."

"Hank Bradley? Good gracious!" Henley said, but he could think of nothing further that would voice the protestations running wildly through his brain.

"Oh, I see you'll oppose it, too," she sighed. "I reckon I've just been trying to make myself believe I ought to go. Hank begged so hard, and—and said such nice things about liking me. I reckon almost any girl would want to believe even a fellow like him, if she'd been a wall-flower all her life, and somehow didn't think she ought to be."

"But did you accept—did you? That's the main thing," Henley asked, and his eyes were fixed on her mobile face where the pink shadows chased one another beneath her long, drooping lashes.

"No, not positive," she said. "I simply couldn't get rid of him to do my work without saying something; so I agreed to talk it over with my folks and let him know after supper. He is to send a man over for the answer. I already see my finish—I see it in the way you are staring at me right now."

"He ain't for you, Dixie," Henley answered, decidedly. "You said once that you looked on me like a big brother. Well, if your brother was to see you driving off that way beside that man—that *sort* of a man—he'd be miserable. I can't do much to show my interest and friendship—though I've tried hard to think of some way. I know you deserve more than has come to you. You are young and full of life, and bright and pretty—so pretty that you'd be the main one in any cluster, and it is hard to think you have to pass your days as you do. But Hank Bradley ain't the one to extend a hand. He ain't—God knows he ain't."

"I know it; you needn't say another word." The girl came nearer. The moon was out now in a clear sky, and its rays fell athwart her face and gleamed in the gold of her abundant tresses. His hand was resting on the top rail of the fence, and she laid her own on it reassuringly. "Don't bother, big brother," she said, in a deep, trembling tone. "I'll write him that I can't go. I'd not enjoy a minute of it knowing that your judgment was against it. Let's not talk about it. Let's talk about something else. I've been thinking all day about that Carlton storekeeper."

"Your ears must have burned." Henley betrayed his relief by the free breath he drew. "I saw him over there, and we talked about you for an hour on a stretch. I wasn't going to see him, but he heard I was in town and sent his porter after me. He wanted to see me about you."

"*Me?* That's funny, if you ain't joking."

"I ain't joking," Henley declared. "He said he'd been unable to get his mind on business like he used to. He says, from what I've told him, that he knows just how you look. He pinned me down again about fetching you over there; and when I told him that you felt sort of backward about taking such a step, he seemed more tickled than set back. He said he'd seen so many women that throwed theirselves at him and interfered with his movements that the hold-off sort was just what he was looking for. He went on and told me about the old maids that knitted socks for him, and the giddy young ones that tittered and looked at him out of the corners of their eyes whenever he passed, and how many widows and mothers of gals was trading at his store now that hadn't before, and how much bother they all was in refusing to let his clerks wait on 'em, and was always coming back to his desk to make him get what they needed."

"Shucks, I'll bet he's had his head turned," was Dixie's comment. "Well, he needn't think he's the whole show; they wouldn't do him that away if he didn't have money. Well, I needn't criticise them, for, as good as I think I am, I don't reckon I'd give him a second thought if he was just a farm-hand at seventy-five a day. Money adds a lot to a person, and I reckon if a girl went about it right and as a matter of duty she could love a rich man as quick as a poor one."

"Well, I simply couldn't head 'im off," Henley resumed. "I couldn't get around his arguments. He said there was a way you and him could meet without compromising your pride, and that was this: he said me and you was good friends, and that if I wanted to make you pass a pleasant day I could invite you to drive over there next Saturday week and see the fire tournament that is to be held."

"Well, he's got cheek enough, I must say," Dixie said. "I reckon he might let you run your own business and extend your own invites. It ain't for him to up and dictate to you—huh! I say!"

"But, you see, I'd already told him that I'd enjoy fetching you over at any time. You see, he knowed it would be a pleasure to me. I'm going over, anyway, and your company the ten miles and back would be a sight better than being alone."

"Well, that's different," said Dixie, "and I really would enjoy the trip. But it would have to be fully understood that I went just with you, and was not going along to exhibit myself, to see if I'd suit him or not."

"Good!—now you've hit it!" Henley laughed. "It will be fun all round. I'm going again to-morrow, and I'll tell him to be—I'll tell him me and you have decided to take in the tournament."

"Yes, put it that way," said Dixie, and she took up her pail. "It may be a flash in the pan, and I'd hate everybody in creation—you included—if I was accused of—of missing fire the *second time*!"

They both happened to glance toward the cottage, and standing framed in the kitchen doorway with a background of light they saw a mute and motionless figure.

"It's little Joe!" Henley exclaimed. "Wait, I forgot what you sent me for." He went to his buggy and returned with a parcel. "I got the Second Reader, and I had the man put in a Geography-book full of pretty maps and pictures. I thought maybe Joe would—"

"He'll be tickled to death," Dixie cried, as she reached for the parcel. "The poor little fellow is watching us now. I told him you'd bring it to-night, and he's been down several times to see if you was back. It's awfully sweet of you, Alfred, to think of the Geography. I need it myself, and me and Joe'll study it together. If that thing we was talking about should happen to go through, the first move I'd make would be to try to get that boy out of Pitman's clutch. I love 'im—he's so gentle and patient that I can't help it."

They heard a step behind them, and, turning, they saw old Wrinkle peering at them through the dark as he stood near the barn.

"If that's you, Alf," he called out, "you'd better come on to supper. After a square meal at the Carlton Hotel you may look on our fare as purty pore stuff. But you may choke it down. It's gettin' cold; the grease in the beef hash is turnin' to tallow, an' the bread was baked yesterday an' is as hard as a brick."

"All right; I'm with you," Henley said, good-naturedly, as he saw Dixie hurrying away.

CHAPTER XVIII

On the morning set for the excursion to Carlton, Henley went down to the stable and harnessed and hitched his horse to his buggy. Old Jason, who was with him, made no offer to assist with the various buckles and straps, but stood leaning in the barn-door chewing tobacco. He was sufficiently courteous, however—as Henley started away with the remark that he was going to give Dixie Hart a lift over to Carlton and back—to slouch in front, his hands in his pockets, his tousled head bared to the slanting rays of the sun, and open the big gate.

Reaching the front-door of Dixie Hart's cottage, Henley had only a minute to wait. Mrs. Hart, followed by her sister with an arm in a sling, came down the steps with a mincing step, her weak eyes shaded by her thin hand, and approached him.

"It's powerful good of you to take my daughter," she said, in grateful tones. "She has so little pleasure in her life, and she's been wanting to go to Carlton for a long time. A place even as much like a city as that is, kind o' interests a young girl. She's always reading about the doings over there among the rich folks."

"I'll see that nothing happens to her, and fetch her back safe," he promised. Then Dixie emerged from the house wearing her best dress, a white muslin, immaculately clean and well ironed, and adorned by broad, pink ribbons which heightened her complexion. Her hat was new and most becoming, and as she rustled out to the gate he felt a thrill of pride in having such a presentable companion. She touched her mother playfully under the chin and kissed her on the cheek.

"Now, Muttie," she said, "you've got to be on your good behavior while I'm off or I'll switch you good when I get back. I have put the exact feed for the horse in his trough, and pumped the tub full of water, and you only have to let down the stable-door bars at twelve and he'll do the rest. The chicken-feed is already mixed in the dish-pan, and you only have to tilt it out of the kitchen-window and they'll divide it amongst 'em."

"Oh, I can attend to everything!" Mrs. Hart remarked to Henley. "I reckon you've found out that she's a regular case."

"Case or not," Dixie broke in, as Henley was smiling and nodding his response, "I'm not through yet. If I don't tell you, you'll be begging for something to eat amongst the neighbors. Your dinner is already cooked and the coffee made. All you'll have to do is to set it on the coals and warm it up. The sugar is right at the coffee-pot, and the cream is in the spring-house to keep it from souring.

"I didn't dare hint to 'em about—about that Carlton fellow," Dixie said, in a confidential tone, as they drove away. She was holding her big hat on to keep it from blowing off in the crisp current of their own making.

"You didn't?" he said, interrogatively, charmed as he had never been before by her propinquity and vivaciousness.

"Not after being sold as bad as I was by letting them know about that other scrape," she laughed, as she glanced at him archly. "Why, they would meet us a mile out on the road to-night—the halt leading the blind—to know every particular. No, I've been burnt once, and I don't want a second coat of blisters."

"You certainly look stunning." Henley allowed his admiring eyes to take her in from head to foot. "You needn't be one bit afraid of what that galoot will say. I tell you I've been about over the country and I know a thing or two."

"Well, I've got my all on my back," she said—"that is, except my wedding outfit. I don't know how I'll ever get my money out of it. I've thought about selling it, but nobody of my size seems to be marrying round here. Even if *this* thing is a go—I mean even if me and Mr. Long *do* come to terms—I don't believe I'd feel just right in using it. It would be sort o' like marrying in widow's weeds, wouldn't it?"

They were now passing Farmer Wade's house, on the edge of the village, and they saw Carrie on the veranda-steps with Johnny Cartwright at her side. The couple stood close together, and Henley saw that the boy was holding Carrie's hands and gazing at her ardently. Seeing the passing buggy, Carrie suddenly drew herself back and stared at them curiously. There was no salutation from either side, and Henley drove on, noting that Dixie kept her eyes on the pair till they were out of sight.

"I thought I'd give her a good, straight look," she said, "so she'd see that I wasn't doing anything I am ashamed of. I know that girl through and through, and you mark my words, Alfred, she'll be low enough to throw out hints about me driving with a young, married man like you. The way she's acting with that poor silly boy is disgusting. His poor old mother is so upset she's talking to everybody about it.

She is afraid Carrie will actually run off with him, and Carrie will, too, if she gets a good chance—she's just that desperate. It's funny how mean, spiteful folks can make other people the same way. Right now, I'd rather have this Long man come out here and take me to meeting where Carrie could see it than to do a kind deed of any sort."

After this, to Henley's mystification, she did not talk as freely as at the outset, and she seemed to be very thoughtful. As they were driving into the bustling town, she looked at him fixedly and said:

"The papers say the programme don't begin till eleven o'clock. That's the hour set for the first race with the reel-wagons. I was just wondering what we'd better do to kill time till then. I hain't got a thing to buy that you hain't got in your stock at home, and I hain't a person to go in and nose about and have clerks pull down a whole raft of bolts and boxes without paying for the trouble. You see, I reckon it ain't later 'n nine o'clock now, and—"

"Oh, I see," said Henley. "Why, Dixie, I sort o' mapped it out this way. You see, knowing how anxious Long will be to meet you right off, I thought we'd drive straight to his shebang and 'light and hitch. He's got a chair or two in the back-end of his shack, and we could kind o' set about, and when he ain't waiting on customers, why, we—"

"I thought you had more sense than that," Dixie burst out with unexpected warmth. "*You* can go there if you like, but I won't go a step! Huh, I say—I *would* cut a purty dash, wouldn't I?—setting around amongst chicken-coops, lard-cans, and salt pork for a fool, vain man to look me over and sniff and feel set back because I didn't happen to—to come quite up—shucks! I don't believe any of you men understand women. Huh! but we understand *you* all right."

"I'm awfully sorry I made you mad," Henley stammered. "You know, Dixie, I wouldn't say a thing for worlds that would—"

Dixie laughed. "You couldn't make me mad at you to save your life, Alfred. I'm mad at myself, that's all, for starting out on such a silly jaunt. I might have knowed that it would be hard to put this thing through in any decent shape. I don't care what Long'll say or think. I come over here to this tournament with you, at your invite, and if he shows by a single bat of the eye that he thinks I meant anything else he'll hear something that will ring in his ears till he's put under ground. I reckon the idea never got within a mile of his brain that he may not suit *me* at all. Why, I may hate the very sight of him."

"You no doubt will if you keep on looking at the thing that way," said Henley, admiring the very mystery that cloaked her words and manner, and quite convinced that she was wiser, in some vague way, at least, than all the rest of mankind put together. "I only thought that would be the best way to start the ball rolling."

"Well, it won't start at all if I have to tote it to the top of a hill and give it the first kick," Dixie said, firmly. "I'm a big fool. I'll bet you haven't a bit of respect for me. That other racket of mine was enough to brand me as the champion woman idiot of the earth, and this goes that one better. What's the use o' being a fool if you don't learn sense by it?"

"Oh, don't talk that way, Dixie," Henley protested, at the end of his resources. "I thought we was going to have such a fine time, and now you hardly know what you want. If you won't go to his store, then I'll tell you what we could do. The public wagon-yard is the best place to see the tournament from. I could unhitch at the edge of the sidewalk in the shade of the trees, and you'd have a reserved seat through it all."

"That's *some* better, anyway," she said, as if relieved. "I come near showing my temper, didn't I? Well, I've got one hid away inside of me, and it kicks up sand sometimes when I'm least expecting it."

Leaving his sprightly charge in the buggy watching the gathering of the festive crowd and listening to the blatant music of the town band from the balcony of the Carlton House, Henley, making some excuse about having to mail a letter, hastened round a corner and down to Long's store.

The young man, in his best suit of clothes and with the odor of bay-rum in his smooth, compact hair, and the barber's powder on his razor-scraped face, was busy giving instructions to his chief clerk.

"Don't come to me to ax a single question," Henley overheard him saying. "This is *one* day I simply will have off. If there is anything you don't know about, let it lie over—tell 'em I'm on the committee of entertainment, tell 'em any darned thing you want to, but don't bother me. Oh!" He had caught sight of Henley, who stood half hidden by a stack of soap-boxes, and came forward, his face falling. "My Lord, Alf, don't tell me you didn't fetch her in!" he panted. "Good Lord, don't say that!"

Henley grinned and explained the situation, much to the storekeeper's relief.

"It don't railly make any great difference." Long twisted his small mustache under its coat of pomade till the ends looked like facial spikes, and pulled at his white waistcoat. "I had a nigger make a bucket of lemonade with ice in it, and left an order at the hotel for three of the best meals they know how to put up. I supply the shebang with produce, and I stand in with 'em. They would spread themselves for me. I was counting on having us all three eat in my back-room. I wanted to do exactly the right thing, you see, so she'd know at the outset that I understand how to make a woman comfortable, and that I ain't a man to split hairs when it comes to a little outlay."

"The back-room wouldn't suit at all." Henley was already a wiser man than when he left home that morning. "I wouldn't think of asking her or any decent woman to eat in a room where you bunk, or where anybody bunks, for that matter—male or female."

"I'll just countermand that order, then," Long said, "and we'll all go to the hotel. We'll see the fust part of the show from the buggy, and then repair to the big dining-room and have our banquet."

"I think she'd really like that," Henley declared, "but I'm going to give you both the slip and take dinner with Judge Temple's folks. They made me promise to come the next time I was in; besides, I want to give you both full swing on this day of days."

"Right you are," Long rubbed his heavy hands together in delight, "and you may have the worth of your meal in the finest cigars in my shebang. Alf, you are my friend. Let's go down where she's at. To tell you the God's holy truth, man to man, I don't feel half as good as I make out. It wouldn't take the weight of a hair to make me show the white feather. I have a sort of forewarning that I ain't agoing to walk straight into this thing. If she'd 'a' driv' right up to the front, and got out and gone back to the rear and set down and looked about like she was taking stock of my belongings, I'd have knowed how to proceed, but this way of having to walk a plank that she's propped up has made me sorter weak at the knees. How do I look, anyway—honest, I don't want any flattery? If you think I'd look better in my silk plug-hat and long Prince Albert I can whisk 'em on in a jiffy."

"You are just right." Henley charitably viewed the individual from his own point rather than that of the over-critical Dixie. "In hot sun like this to-day your straw hat will look better, and that sack coat fits like a kid glove."

"I sorter thought this would be the thing." Long bent down and for the twentieth time dusted his shoes with his handkerchief. "Now get them cigars." He led the way to a show-case near the front. "Help yourself—them's the genuine Havana fillers in the corner. Take good ones—by George, take the best."

"I won't take but one," Henley said, as he opened the case and reached for a cigar. "I don't like to collect pay in advance; and while I don't want to throw cold water on you, Long, I'm free to confess I don't know exactly how she'll act. I always knowed women was curious, but they are more curious about selecting a mate than everything else combined. When I was talking this meeting up at such a rate, I thought I could count on 'er; but, la me! she's got me so mixed that I don't know whether I'm a Methodist preacher or an escaped convict. But let's go down. I want to see what *you'll* make of her."

CHAPTER XIX

As the two friends approached the buggy, Dixie, who had seen them, suddenly turned her head in an opposite direction and seemed to be laughing immoderately at the beginning of a barrel-race. To attract her attention Henley cleared his throat and coughed. But whether she heard he never knew. At all events she was heartily amused, as was evidenced by her free laughter and the sparkle of her merry eyes. As it was, Henley reached the buggy and clutched the front wheel and shook it, while, with his left hand, he held Long's arm in a nervous grasp.

"Oh, it's you!" she said, sweeping him with a careless glance and allowing her eyes to be drawn back at once to the racers. "Ain't it fun? You ought to have seen that boy try to climb the greasy pole just now. He put sand all over his pants to make 'em rough, but he could only go so high, and there he stopped, unable to budge a hair's-breadth. He hung to it for a minute, as red as blood in the face, and then begun to slide down as slow as the hour-hand of a clock till he sat flat on the ground."

"I fetched Mr. Long down; you know—you may remember he wanted to meet you," Henley stammered, under a restraint that was new to him. And, as the couple stared at each other, he finished with a gulp—"Mr. Jasper Long, Miss Dixie Hart—Miss Dixie Hart, Mr. Jasper Long."

Dixie was polite and absolutely unruffled, while Long was one straight flush from head to foot. "Come—come over to see our brag show?" he stuttered, with an untoward jerk of the body, for he had tried to put his foot on the hub of the wheel and missed it. It was a bow so pronounced that Long's hat was dislodged and hurled to the ground. In his shocked sympathy for his friend, Henley was bewildered by noting that Dixie was actually subduing a laugh, her rebellious lips covered with her white-gloved hand. Long secured his hat, drew himself up, and repeated his platitude.

"I thought I would," she said, now gravely studying his face, his hair, his clothing, and his broad, restless hands, on the backs of which rather long hairs lay beaded with perspiration. "Alfred was coming along, and as I have never been to a tournament before, and as he was so set on bringing me, I decided to make the trip. I've heard him speak of you. You are in the bank, ain't you?"

"Why, no, Miss Dixie—" Henley began, but there was a certain warning quality darting from her eyes, now fixed on him, that broke into his puzzled correction, and then he caught the drift of her harmless pretence and obliterated himself with a low grunt of perplexity.

"Why, no, I'm *J. W.* Long, of the 'Live and Let Live Grocery,'" the merchant said. "The other feller is *L. A.* I've had circulars scattered broadcast all over your county. Looks like you'd have seen some of 'em. I believe in lettin' folks know you are alive and in the push. I'm surprised that Alf didn't tell you about me and my business, even if you hain't heard it from others over your way or through the papers."

"There are some Longs that rented land from me a few years ago," Dixie said, evasively. "I wonder if they are akin to you. Seems to me, now I think of it, that you favor 'em some."

"They may be away-off fourth or fifth cousins, I don't really know." Long looked as if he thought the conversation had taken quite an unprofitable turn. "I never was much of a hand to keep track of far-off kin. Folks is liable to want credit on a score like that, and think they never have to settle."

Then the colloquy languished. Henley was plainly not a success as a manager of delicate situations. What puzzled him beyond any mystery he had ever stumbled on in the intricate make-up of his charming neighbor was her evident cool and detached enjoyment of his and Long's awkwardness. At any rate, he reflected with satisfaction, he could extricate himself from the tangle, and in that, at least, he felt that he had the advantage of Long.

"I see an old fellow over there at that covered wagon that was bantering me for a hoss-trade the other day," he courageously threw into the gap. "I believe I'll go see how he talks now. There will be a sight of hoss-flesh change hands to-day. I understand there's a gypsy camp in the edge o' town, and they are the dickens on a swap."

"Hold on a minute!" Long called out, as Henley was moving off, his hat lifted. "I want to see you."

Henley pulled up a few yards away, behind Dixie's back, and Long joined him.

"Are you going to leave me the bag to hold?" Long asked, in a tone of blended gratification and nervousness.

"I don't see that I'm doing you one bit of good," Henley answered, gravely. "This is your day of grace. If you can't fix things up after what I've done we'll have to call it off. I've done my part. I fetched her here, but I can't make women out, and I don't intend to try. Life is too short. When I get bothered about what a woman's going to do or not do I want to get blind, staving drunk; it always has that effect on me, and you know I'm inclined to sobriety."

"The trouble is, I don't know whether I'm welcome or not," Long declared, grimly. "I have never felt exactly that way before. Do you reckon she'd look with favor on the invite to dinner at the hotel?"

"You bet she will!" Henley was more sure of his ground now. "Cooking and fixing up the table is a woman's joy, and they'll go just to see what hotel fare is like, and, as a rule, they will sample every article that's passed."

"Well, I'll risk it on your judgment, Alf. You've stood by me so far like a man and a brother, and I don't believe you'd set a trap for me to tumble in."

"Not me," answered Henley. "But I was wondering what you think of her looks; men differ in tastes, and—"

"Shucks!" Long sniffed. "You needn't ask me that. That'ud be a fool question for a blind man to ask. Why, Alf, she is the stunningest trick that ever wore shoe-leather. She's so dadblamed purty I can't look her straight in the face. There is some'n in her eyes and the way she sets and bends her neck an' cocks 'er head that makes me feel like one of the chaps in olden times that knelt on a strip of carpet at a queen's throne. But it ain't just her looks and trim shape and nobby little feet—it's the woman herself, by gosh! She looks clean through a feller; what she says goes from her as straight as a gun-shot. Well, I'll hurry back and do the best I can. I'm having a big time, Alf—a big, roaring time."

All the rest of the morning, as he strolled here and there through the merry assemblage, Henley managed to keep the pair in sight. Long kept the same position, his right foot on the hub of the wheel, his face upturned to Dixie's. It was the passing of the local military company and the surging of the spectators forward that gave Long a valuable opportunity, for he got into the buggy and sat beside the girl. Henley could see him lashing the air over the dashboard with his whip in a most reckless manner.

"The blame fool!" Henley ejaculated. "He's wearing out that whip. I wonder if he thinks I buy the best whalebone for him to court with. She'd like 'im better if he'd set still, anyway, and not be cavorting about like a jumping-jack."

Noon came, and Henley saw the pair alight from the buggy and walk across to the hotel. Thereupon he betook himself to the house of his friends, and had his own dinner. When it was time to start home he went down to the wagon-yard. He found them seated in the buggy, and, to his surprise, he saw nothing in the manner of either to indicate that any sort of understanding had been reached.

"I reckon it's time we was on the way," Henley announced to her, as he shaded his eyes and glanced at the declining sun.

"Yes, it's high time," Dixie answered, crisply. "I was wondering where on earth you was. I'll have to pay for this jaunt, and the sooner I set in to my work at home the better it will be for me."

Long made elaborate excuses to Dixie for absenting himself, and followed Henley to where his horse was hitched.

"Well," said Henley, as he was putting the collar on the animal, "how did you make out?"

"I hardly know, Alf." Long looked very grave. "There is no use saying she is exactly the thing I am looking for, but, as much as I've seen of her to-day, I don't know any more'n a rabbit what my showing is. She ain't a bit like these town-women; you *can* sorter get at them, for they are on the carpet, and they don't make no beans about it. But this un has a way of making you watch every step you take and every word you speak. I've been in the habit of having women folks listen to all I say, and laugh hearty now and then, but this un has her eyes on everything that is passing, and seems to me to laugh at the wrong time, when there ain't the slightest call for amusement. I reckon maybe I'd have made more progress if we'd been where thar wasn't so much to attract her attention. I don't know—I'm just guessing. But I'm game to the backbone, Alf, and I'm in the race. You hear me? I'm in to stay."

"That's the way to talk," Henley agreed. "A woman that ain't hard to win ain't worth having. These town-gals are after your money; it is my opinion that this one will have to like you a powerful lot before she gives up her freedom."

"She's as independent as a hog on ice." Long smiled, but not at his simile. "I hardly knowed what to do when we got to the hotel. I thought she was accepting my invite, you see, when, lo and behold, at settling time she drawed out her money and insisted on planking down her part to a fraction of a cent. I argued as strong as I knowed how agin it, but nothing would do her but to pay her way. I feel mean about that, Alf. What would *you* have done?"

"Why, it's the part of a gentleman to let a lady have her way in *every single thing*," Henley opined. "If she asks you to get her a drink of water, she wants it; and if she asks to pay her bill at a hotel, she wants that; to accuse her of anything else would be prying into her private matters. If she didn't want to eat at your expense the first day she was throwed with you—well, that was her business. I think it is spunky, myself. I reckon you didn't come right out and talk marrying?" Henley ended with a rather anxious look at his friend.

"No, Alf, I was afraid to—I don't know why, but, as much as I wanted to ease my mind on the matter, I just couldn't get it out. It seemed to lodge in my throat; in fact, I was scared half the time. Every time I'd say a thing, no matter how little, I'd wonder if it injured my case or not. Alf, I'm a goner—a clean goner. I'll never have a minute's peace till she's mine. It's going to be slow work. I asked her if I couldn't drive out to see her next Sunday, but she wouldn't hear to it. She finally said I could come on the first Sunday of next month to hear a brag preacher that is billed to appear for the first time on that date. It's a dern long time to wait, but she's laid down the law, and I'll have to obey it."

During the drive home Dixie seemed wilfully uncommunicative, and she and Henley were silent most of the way. As they were on the brow of the hill overlooking Chester, however, she drew a deep breath and said: "Well, Alfred, I certainly had a bang-up time. Carrie Wade may make her brags of how she runs things, but I certainly had a rip-roaring time."

"But," ventured Henley, his eyes on the jostling back of his horse, "from what Long intimated—at least from what he hinted—it appears that you and him didn't come to any, that is to say, any *positive* agreement."

The girl laughed heartily, covering her face with both hands, and bent downward.

"You men are so silly, Alfred. You want an important thing like that to be over in a minute, while a woman—a woman naturally would like for it to last. If that fellow could insure me, in some shape or other, that he'd keep acting and talking like he did to-day, *after we was married*, I'd be more interested than I am. But hot-headed ones like him cool down about as quick as they get het up. As a general thing the marriage altar seems to rest on a big cake of ice, and overheated couples catch colds that make 'em sniff the rest of their lives."

"I've been waiting to hear you say how he—what you thought of Long's looks," stammered the match-maker; "that always seems the main thing in—in a deal o' this sort."

"Well," she chuckled, "I'm better at making rag-dolls than men, but if men-making was my trade I think I could have turned out a better job than Long. Folks say that to be wide betwixt the eyes shows sense. That may be so up to certain limits, but I'm afraid his are entirely too far apart. Why, when you set close to him you can't see both of 'em at the same time; you have to look first at one and then at the other. I tried to get around the trouble by looking at his nose, but that seemed to be crooked and awful flat. I didn't like them long hairs on his hands; his forefathers must have lived in a cold climate."

"The hairs don't mean nothing." Henley was amused, in spite of his loyalty to his friend. "A heap of men are that way."

"You ain't." Dixie glanced at the rather slender hands of her companion, and then lifted her eyes to his face slowly and studiously. "You haven't got a big chunk of a head, either, and flopping, fuzzy ears, and, above all, Alfred, you ain't dead stuck on yourself. If I marry that man it will be after I've taken him down several pegs. His vanity fairly leaks out of him and stands in a puddle at his feet. Well, that don't matter. When he comes to take me to meeting it will be the talk of the entire community. Carrie Wade will laugh on the other side of her face. I would have let him come earlier, but

I want to take plenty of time to make me a dandy dress and get me a new hat. I'm going to cut a wide swath. That's to be my one big day of triumph and getting even."

CHAPTER XX

It was after nightfall when Henley put Dixie down at the cottage and drove around to his barn. In the stable doorway lurked a shadow of uncertain shape and quite motionless. It turned out to be the form of Jason Wrinkle. The pipe in his mouth glowed like a speeding firefly as he stepped down to the buggy.

"Hello! Well," he muttered, with a low, significant laugh, "you've come back—reports notwithstanding to the contrary, female, legal, or otherwise."

"Yes, I'm back," Henley said, rather curtly. "Anything strange about it?"

"Well, I was just wonderin'. Huh, in this day and time of new-fangled ways and doin's a body never knows what will happen. You'll certainly never know if you listen to talk." Wrinkle peered into the face of his stepson-in-law quite studiously for a moment, and with no little irritation Henley unfastened the hamestring with a downward jerk and began to remove the harness.

"What's the matter with you, anyway?" he asked. "Are you up to another one of your infernal jokes?"

"No, I hain't," Wrinkle puffed. "That one about the baby

was my last one—on you, anyway. You took it like some old, peevish man, and sulked and looked crooked for a week. I've tried to study out just how that happened to go agin the grain so mighty awful, but I'm up agin a snag. No, Alf, you make the bread-and-butter for this shebang, and you work better when you hain't plagued. This time I come as a friend, and maybe adviser—I don't know, it is all owin' to how you'll feel about it. For all I know to the contrary, you may be as innocent as snow that hain't been walked on, and, if you *are*, you ought to know what is going on behind your back."

"Behind my back?" Henley jerked the words from him as he tossed the harness into the buggy and allowed his horse to find his stall unguided. "Well, what's going on behind my back?"

Wrinkle sucked audibly at the stem of his pipe before he delivered himself into the eager expectancy that was massed between him and his companion. "Alf," he began, finally, "you've dealt with humanity, in one shape and another, enough to know that this is a sort of hide-bound community, and, well, you driv' off this mornin' with a good-lookin' young woman, didn't you?"

"Of course I did!" Henley retorted. "What of that?"

"You went toward Carlton, didn't you?"

"I went *to* Carlton," Henley answered, restraining an outburst with difficulty. "I took Miss Dixie over on—on business. It was transacted, and—"

"You didn't tell Hettie whar you was bound for?"

"I didn't, because I didn't think it made any difference. She's never interested in what I do or where I go, and there was no reason for telling her."

"Maybe not—maybe not," Wrinkle answered, aimlessly, "but it wouldn't 'a' done yore case any harm if you had sorter tetched on it before startin' out. You see, Carrie Wade sa'ntered over about eleven o'clock. She hain't been a constant visitor at our house, and as she had a kind o' fidgety walk on her, an' a curious dazzle in her eyes, I knowed she hadn't come to see the pattern of the new quilt as she claimed, and so, bein' a friend of yourn, I set down at the window and listened, wonderin' when she'd quit her eternal preamble an' git down to business. Purty soon I knowed land was in sight, for she said, like she was in a sort of a dream, for she wasn't lookin' at anybody in particular—she said: 'I seed Dixie Hart an' Alfred drivin' off this mornin'. They was headed fer Saunder's Spring, at the foot o' the mountain. She had on her best duds (which ain't sayin' much)'—them was Carrie's words, not mine—'an' a whoppin' big picnic basket full o' good things. That girl will do to watch, Mrs. Henley. As they passed our house the reins was lyin' loose in the buggy, an' Dixie was leanin' agin Alfred like a sick kitten to a hot brick.' It was the fust Hettie had heard of the scrape—the trip, I mean—and I thought she'd flare up, or wilt, or some'n or other, but she was on the job as quick as a flash. On my soul, I don't believe old Het so much as batted her eye, though the revelation must have been as sudden as a mule-kick in the ribs. She give the quilt she was showin' a pull agin the frame like she wanted to straighten out the stitches, an' said, 'Yes, Alf give 'er a lift over to Carlton. I'm awfully glad he had company.' And on that she axed Carrie how her Ma's sore foot was, an' recommended Dr. Stone's hoss liniment, an' cited a good many cases where cures to both man an' beast had been made at a small outlay.

"But Carrie Wade wasn't thar to l'arn how to doctor sore feet. She leaned back in her chair and laffed; you could 'a' heard her this far if you'd 'a' been here an' the pig was asleep. She riz and went and slapped Hettie on the back and said:

'You watch my words, Mrs. Henley, thar's goin' to be talk, an' lots of it. Dixie Hart has got tired o' bein' out o' the ring of young folks, an' is bent on gittin' attention by fair means or foul. Alf's good-lookin', plenty young, an' she's deliberately cuttin' her eyes at 'im. I've heard she goes to the store when she don't need a thing, an' that they sa'nter home together through the woods.'"

"The trifling hussy!" Henley muttered, angrily. "I thought she was a meddlesome busybody, and now I know it."

"Well, you know Hettie don't smile more 'n once a year," Wrinkle tittered, "but this was her anniversary. She was actually one broad grin from ear to ear."

"'I wish somebody *would* stir Alf up a little bit,' she said. 'He's entirely too poky. Carrie, that man is the slowest stick that ever lived. I wish some pretty, dashin' gal like Dixie Hart *would* flirt with him good and hard. If you wasn't so old I'd git *you* to do it. My first husband was different; he was a great ladies' man. That is the only thing that will make married life bearable. A dead certainty in love-matters is killin.'"

"Good!" Henley chuckled. "Hettie saw through her, and headed her off in fine style."

"Well, 'out of the heart the mouth speaketh,'" quoted Jason. "And the truth is, Alf, I railly don't think Hettie would care a hill o' beans if you *did* sort o' prove that you was up to snuff. You ort to profit by what's gone before in matrimony as you have in tradin' amongst men. Dick, when all is said an' done, was her maiden choice, an' if thar ever was a woman roustabout, a feller that had a bow and a scrape for every pair o' bright eyes that come his way, that feller was Dick Wrinkle. He kept Hettie in hot water, and I don't know but what the cold bath you've giv' 'er has sort o' gone agin her constitution. She's a critter that likes what she can't git better 'n what lies right at hand wigglin' to attract attention. No, you needn't be afeard of any family row. The truth is, I think Hettie is some better pleased than she has been for a long time. I reckon she's beginnin' to feel a sort o' pride in you. It ain't from her that you'll have trouble, but from Carrie Wade."

"Trouble, how?" Henley asked, impatiently, as he was turning toward the lights in the farm-house.

"Why, from her clatterin' tongue. If she'll talk like that to us, you know she will about town, and it takes a powerful small spark to set a haystack of scandal afire. Folks think Hettie has driv' you pretty far, anyway, with her odd, graveyard notions, and it wouldn't take much to—to start a ugly report."

Henley furiously tore himself from the old gossip and went into the house. As he paused at the water-shelf and filled a basin to wash the dust of his drive from his face and hands, he saw his wife moving about in the dimly lighted kitchen, and was struck by her easy and obviously gratified bearing. He was drying his hands on a towel which hung from a roller on the wall when Mrs. Wrinkle came out and suddenly faced him. She caught her breath, stared in surprise for a moment, then turned into the kitchen. Henley saw her clutch his wife's sleeve and give it a warning pull. She meant to speak in an undertone, but her piping voice slipped a cog and Henley heard her say:

"They didn't run off; he's back! He's out thar wash—"

"Sh!" came from Mrs. Henley's lips. "Be quiet; you don't know what you are talking about."

"Why, Carrie Wade said him an' Dixie Hart had 'loped away, an'—"

"Didn't I tell you to hush?" Mrs. Henley commanded, in a guarded tone. "You go set down and be quiet for once in your life. You've said enough about this thing."

Henley saw the old woman stand staring blankly for a moment, and then she came back to him in the half-darkness and stood mutely eying him from beneath the black poke-bonnet. Leaving her, he went into the dining-room, where a lamp was shedding yellow rays over the meal his wife had ready for him. He sat down in his accustomed place, and Mrs. Henley promptly brought his coffee.

"It must have been powerful hot on the Carlton road," she said. "We mighty nigh melted here in the shade with every window and door wide open."

"It wasn't so much hotter than common." He put sugar into his coffee, and slowly stirred it. "I reckon moving at a brisk pace through the air keeps you from feeling heat as much as you would if you was setting still. We didn't start back till toward sundown."

"They had some sort of a celebration over there, didn't they?" Mrs. Henley reached over and pushed the biscuits nearer to his plate.

"Yes, but it didn't amount to much."

"I reckon Dixie liked it. The poor girl hain't been away often."

"I think she did," Henley said. "Anyways, she acted that way all through. She had a tiptop seat in my buggy, where she could catch first sight of everything that happened, and she took it all in, every speck of it, even a good dinner at the hotel."

"Oh, I see." Mrs. Henley's brow was furrowed in perplexity. She left the room and returned in a moment with a bowl in her thin hands. "Here is some fresh apple-butter; it's right from the spring. You can put rich milk on it; there's plenty just from the cow."

The wrinkle remained on her brow while he helped himself liberally. She stood and studied his profile from the lighted side. The best reader of her facial expression in the family, had he been a witness, and he doubtless was, as the windows were open, would have found much to rivet his attention in the unwonted solidity of her features. Henley ate silently for several minutes before she spoke again. Then she cleared her voice, drew herself up more erectly, and said:

"You say Dixie set in the buggy all the time? Why, I had an idea from something Pa dropped that she went over there to attend to some er—business or other."

"Well, a body *might* attend to business setting in a buggy," he said, ambiguously and he put a spoonful of apple-butter into a broad smile and swallowed both as he looked at her with twinkling eyes.

The furrows deepened on the austere brow of the woman, and she drew her under lip inward and pressed it between her teeth.

"I don't know exactly what you mean," she said, presently. "I supposed she had things to buy for her farm, or—"

Henley laughed. "I may as well tell you the secret, Hettie. You ain't any hand to gad about and talk, and I know it will be safe with you. The truth, is I'm a match-maker. You've heard me speak of Jasper Long? Well, he's dying to get married, and I've been a sort o' go-between with him and Dixie. He wanted to meet her, and I took her over, and—"

"Oh!" The furrows were gone, the colorless face lighted up from within. "I understand now." She walked round the table and leaned over the dishes toward him and laughed. "Alfred," she tittered, "you certainly are the most goody-goody old poke of a stick that ever wore man's clothes, and you are blind, blind as a day-old kitten. You know men, all grades and styles of 'em, but you are a born fool when it comes to women. When that girl marries Jasper Long—I say, when Dixie Hart takes him, let me know, will you?" and she turned from the room, leaving him more than convinced that he didn't understand women, and certain that he never should try to do so again.

CHAPTER XXI

One morning, in the early part of the following week, as Henley sat working at his desk in the store, and Pomp and Cahews were busy attending three or four elderly women in front, he became conscious that some one was speaking in loud, angry tones near the door. And, rising, that he might look over a stack of soap-boxes which obstructed his view, he saw that a dispute of some sort was taking place between Cahews and Hank Bradley over some cigars that the latter had failed to pay for on a former occasion. Bradley was evidently under the influence of liquor, and he began to swear loudly and threateningly. The women dropped the purchases they were making and shrank back farther into the store.

With a flush of anger over the insult to his house and customers, Henley strode hotly forward and thrust himself between the disputants.

"We'll talk about the account some other time," he said, glaring into Bradley's face. "But right now you get out of this house. You sha'n't stand here spouting vile oaths before these ladies."

"What have *you* got to do with it?" Bradley flared up in his turn, and he whipped his hand back toward his pistol-pocket, only to discover that he was not armed, as he evidently thought he was. However, he kept his hand behind him in a threatening attitude.

"I'll show you what I've got to do with it if you open your dirty jaws like that again!" Henley said, fearlessly. "You dare to draw a gun on me and I'll make you swallow your own teeth. Now, you get out of here!" And, taking him by the arm in a grip of steel, Henley drew him hurriedly to the door and shoved him down the steps.

"This ain't the end of it," Bradley threw back furiously. "You bet it ain't."

"It'll be the end o' *you* if you fool with me!" Henley retorted, and he turned back into the store and resumed his seat at his desk. He had not been there long when one of the women finished her purchases and, with some parcels under her arm, came back and stood timidly by his desk. It was Mrs. Cartwright, the old widow whose son Johnny was so devoted to Carrie Wade. She was short in stature, had iron-gray hair, was slight and stooped, and wore a plain gingham dress and a sunbonnet of the same material.

"It was powerful good of you, Alfred, to do what you did jest now," she said, timidly, as he looked up. "It was like the old-time way men had when I was a girl of takin' up for women. I always heard you was good and kind, and now I know it. A man kin do a lot o' things that women will appreciate, but I'll risk my all that every woman in that bunch down thar will go home wishin' that her husband or brother had done what you did an' in the same sperit. Women love, above all things, to be protected by manly men."

"Well," said Henley, his flush of anger giving way to one of genuine embarrassment, "he was upsetting business, Mrs. Cartwright. I hated to—to git mad that way, but he was running my trade away, and that's a thing I won't let no man do right under my eyes. Set down an' rest, Mrs. Cartwright; you don't look overly stout."

The woman took the chair near his desk, and he heard her sigh as she massed her parcels in her lap with her thin, quivering hands.

"I reckon I don't look well," she said, seeing that his kindly eyes were still on her. "They say worry will kill a body quicker 'n anything else, and, Alfred, I'm worried mighty nigh to death. I don't know which way to turn or what to do. It is all about my youngest child, Johnny. He's took a quar notion to marry Carrie Wade."

"I see, I see," Henley said, sympathetically; "and that's bad. Why, he's hardly out o' the spelling-book class, and hain't a sign of fuzz on his lip. The last time he was in here I know the crowd was teasing him because his voice was in the gosling stage. It had sech a funny way of wobbling about from bass to treble."

"But he thinks he's full grown," the woman sighed, "and won't listen to reason. He keeps declarin' he's older than the way it's recorded in the Bible. This last trouble begun at the Sunday-school Christmas-tree, when Carrie put on an embroidered handkerchief for him. That turned his head, and he hain't hardly let her out of his sight sence. He growed from child to man betwixt two suns."

"They'll do that sometimes," Henley said. "It is surely an odd sort of attachment. She is plenty old to have nursed him. I wouldn't be afraid to say that she was cutting her eyes at men when he was cutting his teeth. Thinking of that ud make some fellers ashamed to act that way, but as apt as not Johnny don't let himself study about it. Somehow I can excuse it better in the boy than in her, because she's old enough to know better."

The old woman nodded and sighed again. "Alfred, sometimes I think I've had more put on me than my share in this world. I've had three sons besides this un, and every last one of 'em give me trouble along at Johnny's age."

"And about women older 'n they was, too, I've heard," Henley said.

"Yes, it looks like it runs in the blood—not in mine, thank the Lord! for I wish nary woman had ever been made; yes, all of my boys no sooner got out o' frocks than they made a dead-run for the first old maid in sight, and marry they would in spite of all possessed."

"And not one got hitched up exactly right," said Henley.

"Not one, Alfred. The two oldest stuck to their hot-headed agreement long enough to feel sort o' tied down, and they went clean off an' left their wives high and dry. Jim is still living with his'n, but I cry my eyes out every time I see the pore fellow. Looks like he hain't got a thing to live for. When a man leaves his own fireside and comes and sets around his mammy's house like Jim does, he hain't got no paradise under his own roof. Ef he'd 'a' had children it mought 'a' been different. I did think I could show Johnny the mistakes of his brothers and make him act different. I've talked it to him sence he was old enough to know right from wrong, but you see how little weight it had."

"Why don't you go to headquarters and call a halt?" Henley's indignation was rising.

"You mean to Carrie? Well, I did, but somehow she manages to git around the question. She jest looks kind o' 'shamed and keeps wanting to talk about other things. I ought to be sorry for her, desperate as she is for attention, but I hain't. She's a tattle-tale and scandalmonger. She never got over losin' that young preacher that Dixie Hart cut her out of, and she spends all her time hammerin' at that pore girl, who is good and decent and noble, if thar ever was sech a thing. Just here lately, because you seed fit to take Dixie with you over to Carlton—"

"Oh, I know—I know." Henley's face grew darker, and he clinched his hand. "I can't think of her bell-clapper tongue without gettin' mad, and I don't like to be that way with a woman. What does Johnny say?"

"Oh, he talks as big as a railroad president; he talks jest the same foolishness as his brothers did; *he's* doin' the marryin'—nobody else has a'thing to do with it. That's what hurts. If I could jest git the pore, simple boy out of her clutches for a month I believe I could open his eyes, but I am afraid at the slightest move they will run off and git married. Sometimes I try to be resigned and argue to myself that maybe him and her could git along together, but when I see my pore baby-boy with that powdered and painted thing out in public I mighty nigh die with mortification."

"We must simply bust it up, Mrs. Cartwright," Henley said, firmly. "That's all there is about it. We must checkmate 'em. Let me study over it. I'll help if I can."

"I wish you would," the woman said, anxiously. "There he is now in the front-door. I'll slip out the side way; he mought suspicion I was talkin' about him."

A moment after her departure Johnny Cartwright came back to the desk. "Jim said Ma was here," he said, glancing around the room.

"She was, Johnny, boy," Henley said, patronizingly, "but

she went home. Ah, ha! I saw you with Carrie Wade the other day—at least it had her look."

"Yes, it was her." A flush of pride rose and spread itself over the boyish face. "I was taking her home from Mrs. Spriggs's quilting."

"I'd bet a hat I know what you wanted to see her about," Henley said, his hand over his facile mouth. "Some of these old bachelors, or widowers with a gang of children to take care of, sent you with some invite or other. When I was a little chap like you I used to pick up a lot o' odd dimes in taking notes to the gals. About ten years from now you'll be spending *your* money that way. You must hear a lot o' funny things if you see much o' Carrie. I'd give a pretty to be near her when she got word from some man or other. She's waited a long time, Johnny. I reckon a proposal at this late day would tickle her to death."

"I don't tote notes for nobody." The boy was white about the lips, and looking as if he hardly knew whether to be angry or not.

"Well, I reckon you wouldn't to Carrie," Henley said. "I hardly reckon anybody has her in mind, now. You know she's been a drug on the market a long time. I wonder if she ever told you about that tin-peddler? It was away back, I reckon, when you was playing with your rattler. Carrie and the peddler had up an awful case—they was going to get married, and open up a tin-shop at Carlton, but a man come along and said the peddler already had a wife or two to his credit, and the skunk changed his route. Lawsy me! how Carrie did take on! We heard her yelling like a knife was sticking in her clean to the sorgum-mill."

"It's a lie! I don't believe a word of it," the boy cried, his face aflame with fury. "She told me she never had a sweetheart in her life—that she hated men."

"She's had good cause," answered Henley. "A woman that don't get a speck of attention will hate anything. I reckon she's passed the line, and nobody will marry her."

"She's going to marry *me*," the boy blurted out, leaning over and striking the desk with his fist, as if to emphasize his words, "and when she's my wife I'll call and make you settle for what you've said. Remember that, sir." And he turned and strode angrily from the store.

"I hated to say it," Henley mused, "but I was doing it for the lasting good of all concerned. It won't do—it simply won't do. That meddlesome old maid simply shall not ruin that boy's life and break his old mammy's heart. I wonder—" He sat staring at the floor for several minutes, and then a smile disturbed the stern lines of his face. "It might work—by gum, I'll try it, anyway!"

Glancing down to the front, he saw that Cahews was disengaged and seated on the end of a counter swinging his long legs to and fro. Henley went to him.

"Say, Jim, Johnny Cartwright and Carrie Wade is driving his mammy mighty nigh distracted with their doings. I don't know when I've ever been so sorry for an old person. I wonder if me and you couldn't put our heads together and—and sort o' bust it up."

"Well, I don't know, Alf—you are a better schemer than I am. I'm willin' to help, but I can't git up nothing. If the boy was mine I'd give 'im a good spankin' in public, and maybe that ud shame Carrie into behavin' herself."

"If I could get you to help I think I could work a change in the thing, anyway," Henley said, persuasively.

"Me, Alf?"

"Yes, it's just this way, Jim, with a woman of that brand and vintage," Henley pursued. "You see, she's gone without the right sort of attention so long that she's kind o' lost respect for herself. Jim, you are the leading young man in Chester, not yet married, and considered a fine catch. I don't know how it will strike you, but you could really do a good turn all round if you'd just pay Carrie a little attention. Take her in your new top buggy to camp-meeting next Sunday."

"Me? Oh, Lord!"

"I don't mean for you to *marry* her," Henley went on, smoothly. "But if I'm any judge of women, I think when a man of your stripe drives out in public with her she'll simply look up again, and, by gum, I believe she'll look clean over that boy's head. I'm asking you to take part in a good deed, Jim."

"I see—I understand pine-blank what you mean, but, Alf, I'm not the man for the job. You'll understand my fix if you'll just study a minute. You know how it is between me and Julia Hardcastle. I'll never marry no other woman as long as the sun shines. She hain't never said the word, nor she hain't plumb pitched me out, either, but she makes me walk a chalk-line. Why, if she was to see me out with Carrie Wade I'd never hear the end of it."

"Julia's going to the camp-meeting, ain't she?" Henley asked, cutting a significant glance at his clerk.

"Yes, she's going with Sam Willis, that Atlanta shoe-drummer. She don't care for him, mind you, Alf, but she likes to have fellows of that sort hanging on. She don't seem half as particular about who she goes with as the company I keep. She's got me where the wool is short, Alf. I wouldn't rub her the wrong way for the world. I hope to get her some day, but I'll have to wait till she gits tired of dashing around."

Henley was looking straight into his clerk's face, a smile twinkling in his kindly eyes. "You are not working that girl right, Jim," he said, decidedly. "She'd have been yours long ago if you'd had more independence. If you keep up that sort of a lick she'll waltz off with some bold and daring chap one of these days and give you the merry ha-ha. The truth is, she wants you, but she wants you to be more of a man. You've tried your sort of way long enough, now switch off and try mine just for one single day, anyway, and see if I ain't right. Solomon himself—and he was the greatest masher in the Bible—even he couldn't win a woman by letting her have her own way. A woman thinks a man is a sissy that gives in to her every whim. You just take Carrie Wade to meeting like any other free-born American citizen has a right to do, and Julia Hardcastle will set up and take notice, and she'll think a sight more of you—that is, if you don't knuckle under and beg her pardon the minute she mentions it to you."

Cahews's jaw was really a massive member, and it looked as solid as stone when he finally answered, which he did when he had stood down on the floor and walked to and fro for a moment in deep and turbulent thought.

"She nor no other woman could make me knuckle if I didn't want to," he said, pausing and resting a steady hand on the shoulder of his employer. "I've been giving in all along, but I'm tired, dang tired. Here she's going with that town-dude Sunday and expects me to drive out there by myself and enjoy the sight from afar. Derned if I don't believe, as you say, that I've been giving that girl too much rein and floundering about too much in the dust at her feet. Alf, I'll write a note to Carrie this minute, and I'll give the old girl a good time if I know how."

"Well, you go back to the desk and write the note," said Henley. "Mark my words, I'll bet, if you hold a stiff lip all through, you'll accomplish in a day what you haven't in all these years."

CHAPTER XXII

The next day, as Henley was walking home in the dusk and was passing Mrs. Cartwright's cottage, she saw him and hastened out to the fence. She was in a flutter of excitement, rubbing her thin hands together in vast satisfaction.

"Alfred," she began, "I want to tell you what's happened. I'm so excited I'm as limber as a dish-rag. Jim Cahews sent a note over by your nigger yesterday to Carrie Wade invitin' her to drive to the campground with him Sunday."

"Oh, Jim's going to take *her*?" said Henley, his eyes twinkling. "He's a sly dog about his doings, and don't tell me all he does."

"That hain't the main thing, Alfred." The old woman raised her hands to her face and laughed immoderately. "Pomp had no sooner gone off with the answer and a big bunch of roses Carrie gathered and sent with it, when she run over to tell me about it and to borrow my cape. She 'lowed it mought be cool drivin' back behind sech a fast hoss as Jim's new one, an' she didn't have a thing heavy enough to throw over her shoulders. Johnny was a-settin' in the corner of the kitchen unbeknownst to her, and heard all she said. An', la me, what you reckon he done? He up an' laid down law an' gospel right on the spot, bless you! Jim Cahews wasn't goin' a step with 'er. Johnny could afford to hire a livery-stable team if he had to borrow the money, an' *he* was goin' to take 'er."

"That was a corker, wasn't it?" Henley exclaimed, with a pleased laugh. "What did Carrie say to that?"

"Looked like she hardly knowed what *to* say," was the old woman's reply. "Him an' her stood starin' smack dab at each other fer a minute, and then—just think of it!—she begun to beg the boy not to interfere with her doin's, and pleaded an' wheedled an' went on at a powerful rate. But Johnny stood as firm as the rock o' Gibralty, an' told 'er, he did, that his plighted wife jest shouldn't run about an' disgrace 'em right on the eve of marriage, and said a lot about folks walkin' over dead bodies an' swimmin' rivers o' blood, an' the like. Well, all that finally made Carrie mad, an' she told 'im he was jest a boy, an' that she had never meant to marry 'im, nohow. An' while he stood gaspin' fer breath she lit in to beggin' him not to tell nobody about the'r little flirtation. She said folks would think it was silly of her, an' if Jim Cahews meant business, which it looked like he did, a tale like that might sp'ile her chances."

"Huh," grunted Henley, "she was getting down to bedrock, wasn't she?"

"Well, I don't blame 'er," said the widow, charitably. "Many a good, married woman wouldn't want all her girlish pranks to reach the ear of the man she finally settled down with, an' I reckon Jim Cahews wants 'er. They say he's tired chasin' after Julia Hardcastle, an' Carrie may suit. Johnny tuck it awful hard. After she went home he come an' laid his head in my lap an' sobbed out good an' strong. I was never tickled by grief of a child o' mine before; but even while my eyes an' throat was full, a laugh would rise in me that I couldn't hold in. But he didn't catch on—he 'lowed I was cryin', too. After a while he set up an' wiped his eyes. 'I reckon,' said he, 'that I've been the fool everybody said I was, but I'm goin' to let women alone till I'm old enough to understand 'em.'"

"He'll let 'em alone a long time, then," said Henley, with a dry smile, as he turned away.

The following Monday morning Henley found Cahews busy in the front part of the store cleaning up and putting things straight on the shelves. As soon as he saw his employer, Jim walked from behind the counter and extended his hand: "Put it right there, Alf, an' give it a good, tight shake," he grinned. "Richard is hisself at last. It's been an awful up-hill fight, but I'm there—gee whiz! I'm there, an' don't you forget it."

"So you really like Carrie? Well, I thought maybe you and her—"

"Carrie, hell! It's the other—damn it! Huh! you may think you know some'n about women, but don't I? I was a long time learning how to turn the trick, but I'm an expert now. I had the time of my life. It was a clean walk-over from start to finish. I had the bit in my teeth, an' I went ahead like the woods afire. I driv' around to Carrie's house, dressed to kill. I had on my plug-hat, silk vest, light-gray pants, dark-blue coat, and my new patent-leather shoes. I put the old gal in by me an' away we shot. I saw that drummer and Julia ahead on a straight piece of road plodding along like they was hauling a load of wood to town, and I chirped to my Kentucky blue-blood, and, with Carrie's ribbons flying in the wind like the flags of a war-ship, we passed like a cannon-ball, leaving 'em in a cloud of dust as thick as a Texas sand-storm. And the funniest part was that I didn't, somehow, care a dern. I was on a new basis, an' believed in it."

"Well, you know I advised—" Henley began, but the eager clerk broke in:

"Yes, that was it; you started me on my new line, and it was the act of a friend. It was that advice that saved me. But I reckon it was the sight of that sap-headed idiot with my girl that did most of it. Well, to come to the end, as soon as Julia and her dude got to the campground she lit out of his buggy and made a bee-line to whar me and Carrie was setting under the trees waiting for the first hymn. She stopped right square in front of me as mad as a wet hen.

"'What did you mean by throwing dust on us?' she asked, as red as a beet, her eyes flashing sparks. Right then I felt just a little inclination to take back water, but I remembered, our talk t'other day, and told myself it was now or never, and that the worm had turned over a new leaf. Carrie had dropped her handkerchief, an' I sprung up and put it back in her lap with a bow, taking a grip on myself while in the act. Then I looked Julia in the eyes and said:

"'I couldn't hold my hoss in, Miss Julia; he's a high-stepper, and it makes 'im hopping mad to see common stock ahead of 'im. The only thing to do was to let 'im pass everything in sight.'"

"She stared at me like she thought I'd lost my senses, and then she said, 'Well, you ought to apologize; any gentleman would after covering a lady with dust from a dirty road.'"

"'But it wasn't my fault,' I told her, with a grin. 'It is my hoss's fault. If anybody apologizes it ought to be him, and he can't talk half as good as he can trot.' Gee whiz, but wasn't she mad? She was splotched with red and white all over, and the purtiest thing, Alf, that you ever laid eyes on. She whirled away and went back to her drummer. He had put the buggy-seat under a tree in sight of where me an'

Carrie sat, and, knowing she was looking, I laid myself out to be pleasant to my partner. I had to pass by Julia and her dude to get to the spring, and I fetched water for Carrie every hour in the day, and always went whistling a jig. At twelve o'clock some of the folks along with Julia come over and invited me and Carrie to dump our basket in with theirs and all eat together, but me and Carrie refused, and had ourn on a grassy slant in plain sight of the rest. It was the first frolic I'd ever had with Julia, and I shore did like it. I dunno, but I reckon it was the way she acted that made me keep it up. Then, after dinner, when Carrie went to Mrs. Wilson's tent to rest up a little, Julia saw me smoking at the spring, and come straight to me. She had a sort o' give-in look, and yet was proud and cold.

"'I want to know,' said she, 'what you mean by fetching that old maid out here.'"

"'I don't know as she's so almighty old,' said I, as independent as a wood-sawyer, and yet scared half out o' my mind. 'I don't know but what it is a sort of comfort to go with women old enough to be sensible once in a while.'"

"That made her madder'n ever, but, you see, I was making her come to me with complaints, and that had never happened before. She stood punching at the ground with her blue parasol and looking every now and then toward Mrs. Wilson's tent like she was afraid Carrie would come. Then all at once I saw that her pretty lips was quivering. I was dying to grab her, Alf, and confess the whole dang trick, but I remembered your talk and helt out.

"'I see,' said she, with a sigh, 'you don't mean what you've been saying to me all this time.'"

"I looked her straight in the eyes, Alf, and let 'er have it right from the shoulder good and fast. 'I tell you, Julia,' said

I, 'I'm a marrying man. I'm tired of living alone in the back end of a store with just a house-cat for company, while men no better are toasting their shins at a cheerful family fire. I'm tired of fooling. Carrie may not have as many dudes at her beck and call as some I know, but she knows what she wants in the man-line and won't take all eternity to decide.'"

"'Oh, you are cruel! You are heartless!' Julia said, and then she busted out crying. Then, before we knowed it, me and her was walking in the woods, 'long a narrow, shady road. She said, Alf, that she'd loved me good and true all along and wanted to quit everything that was foolish and settle down. We are going to be married Christmas, and, Alf, I'm so happy I could holler at the top of my voice. If I don't sell goods to-day there won't be a customer in forty miles of the store."

Henley nodded slowly. "The thing worked," he said, "and I'm glad. The only thing I hate about it is that we had to fool that poor woman to do it. But Carrie was acting wrong with that boy. I had to do it to save him and his old mammy. We must make it up to Carrie some way. We'll find her a husband if we have to advertise in the papers and put up cash inducements. She's got a mischievous tongue and lots of malice, but hard luck fetched 'em on her."

"Alf, you are a good chap," Cahews said, with emotion. "I know well enough you ain't any too happy at home—a blind man could see that—and yet you are always trying to help others."

Henley's kindly eyes wavered as they rested on those of his friend. "My wife is doing the best she can, too, Jim. I don't blame her. In fact, I blame myself. When that fellow went off and died I ought to have left her alone with her grief, but I was blinded by the desire to have what I'd tried so long to win. I reckon I took an unfair advantage of her at a time when she wasn't in a mood to fight off anything. Now, let's get to work. I've got lots to do."

CHAPTER XXIII

As was his custom on Sunday mornings, Henley accompanied his wife and the Wrinkles to church service in Chester on the day Long was expected to pay his visit to Dixie. Henley and the old man fell in leisurely behind the two women. The day was fine, being one of those rare June days which had the moderate temperature of spring.

As they came within sight of Dixie Hart's cottage, Henley noticed a sleek pair of horses and a stylish trap held by a negro boy at the gate, and knew that the girl's suitor had arrived. He fancied that the couple might pass him on his way to church, and in his mind's eye he saw himself waving a cordial salutation to them. It was not, however, until the church was reached and he had conducted his party to their usual seats that Dixie and her escort arrived. Accustomed as the congregation was to direct its attention to the door as much as the pulpit, at least before the services began, all eyes were turned thither when a sudden commotion at the front showed that something of an unusual nature had occurred. The fact was that Long's driver, being unfamiliar with the ways of a place much smaller than his own town, had driven the prancing, snorting pair close to the door in the effort to land his passengers on the steps, and his loud, "Woah dar, blast yo' skins!" rang clearly through the resonant building. As it was, the coming of a bridal pair themselves could not have attracted more attention. Every pivotal head turned on its axis; even the visiting parson, with the huge Bible on his thin knees, half rose that he might peer over the pulpit behind which he sat.

Dixie, in her new gown and new hat, was the very embodiment of easy self-possession as she piloted her escort to a seat in the middle of the room. Long, red and perspiring, and rigged out in all the splendor of the haberdasher's art, even to boots that screamed in pain, had the air of a social laborer who was worthy of his hire. As soon as he was seated he reached for Dixie's fan and began waving it to and fro with the conscientious regularity of a pendulum, thereby increasing his warmth and not lessening Dixie's.

Sheer astonishment clutched all observers. The women bent their necks and stared, and the men winked at one another comically.

Suddenly Henley noticed that Carrie Wade was immediately behind him, and he felt a sharp twinge of conscience over the wan and desperate expression of her face. She had seen, and was staring down into her lap and slowly twirling her bloodless fingers. She had heard of Jim Cahews's engagement and knew that her transient hopes in that direction were groundless; and now this—this of all things—to see her hated rival in such a coveted position in the view of all before whom she had been so systematically maligned.

But Henley's mind refused to be riveted to Carrie's discomfiture. For the first time he was seeing his friend Long through new glasses. He was, indeed, as Dixie had hinted, a rather uncouth individual, and this fault was not lessened by his flashy attire and juxtaposition to so much innate refinement in the person of his companion.

After the service, as they were leaving the church, Henley

saw that three-fourths of the congregation, at least, had deliberately paused outside, and were watching the Carlton man assist his partner into the shining trap. They stood as if transfixed, and regarded the pair till they had disappeared down the road in the direction of Dixie's home.

That morning before sunrise old Wrinkle had gone to his watermelon-patch and plucked a ripe melon. He had put it in the spring-house to keep it cool, and during the afternoon he served it to the family on the back-porch. Henley had enjoyed it with the others, and was idly sauntering about the front-yard when he saw Long leave the Hart cottage and start back to Carlton. Seeing Henley, he told the driver to stop, and sprang down to the ground and came to the fence.

"Well, what progress?" Henley asked. "I saw you at meeting this morning."

"Well, I hardly know yet, Alf." Long clutched one of the palings of the fence with his gloved hand and swung back from it and took a deep breath. "I hardly know what to say. I'm tickled to some extent, and then again I hain't, for I hain't as sure of my ground as I'd like to be. Alf, she's by all odds the finest bolt of calico I ever tried to unroll—I say *unroll*, because if she hain't a tight mystery I never saw one."

"You mean you can't quite make her out?" suggested Henley, with an eagerness for which he could hardly account.

"That's it; you've hit it the first throw out of the box. It looks to me, Alf, like she's always going to do something that she never gets to, and not do what she's sure to do when you ain't expecting it. Now, one thing I counted on as a sure fact before I come out was that after dinner at her house me 'n her would walk down to the woods where it was shady and sort o' stroll about and take in the scenery, but not a peg would she move, although I hinted at it several times. I like old women—that is, you know, I respect 'em in their places—but that pair was too much of a good thing. They set about where me and Miss Dixie was every spare minute. I've seen gals love their kin, but this un fairly dotes on hers. Why, one of 'em couldn't git up to get a drink without Dixie jumpin' and telling her to set still, that she'd get it for her. I'm as good as the average in knowing how to handle a woman, Alf, but I don't profess to know how to court one in a crowd. One of these two is half blind and t'other is lame, but that didn't help me out, for they didn't let their tongues rest a second. They kept alluding to some chap or other that was dead. They said they hadn't ever seen him, but kept talking about his picture and wondering if he looked like me, and how he'd like it to see me there, and so on. Seemed like the girl wanted to shut that talk off, for she told 'em several times to be quiet and to remember what they had promised her."

"Women are all hard to understand." There was a knowing twinkle in Henley's eyes, which he averted from Long's anxious gaze. "I reckon Dixie thought you ought to get acquainted with the family if you and her are to come to any permanent understanding."

"Maybe so," Long agreed, wearily. "But I have enough dealings with old rag-chawers in my business through the week not to want a Sunday off when I get with my own sort. But this un is a prize, Alf, and worth any man's trouble to get her. I'll never forget that dinner if I live to be a hundred. I had to rise early to get a start from town, and the ride kind o' whetted my appetite to a sharp edge, so that I was really ready for anything she wanted to pass; but, geewhilikins! when we all slid our chairs out into that dining-room, where everything was as white as snow and shiny as a new dollar, and where green things was stuck about all around, I begun to know what high living was. And she told me she'd cooked every dab of it herself. Just think of that, and on top of it rigged up like she did and went to meeting as fresh and cool as a rose under dewy leaves! I made up my mind, as I set there and ate all that good stuff, and saw her at the head of the table fingering things in such a dainty way, that I'd have her at the head of my table in a fine, new house, or bust a trace. I'm to come out again next Sunday. In the mean time I'm going to try to think up some way to choke that old pair of hens off my roost."

"Oh, they'll let you alone after a while," Henley said. "You see, you are a novelty right now. You keep on. You wouldn't want a girl that would throw her arms round your neck on the first visit."

"No, I reckon not," Long agreed, slowly, "and still I don't like the uncertainty, either. Looks like she's studying me all the time, and ain't any too well pleased, at that. I don't know; I reckon she's got me rattled to some extent. I know what I want; I want *her*, and the sooner I'm easy in my mind the sooner I'll be fit for business." Long glanced at the sinking sun. "I must be on the move; take care of yourself, Alf, and pray for me. You've put me on the track of a good thing, and if I win I'll be yours for life."

The next morning, as Henley was on his way to the village, he saw Dixie in her peanut-patch on the side of the road. She seemed to be carefully inspecting the vine-covered mounds in the mellow soil, for he saw her stoop now and then and lift the vines and peer beneath them. Vaulting over the fence, he was soon by her side.

"Always at work, rain or shine," he said, lightly, as she glanced up and smiled a cheery greeting.

"I've hit it right on these goobers, Alfred," she said. "I pulled up a vine the other day and washed it in the branch. I'm keeping it for the fair at Carlton. It is a dandy; the goobers on it are as thick as beads on a strand, and already as big as your thumb. Folks laughed at me for putting in five acres in this ground, but I knew what I was about. If they go high this fall, I'll make up for the loss on my wheat and hay."

"From the looks of things yesterday," he said, "it don't seem like you'll have to bother much more about raising anything."

"I saw you looking at us," she returned, gravely. "In fact, I saw everybody in the house. It was an awful day, Alfred, and I wouldn't go through another like it for no sap-headed man that ever walked the earth. I was up before the break of day, scrubbing, sweeping, baking by candle-light, and what was it all for—good gracious, what was it for? For weeks I'd counted on it as a great event, just to feel, down in my heart when it was all over, like a big fool."

"Why, I thought—I supposed—" Henley began in perplexity, but she interrupted him.

"I hate sham, Alfred, and that whole thing was sham—sham, sham, from first to last. Because I've been beat down and sneered at all this time by a silly woman, and because my burden of life looked hard, I let myself be tempted. Do you know, I believe Providence is trying to pound some sense into me. I felt kind o' bad a year ago when that feller didn't come to time, but, Alfred, I know myself better than I did then. I thought I'd have stood up at the altar with a man I never saw, but I'll bet now that I'd have backed out at the sight of him. I was blinded the same way about this last one. When you told me about him, in your kind way, I thought he was just what I was looking for, but when you fetched him to me that day at Carlton it was an awful comedown. I can't explain it to you, but, somehow, I felt like he was butting in with his big head and loud voice between me and another one I was expecting."

"I see, I see. Long don't quite fill the bill," Henley said. "I was afraid there might be a hitch somewhere, and he has all the essentials, too—that is, I mean—" But Henley hardly knew what he meant.

"There is just one main essential, to use your big word," she said, her fine, eyes resting on his in a wise gaze, "and that is love—the genuine article. At one time I thought it was a fine house, and things to wear, and comfort for them I love and protect that I needed, but it was downright, unselfish love for somebody. Alfred, to my dying day I shall shudder over all that parade yesterday. The man or woman who attempts to get pleasure out of sitting in a finer seat, or living in a finer house, or wearing finer duds than his neighbor, or even his enemy, will miss it, unless he is of a low order and taste. When I saw all them good folks gaping and staring at me like I was a comet with a tail, right there in the house of God, while a good man was teaching humility, and prayers, and songs was going up to the throne—I say, while all that was taking place I felt like a cheat and a swindler hiding under plumes, clap-trap flowers, and flounces that ud fade. I looked across and saw Carrie—poor Carrie!—with that blank stare of death in her eyes. She seemed to say, 'You've whipped me clean to the earth, Dix; I'm done; I'm all in; but have mercy, don't you see how awful it is?' She may have thought I was crowing over her, but I wasn't—God knows I wasn't. During the first prayer I knelt down and prayed for her and begged forgiveness for my silly caper. The poor thing has lost even her boy-lover. She's yearning for something she may never lay her hands on. As God is my judge, if I could give her this man that was here yesterday I'd do it at the drop of a hat. Alfred, I don't want him, nohow. I thought I might come round to it, but every word he says, every move he makes, goes against me. If I tied myself to a man like that it would be one continual fight to approve of him. Oh, he was so puffed up yesterday that I wanted to pull his ears and make him see straight—talking all the time about the dash we'd cut and the attention we attracted. I was guilty of the crime and wanted to forget it, but it was all he could talk about—well, that is, except one *other* thing."

"One other thing?" Henley echoed.

"Yes, it was marry, marry, marry; wife, wife, wife—even before the home-folks. He couldn't put a bite of my cooking in his big, red mouth without saying what a blessing it would be to come to a table loaded that way three times a day. I say! I had to laugh. There I was figuring on using him to the end that I could set back in a rocking-chair and fan myself and tell a nigger cook to rake any old scraps together and not bother me with the details, while he saw me with my sleeves rolled up humped over a hot stove, or in a cloud of steam at a wash-tub. He said he could pay me the compliment of being the only girl who loved hard work as much as his mother had till it killed her—*loved* it, mind you! Think of drudging all your life for a man that thought you loved dirty work and was granting you a favor by keeping it piled up around you while he was lying around a store telling a bunch of clerks what to do, and wondering how long it would be before time to eat. Yes, I felt mean all through the service and after he left. Little Joe sneaked over after dark to get me to teach him his geography, and while I was doing it I put my arm around his poor, little, wasted neck and hugged him. He looked up and begun to cry and kissed me. Alfred, there ain't no mistaking the article when you run across it. It is real love I have for that boy—the love of a mother for her child that is suffering. I went as far with him as the fence, and as me and him stood together in the starlight I felt, somehow, that there was just one thing standing between me and God, and that was the unworthy thing I had been doing that day. I am thankful for my burdens, for under them I am free and exalted. Love like I have for Joe shows what the other love ought to be like, and until I yearn to help a man out of his troubles and cling to him and want him by me every minute—until then I'll not sell myself. You can't marry for pay and be honest, for you know you can't give value for value. You'd have to act a part, and that would be a living lie that would pall on you, and sicken your very soul."

"So you're not going to see Long any more?" Henley said, carried out of himself by her winsome logic.

"Yes, he's coming Sunday. I'll get through the day in some fashion or other, but I'm not going to tole 'im along like a pig following an ear of corn. Some girls would, whether they intended to take him or not, but I've been through the rubs and can't afford to be so silly. My natural pride won't let me chop him off after the first visit, for folks would say he turned me down, and, with all my good intentions, I can't stand that. I don't know why, but I can't. I reckon we want what is ours, if it is as empty as a bottle full of wind, and, in the fellow's way, he *does* want me. A girl can be an old maid with much more content if she's had what the world would call a solid chance."

When he had left her and was walking down the road Henley paused and looked back and saw her making her way homeward through her cotton-field. "I might have known she'd kick him," he said, tenderly. "No man alive is worthy of her—no man ever could be. She's a jewel dropped from the skies. She is as sweet and innocent as a baby, and as strong and brave as a lion. I wonder why God didn't let *me*—I wonder why it was that *I* happened not to—"

A flush of shame mounted to his face. His heart seemed to stand still. He trudged onward, his gaze on the ground. "She is doing her duty," he muttered, "and she is not complaining. I must do mine."

CHAPTER XXIV

On the afternoon of the following day Dixie came to the store. At the moment Cahews was busy with some customers on the side of the house devoted to dry-goods, and Henley was at his desk in the rear drawing a cheque to pay for some cotton he had bought from a farmer. Dixie walked straight toward him, but Henley did not see her till she was quite close, then he was struck by the unusual pallor and tense gravity of her face. He sprang up at once and proffered a chair.

"I want to talk to you," she said, her lips quivering, and she motioned toward the waiting farmer. "Finish with him; I'm in no hurry."

Henley complied, a startled concern for her rendering him all but incapable of resuming the business with the customer. He had to go out to the farmer's wagon to read the marks on the cotton-bale for record, and even as he made the notes in his book and directed the unloading of the wagon he was saying to himself: "She's in trouble—something has gone wrong. She never was knocked out like that before."

On his return he entered at the side-door, and as he was crossing the yard to reach it he caught sight of her when she thought she was unobserved. She was pressing her hands to her face, and her whole form seemed to have wilted. She heard his step and essayed to assume a light mood of greeting, but it was a poor pretence, at best. She smiled as she looked up, but it was a cold, bloodless effort.

"I may as well tell you, Alfred, that I'm in trouble," she began, tremulously, as he sat down near her. "You've always said I had a long head on me for a girl, but I reckon I can manage just so far, and not a bit farther. I can plant and sow and gather and reap, and even market small dribs of things, but I'm a fool in big business matters, and I've gone and got my foot in it. I'm up to my neck in the mire, and I'm sinking inch by inch."

"What's wrong, Dixie?" he said, consolingly. "You mustn't let yourself give up this way. It ain't like you."

"Well, it's about my farm," she said, and she paused to steady her voice, which seemed to fail her.

"I see," Henley said. "Old Welborne is charging you too high interest. You ought to shift the mortgage to somebody more human—somebody with at least a thimbleful of soul. That man is the hardest taskmaster on earth. He'd skin a flea for its hide and tallow."

"Mortgage? I'm afraid you wouldn't exactly call it a mortgage, Alfred. Listen; I've just got to tell you about it. You are my friend. I know you'll tell me the best thing to do, and I'll abide by your advice. When I bought the farm from Uncle Tom, who, you remember, wanted to sell out to move to Alabama when the trade was made, I only had a thousand dollars ready money, and the price was two thousand. Uncle Tom was anxious to close out and get away, and so he looked about for somebody that would lend me the balance. Times was awfully hard then, and nobody had any money on hand but Welborne, and he said he'd let me have it at a reasonable rate of interest. Somehow Welborne never would get ready to make out the papers and turn over the money, and Uncle Tom was nearly out of his head with worry over the delay."

"One of the old dog's tricks!" Henley said, angrily. "I know him through and through. But go on; go on."

"Well, it was the last day before Uncle Tom was to go that Welborne finally said he was ready and had us come to his office. I haven't got head enough to tell you all he said, for it was so mixed up. He went on at a frightful rate about how hard it had been for him to call in money enough to accommodate us, and finally made a proposition. He said in order to make himself plumb secure the farm must be bought in his name and mine as partners, with the understanding that whenever I got the money I could buy him out. Somehow I felt uneasy then, but Uncle Tom declared it was plumb fair. Sam Deacon, the young man who was studying law here then, was in the office, and he told me it was all right and perfectly safe, and so under all that pressure I consented. I have never told a soul about it. Somehow the longer it went on the more foolish it seemed for a girl like me to be in partnership with that old money-shark, and I was ashamed."

"Well, even then," said Henley, still perplexed, "your interest must be safe. I reckon you've had your scare for nothing."

"I haven't told you all yet," Dixie sighed. "The big rent I've had to pay him on his half has kept my nose to the grindstone, so that I'm even deeper in debt to him now than I was at the start."

"Rent?" exclaimed the storekeeper, staring blandly.

"Yes, nothing would suit Mr. Welborne but that his part was worth two hundred a year, and he refused right out to trade any other way."

A light broke on Henley. He whistled softly, and his brawny hand clutched his knee like a vise as he leaned forward.

"I see, I see," he panted, his eyes large in pitying surprise. "He was dodging the law against usury. He has it fixed so that he's making no violation of law, and yet he is getting at least two and a half times as much as he'd be entitled to. Instead of eighty dollars a year—eight per cent.—he's getting two hundred. You've already paid him for the value of his part over and over. My Lord, my Lord, and you—you who have had such a hard time! But have you never made any payment at all besides the rent?"

"It was all I could do to rake up the two hundred a year," Dixie answered, huskily. "Once, though, when cotton went high and I had made six bales, I offered him a hundred dollars to lessen my debt, but he wouldn't take it. He said it was too little to count, and that new papers would have to be drawed up to make a proper credit, and for me to keep it and spend it on some implements I needed. But I haven't told you the worst yet, Alfred. He now says land has gone down in value, and that he needs the money he's put in, and that I must buy him out, or him me, he don't care which, but a transfer has to be made. He says if I hain't got the money, and refuse his liberal cash offer, the property will have to be put up at public outcry and settled that way."

"Look here, Dixie, little friend," Henley said, his tense face furrowed with sympathy, "you've been in powerful bad hands. Your Uncle Tom never gave the matter a minute's consideration—all he was after was getting away to his new home, and that young lawyer that advised you didn't have the sense of a gnat, or was in old Welborne's pay. The paper is a legal one, I know, for that old hog has never done a thing he could be handled for. You've committed yourself into the hands of the slyest, most unprincipled old thief that ever blinked under the eye of justice. He is telling you the truth. He can sell you out, according to law, whenever either he or you are dissatisfied with the contract. He knows you've improved that place till it is worth double what you paid for it, and he thinks you are in such a tight place that you'll give up in despair and let him have what you've made by such hard licks. I know that trick, and it is the lowest and meanest one among traders. He's got you in a worse fix than you may imagine."

"But how can the farm be worth as much as you say it is when he says he is willing to take eight hundred for *his* half, which cost originally a thousand?" Dixie wanted to know.

"That's the old 'give-or-take' dodge," Henley explained. "He's kept his eye on you, and he's satisfied that you can't possibly raise eight hundred dollars, and that you will take his eight and be glad to get it. I could help you out of this in a minute—clean out, for I've got the idle money and it would tickle me to death to advance it to you, but he wouldn't sell. He's telling you he'll give or take, but he wouldn't *take*; that ain't his dirty game."

"So he really can sell me out at auction?" Dixie groaned.

"Yes, but that would be his last resort," Henley said. "He thinks he's got you under his thumb, and that he'll scare you into accepting his cash. Wait, keep your seat; let me study over it; there must be some way. The Lord Almighty wouldn't let a grasping old skunk like that rob a helpless girl like you. Welborne didn't make you the give-or-take offer in writing—I'm sure he didn't; he's too slick for that?"

"No, he drove by home yesterday and called me out to the

gate. He says land has gone down on account of the new railroad passing on the other side of the mountain, and that we both made a big mistake in paying as much as we did."

"The old liar!" Henley cried. "The road's coming to Chester, and he knows it. He thinks Chester will grow, and your farm will be cut up into town building sites. He's determined to get your property by hook or crook. Some'n must be done, and that right off. Let me study a minute."

Henley went to the side-door and looked out. Dixie saw him step down into the junk-filled yard, and move aimlessly about from one spot to another, his hands locked behind him. His head was bowed, and his fine, strong face darkened by a steady frown. Jim Cahews came looking for him to ask some question, but he waved him away. Dixie heard him cry out impatiently: "Don't bother me!—let me alone! For the Lord's sake, go back, go back!"

Cahews returned to his customer, and Dixie remained seated, her eyes fixed on Henley. He seemed to have forgotten that she was near; he seemed scarcely to know where he was himself, for once he drew himself to a seat on a big dry-goods box and sat swinging his legs to and fro, his gaze on the cloud-flecked sky. Then the pendulum-like movement, the pounding of his heels would cease; with a hand clutching the box on either side of him he would lean forward, lock his feet together beneath him, and bite his lip. Suddenly he got down and came back to her, a certain light of decision in his eyes.

"I've tackled a heap of jobs," he said, as he sat down beside her, "and I've beat old Welborne more than once, but I generally steer clear of him. I've been trying to think up some way to thwart him, but it is powerful hard to devise any means to get at him. Now, if we just could manage to get him to make his give-or-take offer before a witness we'd have him good and tight, but he'd be too slick to do it. If he did make it, you see, you could plank down the money I'll lend you and settle the thing on the spot. Now listen, Dixie, there is only one possible way open, and that is to trick the old scamp into writing down his offer and signing it. I know something I'd like to try on if you'd forgive me for the—the false light I'd have to put you in for a few minutes."

"False light? Why, what do you mean, Alfred?"

"Why, it's like this, amongst business men"—Henley flushed to the eyes—"now and then two scamps (like me 'n him, for instance) kind o' join forces against a weaker person and work together in harness like. Now, if you just wouldn't think too hard of me, I could sort o' let on to old Welborne, you see, that you was up to your eyes in debt to me, and that—that the thing had been running on till I was—well, was plumb tired out, and ready to come down on you."

"Oh, I see." A faint smile broke over the girl's shrewd face. "Why, I wouldn't care what you did or said, Alfred," she cried. "He's trying to rob me, and I'd have a right to protect myself."

"Well, then, enough said." Henley fell into an attitude of relief. "You set here, and I'll run over and chat with him. I may fetch him here, and if I openly abuse you and dun you to your teeth, you must take it all in good spirit. You can hang your head and pretend to be sort o' shamed, if you like; it will help to carry the thing out. Any girl that could sell that old lion's cage for as much as you did—and in the way you did it—ought to know how to pull the wool over Welborne's eyes. You see, when the old devil is made to believe that I'm down on you and determined to have a settlement, he'll think you are in more desperate straits than ever. Wait!"

Henley went to the big iron safe in a corner of the room and counted out a roll of currency. He folded it tightly and gave it to her. "Stick that down in your pocket," he said, "and have it ready, and, remember, you are to let on all the way through that you are willing to sell out, but before you do so you want his proposition put down in black and white. He may think it is just some cranky woman's notion, and do it—he may, and he may not; our chances hang on that one thing. You are a dead goner if you don't get that paper."

"I understand fully," Dixie said, her lips drawn firmly. "The only thing I don't like is borrowing your money."

"Don't be silly," Henley snorted. "You are good for it, and I'd rather lend money to you than anybody else on earth. Don't let that bother you."

"Well, I won't, then," the girl said. "I know you want to help me, and I'm very thankful for such a friend."

CHAPTER XXV

Crossing the street diagonally, Henley came to a little two-story frame building near the post-office. Pausing before the door, he looked in and saw old Welborne seated at his desk near an open window. The money-lender was thin, had parchment-like skin, massive eyebrows, and long, gray hair, which never seemed to have been trimmed, and was massed on the greasy collar of his faded black alpaca coat. He was past seventy years of age, and the hand which held his pen shook visibly. Henley went in, and as he did so old Welborne laid down his pen and turned round in his revolving-chair. He nodded and grunted, and motioned to a three-legged stool near the desk.

Henley sat down on it, and as he did so he drew out a couple of cigars, and, holding them in the shape of a letter V, he extended them toward the old man. "I'm advertising a new brand," he said, cordially. "Take one, and whenever you want a good smoke drop in. You'll find 'em as free from cabbage-leaves as any in this town. One thing certain, you don't have to bore a hole through 'em to start circulation."

"Drumming up trade, eh?" The money-lender smiled as he took the cigar, and, pinching off the tip with his long thumb-nail, he thrust it between his gashed and stained teeth. "Well, I don't blame any man for trying to turn a penny during hard times like these. But, Lord, Alf, you'd make a living if you was on a bare rock in the middle of the Atlantic Ocean. I take off my hat to any man that could handle a busted circus like you did. I wouldn't have touched that pile of junk at your figure if it had been given to me, and yet—well, every man to his line."

Henley scratched a match on the sole of his shoe and lighted his cigar. "I've been just a little afraid that your nephew—that Hank Bradley may have told you about the little spat me and him had at the store the other day—"

"I heard it," Welborne broke in, with an indifferent smile. "I was standing in the door; he was full; he ought to have been kicked out; you done right; he's a lazy, good-for-nothing scamp, but don't talk to me about him. I pay him what is coming to him, board him for next to nothing, and there my responsibility ends. I'm not fighting his battles—huh, I guess not! How's trade over your way?"

"N. G." Henley puffed, squinting his right eye to avoid the smoke which curled up from the end of his cigar, as he looked absently at the dingy window-panes and the cobwebs hanging from the cracked and bulging plastering overhead. "We can sell plenty on tick, but getting paid is the devil. Jim Cahews is a good man, but he can't say no—to a petticoat, anyway. While I was away he went it rather reckless. Why, he let one little woman that has heretofore been the brag of the county get in clean up to her neck."

Old Welborne ceased smoking; his dim, blue eyes twinkled. "I'll bet a dollar to a ginger-cake I know who you mean," he said, eagerly.

"Well, maybe you do and maybe you don't," Henley said. "But I've had enough of her foolishness and promising and never coming to time. I'm not in business for my health. She's a neighbor of mine, and I always admired her plucky fight, but charity begins at home. I'm not running an orphan asylum, nor an old woman's home. Jim misunderstood me, anyway. I told 'im her account was all right, and for him not to bear down too hard on her, and I went to Texas and forgot all about it. But, holy smoke! when I got home and looked at the books I was fairly staggered at the figures. She's over there at the store now, and I had to talk to her straight, and she won't get a bit deeper in my debt. I've got to call a halt."

"I think I might set your mind at rest on what she owes you," Welborne said, with an unctuous smile. "There is no use beating about the bush, Henley, you know she's in debt to me, and you've come over to see if I can help you out. Well, I can. I am in the shape to do it. Me 'n you have clashed several times in our deals and had hard feelings, but there is no use keeping up strife. We can work together now. Me and her own that farm in partnership, and I've had enough of it. I've made a fair give-or-take offer, and nothing is to prevent her from closing out and paying you what she owes you. I've got eight hundred dollars in cash ready to hand her at any minute."

"You don't say!" Henley's look of gratified surprise was perfect. "Well, she's in a better fix than I thought. She ain't much of a hand to tell her business, and I thought she had—well, about run through her pile."

"She can get the money if she will have common-sense," said Welborne; "but women never know how to 'tend to business, and she may act stubborn to the end and force me to put up the land for sale. It wouldn't fetch much, and you and me'd both lose by it. The best thing to do is to make her have sense, and if you will—if you will talk straight to her about your debt, maybe she'll sell out and be done with it."

"Well, I can talk straight enough, if you'll leave it to me," Henley said, with what looked like a frown of chronic resentment. "It makes me mad to think she'll keep me out of my money while you are offering her enough to square off."

"Well, go over to the store and see what you can do to bring her to her senses," the money-lender proposed, with a smirk which twisted his sallow visage into a grimace. "If you can bring her to reason, we'll both get—get what's due us."

"All right," Henley said, in a tone of gratitude. "You come on over in a minute. I'll tell her I've heard of your offer, and that I won't stand anymore foolishness."

Henley sauntered back to the store. His face was set and colorless as he approached Dixie. She glanced up, and he was shocked by the look of despair in her great, sorrowful eyes.

"He's coming over," Henley said. "Everything is cocked and primed. He thinks you may take his money—he thinks I'm going to *make* you do it. You needn't talk much, but stick to it that you want his offer writ down in black and white and will have it before you'll move a peg. I'll write it and have it ready for him to sign. If he does, we are solid; if not, we are lost. I don't know that I ever tackled anything quite as ticklish as this, for he is as wary and sly as a fox. We mustn't give 'im time to think, if we can help it. Sh! there he is now. Don't mind anything I say, no matter how harsh it sounds—remember, I'm working for your good, and using fire to stop fire."

She nodded and smiled knowingly, but said nothing, for the money-lender was approaching. When Welborne was quite near, Henley suddenly said aloud: "You are a woman, but I ain't going to stand any more foolishness. You've been saying all this time that you can't get the money, and yet here is a cash offer of eight hundred dollars staring you smack-dab in the face."

"I never had the offer until this morning," Dixie said, with what he recognized as astonishing diplomacy. Her face was out of sight under the hood of her sunbonnet, her handkerchief to her eyes.

"She's willing to do what's right," Henley said to Welborne. "The only thing she holds out for is to have the proposition down in writing. Of course, there is no need of it, but women know nothing about business, and will have every detail carried out, and so I scratched it down here. It is a plain give-or-take offer of eight hundred dollars either way, and she ain't in no fix to refuse."

Henley dipped a pen in the ink and held the paper toward the old man. There was an incipient wave of innate distrust in Welborne's manner as he glanced from the bowed form of the girl to that of the waiting storekeeper.

"Let her have her way about it," Henley advised. "Women will have everything complete or you can't do a blessed thing with 'em. It don't mean anything to you; you've made her a fair give-or-take offer."

"Yes, of course I have," Welborne said, conquering his qualms, and with a quivering hand he signed the paper. He had no sooner done it than Henley laid it face downward on a blotting-pad and, with a steady hand, stroked its back. The eyes he fixed on Dixie, who was covertly watching him, fairly danced as he raised the paper and folded it carefully.

"Now, you two have got the proposition down in fair legal shape, and nothing stands between you and a deal. Miss Dixie, you are just a woman, and may not know the ways of the business world, so I want to tell you on my honor that this is what all fair-minded men call an absolutely straight proposition, and when you've acted on it, it would be wrong for you to ever say anybody coerced you or took advantage of you. You understand that you've got a right either to pay eight hundred and own the farm, or take eight hundred and sell your half. Is that plain to you?"

"Yes, I understand it perfectly," Dixie answered, glancing first at him and then at the expectant and suave money-lender.

"And you understand it, too, don't you, Mr. Welborne?"

"Yes, I understand it," the eager old man replied, craftily. "And you know, Alf Henley, that I wouldn't have made as liberal an offer to anybody but this girl. She's in a tight fix and needs the money, and the farm has gone down to less 'n half of what it was worth when me and her bought it."

"Well, then, Miss Dixie," Henley said, significantly, and he held the paper tightly in his strong hand, "you'll have to decide which thing you intend to do."

"I've already decided," the girl said, looking at Welborne with a placid stare, "and I'm going to be satisfied. I know the farm isn't any good now, and will perhaps be lower when the railroad is built the other side of the mountain, but it is the only home we have, and I've decided to buy it."

"*Buy* it?" Welborne gasped, and stared as if unable to grasp her meaning. "You don't mean that you—"

"Well, well!" Henley cried, "this *is* a surprise. Here I've been rowing you up Salt River for your puny little debt to me, and you now say you are able to own a big chunk of real estate unencumbered. Why, you must have struck oil somewhere. My, my, my!"

"I don't tell my business to everybody." Dixie, now standing, had thrust her hand into the pocket of her skirt and was drawing out the bills. "Here's the money, Mr. Welborne."

A snort that could have been heard to the front door issued from Welborne's fluttering nostrils. He pushed the money from him, writhed and tottered, and as he glared furiously at Henley he screamed:

"It's a trick put up between you. I see it, but I won't be buncoed in no such way. Do you hear me?—no such way!"

He was turning off when Henley, now a different man, stepped before him. "You are going to act fair for once, you old thief," he said, a gray look of determination about his mouth and in his fixed eyes. "You've been swindling this orphan girl all these years, and you are going to abide by your own signed contract. You are going to do it, or, by all that's holy, I'll head a gang of mountain-men that will drag you out of your bed and lay a hundred lashes on your bare back."

"I'll see you in hell first!" Welborne shrieked, and, darting past Henley, he hurried from the store as fast as his tottering gait would take him.

"We lost, after all!" Dixie cried, and, sinking back in her chair, the money clutched in her hand, she burst into tears.

"Not yet, not *plumb* yet, little girl!" Henley was unconscious of the vast tenderness of his tone. "Don't cry; be the brave little trick you've always been."

"I'm not thinking of myself, really I'm not," she sobbed.

"But my mother and aunt have heard about it, and they are awfully upset. They love the place, and the thought of leaving and being destitute is running them crazy."

"Look here. Let me have the money," Henley said, his eyes flashing dangerously. "You go home and be easy. Leave him to me. He sha'n't rob you like that; I'll drag his bones from his dirty hide and rattle 'em through the streets before I'll let 'im. This is a Christian community, and God rules."

"You mustn't bother any more," Dixie said, and as she put the money into his hands she clung to them tenderly and appealingly. "Blood has been spilt over matters like this, Alfred, and the whole thing ain't worth it. His nephew—I intended to warn you before—Hank Bradley is your enemy, and now Welborne is, and between them"—she broke off with a convulsive sob, but still clung pleadingly to his hands.

"I don't care if his whole layout is up in arms agin me; he sha'n't rob you. You are the sweetest, dearest, most suffering little girl the sun ever shone on, and I'll fight for you as long as there is a speck of life in me. You go home. I'll come to you the very minute it is settled."

"And you won't—oh, Alfred, please don't—please don't—for my sake, don't have trouble with him. You're hot-tempered, and I've let you get wrought up. Don't you see that it don't make any odds to me?"

"All right, then," he said, smiling, and yet she saw that his smile was only on the surface. "I promise we won't fight about it. I'll try to bring him to his senses in some other way. Now, go home. I'll come out as soon as I possibly can."

It was after nightfall before he saw her again. As he was

nearing her cottage in the vague starlight he saw a figure of some one in the fence-corner of her pasture which touched the road near his own land. He surmised that it was she, and that she was there waiting for him, though her head was bowed to the top rail of the fence and he couldn't see her face. There was a strip of grass on the roadside, and he walked upon it that it might deaden his tread till he was close upon her. As it was, he reached her side without attracting her attention. Then something clutched all his senses and held him like a dead thing in his tracks, for he heard her praying in a sweet, suffering voice that lifted him with it to the very throne of thrones.

"Oh, God, my Maker, my Saviour, my Redeemer," he heard her saying, "give me the strength to bear it and let no harm come to my dear, dear friend. I can bear the loss of my home, but not to have harm come to him. Oh, Lord, help—" She raised her head, and their eyes met and clung together. He had a folded paper in his hand, and he extended it to her. His voice rose and broke in a wave of huskiness: "Here is the deed, Dixie, little girl," he said. "The farm is yours. The transaction is recorded at the court-house. Nothing can take it from you now."

"Mine, Alfred, mine, did you say?"

"Yes, I had trouble; he died hard; he saw it was all up with him after he'd signed that agreement, but it was like pulling eye-teeth to get the deed made out. He'd write a line, and then throw down the pen and cry and whine like a baby. I'm ashamed to say it, but once I got mad and caught him by that slim neck of his and pushed him down under his desk and held him there. My thumb was in his throat. I clutched too tight. I thought I'd killed him. The Lord must have restrained me. He was black in the face and as limber as a rag. It was then that he give in. He'd have held out to the end, but I was holding something over him. Women all over the county are lending him money at a low rate, and I showed him that if this trick of his agin you was published they'd lose faith in him and make him pay up. He saw his danger and give in. But, my! how it rankles. It's the first time he was ever whipped to a dead finish."

With the deed in her hand Dixie stood staring at him, her beautiful mouth twitching with emotion, her great eyes aglow with joy. She started to speak, but a sob rose within her and she lowered her head to the rail. The beams of the rising moon fell on her exquisite neck; her wonderful tresses lay massed on her shoulders.

"Don't—don't cry, Dixie," he said. "I can't bear it." He laid his hand on her head and let it rest there gently.

Presently she looked up, caught his hand in both of hers and pressed her lips to it. "You are the sweetest, best, noblest man in the world, Alfred. I can't thank you. I'll—I'll choke. I'm so—so happy. Good-night."

He stood at the fence and watched her till she had disappeared in the cottage, and then, like a man in a delightful, bewildering dream, he turned his face toward the lights in his own house.

Old Wrinkle was waiting for him at the gate, and he held it open for him. "Your supper—sech as it is—is on the table waitin' for you," he said, picking his teeth with a splinter from the fence. "Ma got it ready for you; I've had mine; I made me some mush out of the yaller corn-meal Pomp fetched from the mill. Mush-an'-milk, with a dab o' cream an' a pinch o' salt, is all right to sleep on. We've had a day of it; Hettie has gone all to flinders, and went to bed at sundown with a crackin' headache, an' eyes swelled as big as squashes. Her uncle Ben is in trouble. He sent her a letter fifty pages in duration by one of his niggers. As well as I can make out betwixt Hettie's spasms her uncle Ben's fine Baltimore lady has turned him down. Thar seems to be a Yankee feller in the way. She advanced a hundred reasons fer deciding not to retire to lonely mountain-life. She's riled up, for one thing, on the nigger question—says she understands a lady has to go armed to the teeth just to walk from the well to the back porch, an' that she never had learned to shoot, nohow. The Yankee feller has more scads than Ben, an' has bought an estate in New York City which he lays at her feet as an inducement. Het an' Ben must be slices off the same block, for his letter was soaked in salt water, an' she had to run a hot flatiron over hern before it would do to send. He writ her that she was the only faithful woman on earth—he was hintin' at Dick's burial arrangements, I reckon—an' that if she was thar he'd put his head in her lap an' have a good cry. They would have had to swap laps if they had been together to-day, for Het needed a foot-tub to take care of her overflow. Well, I'm keepin' you from your royal banquet. You'll find it on the dinner-table, with the cloth all drawed up over it like a bundle ready for the wash. Ma tied it up that way to keep the cat out of it. I don't think the cat 'u'd care for any of it, but I reckon Jane 'lowed the thing mought paw it over in the hope o' strikin' some'n worth while."

Conscious of little that the old man was saying, Henley passed on into the dimly lighted farm-house, experiencing a vague sense of relief that he was not just then to face his wife.

CHAPTER XXVI

One evening shortly after this Henley was returning from the store about an hour later than was his custom. He was nearing Dixie Hart's cottage, when, in the clear moonlight, he saw the girl emerge from the little apple-orchard behind her barn and come rapidly toward him. Her glance was on the ground, and she had evidently not seen him. As she drew near where he stood waiting, he noted that her head was bare, and that she had a medicine-bottle in her hand. He noted, too, from her gait and hurried manner, that she was greatly disturbed. She was about to pass him when he called out, cheerily, "Where away, in such a hurry?"

"Oh!" She looked up and stopped. "You scared me, Alfred. I couldn't imagine who it was. I'm going over to Sam Pitman's. Joe is sick—powerful sick. If I am any judge, it is pneumonia, and a bad case at that."

"Pneumonia!" he echoed, aghast. "I didn't know anything was wrong with him."

"It's been coming on some time," she said. "He caught an awful cold. You know the day it rained so hard and the creek got out of banks? I was trying to cross the ford below Pitman's in my wagon. I thought I could make it all right, but the current washed the wagon in a hole, and old Bob couldn't touch bottom. The wagon was floating like a boat, and he finally got stuck in the mud with just his head and neck out and couldn't budge. Joe was digging sprouts in the field on the right-hand side, and ran down to me. I yelled at him not to come in, but he struck out toward me with his clothes on, swimming like a dog. He got to me and helped me out in the water on a high place, and made me stand there while he worked and tugged at the trace-chains for twenty minutes till he finally unhitched Bob and pulled him out of the mire. Then he helped me out and dragged the wagon ashore."

"Plucky little chap!" cried Henley.

"But he's getting paid for it," Dixie said, bitterly. "He got overheated in the cold mountain-water, and he is in a bad fix, Alfred. I know when a sick person is dangerous, and he is."

She was moving on toward Pitman's now, and Henley was keeping step by her side. "You mustn't take it so hard," he said, in an effort to calm her. "It will come out all right."

"It is a ticklish thing, pneumonia is," she said; "and he hasn't got a doctor. Sam Pitman says it isn't anything but a cold, and he won't send for one. I was over there twice to-day, but he don't even want me to nurse him. I've got my things all done up at home and the folks in bed, and I'm going to stay with him all night if I have to have a knock-down-and-drag-out row to do it. I told Sam Pitman that I'd pay for the doctor out of my own pocket, but that just made him madder. He says I'm trying to come under his roof and run his affairs, and that I sha'n't do it. He may not let me in now. I don't know, but he is one of the devil's imps, if there ever was one. Mrs. Pitman is a little better, but he's got her under his thumb. She won't raise her voice when he is around."

"We must have a doctor, that's certain," declared Henley. "You walk on and I'll run to town and bring Doctor Stone. He knows his business; and he'll take charge of the case if I back him. If Pitman tries to hinder us I'll jail him as sure as he's a foot high."

"Oh, Alfred, I wish you would get the doctor. I'm so glad I met you. I was worried to death. I know how to nurse in ordinary cases, but pneumonia is so treacherous. Hurry, please; I'll never forget you for this."

Twenty minutes later Henley entered the gate of Sam Pitman's diminutive farm-house. Three watch-dogs came from beneath the little front porch, but, recognizing the visitor, they stood wagging their tails cordially and uttering low whines of welcome. There was a broken harrow, with rusty iron teeth, leaning against the house near the log steps; a top-heavy ash-hopper and a lye-stained trough stood under the spreading branches of a beechnut-tree beside a rotting cider-press and a huge pot for heating water during hog-killing or for boiling lye and grease for the making of soap.

As Henley approached the steps Pitman and his wife, hearing the click of the gate-latch, came out on the porch, which was shaded by overhanging vines, and stood staring blankly at him. Henley was a gallant man, for his station in life, and he drew off his broad-brimmed hat and remained uncovered while he spoke.

"I've run over to inquire how little Joe is," he said, conscious of the grim opposition to his visit in the very air that hung around the farmer. "I happened to meet Miss Dixie Hart just now on her way here, and she was considerably upset."

"Nothin' wrong with the boy," Pitman muttered, surlily. "That gal, like most of her meddlin' sort, is havin' a regular conniption-fit over nothin'. I reckon she is afeard thar'll be one less on the marryin' list a few years from now. He was a pesky fool, anyway, plungin' in cold water to attend to her business. He's had croupy coughs before this, an' wheezin'-spells, an' been hot like all childern will when they eat too much, but we never went stark crazy over it."

"Miss Dixie is a purty good judge, Sam," Henley answered, incisively. "She'd be hard to fool if danger was lurkin' around. When she described Joe's condition to me just now I saw she had plenty cause to worry, and so I went straight back to town and left word for Doctor Stone to hurry here as soon as he got home. They was looking for him every minute."

"You say you did!" Pitman came to the edge of the porch, and, with his arm around one of the posts which upheld the roof, he leaned over till his face was close to Henley's. "Huh! you are some pumpkins, ain't you? You can keep me from runnin' an account at your dirty shebang, Alf Henley, but you can't walk dry-shod over me in my own house. A man's domicyle is his castle in law, and I'm goin' to manage mine an' defend it, ef I have to."

"Don't get excited, Sam; keep your shirt on," Henley said, calmly. There was an oblong spot of light thrown on the grass between him and the gate. It was from the attic window above the porch, and across it now and then moved a shadow. He knew that the little room under the roof was occupied by the sick child, and that the shadow was Dixie's. The shadow was now still and bowed at the window in an attitude of attention to what was going on below.

"I ain't excited any to hurt," Pitman went on, his voice rising higher. "You say you've ordered Stone to come, an' I say if he does he won't put his foot across my threshold."

"You've got it in for me, Sam, I see," Henley said, still unruffled, "but this is no time for you and me to settle old scores. The boy is no blood kin to either of us."

"The law gives me full an' complete charge of 'im till he's of age," Pitman snarled, "an' I hain't invited you to put in, an' until I do you'll be a sight safer on t'other side of that fence. I mean the one right thar behind you."

The window-sash was raised above, and Dixie looked out.

"He's just dropped to sleep," she announced in a guarded tone. "Please, Alfred, don't let them talk so loud, and send the doctor up the minute he comes."

"Very well," Henley answered, softly and reassuringly. Then going close to the farmer he said in a low voice, "I want to talk to you a minute; let's walk round the house."

Pitman hesitated, staring doggedly at the speaker, and then shifted his sullen gaze to the face of his wife.

"Go on with 'im," she said, and turned stiffly into the lark doorway behind her.

Silently Henley led Pitman round the house to the little barn-yard in the rear. There was a red-painted road-wagon near the wagon-shed and Henley sat down easily on the strong pole and began to search through his pockets for a cigar and matches. He grunted in disappointment when he found his pockets empty, and then deliberately applied himself to the matter in hand.

"Looky here, Sam Pitman," he began, "for a long-headed, sensible mountain-man you are plunging into more serious trouble than any chap of your size ever got into. I'm going to let you on to a thing that a fellow usually keeps quiet—I'm going to do it because I feel that it is my Christian duty not to be a party to the great disaster you are on the brink of."

"I don't know what you mean, an' I don't care a damn," growled Pitman. "I know what my rights are, an' that's all I'm talkin' about."

"I started to tell you, when you busted in," said Henley, swinging his feet beneath him, "that I'm a member of the grand jury, and you may or may not know that when a fellow is impaneled in that body he's got a sworn job on his hands that is powerful exacting. He is on his oath to report to the authorities any criminal irregularity that comes under his notice. Now! I have had the word and the judgment of a respectable and truthful lady that the boy bound to you by law is dangerously and critically sick, and, calling here in my lawful capacity to look into the matter, I hear you say with my own ears that no doctor shall put foot across your threshold. Now, look at it straight, Sam. Even if Joe was to get well a big, serious case may come up against you—I don't promise that you'll come off free even as it is, but if the child was to *die*—I say if he was to happen to pass away, and I've seen little ones die when half a dozen skilled doctors was standing by—Sam Pitman, in that case, no lawyer on earth could keep you out of limbo. I tell you, you don't know it, but right this minute you are in the tightest hole you ever slid into. A jury in your case wouldn't leave their seats. Men pity helpless children in this life more'n they do big hulking men of your stripe, and they'd sock it to you to the full extent of the law. Even if it wasn't tried at court, take it as a hint from me, the men of these mountains would get together in a body and lynch you. Reports have already been going round to your eternal discredit about this child, and one more act of yours will simply settle your hash. This is me talking, Sam."

"You—you dare to come here—" But Pitman's rage was tinctured with actual fear of the man before him, and his intended threat was not uttered. He was white and quivering, but he was helpless. A sound broke the stillness that now fell between the two men. It was the steady trotting of a horse on the road.

"There's Doc now," Henley announced, and his eyes met Pitman's, which were kindling again.

"Well, I've said he sha'n't—an', by God—" Pitman started toward the house, but Henley sprang up and faced him. Laying his hand heavily on the farmer's shoulder he cried almost with a hiss of fury: "Let that doctor alone, you dirty whelp! He's going to crawl up that ladder to that hole under the roof to see that boy. You and me are nigh the same size, and we can settle right here. You tried me once before, maybe you want another dose. Stir a peg to prevent this thing and I'll drive your head into your shoulders same as I would a wedge in a split log."

Pitman glared helplessly, and then he showed defeat. With his eyes on the ground, and writhing from beneath Henley's hand, he said:

"The boy hain't bad off, nohow!"

"Well, we'll see what Doc Stone has to say about it," Henley retorted. "He's authority, an' you hain't."

Pitman had no reply ready. They heard the gate open and close, and then on the still air came the gentle voice of Dixie speaking from the attic window. "Come right in, Doctor, and up the ladder. Be careful and don't stumble. I'll hold the candle for you."

Pitman sullenly turned away. Henley watched him as he

went into the stall of a stable and struck a match to light his pipe. Leaving him, Henley went back to the farm-house and sat down on the steps of the porch. The light from the attic window lay on the lush green grass before him, and he kept his eyes upon it. There was a tread on the floor behind him as soft as that of a cat. It was Mrs. Pitman in her bare feet. She held her tattered shoes in her hand. She touched him on the shoulder.

"I hope you an' Sam didn't—come to licks," she whispered.

"No, he's all right," was the gentle reply. "I had to talk sharp, Mrs. Pitman, an' I'm sorry it was here at his own house."

"Well, I'm glad the doctor come," she conceded, slowly. "I was afeard to put in while Sam was talkin'. He gits madder at me 'n he does to all the rest combined. I'm sort o' feard the boy is bad off, myself."

"Yes, he's bad off," Henley nodded, grimly. "If it was a light case Doc Stone would have been down before this. You may depend on it, it's serious."

Muttering inarticulately, the woman crept away. Henley remained bent forward, his eyes on the shifting shadows before him. He looked at his watch; two hours had passed. The closing of a rear door and the resounding tread of a pair of hobnailed boots on the lower floor told him that Pitman had entered the house and was going to bed. He saw Dixie's shadow in its frame on the grass, and went out to the fence and looked up. She was there, and she leaned over the little sill and nodded. "I only wanted to know if you was still there," she said, in a low tone. "Joe—" But the doctor evidently had called her, for she looked back into the room and vanished. Henley saw two shadows bending forward, and he strode back and forth along the fence, a fierce suspense clutching his heart. Presently the doctor, a middle-aged, full-bearded man, with a gentle manner, crept down the ladder and walked softly across the porch. Henley joined him at his buggy in the road.

"How is he, Doc?" he inquired, his fears deepened by the physician's silence, as he stood between the wheels of the buggy and fumbled with the reins wrapped around the whip-holder.

"Awful, awful!" Stone said, grimly. "Not one chance in five hundred. Malignant pneumonia. Neglected case. I've left medicine and instructions. I can't stay—would if I could—case of child-labor down the road—nobody else to attend to it. I'll be back before morning. That will be the crisis. He's in splendid hands; a trained nurse couldn't be better."

"Anything I can do, Doc?" Henley swallowed a lump of emotion that had risen in his throat.

"Not a thing; but you might stay right here. Miss Dixie might—if anything happened—she might need you. She's a plucky little woman, and it might be best for her to have some sort of company. She is wrought up. She loves the boy as a mother would her own child, and yet she is calm and steady."

Henley leaned on the fence and watched the vehicle disappear in the misty moonlight which seemed to fall like a mantle from the mountain. He was resting his head on the fence when he felt a light touch on his arm. It was Dixie.

"He is sleeping," she whispered. "The doctor said it would be good for him. Oh, Alfred, it's pitiful, pitiful! I'm glad to see that you feel like you do. He loves you; he has spoken of you scores of times, and, when I told him just now that you was down here watching, he was glad. I wonder why God tears a human soul to pieces like this. If Joe is taken to-night I don't think I could ever get over it. Oh, Alfred, my heart yearns over him. At this minute I could ask for nothing better than to be allowed to work for that child all the rest of my life." Tears stood in her wonderful eyes, and her breast, under its thin covering, rose and fell tumultuously.

"You are a sweet, good girl, Dixie." Henley's voice sounded new to himself. "You are the noblest woman that ever drew the breath of life. As the Lord is my Redeemer, I'd give all I possess on earth to help you to-night."

Their eyes met in a strange gaze of wonderment. "I believe it," she said, simply, while a sad smile touched her pulsing lips. "Yes, I believe it. But I must go back."

He sat under the beechnut-tree watching the attic window till the eastern sky above the mountains began to take on a grayish cast. Now and then through the long vigil Dixie would come to the window and look down on him, only to nod knowingly and retire, as if content with his mute companionship.

It was almost dawn when the doctor came.

"I was delayed," he explained as he sprang out of his buggy; "bad case of labor—had to use instruments, but successful." He hurried to the gate without hitching his horse. "How is he?"

"I can't say, Doc—you'd better see for yourself."

The yellow light was filling all the sky with resplendent glory when Dixie, her face wan and wearied, came down the ladder. Henley's heart sank at the first sight of her, but it bounded when she had seen him, for the rarest of smiles broke about her mouth and eyes.

"He's going to get well, Alfred!" she cried, and she extended her hand with the warm confidence of a child toward a trusted friend. He let it rest in his as he walked with her to the gate, wondering over the good news, wondering over the delight with which her touch was firing his being.

"Yes, the worst is over," she went on. "The doctor says with good nursing and watching he'll pull through. He is going to stay with him while I run home and do up the things, then I'll come back and relieve him. He is going to give Pitman a tongue-lashing, and says he'll appear against him in court if he doesn't act different. As soon as Joe can be moved we are going to bring him to my house. Oh, Alfred, won't that be glorious? There I can give him everything he needs, and a clean, cool, airy room to get well in. Weak as he was, he cried with actual joy when he heard the doctor say he could come. Alfred, do you know we all ought to be ashamed of ourselves for complaining in this life, and wanting more and more of the trashy baubles. Right now I'm so happy I feel like flying. Look at that sunrise! We couldn't have seen it like that if we'd been in our beds with our eyes shut; we couldn't feel this way if we hadn't dragged through all that pain and anxiety last night. I've got to write a letter and mail it before I come back. Jasper Long was to come over Sunday, you know, but I can't give the time to him. I'll ask him to come Sunday after next."

"It will disappoint him mightily," Henley said, a sudden feeling of aversion to the subject on him. "It will break the fellow all up. He's been counting the days and hours."

"I can't help it." Dixie shrugged her shoulders indifferently, her head down. They were now in the little wood that lay between Pitman's farm and her cottage. To the leaves and branches of the chestnut and sassafras bushes that bordered the little-used road the night mists and silvery cobwebs clung, magnified by their coating of dew and the yellow light.

"I don't know as I ever saw a fellow quite so much concerned and anxious," Henley's strangely tentative voice produced. "I saw him over there the other day, and he had lots to say. He means to—to get you if he possibly can. He's planning a fine house, and said he was going to tell you about it when he come over. He says women know better about such things than men, and is going to offer you full sway. To do him credit, there ain't nothing little about Long. He'll do right, I reckon, by any woman he pledges his word to. I'd hate to—to think I'd fetched you together if—if he wasn't all right—that is, honest and upright."

"I know that," Dixie said. "But let's not talk about him, or his fine house, or his money, or his good intentions. He don't seem, somehow, to fit one bit into my feelings this morning. He's a cold-blooded business proposition, and last night's terror and this morning's joy has filled me to here"—she held her tapering hand under her plump chin and laughed—"well, with some'n different from him. The truth is, I don't care if I never see him again. That's a fact, Alfred. I feel like I'm on the up-hill road in single harness, anyway, since I am out of debt to Welborne, and owe you, instead. When are you going to send that note over for me to sign?"

"Never, if I can help it," he said. "I've let men owe me without note or security, why should I make you sign up for a trifle like that?"

"Well, to tell the truth, I like it as it is," she answered, with a fine smile and a rippling laugh that woke the echoes in the quiet spot. "It is such a sweet proof of your friendship. Ain't it funny how me 'n you have been mixed up in things? You know me as well as I know myself, Alfred. You've helped me, and I hope I have you—some. I don't know; I hope

I have."

"More than anybody else in the world," he said, fervently.

They had come to where their ways separated, and, with his hat in his hand, and his heart full of an inexplicable, transcendental something, he stood under the trees and watched her move away.

CHAPTER XXVII

On the day following Long's second visit to Dixie, Henley's affairs took him to Carlton. He was at the cotton-compress making arrangements to have a quantity of cotton prepared for shipment, when he met one of Long's clerks.

"Have you seen Mr. Long?" the young man asked.

"No, I've just got in," Henley answered. He could not have explained the fact, not being given to self-analysis, but he had vaguely determined that he would make every possible effort to avoid the storekeeper. In spite of his good intentions to aid Dixie in the contemplated alliance, he had come to regard it as altogether too incongruous an affair to be viewed favorably. What right had any man to her? What manner of man could possibly be worthy of her, much less the stupid blockhead who was thrusting himself upon her as Long was?

"Well, he's looking for you, Mr. Henley," the clerk said. "It must be important, for he's been to the bank and post-office three times since he heard you'd got in. It really looks like he's in trouble of some sort."

"Business gone crooked?" Henley inquired, as he watched the clerk's face with almost anxious eyes. "Maybe he's been buying futures?"

"Oh no, it ain't that!" the young man hastened to say. "He don't speculate in anything. He's dead sure of everything he touches. No, it ain't that, and business never was brisker, but we boys are doing it all. He ain't much help; don't do anything but write letters and tear 'em up, and talk about marryin' to every man, woman, an' child that happens in. He was all right and sound, and regular as a clock, till you fetched that girl in from over your way and introduced him. Come down right away, Mr. Henley. I'll tell 'im I saw you."

As Henley turned away to attend to his consignment of cotton in the office of the compress he bit his lip and frowned darkly.

"If the dang fool thinks I'm going down there to be buttonholed for hours to hear his tale of woe, he's certainly off his nut," he muttered, angrily. "I've got other matters to attend to. I don't believe she is at all struck with him, nohow. It don't look like she'd put 'im off like she does and keep him floundering in so much hot water if she thought much of him. He was there yesterday. I wonder what ails him now? She didn't take 'im out to church. Little Joe is at her house, but he is doing well enough for her to spare the time; I wonder if she was ashamed to be seen out with him after that first splurge. I don't know; she certainly is a plumb mystery to me."

His business over, he skirted around Long's establishment and made his way through an isolated alley to the wagon-yard where he had left his horse and buggy. He was just congratulating himself on his escape from the storekeeper, when Long suddenly broke upon his vision as he plunged incontinently through the big gateway. With an uneasy look in his eyes, and with a face drawn and serious, the store-keeper came striding toward him.

"Hello!" he panted. "I've been everywhere looking for you.

You are as slippery as an eel, and as hard to catch as a flea. I want to see you bad, Alf. It's a particular matter. I can't let it rest."

"I was busy, and I hain't any too much time left on my hands now." Henley looked at the sun and then at his watch. "You'll have to talk fast, Long. Seems to toe there's a lot o' hitches in my affairs here lately. This 'un to see, and that 'un to talk to, and—"

"I'm in trouble, Alf, old man." Long laid a red, perspiring hand on his friend's shoulder and bore down heavily. "I was out yore way yesterday. I tried to see you as I started home, but didn't know where to find you. Alf, I can't jest somehow make out that little trick. Looks like she's sorter shifty. In the first place, havin' to postpone the trip on account of that sick young brat that ain't no blood kin to anybody concerned sort o' knocked me off my props, and then, when the day *did* come round, very little was done—that is, in the *right* direction."

"You—you'll have to have patience," Henley remarked, insincerely. "If you can't hold in and take things as they come you'd better call the deal off. I started you; I can't lay down everything and keep—keep telling you what to do and say. Life's too short and makes too many claims on a fellow."

"I want you to say a good word for me, Alf." Long wiped his anxious mouth with his bare hand and tugged at his mustache. "She believes the sun rises and sets in you. Looks to me like it's Alfred did this, an' Alfred said that, an' Alfred thinks so and so and does so and so, with every breath she draws. For a while I 'lowed it was because she was grateful to you for helpin' her out in the marryin' line, but she don't seem to want to marry much, nohow. She'd listen to you, though, if she would to any man alive, and something has to be done."

"Well, I reckon the little woman *is* friendly to me." Henley avoided the fiercely anxious stare of his flurried companion. "She's done me good turns, and I've tried to respond."

"She'd fight for you tooth and toe-nail," Long declared. "I know from experience. Why, I just happened to say one little, tiny thing about you, and la! she flew at me like a hen fightin' for her brood. I meant no harm. I'd have said the same thing to your face, as I am saying it now. Me 'n her was talking about the way men dress these days, and I said, without meanin' any harm, that it was naturally expected that chaps here in a town like Carlton would be more up to date than at the foot of the mountains where you live, and remarked that you made no great pretence in the clothes you wore, in fact, that I thought you went just a little bit too careless for a man as young and well-off as you are."

"Huh, you told her that, did you?" Henley's cheeks reddened against his will. "Well, I don't go much on style, in hot weather, anyway. I never did want to be called a dude."

"Of course not, but what you reckon she done? She leaned back in her chair while I was a-talking an' laughed like she'd bust herself wide open. She pointed down at my new tan shoes and green socks and wanted to know if things like them was style, and asked me why I kept my gloves on in the house. She wanted to know if I let my yaller-bordered handkerchief stick out of my upper pocket because I was afraid folks wouldn't see it, an' if I kept a cheaper one to blow my nose on. You may know, Alf, that all the good-dressers here at Carlton—and I pride myself I'm amongst 'em—have their suits pressed once a week to make 'em set right, but she said my pant-legs looked like they was lined with pasteboard, and that my high collar looked like a cuff upside down. Of course, I couldn't get mad, for she was joking all through, and laughin' pleasant-like. But, Alf, I must say she's fallin' off in her meal record. You know she made such a fine spread the first time that I naturally expected some'n out of the common again. I saved myself up for it. I didn't take on a big breakfast before I left home because I told myself, I did, that I'd appreciate her fine fixings all the more. So you can imagine how I felt when she marched me out, with them old women, and set me down to—well, a body oughtn't to criticise what's set before 'em in a friend's house, but, Alf, that really was the limit. I can tell you just exactly what we had. I'll never forget it. It was plain pork and beans, and boiled cabbage, and sliced tomatoes, and hard cornbread. She hadn't put a sign of an egg in it, and cornbread without eggs ain't fit to eat. It looks like Mrs. Hart had had some dispute with Dixie about it, too, for the old lady kept whining and telling me it wasn't her fault, that she thought Dixie was going to set in and fix up proper, but that Dixie wouldn't listen to reason, and why, the old lady said, she was unable to understand, for the like had never happened before. Dixie didn't make any excuses, but set at the head of the table and dished out that stuff as if it was the best afloat. 'Won't you pass yore plate for more beans?' she wanted to know, and 'Won't you try some of the butter with the cornbread?' I reckon I made a mistake by speaking of what a fine spread she got up the last time, for she kind o' tilted her nose in the air, an' said she 'lowed the weather was too hot to stand over a hot cook-stove unless it was some *extra occasion*."

"She's got lots to do," Henley said, his eyes twinkling with amusement. "She's undertaken to nurse that little boy back to health, and he takes up a lot of her time."

"I reckon he does," Long said. "Looks like me an' her'd hardly get settled in our chairs on the porch before her mammy would call out that Joe wanted water, or Joe wanted to set up, or what not. It was more like hard work than any day of courtin' I ever put in. But now, Alf, I'm coming to my chief trouble. I want her, and I want her bad. I hardly sleep at night for thinking about her sweet, pretty face, and industrious habits, and what a bang-up wife she'd make, but I don't get nowhere. The minute I come down to hard-pan she wiggles away like a scared tadpole in shallow water. I done a thing, and I don't know whether it was a big mistake or not, and that is the main thing I want to see you about. It was just before I left, an' we was standin' at the gate, nigh my hoss and buggy. It had got sorter dark, and—well, I'll tell you all about it. Alf, I've heard fellows say (and they was men that had had experience with women, too)—I've heard 'em say that the chap that dilly-dallies with a woman, and always acts as sweet as pie, never makes no headway. Them fellows say you've just got to be sorter firm with a girl that won't make up her mind—that women like to have a man show that he ain't scared out of his senses when he's with 'em. And so I had all that in mind, you understand, when I made my last set at her there in the dark. I saw nobody wasn't looking, and I catched hold of her hand, I did, and held on to it though she pulled and twisted with all her might. I told her I was bound to have a kiss, and I pulled her up agin me and tried to take it. I couldn't manage it, though, and, by gad! she got loose and slid through the gate, and went in the house and slammed the door in my face."

"She ought to have knocked your head off, you low-lived fool!" cried Henley. He was white in the face, and his eyes had a dangerous glare in them. His breath came rapidly and with an audible sound. "For a minute I'd pull you down here and stomp the life out of you!"

"Why, Alf! Alf! have you plumb lost your senses?" Long gasped. "Why, why, good Lord, man! Why, Alf—"

"Don't Alf me!" Henley cried. "Get out of my sight or me 'n you'll mix right here! I didn't introduce you to that gentle girl to have you pull her around like a housemaid and force your foul lips to hers. I introduced you as a *man*, not a bar-room roustabout. No wonder she hain't took to you—no wonder she don't want to tie herself down for life to you!"

Henley had sprung into his buggy and taken up the whip and reins. "Stand out of the way!" he cried. "You've imposed on my friendship, and I don't want you ever to mention this matter to me again. I'm heartily ashamed of my part in it, and I don't want to be reminded of it."

Long tried to stop him, but, still white and furious, Henley lashed his horse, and the animal bore him out of the yard and into the street. "I ought to have given him one in the jaw!" Henley fumed. "I'll be sorry I didn't the longer I think about it—the low-lived, dirty brute!"

CHAPTER XXVIII

All the next day as Henley performed his duties at the store the hot sense of Long's stupid conduct brooded over him. One moment he was fired with fury over the man's sheer vanity, the next he was bitterly accusing himself for having been the primary cause of putting Dixie in a disagreeable position. What would she think of him, he asked himself over and over, for introducing such a despicable creature to her hospitality and good graces?

It was near sunset when he saw her pass the store, going toward the square. He went to the porch in front, unnoticed by the busy Cahews and the drowsy Pomp, and saw her, much to his surprise, enter the court-house yard, a place seldom visited by ladies. She was going up the walk to the arching stone entrance when she met the ordinary of the county, and Henley saw her pause and speak to him. The elderly, gray-haired gentleman stood for several minutes in a listening attitude, his hand cupped behind his ear, for he was slightly deaf. Presently Henley saw the two turn toward the building and enter it side by side.

"I wonder what on earth the little trick's going there for at this time of year," Henley mused. "It ain't tax-paying time."

The sun was down when she came out. He saw her coming and got his hat, timing himself so that he would meet her, as if by accident, and walk home with her. His calculations could not have been more accurate, for she was in front of the store when he came out.

"Oh," he said, "it's you! I thought I saw you pass just now. I'm going your way. I wanted to inquire how your little patient is."

"Oh, he's tiptop!" she cried, a delicate flush of tender enthusiasm on her face, a sparkle in her eyes. "Dr. Stone says he's mending twice as fast at our house because the little fellow is so happy there. When I'm off at work he's petted half to death by them two old women who haven't had anything better than a cat to pamper up since I got out of their clutch."

"And old Pitman let you move him?" Henley half questioned, as he suited his step to hers. "How did you manage it?"

"Me and the doctor put up a job on him," she laughed. "Dr. Stone wanted to help me gain my point, and he had the sharpest talk with old Sam you ever heard. The law was going to take him in hand for violating his contract in regard to the boy, and Dr. Stone would have to appear against him. But he told Sam that if he'd turn the boy over to me till he got well, he thought the whole thing might drop."

"Good job!" Henley chuckled. "Sam's a hard nut to crack."

Dixie raised her long lashes in a steady stare at him. "Guess what I've been doing at the court-house," she said. "I've been engaged in an odd thing for this modern day of enlightenment. Maybe you think slavery is over—maybe you think the Yankees wiped it clean out forty years ago, but they didn't. I've turned the wheels of Time back. I laid down the cash and bought a real live slave to-day. I didn't have to dig up as much as two thousand, which, I understand, was the old price for stout, able-bodied, hard workers, for the one I bought was a little sick one. Alfred, I actually bought little Joe to-day. I paid Sam Pitman twenty-five dollars to get him to release all his claims without any rumpus. I've adopted him. Judge Barton has fixed up the papers good and stout, and says nothing can take him from me as long as I do my part by him. Alfred, I'm so happy that I want to shout at the top of my lungs."

"You have adopted him!" Henley exclaimed, in wondering surprise. "Well, well, what won't you do next? Of all the things on earth this knocks me off my feet, and you already loaded down with responsibilities!"

"I don't care," Dixie laughed. "I'd welcome more like that, and never complain. You ought to have seen Joe when I told him Sam had agreed to let him go, and that I was to be his mother. If you could have seen the angelic look on that thin, white face you would have known that life is eternal, and that the spirit is all there is to anything. He stared straight at me with his pale brow wrinkled as if it was too good to be so, and then when I convinced him, he put his arms around my neck and hugged me tight, and sobbed and sobbed in pure joy."

Dixie was shedding tears herself now, and, with a heaving breast and lowered head, she walked along beside her awed and silent companion. They had entered a wood through which the road passed, and there seemed to be a hallowed stillness in the cool, grayish touch of the coming night that pervaded the boughs and foliage of the trees. Beyond the wood a mountain-peak rose in a blaze of molten gold from the oblique rays of the setting sun, but here the night-dews were beginning to fall and the chirping insects of the dark were waking. In the marshy spots frogs were croaking and snarling, and fireflies were cutting, to their kind perhaps readable, hieroglyphics on the leafy background. Presently she wiped her eyes, and smiled up at him.

"What a goose I am!" she said. "As old as I am, I'll cry if you crook your finger at me. You went to Carlton yesterday, didn't you?"

"Yes," he replied, glad to see her emotion over, uplifting and rare as its nature was.

"Did you happen to see my young man?" A smile he failed to see in the shadows was playing sly tricks with her lineaments.

"*Your* young man? You mean—"

"You know who I mean. I mean my beau—Mr. Jasper Long, Esquire, merchant, cotton-handler, and rich capitalist."

"Yes, I saw him," Henley said, reluctantly. "I didn't make a point of looking him up. He ran about searching for me. I've washed my hands of that—that matter, Dixie. I ain't no hand at match-making, nohow. It ain't my turn. I get all mixed up, and blunder at it. I'll never set myself up to pick out a—a suitable mate for any woman again. There ain't none in existence—there ain't none half good enough for you, nohow. It makes me sick to—to think about a fellow like—well, no better in many ways than this here Long is—having the gall to think he—that you'd be willing to live with him the rest of your days as if there was a single thing in common betwixt you. He told me about what he done—what he *tried* to do out at the fence when he started off the other night, and, *well*—"

"Well what?" she cried, eagerly, the corners of her mouth

curving upward as she eyed him covertly.

"Why, you know well enough what the fool done, Dixie!" Henley said, unaware of the meshes into which her curiosity was leading him. "When he told me about it, in his offhand way, as if he had just done an ordinary, every-day act, I come as nigh as peas mashing his big, flathering mouth. I've been boiling mad ever since. I rolled and tumbled in bed last night, and it's stuck to me all day. Somehow I just can't shake it off."

"You mean, Alfred"—and she paused at the roadside, and put out her hands to his arms, and studied his face with the eagerness of a child searching for the confirmation of something hoped for and yet not absolutely attainable—"do you mean that it actually made you mad when he told you. Tell me how; tell me why. You wouldn't have—felt that way if—if it had been some other girl, would you?"

"How do I know?" Henley cried, hot from the memory of the thing spoken of. "I don't know whether I'd feel mad or not. I never tried it. It is the first time I was ever up against a thing as aggravating as that was. The idea of him actually trying to kiss you, and—and put his arms around you, and holding to you, and—and—"

"He's a bad, mean thing, ain't he, Alfred?" And her merry laugh rang through the quiet wood, plunging him into deeper mystification than ever. "But of course he couldn't know that I'd not be willing to be hugged and kissed right there at the fence, with a crippled woman peeping out at the window, and a half-blind one standing by, begging for a report of what's taking place. Before you married, Alfred, I'll bet you selected a better place than that when you wanted to kiss a girl. That fellow lives in a big town and I live here in the backwoods, but I can learn him a thing or two."

"You can't fool me." Henley was sure of his ground now. "You wouldn't let that chump kiss you at any time or at any place. I was a fool to ever mention him to you; he ain't worthy to tie the shoes of a woman as noble and sweet and pretty as you are."

"Go it, go it, Alfred!" A delicate flush of delight had overspread her face, which was wreathed in smiles. There was a twinkling light in her eyes, and her laugh rang out sweeter and more merrily than ever. "If Jasper Long only knowed how to say nice things in your roundabout way I'd marry him if he was as poor as Job's turkey. You never have told me in so many words that—that you like my looks or—or like *me*, as for that matter; but when you get worked up, the sweetest things in heaven or earth slip out when you don't know it."

But grimly unpleasant thoughts had fastened themselves on Henley's bewildered brain, and he could only stare at her in sheer agony of suspense.

"Then you may—you *may* marry him, after all!" he said, under his breath. "You haven't fully decided yet. You may conclude that you and him—" His voice broke, and, like a dumb animal brought to bay, he stood staring at her, his mouth open, his lower lip quivering.

A great change came over her. She seemed to hesitate an instant, and then she took his inert hand in both of hers, drew it up and held it fondly against her throbbing breast. "Love—the right sort, Alfred—is the sweetest, holiest thing in all the world. It is the first breath of real heaven that men and women feel here on earth. When two people love each other—like we—like they ought to love one another, they both know it as plain as we know that sky full of stars is over us right now. They feel it in the way their pulse beats when their hands meet; they hear it in their voices when they speak; they see it in each other's eyes; they love to be together, and feel like something has gone wrong when they ain't. That's real love, Alfred, and if the man is tied up in a way God never meant him to be, and if the woman is loaded down with burdens till her fresh young shoulders are bent and ache night and day, still the thought of their love may be always in their hearts and make life seem one continual day of sunshine and music."

"Oh, Dixie, you mean—" His voice broke, and he could only stare at her as if waking from a deep dream of perplexity into complete understanding.

She nodded, kissed his hand reverently and released it. They walked on without a word between them till they reached the point where their ways parted. He would have detained her, but she said:

"No, not now, Alfred. I see somebody on your porch. I think it is your wife. We must be careful to do no wrong in the sight of the world. You owe that poor woman all the happiness you can give her. To think of what we might want would be downright selfishness. We know what we know, and that is sweet enough. Don't think of me marrying anybody. I've got Joe and my duties, and—and you know what else. I shall never complain again—never! Good-bye."

CHAPTER XXIX

Across the table at the evening meal Henley saw his wife regarding him stealthily as she served the food to him and the others. Her look had a queer, shifting, probing quality, which at any other time would have inspired investigation, but she failed to rivet his attention to-night. There were other things to think of—things as new and startling as the dawn of day must have appeared to the opening eyes of the first man. And all this had come to him. All these years he had groped in darkness, seeking and never finding till the dreams of youth were dead. But now all was lightness, full comprehension, and joy—joy which all but stifled in its clinging embrace of restitution.

After supper, with a cigar which he forgot to light, he evaded the tentative chatter of old Wrinkle and sought a rustic seat under a tree in the yard. Over the meadow, and piercing the shadows which enveloped him, shone a light from Dixie Hart's kitchen. He fancied that he saw her at work, her strong, lithe form and glorious face emitting cheer, courage, and hope to her helpless charges. He wondered if she was recalling, as he would to the day of his death, the heavenly words she had spoken at parting. The touch of her velvet lips still lay on his hand, sending through his every vein streams of sheer ecstasy. Overhead the sky arched, star-sprinkled, calm, and as full of its untold story as at the dawn of time.

Inside the kitchen near by Mrs. Henley and Mrs. Wrinkle were washing dishes. Wrinkle came from a rear door, a swill-pail in hand, and, bending under its weight, he trudged down to his pigpen at the barn. The clattering in the kitchen ceased; the light went out, to appear again in Mrs. Henley's room. Her transported husband saw her through an uncurtained window. At another time he might have wondered over her present occupation, for, standing before a mirror, she was giving unwonted attention to her toilet. She was fastening a flowing scarf about her neck, pulling at the bow to make it hang to her fancy. She applied white powder to her cheeks and the faintest hint of pink, carefully brushing her hair and pulling down her scant bangs as he could not remember having seen her do since their marriage. Next she threw a light shawl over her shoulders, experimentally drawing it up under her sharp chin, as she viewed the effect in the glass, and then settling it, with final approval, and in easier fashion, farther back upon her shoulders. He saw her raise her candle and turn her head in various ways, her eyes fixed on her twisting image. Then, with a smile of content, she blew out the candle. He saw the tiny red spark which remained on the wick standing guard where she had left it. She must be going to spend the evening somewhere and would demand his company, Henley reflected, in dismay at the thought of his present fancies being disturbed in such a prosaic way. Or perhaps she had taken a sudden whim to go to prayer-meeting—this thought prompted by the dismal clanging of a cast-iron church-bell at Chester. In that case there was a chance of escape, for she would ask Mrs. Wrinkle to accompany her.

Suddenly she appeared on the porch, and came down the steps and tripped lightly across the grass to him. He was conscious of the strange, almost weird, alteration in her manner, and was therefore partially prepared for the change in her voice and intonation.

"Is that you, Alfred?" she inquired, playfully. "I thought you might be here, it is so close inside. You can always catch a breeze on this spot if one is stirring at all."

"Yes, it's me," he answered, pulling his glance from the light across the meadow and letting it rest on her face. "Are you going out somewhere?"

She gave a little mechanical laugh. "Just because I put on this white shawl?" she jested, her thin right hand toying with her bangs. "No, there's no place to go that I know of, and if there *was* I don't feel in the humor for it to-night. Somehow I felt like I wanted to talk to you. I hope Ma and Pa will go to bed; they are getting to be lots of bother in one way and another. They mean well, the dear things, but they are old and childish."

She sat down on the seat beside him and rested her elbow on its back, her face toward him. "I saw you walking home with Dixie Hart this evening," she remarked. "Did she say how that boy is getting on?"

"Why"—there was just the faintest pause on Henley's part; he was conscious that he caught his breath, and that a warm, objectionable flush was stealing over him—"why, I think he is mending purty fast. I—I reckon there is no secret about it—Miss Dixie says she's adopted him by process of law."

"Good gracious! You don't say! Why, that makes *three* on her hands. Well, she's a remarkable girl, Alfred, *and she's pretty.* Don't you think so?" She was toying with the fringe of her shawl, and yet she seemed to hang upon his answer as she gazed straight at him.

"Y-e-s," Henley said. "She really has undertaken a lot, but I reckon she'll pull through, someway or other."

"Pa says she's managed to get out of old Welborne's debt," Mrs. Henley went on, taking her knee in her hands and lifting her foot from the ground and swinging it to and fro. "Lots of folks thought he'd finally sell her out of house and home. I didn't think, myself, that she'd ever pay out, but she seems to have succeeded. I give her full credit for all she is, Alfred. I'm not the sort of woman that underrates another just to be doing it. She's a stanch friend of yours. It is a good deal for me to admit, but she gave me a straight talk once that set me to thinking. I've never let on, but what she said made a deep impression on me."

The speaker paused, as if waiting for her words to take root and sprout in his comprehension, but he said nothing—only sat staring at her, as if trying to divine her subtle drift.

"It was while you was away, Alfred," she continued, "and—and there was so much talk about what I was doing at that time, you remember, to—to show respect for Dick's memory. For a girl as young as she is, she said some powerful strong things. She thought I wasn't acting right toward you, and told me so to my face. I went on with my plans, but I've often thought of her advice. You may have noticed that I hain't talked as much about the—the monument as I did, and I haven't been to see it as often as I used to. Dixie Hart made me look at it from the outside to some extent, and with that I began to be more considerate of you. I saw you wasn't the same as you was at first—I might say, as you was all along when you and Dick was both taking me out, and as you was—for that matter—just before and after me and you got married. In fact, Alfred, you are getting to be a sort o' puzzle to me. Even to-night at supper you seemed to be in some sort of far-off dream or other. You'd lift up a fork or a spoon and hold it a long time before you'd put it in your mouth, and once I caught you gazing straight at me with the blankest look I ever saw on a human face. You don't seem the same. I don't mean that you haven't got a *healthy* look, for that would bother me a lot, but you are—well, you are just different."

"Don't you worry," Henley heard himself saying, aghast at the cliffs and chasms ahead of him. "Don't worry about me if I seem to have my mind off at times. I've made some trades lately, and got the best end of 'em. I'm a natural trader—a born trader, Hettie. They say it is like a mild form of gambling. Just yesterday I made a deal with an old chap—"

"I don't want to talk about trading and swapping, and the like," the woman broke in, firmly. "Besides, no sort of ordinary business ever made a man look like you've looked lately. You used to be sorter active and nervous, but now you set and brood with an odd, reddish look on your face. It ain't natural. It looks like you've resigned yourself to—to something that you didn't exactly like before, and it don't please me to see you that way. Pa's noticed it and mentioned it two or three times."

"There's nothing in the world the matter with me," Henley declared, actually alarmed at the incongruity of his position.

"Alfred," the woman said, contritely, and she bent forward and peered up into his face, "you are a sight better man than I am a woman, and—"

"Shucks!"

"You may say shucks if you want to, but wait till I get through. I reckon, as women go, in the general run, I'm a queer sort of female. I never was just like other girls. For one thing, I always wanted what was out of my reach; not getting a thing, or even having doubts about it, always made me want it more than anything else. I reckon that is why Dick kind o' fascinated me: the girls was all after him, and he seemed a sort of prize to be had at any cost. Even after we was married, as maybe you know, he kept me worried with his attentions to some of the old crowd of girls. But enough of that. When he died and you come back, begging, as you did, to have me consider you, I finally give in and took you. But that wasn't all. I had stood up before a preacher in the house of God and agreed to be your wife and helpmeet, but, as I now see it, I didn't do my duty by you. I made the mistake, I reckon, of thinking too much about what I owed to the dead and gone, and I went so far as to do things in public that actually driv' you away from home and caused folks to laugh at you and make remarks. Dixie Hart was right; I wasn't toting fair with you, and I want to tell you to-night, Alfred, that I see my error, and—and I am plumb sorry."

He turned upon her resolutely. She was looking down, and he fancied she was about to shed such tears as she had often shed early in their married life when Dick Wrinkle's name was mentioned. He had none of the old chivalrous sympathy which such a demonstration had once evoked, nor any of the old indulgence for a love which he had hoped to see die, and yet, just from his passionate contact with Dixie Hart, he was full of comprehension and pity for his wife's plight—at least, as he now saw it.

"Listen to me, Hettie," he began, and his voice shook with deep feeling. "You've been right all along. Don't you bother about that. It was *me* that was crooked. In this life folks don't love in the highest and best way but once—not but once in a lifetime. Dick Wrinkle was your first and only abiding fancy. The feeling that made you turn me down and take him when you was a girl and I was a big blockhead of a boy was born of God in heaven. I was the one that was making a mistake when I come and begged you to marry me while that pure thing was still alive in your heart. A love like that never dies; it is too sweet and glorious to die. I see now, too, that you was plumb right about wanting to take care of his mammy and daddy, and about wanting that sermon preached, and about erecting a lasting monument to commemorate his name. You had to do all them things because they was part and parcel of you yourself, and the constancy God planted in you. I can say honestly that I'm glad you still love him. You wouldn't be a high sort of a woman if you did change. Death can't separate folks that love; they go on and on—side by side, hand in hand, heart to heart—through all eternity."

She actually gasped. She rose, and stood staring toward the door, a deep frown on her face; she shrugged her shoulders; she clinched her fists; she rapped the ground sharply with her foot; then she slowly bent down over him, resting her thin left hand on his broad shoulder while she peered with a stare of would-be incredulity into his enraptured face.

"Look at me, Alfred!" she cried, in a rasping tone. "*You know you don't mean one single word of all you've just said!*"

"Why, I do," he insisted, blandly. "As God is my judge, I do. There ain't no such thing as *two* loves—a first and a second. When the real thing comes to a body he knows it. A feller could be blinded for a time, I reckon, in hot-blooded youth, while he was in close pursuit of a thing that kept slipping away from him, as was my case when Dick and me was going nip and tuck to see which could get ahead; but the genuine, real thing is as different as—as day from night."

She drew herself up straight, and heaved a deep, lingering sigh. "I don't believe you mean a word of what you say," she repeated. "It ain't natural for a man who is as jealous as—as you always have been even—even of the dead—to set up and talk that way."

"Jealous?" he said, half musingly. "I don't think I'm a jealous man. Anyways, I don't think a feller would have the right to be jealous of a man that was dead and under ground. As I look at it now, I don't think a man has a right, in the best sense, to marry a widow; and in the same way a widower has no right to lay aside his past memories if they are the right sort. They ought to be his best company in his loneliness. Of course, now that you and me are linked together by law and religion, we owe it to the community we live in to do our duty and make the best—I mean, to live along as friendly and harmoniously as we can."

She sank down to the seat again, and sat staring at him fixedly. Presently, seeing that he was not going to resume speaking, she said: "I believe, on my soul, Alfred, you have plumb lost your senses. I may or may not be responsible for it; you may have let all this talk about Dick and my—my thinking about him prey on your mind till it is unhinged. Why, what I done about his grave and memory wasn't anything but respect that was due to him, and has nothing to do with our agreement. You've hurt my feelings, Alfred—you actually have."

She rose suddenly, and, with her handkerchief to her eyes, she started toward the door. She moved slowly, as if she expected him to call her back, as he had frequently done in the past; but he seemed to be oblivious of her presence and not to have heard her last plaintive appeal, for he sat gazing at the light in Dixie Hart's cottage like an unwakable man. She came slowly back, now with stiff, indignant strides—strides which dug deeply into the unoffending turf.

"You certainly are either crazy or a plumb fool!" she fired at him. "You said once that folks hinted that I was cracked in the upper story from the way I acted, but the shoe is on the other foot now. If folks don't say you are out of your head it is because they ain't here to listen to your meandering. A man that will set up and hint to a wife who he loves, and always has loved, that he's willing for her to still care for and cherish another person—I say a man like that is in need of a doctor's advice."

"Well, I was just trying to justify you and your acts," Henley answered in pained retaliation, "and to show you that I had no ill-will in any shape or form. You loved Dick in the right sort of way, and I'm just man enough to lay no obstacle whatever in your track. In the next life you and Dick will be reunited, and all things will be made straight. I don't want to fuss with you over it, Hettie. This life is too beautiful, if it is looked at right, to waste time in jowering. You and me can live in harmony from now on if you'll just be reasonable and not fly off the handle when a feller is doing his level best to arrive at some sort of common meeting-ground. All these years I've been fretting and trying to run a race with a dead man when I could have been in more active business. I've give in at last, and I'm going to stay give in. The truth is, I'm just beginning to live. For the first time in my life I'm in sympathy with true, natural-born, well-mated lovers. If they are tied together, all well and good; but if they are parted by some hook or crook, then they are to be pitied, but still they've got the satisfaction of knowing—well, of knowing what they know—that's all."

"Well, I know *one* thing," Mrs. Henley said, and she turned away, angrily. "I know you are simply daft—you've lost every grain of sense you ever had."

"I might have known she'd twist the thing all upside-down and never see it right," Henley mused, as he watched her ascend the steps, cross the porch, and disappear in the house. "I thought that view would hit her just right, but, contrary as she always was, she sees fit to disagree. I reckon if she knew everything there *would* be a row. Huh, I wouldn't risk that with her. She can hold her funeral conclaves, and build monuments to another fellow as high as a church-steeple, and expects me to swallow the dose, but just let me kind o' look about a little, and I'm a fit subject for a madhouse."

CHAPTER XXX

The next morning at breakfast Mrs. Henley seemed to have lost all memory of the angry scene on the grass the evening before. Her countenance was overcast with an expression that her husband would have designated as one of pleasure had he been given to the analysis of her facial phenomena, a pursuit he had long since given up as futile and unprofitable. Her dress, too, showed unusual care, and a crisp, fresh-ironed jauntiness that jerked him back to the past with rather disagreeable suddenness. Amid the white ruffles at her neck she had pinned a large, full-blown rose, and her manner toward the others was a fragile sort of graciousness which would have been a delight if one could have felt that it was permanent. As a rule she passed Henley's coffee to him through the hands of the two Wrinkles, but this morning she rose and brought it round to him, remarking that she had fixed it just to his liking. Old Wrinkle, as his intimates—and many others—knew, was not backward in the use of his tongue, and yet there was something in the unwonted ceremony of the present meal that silenced him. The old fellow, however, was making a record-breaking use of his eyes. Henley saw him taking in every detail of his former daughter-in-law's appearance and mood, and smiling all too knowingly for anybody's comfort as he munched and gulped.

After breakfast Henley was at the gate ready to walk to the

store when Wrinkle came to him and clutched his arm familiarly.

"Wait, I'll go 'long with you," he said. "I want to talk to you some, anyway. Alf, did you ever since the world was made—"

But his words were lost on the morning air, for Mrs. Henley was calling to her husband from the porch, where she stood smiling at him from the honeysuckle vines.

"Don't go yet!" she called out, and she tripped down the steps toward him. She paused at a rose-bush on the way and plucked a bright-red bud, and, bringing it to him, she began to fasten it on the lapel of his coat. "You are getting entirely too slouchy," she mumbled, a pin in her mouth. "You never used to wear such dowdy clothes. You've got to spruce up—ain't he, Pa?"

"Well, it ain't Sunday, nor camp-meetin'," Wrinkle made answer. "He looks well enough for every day; he'd look odd with a long, jimswinger coat on in that dusty store with all them one-gallus mossbacks he makes his livin' out of. Them fellers 'u'd laugh at 'im an' say he was gittin' rich too fast at the'r expense."

As red as the flower with which she was trying to adorn him, Henley pushed the bud away. "I don't want it," he said. "I never was any hand to put on such things. I'd be a purty sight, now, wouldn't I—walkin' in town with a flower-garden pinned to me?"

She submitted to his refusal, deftly twining the stem of the flower into the cheap lace about her neck.

"I've got a favor to ask of you, Alfred," she said, sweetly, "and I don't want you to refuse it, either. This time I know what I want, and I must have it."

"Well, what is it?" he asked, his attention diverted from her by the hungry stare with which old Wrinkle was awaiting the climax of the little scene.

"Why, I want you to take me to drive."

"To drive!" Henley repeated, as much surprised as if she had asked him for a trip to Europe, and he heard old Wrinkle laugh out impulsively and saw him dig his heel into the earth, as, with lowered head, he sought to hide a broad and too-knowing smile which had captured his facile mouth. "To drive?"

"Yes, Alfred, it has been a long time since I've seen anything of the country hereabouts. Why, I've almost forgot how it looks, and this is the best time of the year. It would do us both good to take a little jaunt every day in the cool of the evening. We used to go out that way just before we was married, and for a while afterward, and I want to do it again. We've got wrong, somehow. We are not living like we ought to. I say it here before Pa because I mean it, and know he will see it as I do. Don't you think he ought to take me, Pa?"

"Well, I don't know as I'd sanction your ridin' 'round *late in the evenin'*." Wrinkle now showed no hint of even hidden merriment. "You mought git delayed beyond the usual time and supper would hang fire. Havin' fun an' startin' in to do courtin' over agin is all right an' proper if a body *feels* thataway, but doin' it on a starvation basis ain't good for the health, if it is for the senti*ments*."

"Oh, I'll see that you don't suffer, you old, greedy thing," Mrs. Henley said, playfully, and caught her husband's arm. "I want you to hitch up, and get a new lap-robe, and take me to-day—this very evening."

"To-day? Good gracious, what's got into you, Hettie?" Henley stammered, glancing here and there in sheer helplessness. "I couldn't get off from business. I've got my hands full of deals of one kind and another. Driving around is all right for—for young couples that are sparking, and even for fresh-married ones, but there comes a time when all sensible folks ought to settle down to the—the enjoyment of home life."

"I see—you have changed." Mrs. Henley now drew herself up austerely and glared at him coldly. "You think I'm well enough as a drudge about a dirty old farm-house, but not fit company for riding and driving like any woman as young as I am is entitled to. You never thought that sort of a thing was too frivolous before we married, but now you sneer at it. Well, you just wait till I give you a chance to take me anywhere again. I lowered my pride to ask it this time, but I won't remind you again. No, sir."

With a cloud of fury on her face she whirled, and whisked into the house.

"Come on, Alf," old Wrinkle advised, with a look of amusement in his eyes. "Let 'er sweat it out alone. She's jest tryin' to work on you, anyway. She'll be as smooth as goose-grease by night. Looky here, Alf, I'm an old man, an' you are jest a boy by comparison," he went on, as they walked down the road together, "but what I don't know about women you don't know about hosses, and you know a lot. I've learned women inch by inch all through life. I reckon I got on to it by lyin' around the fire on cold or wet days and listenin' to 'em. They say some men make a study of rocks, ores, plants, an' bugs, but my hobby always was females. Why, I almost know what turn a baby gal will take when it grows up. It was a sort of funny game with me. I set out to see if I'd ever see a woman do or say a sensible thing, an' I hain't won yet. Now, you may not know it, my boy, but you are in hot water, an' it is deep enough to float yore whiskers. You had married life down about right till just a few days ago. You could go and come whenever you liked an' nobody axed any questions. You was about the freest married man I ever knowed, white or black, yaller or red, but yore day of reckoning has come. I knowed some'n was wrong last night when you an' Het had that powwow in the yard, an' I knowed the sun was shinin' too bright this mornin' to do yore crop any good except to burn it up. I know Het. I've watched her bury one man an' start in with another, an' if you had been a worryin' feller she'd have had you mouldin' in the ground long go. As long as Hettie could worry you she was happy. Part of that grave-rock celebration was because she 'lowed it bothered you. I couldn't help hearin' the talk last night. You both spoke louder than you thought, an' the wind was blowin' my way. Why, man, when you set thar last night an' told that woman that her undyin' love for Dick was holy an' godly an' a thing to be kept in a glass case an' looked at every hour in the day—I say when you throwed all that guff at her you sealed yore doom. Them words kicked every prop from under her, an' down she come with a flop that knocked the breath out of all her calculations. She looks fresh and rosy this morning, but she rolled and tumbled the most of the night. I don't sleep sound, an' I heard her. I wondered what step she'd take, an' the breakfast-table grins an' rose-bud and buggy-ride proposition showed her hand. This mad spell is part of the game. She has set in to make you do your courtin' over ag'in, an' you'll find that about as unnatural as wearin' yore vest under yore shirt. No man can court the same woman twice an' put his heart in the job, but a woman is just so constituted that she could *have* it done over an' over by one or a dozen men. I reckon, as Scriptur' says, it is more blessed to give than to receive, but a man 'u'd rather not be blessed in the time to come than to have to make eyes an' say sweet things when he ain't feelin' jest right. Now, I'll turn back; I jest walked out with you to give you what advice I could. Git the bit in yore jaw an' pull yore way steady, an' after a while she'll git tired an' quit naggin' you."

That morning, near noon, as Henley was busy at his work in the rear of the store, Cahews came back to him with a mild look of surprise on his face.

"Your wife is out in front in her uncle Ben's carriage," he announced. "She's dressed for travel—got three or four valises in with her. Warren, must have sent over after her; the team looks like it's been on the go for several hours."

Henley found her in the luxurious seat behind the higher one on which the colored driver, in a battered silk top-hat, sat holding the reins over a handsome pair of blacks. She looked at him coldly as, hatless and coatless, he hurried out to her.

"What's this?" he asked, half playfully. "You ain't going to vamoose the ranch, are you?"

"Uncle Ben's sick," she answered, stiffly. "He sent a note by Ned. He didn't say for me to come, but he hinted at it several times. I'd show you what he wrote, but we haven't time to spare. I packed up as quick as I could. We'll stop at the half-way house for dinner."

"Ben hain't dangerous, is he?" Henley asked, his foot on the brass-tipped hub of the fore-wheel, his hand on the arm of the seat she occupied.

"I don't know whether he is or not," the speaker pulled down the veil under her hat-brim and avoided her husband's eyes, "but he's lonely and heartbroken over the way that unprincipled woman has treated him, and he needs petting and nursing and some company in that big, gloomy house to take his mind off his trouble and humiliation."

"He ought never to have got mixed up with her." Henley was recalling Wrinkle's sage remarks. "Dealing with a woman you've known all her life is risky enough, without going as far as Ben did for an opportunity to get slapped in the face. But he ought to be thankful he found her out in time."

"Finding her out ain't going to lighten the blow." Mrs. Henley shrugged her shoulders. "When a man—or a *woman*, for that matter—has full faith in a person, and finds out that the person ain't anything like he used to be, why, a body hardly knows what *to* think. I'm glad I'm going away, Alfred. You showed me this morning when I give you that chance to take me about a little here and there that you are changed. When I'm away you'll realize what you've missed, and I'll be glad of it. Absence, on my side, is the medicine you need to restore your senses."

"Well, we'll all certainly miss you." Henley was too honest—at least in domestic matters—to know that his assertion was insincere, and accustomed as he was in his dealings among men to assume exactly the shade of tone or set of face that went best with a statement, he now had as complete an air of regret and discomfort as the most exacting of wives could have wished.

"Well, I'm getting the drive I asked for," was her parting shot, and she leaned over and gave him a cold, stiff hand. "I'm taking it all by myself, as most married women have to do if they don't seek the attention of other men. But I'm going to do my duty to a human sufferer, and in that I'll get my reward."

He walked back to the store thoughtfully. "She's gone!" he said to himself. "She's ripping mad and got it in for me, that's certain. She's begun on a new line, and I'll bet she makes me smoke before she's through with me. I know what she wants well enough, but somehow I just can't do it. I might at one time, but I couldn't now to save my neck from the loop. The old man is plumb right. When a feller's love gets cold on the inside he can't warm it up by external applications. He's a matrimonial misfit, and the sooner he realizes it and is resigned the better he'll feel."

CHAPTER XXXI

"Well, the old gal's gone," Wrinkle remarked that day at sundown when Henley came in at the gate and found him seated on a dismantled beehive in the yard. "I reckon you seed 'er spin through town. For a woman goin' out as a sick-nuss or spiritual comforter to a chap kicked by a high-steppin' filly she certainly had a supply of frills and ruffles. Them valises was packed as tight as a compressed cotton-bale. She left behind her one solid wail of woe. Jane is afraid she'll never gratify yore taste for grub as well as Het did, an' she's in thar now humpin' herself to contrive new concoct-tions. Het kept boarders long enough to git stingy, an' I told my wife to turn over a new leaf for a change. I driv' a fat chicken in a fence-corner just now, and held its legs while she chopped its spout off. She knows how to fry 'em, an' if she kin see well enough to pick the pin-feathers off it will be all right. I'd put her biscuits agin any ever baked."

After a really enjoyable supper Henley went out under the trees to get the fresh air which, in invigorating gusts, swept up the valley along the mountain-range. He told himself that his reason for wandering down toward his barn was to avoid meeting Wrinkle, who he knew would soon appear from the kitchen, where he was helping his wife wash the dishes. He was aware, of course, that Dixie Hart's cow-lot adjoined his stable-yard, and he knew that it was the hour at which she went to milk, and yet he would not have admitted that he strolled thither in the hope of meeting her, but, nevertheless, he went.

He saw her entering the lot-gate, a bright tin pail in her hand, and he shielded himself with a jutting corner of his wagon-shed and watched her graceful approach through the dusk. He saw her get the tub of cow's food from the crib and give it to the animal, and then he heard her scream out, and, following her startled eyes, he saw that, having failed to close the gate behind her, the cow's calf had entered and was rushing to its mother. With an ejaculation of impatience Dixie threw her arms about the calf's neck and tried to pull it from the cow's bag, but it was of no avail. The strong young beast would wriggle from her clutch and dart back to its supper.

"Oh, you brat, you are stealing all the milk!" Dixie cried. She picked up a dried corn-stalk, and with it belabored the sleek, brown back of the calf, but she might as well have used an ostrich-plume for all the effect it had on the hungry animal.

It was then that Henley, laughing heartily, sprang over the fence and came to her assistance.

"Let me have the little scamp," he said. And he bent down and took the squirming beast into his strong arms and lifted it bodily from the ground. "Now, where do you want him put?" he asked, as he stood swaying back and forth in his effort to control the wriggling prisoner.

"Over the fence!" she cried, and stood panting in admiration of his cool skill and strength as he walked to the fence and dropped the calf on the other side. He then fastened the gate and came back to her.

"You are doing a man's work, anyway," he said, looking into

her flushed face, "and you ought to call a halt. Life is too short to spend it as you are doing."

"It's all very well for you men to talk that way," Dixie retorted, as she pushed her milking-stool to the side of the cow and sat down with the pail between her knees, "but women, as well as men, want to live, and if there's any way to live without work, and plenty of it, I'd like to find out about it."

"It seems to me that a feller by the name of Long was offering to point out a way to you," he said, with a forced smile.

The back part of her uncovered head was turned toward him. Her shapely hands and bare, tapering arms gleamed like yellow marble through the dusk. He smelled the delightful odor of the warm milk as her deft fingers sent it ringing into the pail.

"Yes, he was offering me a job," he heard her say with a sarcastic little chuckle. "He wanted me to quit working at my old place and set in for him, and nothing particular was said about raising my wages."

"And what are you going to answer him, I wonder?" Henley inquired, as he bent down over her that the noise of the squirting milk might not drown her reply.

She flashed a glance at him; there was an ineffable shimmer in her long-lashed eyes; she made a comical little grimace. "I've said the last word between me and him," she answered. "I got a humble letter from him yesterday begging my pardon for what he'd tried to do, and saying he'd behave like a gentleman from now on, if I'd only let him come out again."

"Well, it was time he was apologizing," Henley cried. "For a little I'd have—well!"

Dixie smiled and looked at him eagerly. "Did that make you mad, Alfred—really mad?"

"I don't think I ever was madder in all my life." He walked unsuspectingly into her trap. "I driv' away soon after or I don't know what would have happened. The more I thought about it the madder I got. Once I started to turn round and go back. I would, if I hadn't thought he was such a weak fool. It ain't done with; I can't think about it without wanting to mash something. I reckon me 'n him had better stay apart."

"We ain't going to have any row about that, Alfred," Dixie said, quite seriously. "You know you would bear a lot rather than have folks say a—a married man was taking up for me in that way. If you ever meet him, and the thing comes up, you must remember that one thing. My character's all I've got, Alfred; if you are what I think you are, you'd think twice before compromising me like that. Carrie Wade *would* talk then, sure enough. Married men don't go about having fisticuffs over girls that live next door to 'em without folks wondering, and I tell you I'm like that fellow Caesar's wife—I'm too good to be wondered about in any shape or form."

"I know it—God knows I know it," Henley responded, under his trembling breath. "You needn't be afraid, Dixie. I'll take care. But you didn't tell me what answer you made to—to Long's apology, or whether you was going to let him come again or not."

"I wrote him a pretty nice sort of a letter." She was laughing as she bent over her pail, but he didn't know it. "You see, Alfred, I was afraid you had hurt the poor fellow's feelings that day, and I thought *somebody* ought to be mild-tempered. I told 'im that wasn't no place or time, anyway, to kiss a girl—right in front of the door of her house—that a girl naturally liked to be wheedled awhile before she set in on such familiar terms, and that if it had been a *third* visit, instead of jest the *second*, that I'd have taken him for a stroll down by the creek. There's a foot-log there plumb hid by willows, Alfred, and I always thought it would be fine to set on it with your feet dangling over the stream and see two sweethearts reflected in the clear water, his arm round her waist and her head on his shoulder. Now, that's the sort of thing this chicken has always had a yearning for, and—" Dixie tittered inaudibly in the pail and said nothing more.

He had drawn himself erect and stood as full of despair as the night was full of darkness. She heard him utter a low groan, but that was all. She peered up at him stealthily, and then, with a face warm with content, she resumed her work. He stood silent till she rose.

"Now that dratted calf can come to the second table," she said, in the most uneventful tone imaginable. "Alfred, will you please let him in? He's about to butt the gate down."

He walked stiffly across the lot and opened the gate. The calf shot past him like an animated cannon-ball. He met her as, with the pail on her arm, she had turned toward the cottage.

"I'm too big a fool to ever understand you, Dixie," he gulped, as they paused face to face. "Since me and you parted the—the other day I—I've been plumb crazy. I got to thinking things that are too far off—too nigh the gates of heaven to be possible—things that made all my troubles fly away, but now I see it was just in my imagination. I'm going to be sensible from now on if it kills me. You can't keep on in the miserable way you are living. You've always thought you'd escape the worst by marrying, and I have no right because this here hell is raging in me to tell you who, or who not, to take. I'd rather see you—you dead in your coffin than the—the wife of that silly fool. But that's your business—that's—that's—" His voice broke and he stood quivering, his strong face torn into shreds by despair.

"You dear, dear boy!" Dixie said, laying her disengaged hand gently on his arm, her own face suffused with a faint glow of uncontrollable tenderness. "I'm only a girl—a natural one, Alfred—and I'm so hungry for love that I try to make you say those things, wrong as they may be. Don't you know when I'm joking? Listen and I'll tell you the truth. I wrote Jasper Long that it was all right about what he'd tried to do. I'd not hold any grudge against him, but that I knew I never could care for him, and I hoped he'd never come to see me again."

"You—you wrote 'im that?" Henley gasped.

"Oh, Alfred," she cried, as she released his arm, "don't you know that I could not marry a man I don't love? Don't you know what has been growing up in me all this time in which you with your unhappiness and me with my misfortune have been drawed so close together? Every night, as I say my prayers and call on God to help you, I wonder what He meant by the bonds with which He's tied me to you hand and foot, heart and soul. When you was trying to find me a husband, and fighting for my legal rights, you thought it was just friendship, and so did I. The world we live in counts it one of the blackest of sins for a married man and an unmarried girl to love each other, but you know we didn't do wrong intentionally. We was as innocent and unsuspecting as lambs in the fold. Right when we thought we was doing our duty the ground was slipping from under us, and we was clutching each other to keep from falling. Now, that's all I'm going to say. I shall never marry any man while this feeling is in my breast. That would be wrong for a dead certainty, let folks say what they please about the other. Your wife went off to-day, didn't she? I saw Warren's carriage drive up and knew something was going to happen; then the old man come over and told us about it."

She had passed through the gate on her way home, and he remained at her side. "I want to stop in after supper, and—and see how little Joe is," he said, hesitatingly.

"No, not to-night, Alfred," she returned, firmly. "He'd like to see you, but don't come the first night after—after she went away. We really must be sensible. Folks don't understand—they never could understand—and we've got to think of them. I may have done wrong in letting you know how I feel, but it will end there."

"I see, I understand," he said, reverently. "They shall never talk about you while I'm alive. Good-night."

He walked slowly toward the lights in the farm-house. He heard the two Wrinkles, with cracked voices, singing a hymn as they sat in their rocking-chairs on the porch. The very stars seemed to hang lower from the darkling mystery overhead; he felt light enough, in his boundless content, to rise to them and drink at their twinkling founts. His soul seemed to swell to the point of bursting. "Oh, God, I thank Thee!" he said, deep within himself. "I thank Thee!"

CHAPTER XXXII

With Henley the next day passed like some fascinating dream. He was busy in various ways as usual, and yet scarcely for a moment were his thoughts away from his new-found delight. He had no hope, bound as he was to another to whom he owed his honor, of ever being closer to Dixie than he was now, and yet there was something in the very purity of his possession of her heart and in her willing sacrifice of so much for the principle which guided her that lifted him into new and untrodden fields of spiritual ecstasy.

It was near sunset, and he stood in the front doorway of the store, looking out into the quiet square, when, to his surprise and with a tumultuous throbbing of his heart, he saw Dixie pass with a letter in her hand on the way to the post-office. She was on the opposite side of the street and did not glance in his direction, and he made no effort to attract her attention. As she passed along by old Welborne's diminutive office Henley noticed that Hank Bradley, who had been drinking about town through the day, came from the doorway and bowed to her conspicuously, his slouch-hat almost sweeping the pavement as he bent downward. She passed on with a bare nod and quickened her step till she entered the post-office, a few doors farther on.

There was something in this, remembering as he did that Bradley had persistently pursued the girl with attentions, which not only angered Henley, but filled him with concern for her safety. The half-drunken brute might take it into his head to follow her down the lonely road which she had to traverse to reach her house. So, with these things in mind, Henley told Cahews that he was going home, and he walked out to the first densely shaded part of the road and, retiring into the bushes, sat on the grass, determined that he would at least follow in her wake till she was out of danger of being accosted.

The sunlight had quite disappeared now, and the fringe of dusk was settling over the silent wood. He was growing impatient, and wondering if anything could have happened to detain Dixie in town, when he beard voices down the road. He stood up and peered through the curtain of wild vines which hung between him and the open. He could see no one, and the voices were so indistinct that he failed to recognize them. But the conversing individuals were evidently rapidly approaching, for their voices were growing louder. Both seemed to be talking at the same time, and Henley was pretty sure that it was a man and a woman. Then the coarser voice drowned the finer and fainter, and Henley recognized it as belonging to Bradley.

"I've been put off and fooled and deviled by you as long as I'm going to be!" the brute cried out. "You are a beautiful young devil, that's what you are. I've offered you every inducement a man could offer. If I'm drunk, you are the cause of it. I can't think of nothing but you—you, with your maddening eyes of fire and cheeks full of hot blood. I want you. I want you every minute I draw breath. You must listen to reason. I've got plenty of money. We could live like a king and queen on the fat of the land, as God means men and women to live, full of joy and life. Stop, you've got to kiss me! We are alone; nobody is about."

"Let me pass, I tell you, let me pass!" Dixie's terrified voice rose to a shriek, and then it ended in a smothered sound as if a hand had been placed over her mouth. Henley was sure they were struggling and he sprang into the road. Swaying back and forth against the dark background of the wood, he saw Bradley with the girl in his arms. Dixie had ducked her head to avoid his repulsive lips, and the assailant's back was turned to Henley. With the bound of a panther he reached them just as Dixie was eluding Bradley's embrace and trying to release her hand, to which he clung with a grip of steel. Neither of the two saw Henley, and it was a crushing blow from the storekeeper's fist against the side of Bradley's head that showed him what he had to contend with. He had scarcely taken another breath before Henley struck him again with the force of a sledgehammer squarely between the eyes. Bradley staggered, swayed, grew limp, and went down. His eyes rolled back in his head till the whites were exposed. He quivered through his whole form, drew his shoulders up once, and then lay still. Henley, his hands clinched, the eyes of an infuriated animal in his head, his great mouth hanging open, stood over the fallen man.

"Thank God, oh, thank God!" It was Dixie's voice behind him, and he turned to see her at the edge of the road, her face as white as death could have made it, her hands convulsively clasped in front of her. "Oh, Alfred, Alfred, if you hadn't come—" She came to him, but, primitive man that he now was, there seemed to be no place in him for tenderness. His great breast heaved, his lips quivered, his eyes bulged from their sockets. She was about to put out her hands in an effort toward soothing him when, glancing toward Bradley, she uttered a scream of alarm. He was rising, a drawn revolver in his hand. Quick as his approach had been, Henley's next movement was quicker; before the weapon was fairly poised he had knocked it from Bradley's grasp. Contemptuously kicking it out of his reach, Henley gave the man a sharp blow with his fist; and while Bradley was impotently shielding his face with his arms, Henley picked up the revolver, cocked it, and directed it toward him.

"Apologize to this lady," he said, huskily, "and do it quick, for I'm going to blow your brains out. Down on your knees, you dirty whelp—down, I say!"

"I'll be damned if I do."

"Then take your medicine, and may God have mercy on your dirty soul!" And, as Bradley screamed out and held up his hands in sudden, overpowering fear, Dixie sprang forward and wrested the weapon from Henley's hand.

"No," she said—"no, you sha'n't kill him. Hank Bradley, go! Go, I tell you! I won't have blood spilt over me. I've got a right to demand that, and I *do* demand it. Go, I tell you! I'm going to keep this gun to protect myself with. I live in a country of outlaws, and I'm going to defend myself from now on. Go! What are you waiting for?"

Muttering and growling in sullen defiance, Bradley got to his feet, his battered face and eyes swollen.

"You've got the best of the game so far," he snarled at Henley, "but it's not ended. You'll hear from me."

"I'll tell you one thing, Hank," Henley said, as he glared at the man, "you are leaving here now, but if I ever meet you face to face in town, or anywhere else, I'll kill you as sure as there's a God. I've said it, and I mean it—I'll kill you as I would a snake."

Henley and Dixie stood in silence and watched him as he entered the wood and strode farther into its depths. They heard the cracking of dry twigs under his feet as he steadily receded, the sound of his untoward progress growing fainter and fainter in the distance.

"I'll be sorry to the day of my death that I didn't kill him," Henley panted, the wild fury unabated in his voice, face, and eyes. "Why, he was treating you like a dog; he actually proposed, actually dared to hint that his dirty money—my God! and I let him walk off on his two feet."

"I know, I know," Dixie muttered, soothingly, and she forced a smile as she looked at the revolver in her hand, "and oh, Alfred, I'm just girl enough to be glad you come as you did, and even to see it work you up like it has; but at a time like this a woman must act and think for a man when he is all wrought up and half out of his head. I couldn't prevent what he done. He was waiting for me at the end of the street and insisted on walking with me. I begged him to go back, but he was talking so loud and rough that I was afraid folks would make remarks. I hated to call for help; I'm neither sugar nor salt, and am able to care for myself. But I'd never seen him as drunk as that before, and, well, if you hadn't come—"

She shuddered convulsively. He looked at her wrist, which she kept touching with her handkerchief; the skin was broken and the flesh bruised where Bradley had clutched it.

"My God!" Henley took it gently in his throbbing hands and looked at it with glaring eyes, "and I let him walk away! He's free now, but, as there is a God overhead, I'll—"

"No, stop, listen—hear me, Alfred!" Dixie entreated, allowing her hand to rest passively in his. "There are some things you men make more of than us women. I reckon it's your natures to be that way. Now, me 'n you have got to settle this thing for good and all right here and now, for if I have to go home to-night with the fear that there is to be bloodshed on my account I'd be more miserable than I ever was. Last night, Alfred, after I left you at the lot-gate, I went home and done my work with an odd feeling on me, I waited on Joe; I fixed the beds and made my mother and aunt lie down, and then I was all alone and had time to reflect over—over me and you. I reckon my thoughts had taken a new turn by just one little remark of yours. Alfred, it was you asking to come over on the—the first—the very first night after your wife left. A girl will do a lot of headstrong things when her pity and admiration are worked up for a man she loves, but now and then, if she's sensible, some powerful small thing will make her think. Alfred, I saw the brink we was standing on, as plain as if we was on a high cliff and there was nothing between us and the bottom, and all sorts of forces was blinding us and pulling and shoving us over. I'm a good, pure girl—no purer, in thought or act, ever lived, and yet I've been in an inch of having a bad character saddled on me for the rest of my life. As I looked at little Joe asleep in his bed and remembered that I had given my word and bond to the law to make a worthy mother to him, as I looked at them two old women who think I'm already robed in the garb of paradise, and realized that one mischievous word started about me and you would ruin me and all the others—I say, when that thought come to me I wondered how I could, in my right senses, have talked to you as I have and let you know my feelings. I can't believe that it is wrong to—to feel as I do toward you, because I was drawed into it by things that I couldn't avoid. You was always trying to help me, and was so sweet and good and manly and respectful that, knowing about your own troubles, I couldn't help myself. Then I saw you loved—liked me, and the—the pure, hungry joy of it—the dazzling glory of it, bound me hand and foot, and I plunged in without thought or caution. But we are cooler now, Alfred, and we've got to keep our heads. To begin with, you have got to let this matter with that scamp drop. I demand it; my good name demands it; I haven't given you the right to fight battles over me, and I don't intend to. I'd rather let that man, repulsive as he is, kiss me a dozen times than have to hang my head before them I love. They would take Joe from me; it would hurry my mother to her grave; it would be a living death. See, here's the revolver." She, forced a white smile as she slid it into the pocket of his coat. "Dispose of it; I don't want to be reminded of what's happened. I'm giving it to you because I can trust you. I know you'll do as I ask."

"Do as you ask me—good God!" Henley bit his lip till the blood ran against his fine teeth, and he fell to quivering. "I see what you mean, and I know you are right, and yet, and yet, I couldn't have let him walk off like that if I hadn't thought—"

"I know—I saw that in your eye," Dixie went on, firmly—"and that's why I'm making you promise now. No matter what happens, Alfred, you are going to avoid that man—you are going to protect me in a higher and braver way than spilling human blood. You'll avoid him, won't you?"

She saw the muscles of his face settle into a rigid grimace, his eyes flared, his great breast heaved, and he nodded. "Yes," he said, "I'll avoid him; that is, I think—yes, I know I'll do it for your sake."

"There, I knew you wouldn't refuse me," Dixie cried, almost merrily. "Now let's walk on. You mustn't go all the way. I'm afraid our dream is over, Alfred. This scare has opened my eyes to our earthly duties. I'm going to think of you just as—as often as I wish, and lo—love you, but we mustn't meet often. I want you to love me, too—that's God's truth, but don't tell me so, Alfred, any more—not a single time."

"How can I help it?" He turned on her, his face full of fire, his voice shaking with passion. He threw his arms about her and was drawing her into a close embrace when she stiffened her body and, with firm hands, disengaged herself, and, as she pushed him back, she said: "No, no! that will not do, Alfred. You must never do that again. It isn't because I don't want you to. If we had the right, I could rest forever in your dear arms; I could—oh, Alfred, what does God mean by treating us like this?"

"He means that we were made for one another," Henley gulped, as his eyes probed her own. "I know it—I know it."

"Yes, maybe," she said, as she moved onward, "but perhaps not for this life, Alfred. Our love is as eternal as that space above is endless. It is spiritual and pure; let's keep it that way. Now I'll leave you. Don't forget."

"I'll obey your commands," Henley answered, fervidly. "I know my duty and I'll try to do it."

She hung back a moment longer, her pretty, arching brows drawn together in thought. "I'm more worried about you and Hank Bradley than you may guess," she said. "Even if you don't meet him, he may do you some other injury. In fact, he once said—" She paused, her eyes on the ground.

"He said what, Dixie?" Henley prompted.

"He said something one day that worried me a lot," she went on, slowly. "It was the day, you remember, when he was drinking and you ordered him from the store. I met him, and he was in an awful state of fury. I didn't tell you about it because I was afraid it would make trouble."

"Oh, I reckon he was mad that day," Henley said, lightly. "He looked it when he left."

"It wasn't that exactly," Dixie said. "He seemed to be under the same impression that lots of folks are, that—that you are very much in love with your wife, and always have been, for he sneered a great deal about it, and finally said he knew something which, if he was not bound by promise to keep, would tear you all to pieces."

"Humph!" Henley sniffed, "I reckon it was some lie or other that Dick Wrinkle told him when they was out West together. You know Dick hated me like a snake. That ain't nothing, don't let it bother you."

"I couldn't help it," Dixie said, as she turned away. "It looked to me like he really meant something important. He seemed so sure that he had you in his power. Now, good-bye. Keep your promise."

CHAPTER XXXIII

Hank Bradley, his face stinging from the bruises he had received, his blood boiling with fury and humiliation, slunk deeper and deeper into the wood. Now he would utter a despondent groan, again a long and resonant string of threatening oaths. As he slowly spat the blood from his gashed lips, he solemnly vowed that he would have the man's life who had dared to interfere with him. To the end of his existence he would see himself sprawling at the feet of the woman whom he had so long and persistently sought—as long as he lived he would see the righteous glare in his antagonist's eyes, the look of grateful relief which lighted the face of the rescued. Plunging onward, he came to a mountain-brook which, as clear as crystal, leaped and rippled, gurgled and muttered down the rugged declivity. Here he paused, whining and bemoaning his luck, and sat down and bathed his face. He was sober now, all too sober, in fact, for his peace of mind. Above the tree-tops he saw the roof and gables of his uncle's house, and, as he mopped his face with his blood-clotted handkerchief, he trudged toward it.

Old Welborne himself was on the lawn inspecting his beehives, near the front gate, when his nephew entered, and he turned toward him, staring curiously.

"Why, what's the matter?" the old man asked. "You look

like you've been run over by a wagon, or kicked by an army mule. Great heavens, man!" Welborne put out his hand as if to touch the purple and swollen spot above Bradley's eye, but with a surly oath the young man drew back.

"Same mule, I reckon, that had hold of your windpipe in your office the other day when you squealed like a stuck pig under the table."

"Huh!" Welborne grunted. "You was in the other room and didn't show yourself when a man less 'n half my age and as strong as an ox was—was—"

"T'wasn't my row, and this ain't *yours*," Hank growled. "I'll tell you that now, and be done with it. I won't take up any fight of yours over your close-fisted, hold-up deals, but I'll see mine through, and don't you forget it."

"You'd better go in the house and put some medicine on your face," the old man advised, "and sleep off that drunk! I smelt you before you opened the gate. I knew when you was kicked out of Alf Henley's store that day that you'd never let it rest till you had another row. You are like your daddy was, always looking for trouble, and, somehow, always finding plenty of it, and doing no particular harm to anybody else. He was always going to kill somebody, but never got to it."

"Listen to me," Bradley snarled; "if I don't kill that dirty whelp in twenty-four hours from now, I leave home for good and all."

"Say, look here," Welborne said, with a change of tone. "I'm not saying this for Alf Henley's sake, for I hate him; he is the only man in this county that ever tricked me out of my rights, and I'll get even with 'im, sooner or later, but I'm thinking now about you. You may be foolhardy enough to try some slip-up game on him. I'm not afraid you'll meet him like a man, for, if it had been in you, you'd have done it before this, but you may think you can do your job in the dark, so listen to me, Hank. You may think you can shoot him from behind, but I tell you if you do you'll swing for it. I've got a longer head than you have, because I've kept it clear, and hate of a man never will get my neck in the loop. Don't you know—can't you see that if anything harmed that fellow now, after this whipping he's given you, that suspicion would be directed to you. He's popular—men on all sides like him—and a jury would not leave their seats to convict you. You'd hang, I tell you, hang till you are dead, dead, dead!"

"I'd rather hang, by God," Bradley growled, "than go through with what I'm going through now. Don't talk to me. Go on with your flea-skinning, and let me alone. I know what I'm about!"

"You don't, for you are too befuddled with liquor to know," retorted the calm old man. "I can remind you of a thing that maybe you ought to recall. There was a white man lynched for a certain offence two months ago. It was done by a mob of eight or ten young devils on a drunken rampage. The authorities was disposed to drop it, because it was believed the man was guilty, but now it is leaking out that he was the wrong party. His friends are working as quiet as moles under ground. They are getting names and stacks of evidence. A man I've done a favor for come and told me to warn you. I didn't think it was worth while, but I do now, because if you fire on Alf Henley from the dark you'll be arrested, and both charges will be saddled on you."

"I don't care a damn about that, either," Bradley spouted, and he turned toward the house. "I'll do one thing at a time, and take the biggest first."

"That's your determination, then?"

"You bet it is. I know my business, and I don't want you to put your fingers in it."

"Well, go ahead with your rat-killing," the money-lender said. "I've given you a piece of sound advice, and, if you don't take it, that isn't my lookout."

Bradley strode heavily and with dragging feet along the gravelled walk to the house. He lunged awkwardly across the veranda floor and went into the wide hallway and ascended the walnut stairs to his room.

An hour later he came down. He had been drinking again from a supply of liquor kept in his chamber. One of his hip-pockets bulged with a flask, the other with a long revolver. No one was on the front veranda or on the lawn. A dim light from a window at the right of the hall told him that his uncle was in his room, perhaps absorbed over his accounts and papers. Passing out at the gate, he took the narrow, private road through his uncle's fields to Chester, the lights of which danced before his unsteady vision. It was Saturday, and, as Henley often went to the store on that night, Bradley concluded that he might be there now. When he reached the square he found few persons on any of the divergent streets. A few strangers and drummers sat smoking and chatting on the low veranda of the little hotel, and in the darkness he passed them without attracting attention. Reaching Henley's store, he glanced in at the front. Cahews and Pomp were putting the tumbled dry-goods department to rights, and sweeping, sprinkling, and dusting. A queer thrill of triumph passed through the watcher as he descried the lamp on Henley's desk and the unruffled face of the storekeeper in its circle of rays.

Fearing that some passer-by might notice him in front, Bradley climbed over the fence at the side of the house and crouched down in the yard, hidden by the shadow of the wall. The village was very still. The clanging of a near-by church-bell calling the choir to practise for the Sunday service jarred harshly on Bradley's tense nerves. Pomp was singing, keeping time with strokes of his broom, and Cahews was whistling an accompaniment. Bradley waited till the bell had ceased its clangor, and then, with a step that was almost steady, he glided along the weather-boarding through the junk-filled yard till he had reached the open window close to Henley's desk. Henley was still there. He seemed to be counting money, for he had a bag of coin near him and the iron safe near by was open. Bradley could see the pigeon-holes and little drawers with their brass mountings gleaming in the light. He drew his revolver and cocked it noiselessly and aimed it experimentally at his intended victim. No better mark could be desired, but the right moment must be chosen. Bradley looked about him, his befuddled brain noting this or that obstacle to immediate flight. He must think; he must make no mistake, for, as his uncle had said, the risk was grave. The sudden report of a revolver would cause that cottage door to fly open; Seth Woods at work in his cage-like shop across the street would run directly over to see what had happened. The loungers at the hotel would appear, Cahews and Pomp, and, and—Bradley recalled Welborne's reference to the lynched man, and shuddered. Yes, drunk as he was, he could see that, easy as the deed was of execution, escape would be most difficult. He told himself, as he thrust the weapon back into his pocket, that the centre of the town was no place for work like this, and that later Henley would have to pass along a lonely road in darkness to get home. Yes, that was the best plan, he decided, and, creeping back through the yard, he regained the fence, and, watching his opportunity, he climbed over into the street and made his way unobserved out into the country road.

Soon he had reached the point he had in mind. It was, by odd fatality, the spot where he had received his castigation only a few hours before. The moon was behind a cloud, and yet the visible stars furnished sufficient light for him to see his way, dulled as his vision was by the spirits he had consumed. Now his plan was complete. He would lie in wait right where the unshaded roadway entered the wood. Henley's form would be clearly limned against the unobstructed horizon. Bradley would fire once, twice, as many times as would be necessary to do the work absolutely. He believed that he would be calm enough, practicable as it would be at that distance from any residence, to step forward and examine the body to be sure that no mistake had been made. Bradley chuckled as he sat down on the heather, and felt a satisfied, even triumphant, glow steal over him. Taking out his flask, he drained its contents, and then threw it into the wood. It whistled ominously as it cut its way through the air and fell with a crash against a bowlder. He drew out his watch and struck a match to see the dial. It was ten o'clock. His victim could not be long now, for Henley never remained late at the store.

"Ah, what was that? Surely it was a man's whistle, and Henley's whistle was a well-known and merry characteristic of himself. To-night it rippled forth more joyously than usual, and this in itself added to the flames in the crouching man's breast. Henley could whistle that way because he had triumphed so conspicuously in the recent encounter. But stopping a man's whistle was a small matter when it was done with a six-shooter by a good marksman, Bradley chuckled, and that wouldn't bother him many seconds. Now he could distinctly hear the storekeeper's step; he would soon be in view there where the fireflies were flashing, and then—but what was that? Something seemed to be lowered from the branches of a tree directly across the road as by a rope, and to hang against the dark background, turning in a gruesome fashion, as if wind-blown, first one way and then another. It was a human body. The feet were tied by a bridle-rein, the hands bound behind by the suspenders the corpse had worn. Bradley had seen the thing in fancy many times before, but never in such grim actuality as now. He strained his sight to make sure. There was no doubt. The thing was actually there—there, there, great God!—there!

"Gentlemen, friends, neighbors"—he remembered the very words that had escaped the lips now grinning at him—"you are hangin' the wrong man. I'm innocent. In the name of God, spare me. I'm the father of six children that depend on me for a living. Give me a chance to prove what I say—oh, God!—oh, God, oh, God, have mercy!"

The hand holding the revolver relaxed. With a subdued cry of terror, Bradley was on his feet, glaring at the accusing sight. He saw Henley enter the wood and move on unsuspectingly toward the horrible spectre which swung across his path. Indeed, Henley passed through it as through a vapor, still whistling. With a cry still in his throat, Bradley dashed into the wood and fled the spot.

Henley heard the sound of pattering feet and paused for a moment, looking about him wonderingly. It wasn't an animal suddenly frightened from its lair, for the weird, guttural cry was human. At the side of the road stood a huge oak, on the trunk of which there was a grayish, barkless strip about the width and length of a medium-sized man, and hanging from a bough above was an uprooted grape-vine. These natural objects would have attracted Henley's attention had he known how they had been masquerading in his behalf. As it was, however, he resumed his whistling, and, barely reminded by the spot of the recent encounter, he cheerfully pursued his way. He was very tired, and looked forward with eagerness to the moment when he could get into bed.

CHAPTER XXXIV

Henley's wife had been gone two weeks and had not written a line either to him or the Wrinkles, when, one morning just after breakfast, as old Jason stood on the front porch, he espied, far down the road, the Warren carriage, with Ned in the driver's seat. The back part of the vehicle was not in sight, but Wrinkle had seen enough to convince him that his ex-daughter-in-law was returning, and he promptly and gleefully announced the fact to his wife and Henley in the dining-room. They all went to the porch and waited for the now-hidden carriage to round the bend. For a short distance Ned's battered silk top-hat and the tip of his whip flitting along above the tasselled corn-stalks which intervened between the house and the road were the only evidence of the vehicle's approach, and then it turned sharply in at the wagon-gate.

"My Lord, the dang thing's empty!" Wrinkle cried. "I wonder if she fell out comin' down the mountain, an' Ned never noticed it?"

A full and rather startling explanation was furnished by the negro, when he had reined in at the steps. Ben Warren was dead and was to be buried the next day. Mrs. Henley had been too much overcome by careful watching at his bedside and grief to write, but she had sent the carriage over for the Wrinkles, whom she wished to attend the funeral. She wanted them to bring a good many things to wear, as they might have to stay some time to keep her company in her loneliness.

When Ned had driven his horses around the house to be fed and watered and rubbed down, and Mrs. Wrinkle, uttering a fusillade of meaningless ejaculations and puffs of gratified horror, had disappeared in the house to pack, old Jason made a wry face and squinted comically at Henley. "I reckon Het wasn't too much overcome to keep 'er from shufflin' 'er cards in her little poker game with you. You notice she didn't include you in the invite. I reckon she still feels sore over that buggy-ride that went crooked, an' has decided that you sha'n't take part in any festivities that she has anything to do with. I like to stay with you, Alf, as well as I would with any feller, but the change to that fine place won't be bad. I'll have a good time, takin' it all in all. Ben has—or had, rather—a fine mansion that is well stocked with grub, an' some nigger women that can prepare stuff to a queen's taste. If Het don't take charge of the pantry, there'll be enough to go around an' plenty over. But we'll see, we'll see."

That afternoon, as Henley and Cahews sat in the front part of the store, the carriage passed on its way over the mountain. Wrinkle and his demure spouse, in their very best clothing, sat on the luxurious leather cushions in the rear, and Wrinkle was smiling broadly and waving parting signals at them. The carriage had passed on, and was about to turn into the first street leading mountainward, when Wrinkle was seen to reach forward and clutch the driver's arm. He gave some command, and the horses were reined in and Wrinkle got out, and as he busied himself rubbing something from the lapel of his broadcloth coat he walked with rather uncertain gait to the store.

"Say, Alf," he began, as he ascended the steps to the porch, "if it's agreeable to you, I'd like to have a dollar for pocket-change. Het's pretty liberal, as a general thing, but Ned says she's powerful upset over her loss, an' I'd sorter hate to tackle 'er the fust day we are over thar, an' I know, in reason, I'll need a few nickels to drop here an' thar."

"Get it for him, Jim," Henley ordered, and, while Cahews was at the cash-drawer, Wrinkle went round the counter and took a plug of tobacco from a box.

"I'd take along a few sticks o' peppermint, too," he said, as he wistfully surveyed the candy-jars, "but I've got so I can't suck a stick without toothache. Ain't a bit o' fun treatin' yore stomach if you have to abuse yore gums while you are at it. Well, so long, boys," he said, after he had carefully counted the coins Cahews had put into his hand and was descending the steps. "Folks says that partin' is always harder on the ones that are left behind, an' I reckon it's so in this case, for it's dull enough here, an' I intend to have a good time. The funeral, and paying due respect to the dead, will occupy me to-day and to-morrow, an' after that I want to take a fish in Ben's brag pond. They say he's got—or did have when he was alive—government trout two foot long, an' oodlin's of 'em, hungry enough to bite anything you stick on yore hook."

If the news of the wealthy planter's death and the departure of the Wrinkles under the high honor which had been conferred upon the unpretentious pair furnished food for gossip at Chester, what may be said of the later report which at first crawled from the bereaved mansion, and then, taking on speed, ran hurtling like wildfire over the country?

Ben Warren, sick unto death, and yet in full possession of his senses, for valid reasons of his own had cut off many anxious more distant relatives and bequeathed all his real estate and personal property to his loving and faithful niece,

"Hester Wrinkle Henley."

Henley himself was disposed to regard the report as a false one, a canard set afloat by the irrepressible Wrinkle, who would joke as readily about the dead as the living. But even the shrewd business man himself was convinced one morning by the appearance of Wrinkle, who had dismountted from a fine horse at the hitching-post and came in lashing the legs of his baggy trousers with a riding-whip.

"I reckon you've heard what's happened, Alf," he began, in a tone in which there was no guile. "It never rains but it pours cats and pitchforks. I'm out o' breath. Forty-six men, women, an' babies met me as I rid in all as eager to know the facts as if they had the'r names in the pot, an' I had to go over the tale so many times that my hoss got so he would nod or shake his head exactly right whenever a question was axed. Them that hate Het would turn white at the gills an' groan, an' the rest would say, 'Oh, my!' an' set in to do it on the spot."

"Yes, we heard the report," Henley made answer, "but we didn't know whether to believe it or not. I reckon you got it plumb straight?"

"Straight as a shingle," Wrinkle said, sincerely. "Het not only told me, but so did the lawyer, a big-bellied chap from Atlanta, in broadcloth and headlight buttons in his shirt. Huh! I reckon you think you know Het purty well, Alf; but you don't. I don't, an' my wife don't. I reckon her Maker sometimes wonders what she'll do in a pinch. I 'lowed she was one woman that 'u'd like to fall heir to a pile o' cash, but they say when Ben sent for her to come to his bed whar the lawyer was ready with pen and ink and paper, an' Ben told her he was goin' to put her in entire charge of his effects, lock, stock, an' barrel—they say when she heard that she begun to wail an' take on at such a rate that they couldn't git her to talk business at all. They had to rub 'er down an' bathe 'er feet in hot mustard-water, an' it was all they could do to keep 'er from crossin' over, hand in hand, with Ben, an' leavin' the boodle to anybody that 'u'd pick it up. The Lord only knows who would have got the swag in that case, but comin' into a fortune don't kill often, an' Het will manage somehow. She et a square meal this mornin' 'fore I started, pokin' it up under her veil-like, in purty good chunks, an' give orders to the niggers like a captain on a ship ridin' high waves. Thar always was only one thing in this life that pestered that woman, an' that was responsebility to the dead. I reckon she thinks the livin' can tote the'r own loads. Be that as it may, she's goin' to see that Ben's shebang an' all pertainin' to it is run jest to a gnat's heel like he would run it if he was alive. But comin' down to brass tacks, she owes her good luck to exactly what most folks thought was a weak p'int in 'er. They say Ben was so all-fired mad at the gal that kicked 'im to death that he said all women was unfaithful, an' he picked Het out for reward because she had showed she was one amongst a million. Then, too, Het kept tellin' 'im he was good for another forty years, while the rest of his kin was sayin' to his teeth that they was sorry he had to go an hopin' that he had his papers in order. If I could get head or tail of the mystery of life, I might be able to tell whether Het was actin' a part or not. I think she simply done it so well that she believed it; anyways, Ben liked it, an' spent his last hours an' every cent he had tryin' to pacify her."

"And he was rich?" Cahews thrust in, tentatively.

"Well, you'd think so," smiled Wrinkle. "He not only had the finest plantation an' house in this county, but he held bank stocks, railroad bonds, warehouses, cotton-factory interests, an' what not."

"And does—does Hettie intend to—to come back *here*?"

Henley asked, a flush of odd embarrassment on his face.

"Well, that's another matter," Wrinkle began, and then he broke off abruptly: "Say, Alf, I've got something private to talk to you about. Jim, I wish you'd give that hoss a bucket of water. I think he's dry."

With a knowing laugh the clerk turned away, and Wrinkle caught Henley's suspender and gave it a familiar tug. "I didn't want to discuss family affairs before a third party," he explained. "The truth is, Alf, I've always been interested in yore little ups an' downs with Het, an' right now I'm curious to see how prosperity will affect her. Up to now, you see, she was dependent on you for funds, an' sorter had to go slow on some o' her fancies, but now the shoe is on t'other foot, an'—"

"That is not answering the question I asked," Henley broke in, quite out of patience. "I asked you if she intended to—"

"I knowed what you axed me, an' I intend to answer at the proper time an' place," Wrinkle went on, quite unruffled by the reproof. "I never begin to unravel a sock at the top or the middle. The toe is whar the work begun, and therefore the toe is the only natural an' sensible place to—"

"You make me tired!" Henley retorted, impatiently. "You take all day to tell a thing."

"Well, if it won't hurt yore pride I'll tell you what I think is her little game." Wrinkle smiled unctuously and rubbed his hands together. "She left here when that little tiff was on with you about a buggy-ride or two that was hangin' fire because you couldn't spare the time, an' I think her present object is to make you do some knucklin' down. You see, Alf, she's a fine lady now, an' a big heiress, an' naturally is now a woman to be treated with respect by you or me or anybody else. She's the head o' that whole thing over there, an' you'll have to fall in line with the rest of us. She's in deep mournin', an' considerably overcome, but she hain't forgot them buggy-rides. She's brought 'em up a dozen times, an' always with a sniff an' a sneer. She sent me over to git all our leavin's in shape for shipment, an' she's goin' to send a wagon over after 'em."

"So she intends to make that her future home?" ventured Henley, a frown of perplexity on his face.

"Yes, she says it would be out of all reason for the head of sech a big thing to live away over here, an' that you kin sell out yore little shack an' move thar. She's installed me an' Jane in a big room overlookin' the river, an' has one set aside for you that is every bit as good. I reckon you'll be made to feel like a common chap that has married into a royal family, but I wouldn't let that bother me if I was you. You are in luck, Alf. When you took her she didn't have a red cent, an' now just look at her. If Dick had knowed this thing was in the wind, he'd have stayed at home an' put up with a lot that he used to kick agin. She sent you one positive message, an' that was to be sure to come over next Saturday an' spend Sunday. She said you mustn't make it later 'n that, because folks would be sure to talk, an' that she don't want to be talked about, especially while she is in black."

"Well, I'll go over, then," Henley said, with sarcasm that was lost on Wrinkle. "You may tell her that I have accepted her kind invitation." And he turned to his desk and sat down and began to work.

CHAPTER XXXV

That night at his uncle's house Hank Bradley, still wearing traces of his encounter with Henley, sat reading a newspaper and smoking in his chamber at the head of the stairs. A half-empty whiskey-flask and a glass of water were on a table at his elbow, and torn and soiled playing-cards were scattered about the floor.

Presently his attention was drawn to the outside by a sharp whistle which was evidently familiar, for he dropped the paper and went to a window which looked out on the front lawn. At first he could see only old Welborne at a potato-bed on the right, but as his sight became used to the outer gloom he descried a man leaning on the fence near the gate. The fellow wore the broad-brimmed felt hat of the mountaineers; his pants were tucked into his high-top boots and he wore no coat, but a gray flannel shirt with a leather belt and a flowing necktie.

"It's Rayburn Hill," Bradley ejaculated. "What the devil can he want? He must have come thirty miles."

Descending the stairs, and looking furtively at his uncle, whose back was turned to him, Bradley tiptoed across the veranda and gained the grass sward, across which he walked noiselessly.

"Hello!" he said, in a gruff tone; "what are you doing over here?"

"Come to see you, Hank." The man, who was under thirty and tall and strong of limb, thrust out his hand and shook that of his friend. "I left my horse down at the square."

"What do you want to see me about, Ray?" Bradley's voice almost shook with growing perturbation. "You told me last week that you never would come this way again—that the more we all was scattered the safer it would be."

"I'm on my way to the nighest railroad, Hank."

"You say you are?" Bradley leaned against the fence, and his face turned white. "You don't think it's as—as bad as that?"

"Don't I? Huh, I only hope I'll catch that twelve-o'clock flyer! I wouldn't be here now but I told you I'd never act without reporting to you, and that's what I'm doing, Hank."

"But what's—what's happened to—to scare you up so?" Bradley stammered.

"Hank, that fellow's kin are on our track like a pack of thirsty bloodhounds. I got onto it by accident. They have smelt blood, and they are going to drink some. We got the wrong man; I know it damned well now, and you and me was the ringleaders. You know the West, Hank. I want you to show me the way. Git a move on you. You haven't a minute to lose."

"I'll have to raise some money." Bradley looked toward the dim form of old Welborne through the darkness. "Go back to town, Ray. I'll see my uncle and pack and meet you at the train. I'm sure you are right. I've seen bad signs myself.

I'd have lit out before this, but there was a skunk here that I wanted to settle a score with."

"I know, but you'll have to cut that out, Hank. This is no time for revenge. Hurry up. I'm off. I've got to get a man to take my horse home."

When his accomplice had gone away, Bradley crossed over to old Welborne.

"You remember," he began, "that you advised me to leave here the other day?"

Old Welborne stared at him steadily for a minute, and then shrugged his decrepit shoulders. "I have been expecting to hear you say you'd settled with the jackass that gave you that licking that day. I don't want to see you get into more trouble, but that fellow ought to be pulled down from his lordly perch. I never see him without feeling his hands on my throat. He's the one man that has always stood in my way. And now, just look at him! He's in big luck again, and can sneer in his high and mighty way at all of us. That fool woman he was so crazy about as to marry when she loved another man has come into a great big fortune, and he walks about with a strut as it he was a king and we all was common trash 'way beneath his notice. I saw him talking to Dixie Hart this morning in the post-office. His face was shining, and his eyes twinkling over the news of his wife's big haul. Me an' him have had it nip and tuck here ever since he set up in business, and he has always thwarted me. I've pinched and delved to save a few dollars, and his comes to him in rolls and wads. Folks say he's going to sell out and live over there in ease the rest of his life. I don't care how soon he leaves, but I'd like to wipe that grin off his gloating face."

"I've got to go, uncle," Bradley said. "It's too hot for me

here. But I need some money, and I must have it to-night."

"Money? Good Lord! How much do you want?"

"Five hundred. I'm going back West. I know the country, and I'll settle there. As for Alf Henley, I've got something up my sleeve for him. He's chuckling now over his wife's big luck, but I'll knock that higher than a kite; he'll never live on that plantation or spend any of that cash. You listen close and you'll hear something drop with a big clatter before many days."

"What are you talking about?" the money-lender asked, bending forward and peering eagerly into the bloated face of his nephew.

"I know what I'm talking about," Bradley replied, still evasively, "and that will be the first thing I attend to when I get where I can breathe fresh air. Say, uncle, I've had a secret in my hold for several years. It is about Dick Wrinkle. If I thought you could hold your old tongue—"

"Hold my tongue?" Welborne broke in. "Did you ever hear of me telling anything?"

"Nothing that concerned you, and this does, to some extent, I'll admit," Bradley said. "Listen, uncle. How would you like to hear that Alf Henley ain't that woman's lawful husband? Dick Wrinkle is alive."

"Good Lord!" The old man's eyes gleamed even in the starlight. "You don't mean it? Surely, surely, you don't."

"Yes, he's alive. He was in Oklahoma when I last saw him. He was done with everything back here—bored to death by his wife and her odd ways, and wanted to shake it all off. He had done me a good many favors. He was hurt in that big storm and reported dead, and got me to confirm it back here. I did the job right. You are the first one I've told the facts to. I get a letter from him now and then, and know where he is. He's made enough money to own a bar in a little place near the Texas line."

"Well, well, but what has that got to do with Henley?" Welborne wanted to know.

"It's just got this to do with him," answered Bradley. "Dick Wrinkle can simply wrap the woman round his finger. She would fall on his neck at the drop of a hat. If Dick came back she'd have a fit of joy and kick Henley clean out of the house. I know women, and Dick has told me lots about his hold on this one."

"But would he come back?"

"Would he? Humph! He's so homesick he thins his ink with brine when he writes to me. He's known all along that she'd take 'im back, but there wasn't any special inducement till now. I have an idea that when he is told—and told in the right way—of this big haul of hers he'll come back to life with some tale or other to square it, and hurry home and claim his rights."

"And you want to start to-night?"

"If you'll get me the money. I've overdrawn my account like thunder, uncle, but I'll not bother you for a while. Get it for me. I've got to go."

The old man looked at the ground hesitatingly, then he shrugged his thin shoulders. "Well, go ahead and pack. I've got that much in the safe at the office. I'll meet you down there. But I'm going to count on you to—to put this thing through."

"I will if I possibly can," Bradley said. "I think he'll do as I tell him. He's always listened to me. I know how to work him up. Don't keep me waiting. I'll pack in twenty minutes."

"Good Lord," the old man chuckled, as he stood alone in the dark. "If Dick Wrinkle comes back and claims his wife, Alf Henley will take a tumble from the highest peak he ever stood on. Won't I laugh at him then? Say, won't I?"

CHAPTER XXXVI

The following Saturday afternoon Henley set out in his buggy to accomplish, in some fashion or other, the disagreeable task of paying his first visit to his wife in her new home. His chagrin could not be imagined by any one less closely concerned in the affair than himself. He had been taught to regard divorce laws as a veritable abomination, and had never for an instant allowed himself to think of freedom from shackles which goaded and chafed his body and soul. And now the situation was even more irritating. His proud spirit rebelled against the unlooked-for circumstances that had made him the husband of a wealthy woman. Heretofore he had been able to realize that if he had made a serious mistake in his marriage, he was, at least, helpful to the woman he had chosen.

From a hill half a mile to the west of the Warren plantation he drew rein and all but bitterly surveyed the vast possessions of his incongruous spouse. In a grove of primitive oaks, near the main-travelled road, against the misty blue background of the distant mountain-range, stood the stately white residence, with its long veranda supported by dignified Corinthian columns, its steep roof, quaint dormer-windows, and central cupola.

"What a joke!" Henley said, with a wry smile, as he started his horse slowly down the incline. "And she's the mistress of it all. I wonder if she'll expect me to get down on my all-fours and crawl in at the back-door."

Old Wrinkle must have been on the lookout for him, for, in his best clothes, he was standing at the carriage-gate in the nearest corner of the grounds. His beard had been trimmed, or awkwardly chopped off, by the unsteady fingers of his wife, and his grizzled hair was plastered down over his dingy brow flatter than it had ever been before.

"Hello!" he called out, merrily. "I 'lowed I'd warn you to enter at this gate an' not drive on to the little one in front of the mansion. That's for foot-passengers," he explained, as he swung the gate open. "Het's mighty—I mean Hester; she says I mustn't call 'er Het any more; she says it will make the nigger help disrespectful. It ain't Pa and Ma any more, either, bless yore life! but father and mother. The other day at the table, before we had lifted our plates, she started in to father me, solemnlike, an' I ducked my head, for I thought she'd set in to ax the blessin'. I started to say that she was mighty particular about the way things are run. Ben had rules an' regulations, you see, an' she is carryin' 'em out an' addin' on more. I seed 'er git as red as a turkey-cock t'other day beca'se a nigger-wench rung the front-door bell. She made the woman hump 'erself round to the kitchen double quick. She's got a new toy to piddle with, an' it's a whoppin' big un. She says things has to move accordin' to the clock on this gigantic place, an' so far it's doin' it. Wait, I'll shet the gate an' ride to the barn with you.

"You've got a lot to learn, Alf," Wrinkle resumed, as he climbed into the buggy and the horse started, "and you might as well set in to do it. I told my wife I was goin' to git you off on one side an' give you a few hints so you won't make the mistakes we did at the outset. About eatin'-time, for instance—no matter what meal is on—we are instructed to listen for bells. It's that big un that presides at the kitchen-door. Thar's always a fust un an' a last un—a number one an' a number two. The fust is to wash an' comb by; the next is to come in the dinin'-room, but, mark you, not in a hurry. I'd lafe a heap o' times if she wasn't so all-fired serious over it. Goin' to school ain't in it. In her thick black she looks as important and stern as a judge in his robes."

They had now reached the barn, a great, rambling structure that was well-painted and well-kept.

"Thar's the stables," Wrinkle said. "It might as well be called a hoss-hotel. It really is a finer shebang in many ways than the house we all lived in till this happened. I ain't criticism' yore place, Alf. It was the best you had to offer, an' nobody could be expected to do more 'n that. But Ben went in for show, an' he added to an' tuck away till the day of his death. This barn has been painted so many times that dry sheets of paint would fall off if you kicked the weather-boardin', and inside—well, jest wait till you see it."

They had descended from the buggy, and Henley was about to unhitch the traces when Wrinkle laid a firm, even agitated, hand on his arm.

"That's another thing," he said; "don't tetch it. You'll break a rule. No member of the family—an' that means me an' you, for we can claim kin by adoption, if not by blood—no member is allowed to do dirty work o' any sort. Ben never allowed it, an' Het says the same rule must hold. She says it would spile the help an' git 'em out o' the right sort o' habits. She told me to whistle whenever I wanted a thing done, and Rastus, or Lindy, or Cipo, or Ned would come on a run. That's sort o' makin' bird-dogs out o' two-legged creatures, but I kind o' like it. But, mind you, Alf, don't whistle for 'em inside the house. You will find a fancy rope with a tassel on the end of it in every room. Give it a light tug an' let it loose. Thar, I see Cipo now. Watch me!". Wrinkle spat on the ground, wiped his mouth with his hand, and puckered up his lips and whistled keenly. "He's comin'; watch 'im hop; he knows better than to dally when I give that sound. He's slow, though; walks like he had lumbago or locomotive attachment. Say, Cipo!" as the tall, elderly negro arrived, holding his tattered hat in his hand, "this is Mr. Alfred Henley, an' this is his hoss. Orders is out from headquarters to give both of 'em every needed attention. It ain't any o' my business, Cipo. I'd give all o' you coons a rest if I had my way. Life is too short to bother about puttin' on style an' tyin' a bow of ribbon to every act."

With the broadest of grins the negro, whose splaying feet were in remnants of shoes that were tied with white cotton strings, detached the horse from the shafts and led him away.

"Now, come on," Wrinkle said. "I see Ma in the back veranda waitin' for us."

As they reached the house the old woman, with timid, halting steps, and better dressed than Henley had ever seen her before, came forward and extended a limp hand. "Howdy do? How did you leave Chester?" she inquired.

"All right," he answered. "Where is Hettie?"

The question was addressed to her, but she stared mutely, and with some agitation looked at her husband.

"I forgot to tell you." Wrinkle glanced up at the sun. "This is her nap-time. That used to be the order in Ben's day, an' she's holdin' to it. Just after dinner all hands are expected to unstrip an' lie down till the cool of the evenin'; then you are free to walk about, but you ought to be ready for supper so you won't have to wash at the last minute, an' come in in a scramble. We don't see Het at breakfast. Ben had a habit of stayin' in his room an' havin' a nigger fetch his up on a waiter, an' Het feels like it is her duty to do likewise. She sets up thar, they tell me, in easy, roustabout clothes, an' attends to the business of the day—sech as readin' the mail, answerin' letters, an' listenin' to complaints from overseers an' land-renters. Ben advanced cash, in dribs or wads, accordin' to needs, an' kept a set o' books. Het's got all that an' more on her conscience, an' she's gittin' as thin as a splinter over it. Folks say she's a regular hair-splitter when it comes to settlements. She would divide a copper cent into several parts if the Government would let 'em pass that way. Come in the parlor, Alf. I want you to take a peep at it. You've travelled about some an' seen sights, but for a place jest to live in, I'll bet you'll admit this caps the stack. If a royal emperor was to kick at a home like this it would start a revolution amongst his subjects."

Henley and the demure little woman followed at the talker's heels. He led them into the main entrance-hall, a spacious, oblong room with colored-glass windows on both sides and above the heavy Colonial doorway. A massive stairway with a carved newel and balustrade of black walnut wound gracefully up to a companion hall above. Piloting the others around this, Wrinkle pushed open a big, white door and led them into the parlor. It was really a spacious room of good design, the walls and woodwork of which were ivory-white. It was, however, furnished with execrable taste. There was an old-fashioned rosewood piano, a row of modern bookcases of oak, rocking-chairs of ancient mahogany, cheap oil landscapes in cheaper gilt frames, a worn carpet of shrieking colors and a design which maddened the vision. There was one spot which would have soothed the trained eye—it was the wide mantelpiece, on which stood a quaint, glass-doored clock and a pair of tall, brass candlesticks of simple form. The fireplace was deep and wide and held a pair of fine, old brass dogs with an appropriate open-work fender.

"I jest want you to take a glance at that big lookin'-glass." Wrinkle pointed at a fine gilt-edged pier-glass which reached from the floor to the ceiling and filled all the space between the two windows at the end of the room. "I'm callin' yore attention to it so you won't be fooled like I was when I fust saw it. They had the funeral in here, an' me an' Ma was axed to set over thar agin the wall. Well, you may believe me or not, but I thought the lookin'-glass was a wide door into another room the same size as this; an' all the time the folks was gatherin' I was watchin' it, for it was fillin' up an' I couldn't make out whar the folks come from. Then all at once I was scared mighty nigh out o' my socks, for the crowd sorter shuffled, to make room, an' I seed another coffin. If I'd been a drinkin' man I'd 'a' been sure I had the jimmies. I wanted to p'int it out to Ma, but I was afeard it might go hard with 'er, for she's a believer in hobgoblins, an' might 'a' raised a noise. So I jest set thar wonderin' who else could be dead, an' why I hadn't heard about it, an' thinkin' maybe that it was the style to bury a rich man in two boxes, though they looked to me like they was the same size an' had the same trimmin's, an' was piled up the same way with flowers. Then I said my prayers in dead earnest, for I seed Het come in on the preacher's arm facin' me in t'other room, while they was walkin' with the'r backs to me in this un. I reckon I'd a been fooled till now if the preacher hadn't begun to hold forth. I could see two parsons as plain as life, but only heard one voice, an' so I discovered my mistake just in time to keep from goin' stark crazy."

At this juncture, Lucy, a young mulatto, came and touched Mrs. Wrinkle on the arm, with the regretful air of one not wishing to disturb her superiors.

"Miss wants to know who's got here," she said.

The little old woman started, looked nervously into the faces of the others, and then ejaculated, "It's Alf; tell 'er it's Alf."

"'Miss'?" Henley repeated, as the girl was withdrawing, muttering the monosyllabic name to herself to fix it on her memory—"who's 'Miss'?"

"Why, it's Het herself," Wrinkle explained, readily enough. "You see, the niggers all used to call Ben's mother 'Old Miss' till she died. I'm told they started in to call Het 'Young Miss,' but when she put on crape an' begun to fling orders about they cut off the 'Young' part. I reckon they'll call you some'n or other to fit the dignity of yore position when they git it into the'r noggin's jest how close you stand to the prime head of it all. They know who me 'n Jane are, you bet yore life, an' when we call 'em they come in a tilt with the'r hats in the'r hands. I never lived before, it seems to me, an' I care less than I ever did about the future state. This is good enough for me. If it will just go at the present pace all the time, I won't care to git cold feet an' retire to a soggy hole in the ground."

Wrinkle suddenly took on a look of attention to external sounds, and he went to the door and peered cautiously up the stairs.

"I think I heard 'er walkin' about," he called back, and he waved his hand downward as if commanding silence. "Yes, she's comin'. Ma, you 'n me had better make ourselves scarce. You see, Alf," he went on, in a rasping whisper and with a very grave face, "we don't exactly know when we are wanted an' when we ain't. It wouldn't be so awkward if she'd lay down some positive rule. She's different under every change, an' the Lord knows she changes often enough."

With a frightened mien Mrs. Wrinkle lowered her head and glided quietly from the room through a door in the rear.

"Take a cheer," was the old man's parting injunction to Henley. "Throw yoreself back, an' cross yore legs, an' let 'er know at the outset that you ain't beholden to 'er, an' that her rise in life don't make no odds to you. That's the way Dick would act if he was alive. He'd 'a' been cussin' these niggers about an' tellin' Het to git out o' that bed an' fix some'n to eat. That's the way he worked 'er, an' she was jest so constructed that she liked it. Take my advice an' turn over a new leaf; you'll have trouble if you don't."

Henley made no reply, and he found himself alone in the big room. The lace curtains of the windows which opened like doors on the front veranda were gently blown in by the cooling breeze, and into the white surroundings came the grim, black-draped figure of his wife. She advanced toward him, her hand stiffly extended. He took her cold fingers into his and awkwardly pressed them. Her eyes rested only a moment on him, for she was looking critically at the carpet.

"Oh, I'll never get things right!" she cried. "Look at the stable-mud on the carpet. I've told 'em an' *told* 'em not to come in here without wiping their feet, but it goes in at one ear and out at another. They've tracked it all over, and this ingrain carpet can't be cleaned. I'd shut the room up and keep the key, but Uncle Ben always had this room open for visitors, and I want to carry out his plans in every detail. Oh, Alfred, I'm afraid this awful responsibility will kill me! You have no idea of what it all is. I used to think you had enough to do, but your affairs are simply child's play to this."

"I suppose so," he said, "but you never took hold of mine. That's why you think this is so awful. It is on your shoulders like my business is on mine."

She shook her head and sighed as if his remark were not worthy of serious notice, and sat for half an hour going into all the details of Ben Warren's last illness and his wonderful faith in her. "He simply *would* leave me in charge." She applied her handkerchief to her moist eyes and choked down a sob. "I tried to get him to see that I wasn't at all worthy, but it only made him more determined. The lawyer told me to stop arguing, and the doctor said I was hastening his end, and so I let him have his way. He died like a trusting child, Alfred. I held his hand to the last."

"It was sad," Henley managed to fish out of his confused brain. "He was a young man to go so suddenlike."

"That woman killed him, Alfred." The handkerchief was applied again, though the voice of the speaker rang with rising indignation. "He had me read all her letters over to him, and I followed the outrage from the beginning to the final blow she dealt. She led him on and on, just holding him as a certainty till another man proposed and she got what she wanted—a home in New York. He couldn't stand up under it; she was poor uncle's very life, and when she went out of it he wilted like a delicate flower. I've ordered his monument; it will be the most beautiful thing in the State. He had plans for a church to give to the people in the neighborhood, and I'm going to see to the building of it. I'll have to cut household expenses in a good many ways to do it, but the edifice must be built. I get out the plans every day, but I shed tears so that I can't hardly see the lines. This brings up what I wanted to ask you, Alfred."

"To ask me?" Henley echoed, and he moved his feet and hands uneasily.

"Yes. I'll need the aid of a man over here, and, well, really, it would look better for you to be here than over there. Jim Cahews managed for you while you was away in

Texas, and—"

"I know what you mean," Henley stammered. "I understand precisely, but the truth is, right now, at least, I've got so many deals of one sort and another on hand that—"

"I see. I might have known it." The woman sighed, avoided his helpless stare, and tossed her head resentfully. "You never loved him as I do, and you put your own selfish and worldly aims first." She rose stiffly and stalked across the room to the silken bell-pull and gently drew it downward. "You'll want to go to your room before supper. Lucy will show you where it is. I hope everything will be in order up there. I have had so much to worry me that I couldn't see about it myself. I'll meet you at supper. I'm going down to the barn to see if they are taking care of Jack—uncle's favorite horse. I haven't let anybody ride him since he died. I don't know who would be worthy of it. Never mind, Alfred, this is the second request I've made of you lately. I doubt if I'll ever make another."

An impatient retort was rising in the man's breast, and it might have found an outlet if she had not left him at that instant to give an order to the girl who had come in response to her ring.

CHAPTER XXXVII

It was the second night after Henley's return to Chester. He was alone at the farm-house. It was a desolate place now, despite his constant self-assurance that he was accustomed, in his travels, to depend upon his own resources for company and entertainment, and would now find nothing lacking. He was in the kitchen cooking his supper in the same crude way he had cooked his meals in the Western mining-camps where he had once prospected.

He took down a rasher of bacon from a hook on a rafter, and with his big pocket-knife deftly cut some thin slices into a frying-pan on the smoky stove, and into the hot grease he broke some fresh eggs which he had purloined from a hen's nest in the stable-loft. He had a loaf of baker's bread, and he made some coffee of exactly the strength he liked. These things ready, he took them to the big, empty dining-room, resting the smoking frying-pan on an inverted plate on the clothless table. He sat down and ate and drank, but somehow not with his usual relish, for there was upon him a heavy sense of isolation from his kind. In spite of his effort to regard his condition in a philosophical light, he found himself unaccountably depressed. After all his youthful dreams of the domestic happiness which was to round out his life, it had ended in this. He could, he knew, go to live on the big plantation his wife had inherited, but it would be at the cost of the pride of manhood which had been his mainstay so far. She was acting out the part which had fallen to her, and what was there to justify him in altering his plans—in giving up the mode of life which had become a part of himself? Marriage, such as his had become, through no fault of his own, was an acknowledged failure.

Lighting his pipe, he blew out the lamp and sought the cooler air of the front porch. There was something depressing, rather than helpful, in the profound stillness of the night, the expanse of the star-filled heavens, the shadowy outlines of the foot-hills of the invisible mountains beyond. He heard his horses pawing in their stalls, old Wrinkle's pig grunting in its pen; the chickens roosting in a cherry-tree hard by chirped and flapped their wings as they jostled one another on the boughs; all nature seemed normal and at peace save himself. What was wrong? How could it go on? Where was it to end?

Presently his attention was drawn to a figure advancing along the front fence to the gate. The latch was lifted; it was opened, and the figure, with a light, confident tread, began to cross the grass toward him. It was Dixie Hart, and he rose from his chair and went to the steps, a throbbing sense of relief upon him.

She laughed softly, with a slight ring of affectation in her voice, as she paused with her foot on the lowest step. "You must excuse me, Alfred," she said. "I ought not to have come. I ought to have waited till to-morrow, but I'm getting to be a regular slave to Joe. He was worrying over you, and I was afraid he wouldn't go to sleep at all unless—unless I set his mind at rest. Children are so funny."

"What's wrong with the little chap?" Henley came down the steps and stood beside her. There was an inverted flour-barrel on the ground near her, and Dixie sat upon it, and swung her feet back and forth for a little while without seeming to have heard his question. He repeated it, bending toward her the better to see her face in the starlight.

"Oh, I hardly know how—how to say it." She was studying his face with a strange, hungry eagerness, which he failed to fathom. "Children are so odd, Alfred, and have so many fancies that they conjure up themselves. I reckon he's heard Ma and Aunt Mandy talking about—well, about the big piece of luck that has come to you all. You know women that have never had a windfall in any shape through their whole lives naturally make a lot of the good-fortune that comes to a neighbor, and little Joe has just set and listened to it all till—well, I reckon even you've changed from—from his plain friend to—well, something like a king in royal robes."

"The little goose! Besides—" But Henley's resources furnished no further comment.

"He actually cried over *one* thing," Dixie went on, avoiding Henley's helpless stare. "It was when Aunt Mandy said that, while maybe you and your wife had not been *quite* as thick as—as some couples are, that now, in all her wealth and splendor, you'd be like every other *natural* man, and be more attentive and—and—even loving."

"How ridiculous!" Henley exclaimed. "Why, Dixie, that money and place ain't anything to me. It comes to *her*, not to me, and, while I'm glad, of course, for her sake, still—"

"Joe cried," Dixie broke in, with a cold, resentful shrug. "You see, Alfred, he felt bad because Aunt Mandy hinted that you'd have to live over there now, and move away from this farm. You see, as she told Joe—I wasn't there—I don't listen to their silly gabble, anyway—but, you see, Alfred, when the little fellow gets an idea like this in his head and keeps hammering and hammering on it, there ain't nothing to do but try to pacify him—as Aunt Mandy told Joe, your interests are so whopping big over there that you will naturally have to be on hand to look after 'em. Your wife—Mrs. Henley hain't got your head for business, and it will be your bounden duty to help her run things. Of course, you *do* love money. A man would be unnatural that didn't, in this day and time, when it is the main thing all humanity is out after. And—and—" Her voice broke. She coughed and glanced aside.

"I'm not going over there, Dixie," he said, firmly. "I'm going to stick right here, and do the best I can. Folks may talk some about me and Hettie not living together, but I can't put up with all that rigmarole over there. It would kill me."

"Aunt Mandy said you might say that at *first*." Dixie steadied her voice. "She told Joe so in my hearing. She said it kinder nettled *some* proud men to have it said they was beholden to their wives, but she said—*she told Joe*—that the proudest man would give in to a situation like that sooner or later. That's why the boy felt so bad, I reckon. He's sure you are going to leave this measly little hole, and that he'll never lay eyes on you again. I've tried to pacify him; but what can I do? I wouldn't advise you to—to do a thing against your best interests, either. You've made a good deal of money, and, like most men, you know its value. As Aunt Mandy told Joe, in case of your wife's death you'd get it all—that is, if you kept on the right side of her and indulged her whims. It seems queer, Alfred, to be standing here in my plain dress before a man as rich and high up in the world as you are."

"Dixie, listen to me!" Henley tried to take her hand, but she drew it from his clasp stiffly and stared sharply into his face. "Dixie, you said, not many days back, that me and you understood one another perfectly, and that nothing would ever change our feelings. I can't make out what you are driving at in all this roundabout palaver, but I know I'm just pine-blank as I was, heart and soul and body. Going over there made me miserable. I never spent such a day in my life. In all that red-tape splendor and high doings I wanted my old ways and nothing else."

"You'll get used to it," the girl said. "Aunt Mandy told Joe, you remember, that you wouldn't like it at first, like any proud man, but that the feeling would wear off. She says your wife ain't a bad-looking woman, and that, in fine clothes and with fine things about her, she will be different from what she was here. Money is power, Alfred; it will have its way in this world. A man might sorter *fancy* he couldn't get along with a woman on his own level, but let her rise high above him, and he won't be exactly in the same boat. He'll naturally think more about her, and, in thinking more about her, and trying harder to please her, his old love will be revived—that is, *if it ever died.* Who could tell? I couldn't."

"Look here, Dixie, listen to me!" Henley's voice shook with subdued passion. "I've never felt like it was exactly honorable, fixed like I am, to tell you—to talk out plain to you about—about how I feel toward you, but you are nagging me on to it. I can't help it. Right now it is burning me up inside. I love you more than a man ever loved a woman. You are in my mind day and night. Standing here before me now you seem as far-off and precious as an angel of light. I want you. I want you from the very bottom dregs of my suffering soul. She asked me to move over there, and when she did it the thought of getting farther away from you made me actually sick. I'd rather live here on a crust of bread than to rule a nation away from you. I may as well confess it. I don't love her. I couldn't in a thousand years. She killed the love I once had. She was slowly killing it by her strange ways while you was growing into my heart by your sweet, brave, unselfish life. Now, I've said all I can. I have no hope of ever having you all for my own, but I can love you—I can worship you, and no earthly power can prevent me."

Even in the starlight he could see the color rising in her face and the shimmer of delight in her eyes. She laid her hand on his tense, throbbing arm. "I see," she said, a sweet cadence in her voice. "I've had all my scare for nothing. Oh, Alfred, I've been nigh crazy. I doubted you. All the talk about your wife's wonderful luck went clean against my better judgment. I kept telling myself that you was different from ordinary men, but, somehow, it wouldn't stick. I may as well tell the truth. That's why I come here to-night. I've been unable to sleep—I was going crazy. You are mine, Alfred, all mine—ain't you?"

He felt her throbbing fingers on his wrist and saw her shoulders rise convulsively. An overpowering force within him urged him to clasp her to himself. He opened his arms, but she deftly caught his hands and held them tightly. "No, no," she said, firmly, "not that—not that! Folks say men and women fixed like we are can't love one another without doing wrong; but they can. The strong ones can, and we are strong, Alfred. Our love is sweet enough as it is. It is of heaven; let's keep it right. You might think you'd respect me if I let you hold me in your arms—here at your own house, with your wife away, but you wouldn't—down in your secret soul you'd feel that I was—was tainted."

"Forgive me, Dixie, darling," he cried. "My blood's in my head; I'm dazed and dazzled by you, little girl; but you know best. I wouldn't do a thing you didn't approve of for all the world."

She released his hands with a little, satisfied laugh, and stepped back toward the gate. "Well, I got what I wanted," she said, frankly. "I've been more in the clutch of Old Harry since you went over there than I ever was in all my born days. All day yesterday and to-day I've brooded and brooded and had evil thoughts, till—well, I'd have gone plumb out o' my mind if I hadn't come straight to you. I may as well tell the truth; I don't want a lie, even a little, tiny one, to smut the confidence between us. Alfred, Joe wasn't worrying so—so *very* much. I was attending to that job. What I said about him was to pump you dry and make you ease my mind. I feel better. I can sleep now. Oh, Alfred—Alfred—good-night!"

He threw out his hands impulsively, but she had evaded them, and, with lowered head, was scudding across the grass toward the light in the cottage.

CHAPTER XXXVIII

The bar in the Oklahoma village kept by Dick Wrinkle was in the centre of the place. It was a narrow, one-story shanty built of undressed boards, the roof of which sloped from the front to the rear. It was devoid of the conventional door-screen, the rough, unpainted shutter, with its padlock and chain, swinging back against the inner wall.

It was early in the morning. The proprietor, a fat, partially bald man of forty years, without a coat, his shirt-sleeves rolled above his elbows, was sweeping into the cracks of the floor the tobacco-quids, stubs of cigars, and remnants of matches left by his carousing customers the night before. He had just tossed his broom into a corner of the room and was looking out of the door when a dust-laden, travel-worn individual with a familiar look slouched around a corner and said:

"Hello, Dick! Don't you know a fellow?"

"By gum!" Wrinkle cried. "Where the hell did you blow from?"

"Georgia—from back home, Dick. Just got here on the night mail-stage. Gosh, what a ride! My windpipe is lined with dust. Quick! Gimme something to wash it out. Three men on the stage, and not a drop in the bunch. I'm burning up."

"By gum!—by gum!" Wrinkle muttered, as he slid behind the counter and set out a long bottle and glasses. "Help yourself, but I'll tell you now it ain't any o' the simon-pure moonshine we used to get in the old red hills. And you say you are direct from there? My Lord! It seems funny to see a man in this God-forsaken place fresh from them old mountains. Since I clean cut myself off—burnt my bridges, as the feller said, I kind o' realize what I lost. Say, Hank, you didn't give me away, did you?"

Bradley drank a half-tumbler of the whiskey, and took a sip of water and cleared his throat. "No, I kept mum, Dick. I said I would, and I did. It wasn't anything to me, nohow. I ain't no gossiper. That was your game, and I saw no reason to spoil it. Shucks! you needn't worry; you are deader back there than a door-nail. Where is that old pal of yours?"

"Dead." Wrinkle raised his hand warningly. "Don't talk about him. He was a good chap, and stuck to me like a friend and a brother."

"Gee! then you must be lonely, away out here—"

"Don't talk about it. Cut that out, Hank. I'm blue enough as it is." Wrinkle moved the bottle and glasses to a crude table near the door and took a chair. Bradley drew up another and sat down. The rising sun blazed in at the open door, and flared like flame in the gilt-framed mirror back of the bar.

"All right. Out she goes. I didn't mean to touch on a sore spot, but I didn't know. You didn't write often."

"I was afraid my letters might be opened by somebody else. I wanted all that to stay wiped out, Hank. I didn't care so much for Het as I did for the old man and woman."

"I wrote you about your wife marrying again?" Bradley said. "I reckon that ain't news?"

"Oh no." Wrinkle had inherited his nonchalant smile and care-free tone from his father. "The damn fool was welcome to 'er. In fact, I owed him that dose. He's the only man I ever had a grudge against, and I was glad he got her. He thought she was exactly the thing he was looking for; I reckon he knows what he got by this time. Marrying her was the foolishest thing I ever was guilty of, and I think I done it to spite him. I ought to have let 'im marry 'er an' then 'a' took 'er away from him. I could 'a' done it as easy as falling off a log. She was plumb daft. I reckon she cut up considerable when the news was spread that I was done for."

"It was the talk of the county, Dick. Folks thought she'd have to be sent to the asylum. Her uncle, Ben Warren, who was so rich, you know, took pity on her and made her come visit him so she could get her mind off her trouble. When she got back, Henley made a dead set for her. But while he got her, Dick, she never cared for him. I reckon you never heard about what she done last summer."

"I haven't had a line from home in two years, Hank. She didn't quit 'im, did she?—she didn't throw 'im clean over, after all, did she?" And Wrinkle laughed expectantly as he pushed the bottle toward his companion.

Bradley's eyes shone; the neck of the bottle in his unsteady hand tinkled against the edge of the tumbler as he poured out another drink.

"No, but she come nigh to it. She drove him off to Texas, where he pretended to have some business or other. Dick, she erected a monument to you that cost a stack o' money.

You can see it from the Chester square, looming up like a ghost."

"The hell you say!"

"Not only that, but she sent off for a silver-tongued preacher and had your funeral preached in bang-up style."

"Good Lord! What did she do that for?" Wrinkle groaned, and his mouth set rigidly.

"Because the notion struck her," Bradley smiled. "She made a mark for herself. She's the pride of all the women in that section. Whenever a woman is accused of being changeable, your wife is pointed at to give it the lie. You knew she was looking after your father and mother, didn't you?"

"Yes, yes, you wrote about that," the barkeeper answered, his eyes sullenly averted. "I thought she'd do something of the sort."

"And she has done it right, Dick; they are as rosy as two babies. Henley makes plenty of money in one way and another, and he foots all her bills, or did till—till—well, I haven't told you all the news yet. Dick, neither one of us likes Henley. He's crossed me several times in his high and mighty way, but he's got us both down now and he can sneer at us all he wants to. No wind ever blowed that didn't blow profit to him. You thought you was handing him a gold-brick when you left him your wife, but, la me, Dick, you done him the biggest favor that one man ever done another."

"What the hell you giving me?" Wrinkle raised a pair of wondering eyes to Bradley's design-filled face, and fixed them there anxiously.

"Dick," Bradley toyed with the tumbler, turning it upside-down and stamping rings of liquor on the table—"Dick, Ben Warren died and left her every dollar of his estate. She's as rich as cream, and Henley—huh! he's so stuck-up he can't walk. His lordly strut fairly shakes the ground when he goes about. That fellow's as deep as the sky is high. Folks think now that he knew she would come into that money away back when he first set out to catch her. They don't know how he got onto it, but it looks like he had a tip from some source or other."

With the lips and throat of a corpse, Dick Wrinkle swore; the pupils of his eyes dilated; his yellow fingers, like prongs of dried rawhide, clutched the edge of the table, and the tremor of his body shook it visibly.

"I see it all now," he gasped. "He must have known it; he was crazy to get her, and—and he took her as soon after—after I left as he could possibly manage it. The Lord only knows what means he used, for, as you say, she still loves me."

"Folks say Henley turns up his nose at common folks now," Bradley went on. "He's planning a great stock-farm, and going to keep fine-blooded race-horses, and him and his wife is going to travel about and see the world. Things certainly run crooked in this life." Bradley laughed significantly, his studious eyes on his victim's tortured visage. "Here you are, all alone away out here in a measly little joint like this when your old enemy is living like a king in the bosom of your family. Why, he's even robbed you of your daddy and mammy. You are dead, buried, and laughed at, Dick. I reckon you are not making much out of this thing?" Bradley swept the meagre stock and cheap fixtures with a contemptuous glance.

"Don't make my salt!" Wrinkle groaned. "Nothing is

coming in, and no prospect of a change. New town, Citico, drawing all the trade. I've thought of selling out. There's a fellow here that has made me a cash offer for the whole shooting-match—a thousand dollars down. He's a gambler that is at the end of his rope; his wife says she'll quit 'im and marry another man if he don't get into something more steady. She's willing to put up the money if he'll buy me out. He's crazy for a deal. He's got friends and can make it go. His wife's kin live here and she won't move. He's in every hour of the day, shaking his wad in my face. I saw him just now as I come down to open up. I'd let him have the dang thing, but I don't know where to go. I'm sick o' the game, Hank. I've had enough of the wild and woolly West. I've laid awake many and many a night, by gosh! mighty nigh crying for the old life in the mountains. Lord, Lord, I set here sometimes when there ain't anybody about except a drunk Injun or cowboy and git so blue and lonely that it leaks out of me like sweat and drops on the floor. I reckon it is kinder natural for a feller to want what he's been brought up on, especially if he has, by his own act, cut it out and signed his death-warrant. Oh, that was a fool thing, Hank—a blasted fool thing! It seems to me that I dream o' them damn mountains and blue skies every night hand-running—and the good, old-fashioned grub we used to have! And, Hank, I hain't just a dead man—another feller has took my place and, as you say, is gloating over me."

"Oh, well, as for that matter," and Bradley looked idly out through the doorway, "you ought to settle his hash—pull 'im down from his perch."

"Yes," ironically, "now that would be a good idea, wouldn't it?"

"The easiest thing on earth, Dick. Alf Henley ain't legally married to your wife. He's living with her, but they hain't been tied by law."

The barkeeper stared blankly; his features worked as if he were trying to solve a mathematical problem. He started to speak, but his mouth fell open and remained so; his lower lip hung wet with saliva.

"Why, no," Bradley went on. "No woman can legally marry another man while her husband is alive. She didn't get no divorce. She's your wife yet, and Alf Henley has simply slid in and taken possession of all you got on earth. I know what I'd do; I'd hike back there and walk in as if nothing had happened, and I'd kick that skunk out, too, or shoot the top of his head off. Dick, she never loved anybody but you; she'd be so glad to have you back she'd throw her arms round your neck and hold you tight. It is the talk of the whole county about how true she is to your memory. It has driven Henley mighty nigh crazy."

Wrinkle stood up. He was shaking like a man with palsy. He leaned over the table and gazed almost tearfully into the designing eyes before him.

"Yes, old Het's a good girl," he muttered. "She was always the right stuff. I know in reason that she'd be the—the same as she was. I know her through and through and exactly how to manage her, but, Hank, they all think I'm—dead!"

"Folks have made mistakes before," Bradley argued, in a tense and yet plausible tone. "You was hit in the head by a falling beam in that storm. You told me so. You was laid up with a lot of others in the hospital, and for a solid month didn't know your hat from a hole in the ground. That's how the report went out that you was done for. Why, Dick, there have been no end of cases where men have not known where they belonged for half a lifetime, and then got it all back in a flash. Nobody would doubt that you was in that fix. I'll help you work it. I'm your friend, and I want to see you get what is due you. That man's robbing you, choking the life-blood out of you. You've simply got to go back and claim your rights."

"I couldn't do it, Hank." The barkeeper sank back into his chair, and, with his elbows on the table, he ran his blunt fingers through the fringe of hair around his glistening pate. "I'm in a hole. I'm clean done for. I wouldn't be good at such a racket as that. I wouldn't know how to fix it. I'd forget my tale; I ain't got much memory. Hush, I saw that gambler turn the corner. He's headed here."

"Dick, you'd better take my advice and sell out," Bradley advised. "You'll be a damn fool if you don't. It's the chance of a lifetime."

"Sh!" Wrinkle hissed, warningly, as a shadow fell athwart the floor and a tall, middle-aged man, with dyed mustache and whiskers, sauntered in at the door. He was jocularly called "the Parson," owing to his dignified and clerical appearance. His trousers were neatly folded into the tops of his very high boots, and his shirt-bosom was broad and none too clean, and his flowered silk waistcoat was cut so low that two buttons sufficed to keep it in place. He wore a flowing, black necktie, glistening foil-back studs, and rings of the same quality.

"I'm up early," he laughed, nodding to Bradley as a stranger might. "My wife pulled me out o' bed. She has got Shanks to agree to sell me his grocery, part cash and part on tick, and she wants me to watch and see what sort o' early-morning trade he's got. She knows I don't know as much about that line as this, but she thinks I kin learn, and maybe keep better company. I reckon it will be a deal betwixt now and ten o'clock—that is, unless you make up your mind to sell out."

Dick Wrinkle was looking into the speaking eyes of his old

friend across the table. He knew well enough that the gambler's remark was merely a poker bluff, and yet it stirred certain natural fears within him.

"You can't root me out of a good thing with a little wad like that, Parson," he said, rising and going behind the counter and briskly wiping off its surface more from habit than necessity. "I've just met an old friend of mine from back in God's Country, and we was just talking over old times. What'll you have?"

"The one next the jug," the gambler said, and Wrinkle set the bottle before him, watching him fill the glass with unsteady eyes.

"I don't think Dick is in a trading humor," Bradley informed him with a cordial smile. "We've been talking over old times, and he's hot under the collar. He's got an enemy back home that has been throwing dirt on him. If I was in Dick's place I'd go back and call him down."

"I don't know anything about that," the gambler said, and he drank, wiped his lips on his hand, and stepped to the centre of the bar and peered out. "I see Shanks in front of his shebang now. If I make him an offer and he accepts it, it is all off between us, Wrinkle—you understand that. I've got to settle down at something, and I'll do it without delay. What do you say?"

"Oh, I've said all I'm going to." Wrinkle tossed his head and applied himself to restoring the bottle and washing the glasses beneath the counter.

"All right. Good-day." He stepped out of the doors

Wiping his hands on a towel, Wrinkle came round to the table and leaned on it.

"You damn fool!" Bradley cried, in disgust. "That's all I've got to say."

"It's gone too far, Hank," Wrinkle groaned. "It was my own doings; I've got to take my medicine. He's gone, anyway."

Bradley stared at the floor and pointed grimly at the gambler's tell-tale shadow. Then he whispered: "Don't be a fool; close with him. Secure his money, and I'll help you get your rights—don't lose this chance. A thousand dollars is a lot of money back home. Call him in."

A change crept over Wrinkle's visage; he glided back behind the counter, picked up his towel and began wiping the counter's top till he was in a position to see the gambler. He caught the man's eye and laughed tauntingly:

"Hey, Parson, you are always making your brags," he called out. "I'll bet you haven't seen a thousand dollars in a month of Sundays."

"You think not, eh?" And the tall man stalked back into the room, whipped out a roll of bills, and tossed them on the table in front of Bradley. "Say, stranger, umpire this game—count it. I'm ready, but I won't be ten minutes from now."

Bradley smiled easily and counted the twenty fifty-dollar bills.

"It's all right, Dick," he said. "You don't know what to do. I'm going to close it for you. He'll take it, stranger." Bradley's eyes were on the startled gambler. "I'll act for him."

There was a pause. Wrinkle's face was set under an expression of blended fear, doubt, and half-willingness, but he said nothing, simply staring at Bradley as a subject might under the spell of a hypnotist.

"Yes, he'll take it," Bradley repeated. "Get your hat, Dick, and leave the gentleman in possession—the agreement sweeps everything, doesn't it?"

"Yes, lock, stock, and barrel." The gambler was trying to conquer the look of elation which had captured his features.

"All right," Wrinkle gave in, doggedly, and he reached for the money and counted it. When he had finished he took his hat down from a nail on the wall and extended his hand. "Luck to you, Parson," he said. "I reckon I'll shake the dust of this place off my feet. I've got work to do at home."

CHAPTER XXXIX

Dick Wrinkle, travel-stained and covered with dust, a small valise in his hand, trudged down the declivitous footpath of the mountain amid the splendor of late summer leafage and occasional dashes of rhododendron and other wild flowers, the color and scent of which greeted his senses, dulled as they were to the finer things of life, as a subtle something belonging to the past which had been lost and was regained. Now and then he would stop, rest his bag on the ground, and breathe in the crisp air as if it were a palpable substance that was pleasing to his palate. At such moments, when the open spaces between hanging boughs, tangled vines, and trunks of trees would permit, his glance, half doubtful, half confident, would rest on the palatial residence in the valley below, which, at every step, had been growing nearer and nearer.

"Yes, that's the place," he said once, in a certain tone of exultation. "It must be; I've followed the directions to the letter, and there couldn't be two such dandy houses as that round here. And it is hers, in her own right, to boss over and to keep or to sell or to do as we please with."

When he had reached the level ground he found himself in a broad, well-graded road that led straight to the gates of the mansion, and when he was quite near to it he observed on the right-hand side an extensive peach-orchard. It was the gathering season, and in a shed open at the sides, and containing long, canvas-covered tables, several negro men and women were busy packing the ripe peaches into new crates which were being nailed up by a white man in overalls and a conical straw-hat. The pedestrian leaned against the whitewashed board-fence and scanned the group, seeking a familiar face. But those before him had a strange look. He was wondering if he could be mistaken in the place, after all, when, his glance roving to the nearest row of trees, he saw an aged man emerge with his arms full of peaches, which he took to the nearest negro packer. Dick Wrinkle didn't recognize him under his broad hat and in his fine clothes, but a thrill went through him when he heard him address the servant.

"Put these jim-dandies on top with the yaller side up," he commanded. "They are a lettle mite soft, but they've only got to go over the mountain. They are for the head boss, an' you'd better pack 'em right. He's powerful fond o' good ripe peaches. I've seed 'im eat 'em with the skin on, an', as much as I like 'em, I can't do that. I'd as soon chaw sandpaper."

"It's Pa," the man at the fence said, in a tone of relief. "I'd know his voice amongst a million. He looks younger by ten years than he did. I reckon high living did it. Well, it's my turn at it, an' it won't be long 'fore I set in. I may have trouble at the start, but I'll weather the storm. I know who I'm dealing with. I didn't live with 'er as long as I did without learning a few things."

Dropping his bag over the fence, he climbed over after it. He stood for a moment, hesitatingly, and then, taking out his pocket-handkerchief, he flicked the dust off his coat and trousers and new shoes. He was well and rather tastily attired. He was shaved, and his scant hair showed that it had been brushed. He wore a heavy gold chain, which had a prosperous look stretching across his black waistcoat. The old man had turned back toward the trees, and, without being noticed by the active packers, his son followed him, bag in hand. Old Jason, his eyes raised in searching for the choicest fruit among the low branches of the trees, did not see his son till he was close behind him.

"Now, Pa," Dick Wrinkle began, calmly enough, "don't jump out o' your hide. Reports to the contrary, I'm alive and kicking."

Turning at the sound of the familiar voice, the old man started, an exclamation, half of fear, half of gratified wonder, escaping his lips. He stared fixedly, and his mouth fell open, exposing his quid of tobacco. The peaches in his hands rolled to the ground, and, utterly bewildered, he stooped as if to pick them up, but paused and stared again. "Lord, have mercy!" he cried. "Lord, have mercy, who'd have dreamt it—you back—you—you here! Why, we all heard—we all 'lowed—we all was plumb sure you was—"

"I know. Never mind about that," the younger said, with a shrug meant to shake off the topic. "Where's Ma, and—and Hettie?"

"Your Ma?—your Ma? Why, she's down at the spring-house watchin' 'em try a new-fangled churn, or—or was a few minutes ago. Why, Dick, we all thought you was—was—"

"Oh, I know, but where is Hettie?"

"Hettie? Oh, my Lord! Why, Dick, boy, hain't you heard a thing?"

"I've heard a sight more 'n I want to hear or will again," Dick Wrinkle said, with lowering brows and a voice which seemed to bury itself in a mass of inner threats as to dire approaching events. "I've come to propose a—a settlement, without blood if it can be arranged; if not, we kin spill plenty of it in the up-to-date Western style. I've been away, and was detained longer 'n I expected by circumstances over which I had no control, and in my absence, I'm told, my household—an', by gosh, my honor!—has been stained. I'm not out looking for trouble, but trouble may throw itself in my way. I'm prepared to do an outraged man's part. I've got a medium-sized gun in my hip-pocket and a young cannon in this valise."

"Oh, Dick, Dick, we mustn't have blood spilt, for all we do!" Old Jason's display of actual concern was the first ever wrung from him. "Besides, the law—the law must be considered."

"Oh, I'm willing to consider the law," Dick said. "I'll do a lot o' things if I'm not made any madder 'n I am right now. I'm glad to git back, an' I don't want to be mad. I'll do as much toward keepin' peace as any other man. There ain't anything so awfully unheard of in what happened to me. Fellers has been off from home before, an' the whole world wasn't plumb upset by it."

"But they didn't rise from the dead," old Jason submitted, argumentatively. "How on earth did you manage to do it? I mean—"

The son's glance for the first time wavered. He looked toward the towering mountain as if for moral sustenance. His lips mutely moved as if he were conning a lesson he was learning by rote, and then, seeing the question still in his father's blearing eyes, he began:

"I met with trouble, Pa—I reckon some would style it an accident. When that big tornado struck the country out there and so many was blowed to smithereens and never had even the pieces of 'em put together again—I say, Pa, when all that happened I was struck in the back of the head by a rock or a beam or a plank—I never knew exactly which—and never got my right senses back for a long, long time afterward. In fact, I didn't even know my own name or even recall you and Ma, or my old home back here. I say, it was all a plumb blank till—till—"

"I know, till you heard about Hettie and—and—but go on. I'm a listenin'."

"Well, there ain't much to tell." Dick Wrinkle was perspiring freely. He took off his hat and wiped his red neck and bald pate with an impatient hand. "Being hit that way, you see, was the last thing I remembered. Folks say I must have wandered about over the plains like a wild animal that didn't know how to do a thing but eat and drink what I could run across. Some cowboys tuck me up and l'arned me to cook, and I followed that for a long time. Then, t'other day, they put me on the back of a bucking bronco, just for the fun o' the thing. I stayed on as long as I could, but he finally flung me over on my head. That fetched me to. The whole thing come back like a flash. Several years had slipped by, but when I come to my right mind I thought that same storm was raging. I refused to believe so much time had passed till a cowboy showed me the date on a newspaper, and that plumb floored me."

"You don't say!" Old Wrinkle stroked his beard thoughtfully and, in paternal sympathy, avoided his son's anxious eyes. "Well, well, that was all-powerful curious, but—but I've read of sech things, and maybe Hettie has, too; if she hain't, I'll try to show her that—I mean—but I reckon I'd better trot over to the spring-house and kinder lead your Ma up to it, and not have it sprung too suddenlike. She ain't one o' your weak sort that flops down at the slightest report of good or bad luck, but we'd better be on the safe side. I'll tell yore Ma, I say, an' then I'll go up to the big house an see if I can do anything with Hettie."

"Well, maybe you'd better," Dick Wrinkle agreed, slowly, "and I reckon you'd better give her a full account o' how it all happened. I don't want to be eternally going over it. I've had enough of it myself."

"You mean about—yore crazy spell?" The old man stared inquiringly.

"Yes, about all that. I've told you—I've done give you full particulars. You know as much about it as I do. A man out of his right senses don't remember anything worth while, nohow."

"Well, I hope I'll git it straight, an' not backside foremost. It would be funny if I begun it whar the bronco throwed you and ended up in the tornado. Het will have to be worked fine, Dick. She sorter feels 'er oats now. She always did hold 'er head in the air, but it's higher now since she got rich. She mought take a fool notion that the bronco throwed you powerful soon after her change o' luck."

"I don't want 'er dern money!" Dick Wrinkle snarled, his glance shifting unsteadily. "I don't need *anybody's* cash. I've got a thousand dollars in my pocket now."

"You say you have?" The eyes under the bushy gray brows fluttered thoughtfully. "Well, if I was you, I believe, Dick, that I'd not haul it out an' make a show of it. You see—well, you see, it's like this: Het's a thinkin' woman, an' sorter keen-eyed at times, when she wants to be, an' lookin' at a wad like that mought—I don't say, it *would*—but it mought, bein' a sort o' money-maker herself, it mought set her to wonderin' how a feller clean out o' his senses could accumulate so much cash in times as hard as these. If crazy fellers kin load up like that out thar, men of brains could walk clean off with the State."

Dick Wrinkle started slightly and let his glance trail along the ground, in several directions before lifting it again to the would-be helpful countenance before him.

"I made it *after I got my senses back*," he said, finally, and rather doggedly.

"Well, I don't believe I'd let that out, *nuther*," said old Wrinkle, in a tone that was meant to be kindness itself. "You see, Dick, the bronco throwed you just t'other day, an' a thing like that is liable to git you all balled up. A woman like Het mought ax a heap o' fool questions, an' you hain't had yore right mind back long enough to go into a game like that yet awhile."

"Oh, I don't give a damn, one way or another!" the younger snorted. "It ain't any o' her business, nohow where I was nor how long I was gone. She's my wife, I ain't the fust man that ever went away for a spell and then come home."

"I was jest wonderin'," the old man said, soothingly, "if yore old high-an'-mighty way wouldn't be best, Dick. All the tornado an' buckin'-bronco business may be a waste of talk. Het tuck to you in the fust place beca'se you sorter held a tight rein over 'er, an', if I'm any judge, Alf Henley, with all his easy ways an' indulgence, hain't driv' her over any smooth road. I've heard it said that a woman will kitten to a man that beats 'er quicker 'n she'll kitten to one that kittens to her; an', if you set in on this fine place with a bowed head, you'll be duckin' at every turn."

"Well, you go on an' tell her I've got home," was the request of the son. "Tell 'er I want to see 'er, too, an' that right off. You may tell 'er I'm loaded for bear—that I've heard about the way she's been going on with Alf Henley behind my back, an' that a day of reckoning has arrived. It's been delayed, but it's here."

"All right," old Wrinkle said, gravely, "that's the best way. You are comin' to yore senses, Dick. It wouldn't be natural for you to let a fine place an' a little money scare the life out of you. It's lucky Alf ain't here. I don't think he'll give you any trouble, though. Some thought Het's good luck would spoil 'im, but, if I'm any judge, he seems sorter 'shamed about it. He hain't been here but once, an' then acted like a fish out o' water. He's a money-maker, an' too live a chap to want to put on a dead man's shoes. You've come in good time, an' if Het will let you stay you'll be in clover the rest o' yore days. Between you an' Alf I naturally favor *you*, of course. Me 'n yore Ma felt all right here, but we *did* have a shaky sort o' claim, you'll admit, bein' akin to the fountain-head in sech a roundabout way, an' with Alf Henley's name in the pot, too. Well, I'll be goin'. Watch the back porch, an' if you see me wave my hat up and down, this way, you come right on. If I was to wave it to one side, like this—but never mind; we'll do the best we kin."

"All right," agreed Dick. "I'll go pick me some ripe peaches. The very sight of 'em makes my mouth water."

CHAPTER XL

One clear, warm evening three days later, on his return to his lonely house, Henley went into the kitchen and prepared his simple meal, and, after eating it, he went to his room to get his pipe and tobacco for a smoke. He had no sooner entered the room than he noticed that it had undergone a change. Some one had taken the white lace curtains from his wife's room and put them up over his windows. Pictures in frames which had been ill-placed in the parlor now hung by his bed and over the mantelpiece. A neat-colored rug from Mrs. Henley's room ornamented the floor, and on it stood a table from the hall, holding the family Bible, an album of photographs, some other books from the parlor, and a vase containing fresh roses. The open fireplace was filled with evergreens, and the rough, brick hearth had been whitewashed, the lime giving out a cool, pungent odor.

"She done it!" he exclaimed. "Nobody else would have thought of it." And he sat down in a rocking-chair, in which some cushions had been placed, and, not wishing to contaminate his surroundings by smoke, he leaned back and enjoyed it as he had enjoyed few things in his life. "Yes, she done it," he kept saying. "She slipped over here, busy as she is at home, and done it just to please me. She is a sweet, good, noble girl."

As the dusk came on he went outdoors, lighted his pipe, and

strolled down to the gate. Leaning on it, he looked toward the mountains, which were rapidly receding into the night. How majestic and glorious it all seemed! How soothing to his sore spirit was the gift which had been so delicately bestowed and which nothing should ever take from him! He wouldn't have admitted to himself that he was there at the gate because it was the hour at which Dixie drove her cow up from the pasture across the way, but he was there with his glance on the pasture-gate. He saw her coming presently, and went to meet her. Her color rose as she recognized him above the back of the waddling cow, and she assayed a mien of casual indifference as she returned his smile.

"I have to tell you," he began, as he turned and suited his step to hers, "how tickled I am over the way you fixed up my room. I'm certainly much obliged to you. It's a different place altogether."

"I'm glad you didn't scold me for the liberty I took," she said. "I saw your front-door wide open, and—and, well, I just couldn't help it. I never saw such a mess in all my life. It made me sick to look at it. I simply had to clean it up. Oh, Alfred, you are just a big baby, and it's a pity to see you left this way."

"And to think that you done it!" Henley said. "With them little hands, and—and for a big, hulking chap like me."

"Oh, it was fun," she answered. "Joe was with me; he whitewashed the hearth and cut the pine-tops for the chimney. He'd have moved every stick of furniture out of the parlor if I'd 'a' let him."

"I kept bachelor's hall for years," Henley said, "but I never once thought of fixing up the room I occupied. I can see now how much difference it makes. La me, Dixie, I could set there by the hour and just—just enjoy it, knowing that you—"

"Don't talk about it any more," she interrupted, with a wistful, upward glance. "It makes me feel sad to think that after all you've done for other folks you should make so much over what you ought to have by rights. I actually cried the other night. I was driving the cow 'long here and saw you through the window in the kitchen cooking your supper. A woman's heart is tender toward children and to a man that she—to a man that is plumb helpless and bungling about over things he has no business to fool with. Alfred, your frying-pan had a sediment of eggs, meat, grease, and pure dirt on the bottom as hard as the iron itself. I had to chop it out with a hatchet. Your coffee-kettle was full to the spout with old grounds, and you left a ham of meat lying flat on the floor, and the flour-barrel was open for the hens to nest in."

"So you was there, too," said Henley. "I thought Pomp done it."

"Pomp? He's a man, if he is black," the girl sniffed. "He wouldn't have thought anything was wrong if he'd found the house-cat sleeping in the bread-tray. No, you've got to be attended to some way or other. I don't know how, but it's got to be done."

"I'll make it all right," Henley declared. "I'm used to knocking about."

Dixie shook her head. They had reached his gate, and she paused, allowing the cow to trudge on homeward. "You may not know it, Alfred," she said, "but you are changed. You look restless and unsettled. You made one of your best trades the other day in buying them mules, but you haven't been to see 'em once since you turned 'em in the pasture. It ain't like you. You used to be so full of fun. This money your wife has come into has upset you. You don't feel exactly right about it."

"I'll admit it," he said, softly. "I want her to get all she can out of the good things of this world; but, somehow, that knocked me out—clean out. I've made my own way in this life, and I want to keep doing it. Men come to me every day and wish me joy in another man's death. I get mad enough to slap 'em in the mouth. One fool said it was silly of me to keep working when I had such a soft bed to lie on."

"I knew you'd feel that way," Dixie said, her eyes full of sympathetic tenderness. "I was just thinking to-day of how many trials we've been through together. I've helped you a little, maybe, and you've been my mainstay. There is only one thing I'm plumb ashamed of, Alfred, and when I think of it I get hot enough to singe my hair."

"What was that?" he asked in surprise.

"You remember—the time I engaged myself to a man I had never laid my eyes on." And Henley saw that she was blushing. "I'd give my right arm, and do my work with my left, to wipe that off my slate forever."

"Don't bother about that." He tried to comfort her. "You only come nigh making the mistake I actually tumbled into. You ought to be thankful you escaped the consequences that I had to shoulder. I didn't know Hettie, and the only true love is the sort that comes from a deep knowledge of a person's character. You see, I know you, little girl, through and through. I've seen you in trouble and in joy, and found you all there—true blue, the sweetest woman God ever made. If I'm out o' sorts here lately it is because I can't keep from seeing what an awful, life-long mistake I made. It is seeing the thing you'd die to have, but which is out of your reach, that makes you see how empty the whole world is."

"Don't say any more." Dixie impulsively touched his arm and then drew her hand away. "I could listen to you talk that way all night, but I must do my duty to you and me both. Talking of what we've lost won't bring us any nearer to it. As for me, well—I'm a sight happier than I was before she went off. I don't exactly know why, but I am. Every night before I go to bed I tuck away my two old folks, and then hear little Joe say his lessons and his prayers, and then I go out in the yard and look at your light gleaming and twinkling through the vines about your window. Then my heart gets full of a feeling so sweet and soothing that when I look above the whole starry sky seems to shower down comfort and blessings. Then I thank God, Alfred—not for giving you to me like other women get their partners for life, but for giving me a love that can't die as long as the universe stands."

He saw her breast heave with emotion. He tried to find his voice, but it seemed to have sunken too deep within his throat for utterance. The vague form of a horse and rider appeared outlined against the horizon down the road. She was moving away, but he touched her arm and detained her.

"Wait till he passes," he said. "Don't go yet—not just yet!"

"I ought not to be here talking to you after dark," she mildly protested. There was a pause, during which the eyes of both were on the horseman. "Why," she cried, "it is Mr. Wrinkle!"

And so it was. The old man reined in his sweating mount, and, throwing a stiff leg over the animal's rump, he stood down beside them.

"Howdy do?" he greeted them. "I've just started to yore house, Alf. I'm totin' a big piece o' news. I'm late. I had to stop an' tell it to a hundred, at least, on the way. You mought guess all day and all night an' never once hit it. Alf, we've had an increase in the family—but hold on, hold on! it hain't that—it hain't another one o' my baby jokes. I know better 'n to try a second dose on you out o' the same bottle. Alf, Dick Wrinkle hain't dead."

"Not dead?" Henley and Dixie repeated the words in the same breath as they tensely leaned forward.

"No, an' that ain't the only thing to be reckoned with. He's over at home now, stouter and in better trim than he ever was in his life. He appeared to me in the orchard whar we was packin' peaches, an' I was plumb flabbergasted. It seems that he would have reported sooner if he had been fully at hisself. He wasn't actually killed in that tornado, but blowed off somers an' got a hit in the skull and was fixed so that his remembrance played tricks on him. At one time he imagined he was a cook for some cowboys, and a lot more fool antics. He would have been that way yet—I mean in his crazy fix—but he says a pony throwed 'im an' it all come back. You'll have to get him to tell you about it. I've got it all mixed up."

Henley's wide-staring eyes sought Dixie's face. She was pale, still, and mute.

"Well, I've got to be going," she said, in a quavering voice to old Jason. "I haven't had a chance, Mr. Wrinkle, to ask you how Mrs. Henley likes it over there. I hope your wife is well. They say the water is freestone on that side of the mountain, and that is better for the health than our hard limestone. You must tell them both that we all miss them every day."

"Hold on! hold on!" Wrinkle said. "You'd better hear the straight o' this thing. You'll wish you did, for folks will have it all lopsided by to-morrow, an' I'll give you dead cold facts."

"But I've got my cow to milk," Dixie faltered, her color coming back, "and it's growing late."

"I was going to tell you how Het tuck it," Wrinkle ran on, and there was nothing for the girl to do but remain. "Dick told me to go on up to the big house an' hand in his report in as fair shape as I could, an' I sent his mammy, who was havin' ten fits a minute, to him, and went up to Het's room, whar she lies down at that time o' the day. She's as tough as rawhide, you know, an' I wasn't afraid she'd keel over, so while she was frownin' at me like she thought I ought not to have butted in on her privacy that way, I up an' told her the news. Well, sir, it plumb floored her. You kin well imagine it would take a big thing to down Het, but that did. She set up on the edge o' the bed, makin' wild stabs with 'er feet at 'er slippers, and lookin' wall-eyed an' scared.

"'Pa,' says she, 'this is one o' yore jokes.'"

"'Joke a dog's hind-foot!' says I. 'If you think it's a joke you jest step to that thar window an' look down at the peach-packin' shed.'"

"Well, sir, you don't have to tell a woman twice how to verify an important report. She riz like she was on springs, an' thumped across the room in her stockin'-feet, an' looked out o' the window, with me right in her wake. An' thar, as plain as a sheep in the middle of a stream, stood Dick a-pealin' an' eatin' the peaches his mammy was fetchin' him. An' now comes the part that may not suit you, Alf, one bit; but I've come to fetch the whole truth an' nothin' but the truth. In consideration of what Het has fell heir to, an' one thing an' another, it may not be good news to you to hear that, instead o' lookin' sorry, Het actually chuckled an' reddened up like a gal in her teens.

"'It's him!' she said. 'Thank God, it's Dick—it's Dick!'

"I couldn't pull 'er away from the window. She jest leaned agin the sash an' stared, an' rubbed 'er hands together, an' went on like she was gettin' religion. Then I set in, as well as I knowed how, to tell 'er about Dick's mishap, but she waved her hand backward-like, an' stopped me. 'Leave all that out,' she said, sorter impatient, as if she couldn't think of but one thing at a time. 'You needn't tell about that—he's alive, that's enough—Dick's alive!' And, would you believe it, folks? She flopped herself down in a chair an' cried and tuck on at a great rate. It upset me so that I give up the whole dang business. I went down an' told Dick he'd better go attend to 'er. He axed me how the crazy spell went down, an' I told 'im I didn't think she'd even heard it, or ever would, for that matter. Women seem to scent a thing from far off that they don't want to believe, an' close every pore of their bodies an' eyes an' ears so it can't get in."

"Well, what was the final upshot of it all?" Henley was quite calm, though a great new light was flaring in his eyes as they rested on Dixie, who was looking off in the direction of the mountain, her little hands grasping the palings of the fence, her tense body thrown slightly backward.

"Dick's my own son," Wrinkle made answer, "but I got out o' all patience with him. He ought to 'a' let well enough alone, bein' as Het was willin' to let bygones be bygones. But not him. As me 'n him walked up to the house, an' he looked over them broad acres on all sides, an' as we went in at that fine door, he seemed to get back to his old self—an' that is one thing that sorter makes me believe a little in the crazy spell, for he looked like a man that had just waked up from a long nap, shore enough. He was the maddest chap I ever laid eyes on as he went up them steps to her private quarters. I followed. I wasn't wanted, I reckon, but I had to see the thing through. She come up to him, Het did, all wet from head to foot with tears, and tried to throw 'er arms around his neck, but he shoved 'er off, he did, an' begun the awfulest rip-rantin' jowerin' you ever heard, about the scan'lous way she'd carried on with you while he was off. He didn't say nothin' about his spell—he had no apologies to make. Accordin' to his way o' lookin' at it, she'd blackened the white purity of his home while his back was turned, an' nothing but blood, an' whole gurglin' streams of it, would suit him. Well, they had it nip and tuck for fully an hour, an' then they come to an agreement. They was to drive over to Carlton the next day and ax Judge Fisk if Het had disgraced 'erself past recall; and so we hit the road bright an' early. The judge was mighty nice. He said a big mistake had evidently been made, but it was one that the law could rectify if Het 'u'd just grease its wheels properly. He said he'd quit settin' on the bench hisse'f—bein' beat by the Prohibitionists in the last election—an' had gone back to practise at the bar, an' would gladly take the case in hand. He saw plainly, he said, that it was Het's duty, havin' come into sech a big estate as that, to clear her record all she could, even if it *did* cost her considerable outlay, first an' last. He summed the whole thing up as calm, an' bent over with his pencil in his hand, an' peepin' above his specs, just like he was deliverin' a charge to a jury in a murder case. It was for Het to weigh the evidence pro and con, an' consider, an' deliberate, an' make her final choice betwixt the two claimants she had got tangled up with. He didn't know, he went on to say—an', of course, he must have suspicioned that she'd already made up her mind, bein' as she had fetched Dick along an' left you out in the wet—he didn't know, he said, but what jestice sorter leaned to the prior claimant, possession bein' nine parts of the law, an' Dick bein' incapacitated an' rendered null an' void fer the time involved. As to the crazy spell Dick had, he gave it as his opinion that such things had been heard of often. He'd 'a' made a good doctor, that judge would; he said the brain was the finest constructed part of the human an—an—anatomy—that's it,—anatomy. He said it was made up of a bunch of fibres an' strings as thin as spider-webs, an' that an expert with the saw an' knife could open a man's skull an' tickle the ends of 'em an' make the patient cut a different caper for every nerve he touched. He said that's why human nature was so varied. He said, with all fees paid, that Het could suit her own tastes an' inclination. He said that she could claim that Dick's quar condition an' his disinclination to furnish a support equal to her reasonable demands justified her in callin' the fust deal off; or, on t'other hand, that she could regyard it as the only obligation to which she was bound by law or religion, an' that he would set about—after the fee was paid in cash, or by check on any good, reliable bank, or even by a solid, negotiable note—he would set about to have the second weddin' set aside, and an-an—"

"Annulled," Henley threw into the gap.

"Yes, that's it—annulled," Wrinkle echoed. "An' he advised her to have it docketed for next week's special term o' court, and that he'd promise to rush it through without hitch or bobble. Dick seemed better satisfied after they left the judge, an' they driv' back home without any more wranglin'. Dick has bought him some new fishin'-tackle, an' is off to the river to-day. He has a natural pride in the big plantation, and rid all over it this mornin'. He says he has some new ideas that he picked up in the West—before he had his spell, I reckon—which he intends to apply there."

"Well, I really must hurry on," Dixie said, turning away. "Give my love to your wife and to Mrs.—to your daughter-in-law. Good-night."

The two men saw her hastening away in the thickening shadows. There was a vast throbbing within Henley's breast. The whole firmament above seemed to be shimmering with a subtle, spiritual light. He laid his hand almost affectionately on the old man's shoulder and beamed down into his eyes.

"It is all for the best," he said. "I had no right to Dick's place. I found that out long ago."

"Thar's one thing I don't like about it." Wrinkle was thoughtful, and a rare mood it was for him. "I was thinkin' about it ridin' over here. Alf, I don't like to give you up. As God is my holy judge, I like you—I like you plumb down to the ground. You are a man an' a gentleman."

"Thank you." Henley's voice rang with a triumph he strove hard to suppress. "Come in and put up your hoss and stay all night. I'll cook you some supper and you can sleep in your bed, like old times."

"Much obliged all the same, Alf, but I reckon I can't. Het an' Dick both laid down the law on that particular point. He's throwed that at 'er several times already—I mean about lettin' you support me an' his Ma. Seems like that sorter hurts his pride. He's threatened several times to come over here an' instigate a civil war, but he won't do it right away. He knows what a temper you got, an' I reckon he don't like the idea o' that big tombstone already marked in Welborne's new graveyard. No, I can't put up with you to-night. Het give me a five-dollar William to defray expenses at the hotel, an' I sorter like the idea o' makin' a splurge for a change. I'll make 'em give me the best drummer's quarters, an' I'll order just what I want to eat."

Henley watched him remount and ride away, his legs swinging back and forth against the flanks of the animal. He heard little Joe calling to Dixie from the kitchen-door, and from the cow-lot her clear answering "Whooee!" which came again in a softer echo from the nearest hill.

"I wonder what she is thinking?" he mused, the hot blood

from his surcharged heart tingling through his entire body. "I'd go to her now, but she'd not like it. She wouldn't look at me while the old man was talking. The sweet little thing is scared—she don't know what at, but she's scared."

CHAPTER XLI

Although Henley, now grown oddly timid himself, made several efforts within the next week to catch sight of Dixie, he failed signally. He began by haunting the cow-lot at milking-time, but she did not come as usual. From the front porch one evening he observed something that explained this to him. It was the sight of little Joe driving the cow up to the house instead of into the lot.

"She's milking up there to keep from meeting me," Henley said, his heart growing heavy. "Maybe, after all, I've been hoping too much. Maybe she sorter thought she'd like me well enough when I was bound to another, like I was, but now she sees it different. Folks is likely to think twice in a matter like this, for I mean business, an' she knows it. My God, I may lose 'er—actually lose 'er, after all!"

For the next week Henley really suffered; the gravest doubts had beset him; as close as Dixie had been to him, she now seemed farther away than ever. He was constantly wavering between the hungry impulse to go directly to her and the abiding fear that such an intrusion might offend her beyond pardon.

One day, however, he felt that he could stand his suspense no longer. It was the day his lawyer at Carlton had written him that he was a free man. Surely, he argued, he would have the right to inform her of such an important fact, after all that had passed between them, simply as a friend, if nothing more. He left the store early in the afternoon, and on his way home, and with a chill of doubt on him, he stopped at Dixie's cottage.

Mrs. Hart was seated behind the vines on the little box-like porch, and she rose at the click of the gate-latch and stood peering at him under her thin hand.

"Oh, it's you, Alfred!" she cried, in pleased surprise. "I was just wondering what had become of you. Did you want to see Dixie?"

"Yes, I thought I'd ask if she was about the house," Henley made reply, in a jerky sort of fashion. "There is a little matter I wanted to speak to her about."

"So the poor child is right, after all," the old woman sighed. "Well, I reckon you must protect your own interests, Alfred, let the burden fall where it may. She's done 'er best to pay out, an' if she can't do it, why, she'll have to give in, that's all. She's undertaken too much, anyway."

"I don't understand, Mrs. Hart." Henley was unable to follow her drift, and, with his hat in hand and a puzzled expression on his face, he stood silent.

"Why, for the last week, Alfred, Dixie hain't done a thing but fret and worry about the money she owes you," Mrs. Hart explained, plaintively. "Why, when you advanced the money to get her out of old Welborne's clutch she was so happy she sung day and night, and me and her Aunt Mandy thought the worst was over, because—well, because you seemed so kind and friendly that we felt like you would not push her, that you'd give her plenty o' time to make the payments. But now that her cotton fell short of her expectations and the overflow killed half her potato-crop she's all upset. She didn't say, in so many words, that you was going to sue for your rights, but we couldn't, to save us, see what she was so upset for, if you hadn't, at least, hinted about it. My sister thought that maybe—that maybe, now that your wife's big fortune had gone off in an unexpected direction, that you was obliged to raise money to make good some investments that you made while you was counting on things remaining the same. We couldn't talk it over with Dixie, because she'd get out of patience every time we'd bring it up."

"You are quite mistaken, Mrs. Hart," Henley said, his face aglow from a new light on the situation. "I don't want to collect any money from Dixie. She can keep it as long as she wants it. If she thinks I want that money, she is away off from the facts. Is she about the house?"

"No, she ain't," Mrs. Hart fairly gasped in relief. "Her and Joe went down to the creek to fish. They are at the first bend; you can see the spot from the gate. So that was a mistake! Well, I certainly am glad. I reckon she just imagined it. She's acted funny for the last week, anyway—sometimes just as happy and jolly as you please, and then bringing up this money question—sayin' that she couldn't bear to be in debt, and the like. She said if she could just sell the farm for anything near its worth she'd do it and pay all she owes."

"She could easily sell it," Henley said, "but she won't have to do it to pay me. I'll go down there, I believe, and see if they are having any luck."

He walked away slowly, for the burden of doubt as to his chances was still on him. From the bend of the road he looked across the level pasture and hay-land to the green line of willows and canebrake that marked the course of the stream. At first he saw nothing but his grazing horses and mules, some of Dixie's sheep and lambs, and then he descried a purplish blur against the living green, and recognized it as the girl's sunbonnet, the back part of which was turned toward him. Across the uneven ground, his feet retarded by creeping earth-vines and furrows where grain had grown and ripened, he strode, his doubt and awkwardness increasing with every step.

She saw him as he was nearing the grass-covered bank upon which she sat, an open book in her lap. It was quite clear to him that she, too, was embarrassed, for a violent color rose in her cheeks, and her glance deliberately avoided his. She called out quite distinctly and irrelevantly to Joe, who sat on a log which jutted out into the stream, telling him to be careful and not fall in. Henley saw the boy shrug his shoulders and heard him laugh contemptuously, as he whipped his rod and line into the stream and reseated himself, his bare feet sinking into the cooling water. "Why, it ain't up to my waist," he said. "I could wade across."

"No, he's safe enough," Henley heard his coarse voice saying, as he stood over her and looked down on her expressionless bonnet.

She looked up and pushed her bonnet back farther so that a wisp of her beautiful hair was exposed to the sunlight against the shell-like pinkness of her neck. "He hasn't caught a thing," she said; "but he's had some bites that was just as much fun."

"I'm sorter tired," he ventured. "I've been on my feet all day, running first one place and another. This is your picnic, and you are the boss. I wonder if you'd care if I set down a minute."

"It may be my picnic, but it happens to be your ground,"

she laughed. "There's a sign up at the fence that no trespassing is allowed, but me and Joe neither one can read, and so we came right in and helped ourselves."

He lowered himself to the grass at her feet, glad that he had it, and yet almost afraid of the full view he now had of her face when he dared to look directly at her. He leaned forward and began to pluck blades of grass and twist them nervously in his fingers.

"You are powerful good to that boy," he said, after a silence through which several kinds of thoughts percolated. "His own mammy couldn't treat him better."

"I don't know whether I'm spoiling him or not." He detected a slight quavering in her voice which was not exactly that of her usual composure. "Some folks say I am. I know I can't bear to have him work hard, although he is plumb well now. He had such a hard time under Sam Pitman that, somehow, I want him to have a good, long vacation. Alfred—" She raised her hand to her lips impulsively, colored vexatiously, and then with a shrug, as if the familiar use of his name were a matter that could not be remedied, she continued; "I started to say that it makes me awful sad to think of the slavery that child went through, short as it was. It might have made a scoundrel of him, in the long-run, for he was getting hardened."

"And now he's just the reverse." Henley meant it as a tribute to her, and it was as bold a compliment as he would have dared to pay her in the dense anxiety through which he was groping. "He's a manly little chap, and is sure to come out on top. I've been studying over it"—Henley was growing a trifle bolder—his eyes met hers—"and I've wondered if you'd get jealous if I said that I want to do something substantial for him. He'll need good schooling, you know, and a lot o' things to start 'im out fairly."

"You? Why, Al—why, surely you don't mean it—you don't mean *that.*"

"Why, why not, Dixie—Miss Dixie?" he corrected, as his warm, anxious gaze rested on her lowered lids, for she was turning the pages of the arithmetic in her lap. "You see, I'm not exactly a poor man; the Lord has been powerful good to me, and—and you see, now I'm all alone in the world. I—I got news to-day about—about, well, I'm a free man now, with no responsibilities on me, and—well, you see how it is."

"I don't know what to say about it—about Joe." She lowered her head over the book. "It would be wrong for me to stand in his way, and I won't. He was helpless on the world when I took him, and he is yet, for I'm over head and ears in debt. I thought I could do wonders by buying land on a credit, but I'm as near a bankrupt as could be possible. I'd be down and out now if others got what was coming to them. As proud as I am, and as hard as I've worked, I'm right now living on charity."

"Shucks! Don't be silly, Dixie!" burst from Henley's lips with considerable warmth. "You sha'n't set here and talk such foolishness; you've done more than thousands o' men could have done. You are a plumb wonder."

"All you say don't alter facts," Dixie sighed. "I know that I've got a big debt to pay, and it's got to be paid by fair means or foul. Let's talk about something else. I've been setting here an hour trying to work this example for Joe. It looks as easy as two and two make four, but it ain't; it's simply terrible. Listen: 'Sixty is two-thirds of what number?'"

"Let me see." And Henley crawled to her aide till he could see, as he rested on his elbow, the page and the lines at which her finger pointed. "That's easy enough, I reckon. 'Sixty is two-thirds of what number?' Why, it's—" His eyes became fixed in vacancy, as he gazed at the blue sky above the tree-tops, and then at the ground. "Why, it's a fool thing—it must be a misprint. You often find mistakes like that in school-books. I know my teacher used to write the correct thing on the edge of the page."

"No, I reckon it's all right," Dixie argued. "It's a funny thing, for every minute I seem to be on the point of catching it, and then it slips away. You see, it has been so long since I went to school that I can't remember how such sums are done."

"Well, I can work any sort o' example that I have use for in my business," Henley defended himself as well as he could, "but the Lord knows I never had any use for a—a thing as silly as that is on the very face of it. Huh, I say—'Sixty is two-thirds of what number?' Why, the fool don't even give the number he asks you to divide. How can you divide a thing that hain't been seen, measured, or weighed? It is as silly as asking how many inches long is two-thirds of a piece of string, or how many bushels of wheat in two-thirds of a barn that's twice as big as four-fifths of one that never was built."

Dixie laughed heartily. "It does seem that way, don't it? But, after all, you do know that sixty must be two-thirds of *some* number, for every number is two-thirds of something, ain't it?"

"By gum, yes!" he exclaimed, with a start. "You are sure right. Ah, I see now. By gosh, I've got it! No, it's gone already." He had reached for her pencil and paper, but his hand fell idly on his knee. "Good gracious! Some'n is dead wrong with me."

"I think it can be done," Dixie declared, her brow furrowed. "You see, since sixty must be two-thirds of some number, I'm picking different numbers and dividing by three and multiplying by two. The last trial I made was one hundred, and I got sixty-six and two-thirds for the answer. You see, that ain't so powerful far off."

"I see, I see," Henley cried, eagerly. "Now, what you want to do is to keep getting lower and lower till you hit the nail on the head. I reckon it's one o' them sums just got up to make the sprouting intellect hop and skip about for practice. Suppose you try ninety-nine next? It's better to go slow, and be sure, than to have to go back. Le'me see: three into nine, three times and nothing to carry; three into nine again—there, you've got thirty-three, and twice thirty-three are sixty-six. See, we are still closer to the mark, for we have already wiped off the two-thirds."

"We are warm!" Dixie cried, with the laugh of a child playing a game. "Now let's try ninety-six."

Henley made a rapid calculation. "Sixty-four!" he cried out, gleefully. "We are closer. Now let's take a stab at ninety-three." And he began to figure, but she stopped him.

"My judgment is ninety," she said. "One-third of ninety is thirty and twice thirty is—glory, Alfred, we've nailed it! We've got it—we've got it! And we thought it couldn't possibly be done."

"That's so," he admitted. "But I'd hate to make a hoss-trade by such figuring as that. The feller would back out or the hoss would git too old."

The conversation languished. He had a feeling that she might object to his closeness to her, and yet he hardly knew how to draw away without attracting undue attention to the act, so he took the book into his hands and began to look through it. And then he remembered what Mrs. Hart had said about Dixie's desire to sell her farm, and a slow twinkle of a set purpose began to burn in his eyes. "It might work," he said to himself. "Anyways, that debt notion has got to be got out of the way or I'll never make any progress.

"I was just wondering whether I oughtn't to give you a piece of advice, in a business sort of a way," he said to her, his fingers rapidly twirling the pages of the book. "You see, a feller that trades as much as I do in all sorts of things is calculated to know the drift of the market better, maybe, than a girl like you. You was speaking about how you hated the idea of being in debt just now, and your mother says you want to sell your farm—the fact is, I don't see why you don't sell it and quit working like an ox in a yoke. It's plumb wrong; you oughtn't to do it, that's all."

"Sell it? Why, Alfred," and she looked at him eagerly, "I'd only be too glad to do it if I knew any one who would pay anything near its worth. You see, it's cost me first and last something over two thousand dollars, and if I could get that much—"

"That much!" he sniffed contemptuously. "Why, you'd be crazy to sell at a figure like that. You see, I know the field pretty well. I rub against moneyed men every day who are simply itching for something to invest in. The most of 'em believe the new railroad will eventually strike Chester on its way to hook on to the trunk-line through Tennessee and North Carolina, and they are willing to bet on it. You know old Welborne wanted your farm, and it nearly killed him to lose his hold on it. But—while I ain't exactly free to use names—I know a man right now who wants your property. He'd pay you three thousand dollars in cash right down."

"Oh, Alfred, you don't mean it—surely you don't!"

"You say you'll take it," Henley laughed, though the edges of his mouth were drawn tensely from some inner cause, "and I'll close the deal before you can say Jack Robinson."

"Take it?" Dixie cried, and in her eagerness and gratitude she actually laid her hand on his arm. "Oh, Alfred, if you'd only do that for me I'd be the happiest girl in the world!"

"Well, it will be done to-morrow morning early," Henley said, a certain purpose rendering his face rigid, his eyes fixed as if a great crisis had arrived in his life. "The only thing is, that I'd naturally feel like I'd be entitled to some commission—" He tried to smile into her staring eyes, but failed. He caught hold of her hand and she seemed wholly unconscious of the fact.

"Why, of course," she groped, "I'd be willing to pay all costs and anything else you'd ask."

"There is only one thing I could want, or would ever care to have," he swallowed, "and that is you, Dixie. You must be my wife. I'm free now. Nothing stands between us. I want you, sweetheart—I want you!"

Their eyes met, volumes of tenderness sweeping to and fro between them. A great light had taken possession of her face. He felt her lean against him confidingly, and he put his arm around her and drew her head to his shoulder, and then, with a boldness he would till now have ascribed only to a god, he put his hand under her warm face, turned it upward and kissed her on the lips. She nestled closer to him and shut her eyes, remaining still and silent. He felt her warmth striking into his body.

For several minutes they sat thus, and then she opened her eyes and smiled.

"Oh, Alfred, I'm so happy!" she said, softly.

"Well, maybe *I* ain't," he said, huskily, and then he kissed her again.

"I'm so glad about the farm," she said. "I can come to you now freer. I couldn't bear the idea of being in debt to the man *I* was going to marry. I've been independent so long that—that it actually hurt me. Are you plumb sure you can sell it, Alfred—absolutely sure?"

"Absolutely," he answered. "The only thing that's bothering me is that it's worth more."

"Never mind about that," she cried. "But tell me who is to take it, Alfred?"

Their eyes met again steadily, a warm, confident, fearless smile lighted up his face. He put his arm about her again, drew her close to him, and held her cheek in his hand.

"There ain't but one man under God's eye that's got a right to own the land you toiled on like you did," he said, "and that is the man that worships every hair on your head and every drop of blood in your veins. I'm the feller, Dixie."

"Oh, Alfred!" she cried out, but, seeing his eyes burning into hers, she smiled, nestled closer into his arms, and said: "Well, what's the use? My fight's over. I've got you, and nothing on earth can take you from me."

THE END

Friedrich Kerst
Friedrich Nietzsche
Fyodor Dostoyevsky
G.A. Henty
G.K. Chesterton
Gabrielle E. Jackson
Garrett P. Serviss
Gaston Leroux
George A. Warren
George Ade
Geroge Bernard Shaw
George Cary Eggleston
George Durston
George Ebers
George Eliot
George Gissing
George MacDonald
George Meredith
George Orwell
George Sylvester Viereck
George Tucker
George W. Cable
George Wharton James
Gertrude Atherton
Gordon Casserly
Grace E. King
Grace Gallatin
Grace Greenwood
Grant Allen
Guillermo A. Sherwell
Gulielma Zollinger
Gustav Flaubert
H. A. Cody
H. B. Irving
H.C. Bailey
H. G. Wells
H. H. Munro
H. Irving Hancock
H. R. Naylor
H. Rider Haggard
H. W. C. Davis
Haldeman Julius
Hall Caine
Hamilton Wright Mabie
Hans Christian Andersen
Harold Avery
Harold McGrath
Harriet Beecher Stowe
Harry Castlemon
Harry Coghill
Harry Houidini
Hayden Carruth
Helent Hunt Jackson
Helen Nicolay
Hendrik Conscience
Hendy David Thoreau
Henri Barbusse
Henrik Ibsen
Henry Adams
Henry Ford
Henry Frost
Henry James
Henry Jones Ford
Henry Seton Merriman
Henry W Longfellow
Herbert A. Giles
Herbert Carter
Herbert N. Casson
Herman Hesse
Hildegard G. Frey
Homer
Honore De Balzac
Horace B. Day
Horace Walpole
Horatio Alger Jr.
Howard Pyle
Howard R. Garis
Hugh Lofting
Hugh Walpole
Humphry Ward
Ian Maclaren
Inez Haynes Gillmore
Irving Bacheller
Isabel Cecilia Williams
Isabel Hornibrook
Israel Abrahams
Ivan Turgenev
J.G.Austin
J. Henri Fabre
J. M. Barrie
J. M. Walsh
J. Macdonald Oxley
J. R. Miller
J. S. Fletcher
J. S. Knowles
J. Storer Clouston
J. W. Duffield
Jack London
Jacob Abbott
James Allen
James Andrews
James Baldwin
James Branch Cabell
James DeMille
James Joyce
James Lane Allen
James Lane Allen
James Oliver Curwood
James Oppenheim
James Otis
James R. Driscoll
Jane Abbott
Jane Austen
Jane L. Stewart
Janet Aldridge
Jens Peter Jacobsen
Jerome K. Jerome
Jessie Graham Flower
John Buchan
John Burroughs
John Cournos
John F. Kennedy
John Gay
John Glasworthy
John Habberton
John Joy Bell
John Kendrick Bangs
John Milton
John Philip Sousa
John Taintor Foote
Jonas Lauritz Idemil Lie
Jonathan Swift
Joseph A. Altsheler
Joseph Carey
Joseph Conrad
Joseph E. Badger Jr
Joseph Hergesheimer
Joseph Jacobs
Jules Vernes
Julian Hawthrone
Julie A Lippmann
Justin Huntly McCarthy
Kakuzo Okakura
Karle Wilson Baker
Kate Chopin
Kenneth Grahame
Kenneth McGaffey
Kate Langley Bosher
Kate Langley Bosher
Katherine Cecil Thurston
Katherine Stokes
L. A. Abbot
L. T. Meade

L. Frank Baum
Latta Griswold
Laura Dent Crane
Laura Lee Hope
Laurence Housman
Lawrence Beasley
Leo Tolstoy
Leonid Andreyev
Lewis Carroll
Lewis Sperry Chafer
Lilian Bell
Lloyd Osbourne
Louis Hughes
Louis Joseph Vance
Louis Tracy
Louisa May Alcott
Lucy Fitch Perkins
Lucy Maud Montgomery
Luther Benson
Lydia Miller Middleton
Lyndon Orr
M. Corvus
M. H. Adams
Margaret E. Sangster
Margret Howth
Margaret Vandercook
Margaret W. Hungerford
Margret Penrose
Maria Edgeworth
Maria Thompson Daviess
Mariano Azuela
Marion Polk Angellotti
Mark Overton
Mark Twain
Mary Austin
Mary Catherine Crowley
Mary Cole
Mary Hastings Bradley
Mary Roberts Rinehart
Mary Rowlandson
M. Wollstonecraft Shelley
Maud Lindsay
Max Beerbohm
Myra Kelly
Nathaniel Hawthrone
Nicolo Machiavelli
O. F. Walton
Oscar Wilde

Owen Johnson
P.G. Wodehouse
Paul and Mabel Thorne
Paul G. Tomlinson
Paul Severing
Percy Brebner
Percy Keese Fitzhugh
Peter B. Kyne
Plato
Quincy Allen
R. Derby Holmes
R. L. Stevenson
R. S. Ball
Rabindranath Tagore
Rahul Alvares
Ralph Bonehill
Ralph Henry Barbour
Ralph Victor
Ralph Waldo Emmerson
Rene Descartes
Ray Cummings
Rex Beach
Rex E. Beach
Richard Harding Davis
Richard Jefferies
Richard Le Gallienne
Robert Barr
Robert Frost
Robert Gordon Anderson
Robert L. Drake
Robert Lansing
Robert Lynd
Robert Michael Ballantyne
Robert W. Chambers
Rosa Nouchette Carey
Rudyard Kipling
Saint Augustine
Samuel B. Allison
Samuel Hopkins Adams
Sarah Bernhardt
Sarah C. Hallowell
Selma Lagerlof
Sherwood Anderson
Sigmund Freud
Standish O'Grady
Stanley Weyman
Stella Benson
Stella M. Francis

Stephen Crane
Stewart Edward White
Stijn Streuvels
Swami Abhedananda
Swami Parmananda
T. S. Ackland
T. S. Arthur
The Princess Der Ling
Thomas A. Janvier
Thomas A Kempis
Thomas Anderton
Thomas Bailey Aldrich
Thomas Bulfinch
Thomas De Quincey
Thomas Dixon
Thomas H. Huxley
Thomas Hardy
Thomas More
Thornton W. Burgess
U. S. Grant
Upton Sinclair
Valentine Williams
Various Authors
Vaughan Kester
Victor Appleton
Victor G. Durham
Victoria Cross
Virginia Woolf
Wadsworth Camp
Walter Camp
Walter Scott
Washington Irving
Wilbur Lawton
Wilkie Collins
Willa Cather
Willard F. Baker
William Dean Howells
William le Queux
W. Makepeace Thackeray
William W. Walter
William Shakespeare
Winston Churchill
Yei Theodora Ozaki
Yogi Ramacharaka
Young E. Allison
Zane Grey

www.ingramcontent.com/pod-product-compliance
Lightning Source LLC
LaVergne TN
LVHW090549110826
845146LV00001B/76